The Bone Bearer

Book Three in the Telesā Series.

Lani Wendt Young

ISBN: 978-1490948713

Printed and bound in New Zealand by Kale Print, Tauranga.

Cover Design by Talia Design, NZ.
Photography by Penina Momoisea.
Model, Stacie Ah Chong-Levi.

Dedication

For my friend, my sister – and a true example of beautiful,
fierce, fiery and fabulous womanhood,

Elena Peteru

Without you, this book would never have been written. Time
and again, you help me find my way. Better than a happy pill;
your insight, love and support keeps me from falling away from
the straight and narrow (or at least not *too* far away!)

PELE

The Legend of Pele, the Fire Goddess. As told by the Telesā.

Pele was born in the fabled islands of Hawaiki, an Ungifted child of Noalani – the Covenant Keeper for the ruling fanua afi in the Pacific and as such, the holder of the Tangaloa Bone. Noalani hoped, watched and waited for her daughter's Gift to manifest. But her hopes were in vain. Pele grew to womanhood with barely a whisper of fanua afi capabilities. According to the Telesā custom, Noalani should have sent Pele away. Given her to a good foster mother somewhere so she could find a place in the world, as a healer, a wife, a mother. So that she could find happiness. But Noalani loved her daughter too much. She could not bear to part with her and so she kept Pele with the Fanua Afi Sisterhood. In this, Noalani did her a great cruelty because Pele grew up a stranger amongst her own kind. As a child, she was scorned by her sisters, pitied by her elders and mocked by her community who knew that she was a fanua afi without fire.

Wracked with guilt and sorrow for her daughter's pain, Noalani did the unthinkable. She gave the Tangaloa Bone to Pele and showed her how to use it to take the Gift – and thus the life – of one of the youngest and newest telesā fanua afi.

"There my daughter. Now you have the Gift of fire and you can walk tall amongst your sisters. Put aside your sorrow. Embrace who you are. My daughter."

For a time, Pele was content to be the same as her sisters. But like a tree maggot, the hunger for power ate away at her soul. She nurtured a growing hatred for her sisters, they who had scorned her, mocked her, and pitied her. She took the Tangaloa Bone without her mother's knowledge and secretly used it on another young girl in the Citadel. And then another. The string of mysterious deaths had the whole island confounded. Who was killing their daughters?

Suspicion grew in Noalani, a tree fern unfurling its leaves in the sun. She confronted her daughter. No-one knows exactly how it happened but Pele stole her mother's Gift. And her life. The girl who was born the weakest among them, was now the strongest telesā fanua afi in Hawaiki. She could have been the Covenant Keeper. There were none who dared to oppose her. But Pele did not want to belong to a family that had spurned her. She did not want to belong to a sisterhood. She wanted everyone to suffer for her childhood of pain. Vengeance was her enduring thirst.

And thus began the dark time in telesā history. Pele sought out the fanua afi, and drained them one by one, taking their power and their lives. But she was not content to stop there. She wanted to rid the world of every fanua afi in existence. She hunted them in Tonga, Samoa, Fiji and Tahiti. And with each kill, her powers grew. She turned her gaze to the other elements. Using the Tangaloa Bone, she then hunted the Vasa Loloa and Matagi who dared to oppose her. It was a time of fear and suspicion.

Pele's unquenchable thirst for power proved to be her undoing. She stole so much of the Earth's raw power that a body of flesh and blood could no longer contain it. One crimson spangled day, Pele erupted into flame and her body was no more. She was consumed by a volcano unlike any other. The event triggered a mega-tsunami which swept across the Pacific Ocean, drowning atolls and laying waste to entire island chains. Pele's essence fused with the very heart of the volcano she ignited and she was bound forever to the earth which she had stolen from.

She lives still. In raging rivers of molten red lava. In shimmering bursts of cindered light. In the raging violence of earthquakes.

She is Pele, the Fire Goddess and she festers beneath the earth's surface. Brooding, innately powerful but forever wanting that which she does not have.

A body.

They say that the Pacific Council of telesā met after Pele's demise. The Council agreed that the Tangaloa Bone must never be held by any single telesā again, the lure of its power too great. It must be hidden away for the time spoken of in prophecy, when the Bone would be used to bring together all telesā as one heart and one mind. The Bone was broken into three pieces and ageless guardians appointed to watch over them. The elements of Air, Fire and Water – forever separated.

Waiting for the coming of the Bone Bearer.

Ha. Legends. Myths. Lies and half-truths. What do people a thousand years away from my life really know about me? About my reality, my struggles? What do they know about my mother, or my sisters, our way of life?

Nothing.

But then, what is a legend if not a people's attempt to make sense of the unknown? What is a myth if not an attempt to reason the unreasonable? All legend is nurtured by the sweet rot of lies. All mythology is fed with the rich fat of fear. Let's take the legend of Pele for example. The story of me. And my descent to hell.

Yes, it's been a long time. I am old. Very old. There is none other who has seen as many earth beats as I. Yes, I've forgotten many things. Inconsequential things. But there is much I do remember. After all, what else is there to do when you are condemned to burn beneath the earth for all time? What else is there but memory?

This is my story. The story of Pele.

I am broken. Incomplete. Missing the most essential part of me. That which gives me a voice. I am the oyster missing the treasured blackness in my most secret, wet heart. Harvested from the ocean depths at great cost, opened with great tenderness and then, disappointment. Destined to be discarded.

My mother tells me she loves me still. Even as she tries and fails to coax from me the fire that would make me her child. She hides the disappointment in her eyes. But I see it in the still surface of the Loahine Pool. Staring back at me.

She tells me I am precious. Her Beloved. She saves her tears for the quiet side of midnight when she thinks I am asleep. But I hear her still. Because her tears are my own.

I am Pele the daughter of Noalani the Bone Bearer. I am the Beloved.

But I am still broken.

We are Keawe, worshipped and revered by all. Our feet dance with strands of fire that tug their fury from earth's heart and our hands burn with the flames of the very stars themselves. We speak for earth. We speak for the stars.

We are gods.

Well, *they* are. Them. My sisters. My cousins. My aunts. My mother. But I? I am only a girl. Seventeen years and I'm still ordinary. Nothing and nobody. I'm only a girl who walks with the gods. Seventeen years and I still show no signs of my heritage, no hint of my mother's fiery blood. I look like her. But I don't. We are tall with thick black hair and cinnamon skin. Admirers say my mother's lips are 'lush like ripe mango' where I am teased mercilessly for my 'fat lips like shellfish swollen with rot.' Her eyes are 'liquid pools of midnight a man could get lost in.' While my name all through my childhood was 'Mata Lulu.' Owl eyes. But that's what godhood does. It transforms the ordinary into the magical. I love the beauty, the majesty and the power that is my mother.

But I hate her too. Because her perfection reminds me every day of what I am not.

My mother is the Covenant Keeper of the Keawe. As such, she is also the Bearer of the Tangaloa Bone. They say her mother was given it by the hand of Tangaloa herself. Keawe are the chosen of the gods, entrusted with earth's fire so they can stand as guardians of the land upon which we walk, live, and love. Keawe say they are the most powerful of the elements, the most sacred of all the guardians. But I have never met any of the Ocean people. Or those who speak to storms. So I couldn't tell if that is but a wishful claim!

I can tell you Keawe are revered and feared as both destroyers and creators of life. I have seen Noalani summon new lands from beneath a boiling ocean and the grateful adoration of a people hungry for new space to settle. Their tears of gratitude and reverence. I have also seen their terror. A people brought to their knees as she shreds the earth beneath their feet and razes it with fire when they have broken a taboo or displeased her in some way. My mother is a woman of many faces. A fearful tyrant. A benevolent leader. Perhaps all gods are made that way? For where there is no fear – how can there be any respect? Any order?

But the face she always showed me is of a gentle mother. I remember as a child, how she would chase away nightmares with a gentle flame in the palm of her hand. She would hold me close in her arms and light up the air above us with a radiant scattering of dancing sparks. She smelled of vanilla and sweet chili like all Keawe but with a hint of something extra – citrus. Ripe oranges and tangy lemon. To me, her fire was always comfort, love, and peace. She was the bringer of happiness and the light that kept the bad things away.

There has never been any doubt that my mother loves me very much. It is a fierce kind of love that defies the rules. Because I am Ungifted, my mother was supposed to give me away. Send me to one of the villages on the outer islands, far away from all the things that I could not be, all the reminders of who I could never be.

But she kept me with her. It was a decision that displeased the Elders, particularly those who had given away their daughters in the past. They never let her see their disapproval because her word is law, her fire is mightier than all of them. The more sisters that covenant with a Keeper, the stronger her Fire burns, the clearer her connection is with our Mother Earth. A Keeper's strength comes from unity and harmony as she is the one who stands as the heart of them all, the kava bowl that holds their gifts as one. My mother has lived a long time and she has tied many Sisters to her in the Covenant.

My mother has also had other daughters in her many years. Some gifted and some not. I have sisters who can make fire their own and I have also seen sisters sent away. I heard their weeping as they left with kind women who were grateful to have the privilege of mothering a daughter of a Keawe. But not me. Everyone knew I was her favorite. She had named me 'Pele' which means precious and beloved – for a reason.

I was eight years old when I first found out why. She took me to a quiet grove of frangipani trees. There under the pale grey branches heavy with sweet bursts of color she showed me a burial spot. A bone shard etched with a sun marking. She took me in her arms and held me close. Her cheeks were damp with tears.

"His name was Richard. Your father. He loved me very much. Even without Keawe potions. He came to us across the ocean in a big ship with white sails."

"Why did he die?"

My mother hesitated. I know now that her answer was a lie. "He was very sick. We couldn't heal him. He died when you were just a baby."

It wasn't the only time my mother told me about the father I never knew. She liked to talk about him but only when we were alone. "Richard had hair the color of sunshine. His eyes were blue like the sky on a perfect day and he laughed more than any man I've ever known. So many jokes, so much laughter, so much teasing. He liked to make me laugh. Said I was far too serious all the time." A sadness in her eyes. "I told him I was the leader of my people and I couldn't spend my days laughing. You know what he said to that?"

She didn't wait for my reply. "He said, *Life is for laughing and loving. If you can't do that, then you may as well be dead.*"

"Where did he come from?"

"A land far away, far across the sea. A place called England. He said it was a dirty, gray place that I would hate. But with many marvels and wonders. Like metal horses that breathed smoke and fire. Big ships like his that moved on land. Tall houses that touched the sky. His people had captured pieces of the sun and put it into bottles so they could have light whenever they wanted. Light in the darkest nights. England also had something called snow. When the air got cold, so very cold that you could hardly breathe it because it hurt your insides. So cold that water hardened and turned to white and fell from the sky. So cold that people without fire, without coverings – they would turn to stone. Cold stone.

'Ah your fire would be such a gift in the winter my love. We would never be cold. You could fuel an entire city I'm sure!'

Men were a mystery to me then because they did not live among the Keawe as equals. Some Keawe would choose men as consorts for a time but they were good only for serving as war and field slaves. And for other night duties. It was an oddity to hear my mother speak of a man with affection. Kindness. With love.

With remorse?

Much later I found out what really happened to the man that had tried to make my mother laugh. Noalani had made the mistake of falling in love with the man she had taken to her bed. She had allowed him to stay with her for longer than was deemed acceptable. Her people had watched as their Covenant Keeper laughed, loved and delighted in the man with hair like sunshine and eyes like the sky. Richard's ship left the island but he had stayed behind, because he loved a woman of the Keawe and mistakenly believed that she loved him too. Loved him enough to defy the law. Her belly swelled with his child and he had rejoiced. Did my father know he was doing a dangerous thing? Did he know what he risked by staying? Did he know what Noalani risked on his behalf? Did they discuss it when they weren't laughing in the moonlight?

I will never know. What I do know is that according to Keawe law, Richard was put to death on the day I was born. Keawe law is much more formidable for a Covenant Keeper than for a regular sister. It dictates that once a man has served his purpose and provided her with a daughter – then he must be killed. By the Covenant Keeper herself. Who knows how many men my mother killed in her ageless lifetime? Sometimes, when I feel a lingering unpleasant taste of guilt at what I have done – I remind myself that my mother was a murderer before me. A killer. Sometimes it helps.

But only sometimes.

I would venture to say that Richard was the only man my mother ever loved – well, as far as she was capable of loving a man anyway. She did kill him after all. I wonder if she smiled as she did it?

The man with sunshine hair and sky eyes is the reason I was always my mother's favorite. Perhaps it was to honor the gift of laughter he had given her, no matter how fleeting. Whatever it was, my mother refused to send me away when time revealed that I was useless as far as Keawe go. I couldn't spit fire, or make the earth move beneath anyone's feet, no matter how hard I tried. No matter how much my mother wished it. No matter how much laughter my father had invoked. So Richard had the last laugh after all from beyond that grave under the frangipani trees because the child he had given to Noalani, this child she cherished – was cursed with Ungiftedness.

I have wished a thousand times that I could bring my father back to life. So I could look into his sky blue eyes and stab him myself. It was his fault that I was Ungifted. Of what use is laughter when it can't touch the stars or talk to the earth's heart?

I grew up hating who I was. And hating who I wasn't. The sisters I lived and trained with – they all knew I lacked that essential thing which would make me one of them and they never let me forget it. The worst of them all was Melita. She was the first one I killed. With my mother's help. With my mother's permission.

It's vital you remember this. In generations to come when they talk of my journey of blood and fire, remember, it was my mother who started it.

The journey began one happy afternoon of celebration. It was the Covenant Day when new sisters received their ink marking them as sisters. The day they covenanted with my mother, adding their power to hers in exchange for her vow that she would never use Fire against them. I watched from the window of my mother's chambers as each girl went forward to receive her marking. A curved hapu'u leaf frond with the bold stamp of the red Ohelo'Ai berry at its peaked edge. Girls flinched under the determined tapping of the chisel and adze. Some cried. I wouldn't have cried. Their weakness made me sick to my stomach. How could they be Keawe when they were so weak?

I wanted a Keawe tattoo and I would never have one. This day of celebration would never come for me. Whatever hope I had nurtured, whatever whisperings of prayers to gods I still had within my breast – they all died there on that day. No-one had ever heard of a Keawe who reached her seventeenth birthday without finding her Fire. If it hadn't happened by now, it never would. The relentless tapping of the tattooist's instruments were sealing my fate. My destiny. I would always be Pele the Ungifted, the Broken daughter of Noalani the Covenant Keeper.

A failure.

I cried there in my mother's bedroom until the sun had long set. While the sounds of celebration, resounded from outside. I hugged Noalani's pillow and breathed deeply of her familiar scent. The scent that reminded me of my mother's love for me. That's where she found me later that night. Alone. Crying.

"Oh Pele, what is it?" She could speak soft and gentle when she wanted to, my mother. She raised my face to hers and wiped away my tears.

"Mother please, send me away from here. I can't bear it. I can't stay here anymore where I don't belong. It's killing me!"

If I had asked for anything else other than that, perhaps my mother wouldn't have done what she did. But I was desperate. When I asked my mother to send me away, I meant it.

She sat me up and gave me a rough shake. "That's enough. You are my daughter and the daughter of the Covenant Keeper does not waste her time on empty tears and regrets. She doesn't pine wishing for things. She makes them happen."

"I've tried. I've done everything. You've seen me at my lessons. I pray to Tangaloa. To our earth mother. I study all the sacred writings in the temple. I am the best at Lu'a. Nobody trains as hard as me. It's not working. I don't belong here and I'm begging you, please let me go."

She pulled me to my feet. Her grip was a vice leaving red imprints on my wrist. "Enough of this. Come with me."

Noalani took me to the room where she kept the Tangaloa Bone. I had seen her use it many times. It was a weapon as well as a ceremonial tool. It was almost as long as she was tall. A staff made from interlocking pieces of carved materials. Some I could recognize – whale bone, boar's tusk, pearl shell, black coral, jade stone, swordfish hook. Others I didn't know. It looked heavy and cumbersome but when lifted, it was surprisingly lightweight and easy to maneuver. She had taught me the knife dance using the Tangaloa Bone and no staff could equal its graceful flow and ease in my hands. When Noalani wielded the Bone, the markings would glow with red fire. A complement to the patterns of her Keawe tattoos. She said it was her Keawe Gift speaking to the fire within the bone. But when I touched the staff, it did nothing.

She held the Bone lightly and closed her eyes for a moment, savoring the rush of power that it always gave her. Like a lover's welcome she once described it to me. A moment of contemplation – that was all it took for my mother to decide our fate.

"Give me a name."

I was bewildered. "What do you mean?"

She drew me to stand beside her at the window, gestured outward. "Choose. It shouldn't be difficult. I know many of them have made your life miserable. Choose one. The one who has made you suffer the most."

"I don't understand. What are you doing?"

There was an uneasy edge of danger in the air. My mother was angry. But at who? And something else – my mother was afraid. But of what? "Quickly. Choose. Give me a name. Think! Who has hurt you the most?"

The name came easily to my lips. "Melita."

Noalani nodded. She took my face in her hands and her words were a fierce breath uttered in the night. "I do this for you, Pele. You are my Beloved. You belong here by my side, with me. For always. Never doubt that. Never question your place in my heart. At my side. I do this for you." She placed a kiss on my forehead and then slipped out of the room. "Wait here."

It couldn't have been more than a few minutes but when I look back at my memories across the chasm of several centuries – it seems like I stood there waiting for my mother for hours. It's a moment that is frozen in place in my mind because of what came next. It's a moment that marked the point of no return. It's a moment that has brought me here today. Living in a dead girl's body.

Noalani returned with Melita. The girl was eager and acquiescent – as they always were in my mother's presence. A woman who can melt your bones with a thought tends to have that effect on people. She left her standing in the center of the room and called to me. "Pele, come here."

"Thank you for joining us Melita. Congratulations on your admission to the sisterhood. You have worked hard."

"Thank you. I'm very excited to be part of the sisterhood. So very honored to be making my covenant with you." Melita was practically wriggling with enthusiasm. She was so happy to be in the same room as her idol. To be having a private audience with her. The fact her defective daughter was there too was not even worth a mention. I was a fungus growing on the walls.

Noalani didn't look at her. Instead, she stared outside at the splayed night sky. "But it wasn't all your efforts that got you here, was it Melita?"

The girl was puzzled. Her smile faltered. "I'm sorry Keeper, I don't know what you mean?"

Noalani turned back to face her and this time there was no pretense at a smile. "I mean that you are here because of some trick of birthright. Yes you have worked hard but you haven't worked as hard as my daughter Pele. You have not bled and sweat with every fiber of your being for Fire. You have not cried for it. Begged for it. Pleaded with the earth mother for it. Have you?"

Melita stumbled over her words, "No Keeper. I … I'm sorry, I don't understand."

Noalani raged then. Her voice bore down on the girl that quaked before her. "No, what I don't understand is why, when you have been given everything that you would go out of your way to hurt my daughter. Why? You think I don't know the things you have done to her? The words you have spoken against her? An offense against my daughter is an offense against me. Do you deny it?!"

Melita shook and tears spilled from her eyes. "No. I'm sorry. I made a mistake. I'm sorry. Please forgive me."

There was a glint of triumph in Noalani's eyes. She had gotten the admission she wanted. "Pele, bring me the Tangaloa Bone."

I promise you I still had no inkling of what my mother intended. Even then. I look back and I search for hints in my soul. Did I know what Noalani planned? Did I want it then? Could I have stopped her? Was it my fault? I look back and I'm not even sure why it matters now. A thousand years later.

I walked to Noalani with the Bone. She didn't take it. Instead she moved to stand behind me and gripped the staff, one hand side-by-side with mine so that we held it together. Mother and daughter. Together we confronted the crying girl before us. One of us vengeful and loving. The other … unknowing?

"Melita, you have committed an offense against the Covenant Keeper. As such, your life is forfeit. As such I call upon our mother earth to relinquish her Fire in you. I – we – take it from you."

The Bone glowed a fiery red. It burned in my fingertips. It burned. I wanted to let go but my mother wouldn't let me. She released her grasp on the staff and instead she covered my fingers with hers, clasping them tightly so that I couldn't let go. So that it was ME who stood there as the Bone Bearer and not her. The smell of burning flesh was sickening. I was burning. I hurt.

Melita screamed. So did I. But her scream ended abruptly as a white light filled the room. Where did it come from? It came from the center of her chest, from her core. Melita's body lit up and began fragmenting at the edges. Like soft tapa cloth slowly but surely catching fire. Skin curling in on itself. Dissolving in soul-hazing heat. Her face melted. I could see her bone outline and hear her frozen cry. I turned my head away but my mother was standing straight and tall against my back. Her order was brutal. "Do not look away. Take the gift I give you Pele. Take it!"

The pain in my hands was forgotten as something else began to burn inside me. A stone knife pierced my throat and slowly began to rip through my chest. Downward. It was a knife of scorching suffering that carved me open so I could accept the fire that wanted entry. I screamed again. I looked down, expecting to see my entrails spill out on the ground but all I could see was a blaze of red fire that connected me to what was left of Melita. I choked on bubbles of blood. Hers and mine. Or perhaps I only imagined it. Perhaps I only wished it. Because surely one should hurt when one is sucking the very life force from another? Surely one should experience some measure of pain if they are draining another dry?

Time and sound rushed and roared in my ears. In my brain. Just when I thought I couldn't endure the agony for one moment longer, it stopped. Melita crumpled into a loose pile of ash. There was no more light. No more pain. No more screaming. Just the sound of my mother's breathing against my ear. As she held me close. A whisper. "Do you feel it Pele?"

I wasn't sure what I was supposed to be feeling. But before I could shake my head in answer, it happened. A growing surge of delicious pleasure that pooled deep inside me. It was warm and sweet. I could feel it everywhere. I could taste it on the air. In my mouth. On my skin. Glorious. Joyous and unbelievably good.

Noalani released my hands and backed away. She walked around to face me, peered into eyes, "Do you feel it?"

Yes I felt it. And my world would never be the same again.

I raised the Bone and gazed at the fiery patterns in wonder. They were lit up, for *me*. I looked around. Everything seemed to have a sparkling new edge to it as if the world was waking up anew. I gazed out at the stars and even they seemed to burn far brighter than I had ever seen them before. Time slowed to a still. I breathed in deeply of the night air and for the first time, I could feel my Mother earth. The very air pulsed of her. It hummed of her essence. Of her presence. She could feel me, I knew that now. A feather light touch caressed my skin, knowing every pore, kissing every nerve edge, licking every sinew line. How could I have existed before this without her? How could I have lived without knowing this oneness, this unison with the earth that had born me? This earth that breathed with me and for me? I walked over the dustings of ash uncaring of what it had been.

I reached with my heart, my mind, my soul – for Fire. And she answered me. The staff in my hands glowed with love for me and a single cord of flame sparked and crackled from my fingertips. I turned to Noalani. "Mother look! I am Keawe. I have the gift."

She wept. My mother the Covenant Keeper of the Keawe stood there and cried with happiness. "You are so beautiful. So strong, so powerful. I'm so happy for you."

We embraced. My heart overflowed with gratitude for the gift my mother had given me. I was Broken no longer.

"Now, remember you must not speak of this to anyone. We will wait for a time before you reveal your gift. Yes, it has manifested late in you, but so be it. You are my daughter and they will just have to accept it. No one can argue against this. I am the Bone Bearer after all."

I think she blocked it out after that. The how and the why and the where her Ungifted daughter had suddenly got her Fire from. I think in her mind, she truly did believe that I was merely a 'late bloomer'. We didn't speak of Melita or what took place that night. Was there even a search for the missing Keawe girl? I can't remember. I didn't even care. Melita had been a thorn in my side for so long. I was only too happy to be rid of her.

We waited a few weeks and then I presented myself to the Elders. "I have found my Fire. See?"

I did all the drills. I passed all the tests. I had wished and hoped and dreamed of Fire for so long that it wasn't difficult to master it when I finally got it. Melita had been one of the stronger new acolytes. Combined with my determination it wasn't long before my aptitude for Fire made me the leader of the class.

But it wasn't enough. Girls who had scorned me before, now wanted to befriend me. But I could see through them. They only wanted to ally themselves with me because they hoped to ingratiate themselves with my mother.

There's something very seductive about a Gift. Feeling the earth mother's power within you. Your senses are heightened tenfold and you are aware like never before – of the power in the very air around you that you breathe. The ground you walk on. In the leaves, the flowers, the plants, the trees, the water. Everything resonates with a glow, a wired edge. Sensing it, feeling it all around me made me hungry.

For more.

Yes, I wanted more. I wanted to be as strong as my mother. I wanted to be consumed and enveloped by the force of earth. I would lie awake at night, thirsting for it. That rush, that sweet pleasure when Melita's life force had become mine. I could taste it in my mouth. It was a constant physical ache and longing. I couldn't understand why my mother didn't make use of the Bone more often. Yes, she was powerful but how could she resist the lure, the delicious taste of even more power?

The moment when it came was deceptively simple. Noalani was away from the Keawe Citadel on one of her many visits to the outer islands. She took these trips often with some of her closest circle so they could see and be seen by those who worshipped us. Keawe visits were a reminder of who we were and what we could do. Wherever they went, people would bring their daughters to them, hopeful they would be found blessed with a Gift of Fire, eager for their child to gain admission to godhood. It was considered an honor above all others for one's child to be chosen by the Keawe. Even if it was just to prepare their food, clean their houses and wash their clothes. Besides, families were also given compensation for their daughters. I had seen many girls come to the live among the Keawe. They came eagerly. To live as a commoner after all, meant an early arranged marriage for many and a life of harsh toil and struggle in the fields, risking death many times over to bring yet another squalling infant into the world. Most girls who came to the Keawe came happily, with gratitude and relief at the blessing of being chosen.

Except for Anuhea. She had been brought in with the last intake and she stood out for me because where everyone else had been alive and lit with the excitement of seeing what it was really like behind our walls – Anuhea walked with eyes downcast and feet dragging in the dust. When they called her name in the ceremony, she was slow to respond.

"Anuhea."

She walked forward to receive her initiate necklace from Ikaika the lead instructor. There were dried up tears, wet and dirty on the new girl's face. "Welcome to the Keawe." Ikaika intoned. "You will walk among us and learn how to speak to the Fire that burns within you. If your progress is pleasing to the Earth Mother, you will unleash your Gift and covenant with us as a true Keawe sister."

No response.

They gave her a red carved wood necklace, identifying her as a Keawe initiate of the highest degree which meant she was not destined for housework or cleaning duty. If all her study and training paid off, she would be a Keawe Sister in the same circle with my mother. One day. Yet there she stood, crying. I was disgusted. Didn't she realize how blessed, how precious her Gift was? How much power and authority would be in her future? In all the years I had seen the new girls brought in, I had only ever seen four red necklaces bestowed and each of those four had gone on to be admitted to the Sisterhood and become leaders in their own right, surpassing Keawe much older than they.

It was time for the girls to be shown to their house where they would live for the duration of their training years. Anuhea's tears intensified and she cried loudly, not bothering to even try to hide her agitation. I watched her walk past and my anger grew. She was a chunky girl with broad shoulders, thick arms and legs. Her clothes were ragged and worn. Clearly she was from the poorer class. This made her agitation even more of a mystery to me.

I watched her from a distance over the next few days. Her sadness didn't go away. She was morose and sour with a glassy stare during lessons. She sobbed whenever anyone spoke to her.

"What's wrong with her?" I asked Ikaika. "Doesn't she know what her red necklace means?"

Ikaika was very old. She had been working with new Keawe for many generations so perhaps that explained the patience I didn't have. "Her heart sings for her family. She wants to go home."

I scoffed. "Her family could never give her what the Keawe can. What a fool."

Late one night, I went to Anuhea's sleeping mat. She lay with her face to the wall and her shoulders shook as she cried. *Ugh.* Did she do nothing else besides cry useless tears? "Stop that right now."

The girl turned to look at me. She didn't speak. Just kept crying big fat tears of hopelessness. I stamped my foot. "What's wrong with you? You have been chosen by the Keawe. You are a red bone initiate. Don't you know what that means?"

"I don't know and I don't care." She turned her back on me.

I knelt down beside her, trying not to curl my lip at the smell of her. I don't know when this girl last bathed but she stank. How could our mother earth give so much of her Gift to one such as this? A plodding, sniveling wretch. I tried to fake kindness I didn't feel. "You should care. There hasn't been a red bone initiate since I was a little girl. It means your Gift is very strong and one day you will be one of the Keawe of the inner circle with the Bone Bearer herself. The power you will have – it will be so, so good." For a moment I was lost in the memory of that night when I had savored in Melita's Gift. How good it had felt. How badly I wanted to taste more of it. "Don't think of the family you used to have. Think instead of what you will have here."

Anuhea sat up and her ugly face was even uglier in all its splotchy redness. "I don't want to be Keawe. I want to go home. I want my family."

"Well they didn't want you, did they? That's why you're here."

Her whole body crumpled as a fresh wave of sobs wracked her. "My father said no. My mother knelt and begged them not to take me."

"Don't lie to me or to yourself. Everyone wants their daughter to be chosen by the Keawe. Everyone. It's an honor above all others to live with the gods and even more rare to be admitted to their inner circle. Besides, your family is poor. They would have wanted the Gift price."

Anuhea shook her head. "No, my parents didn't want this for any of us. For any of their daughters. They hid me and my sisters from the Keawe every year so we couldn't be taken."

"But why? If you are Keawe you can have everything you've ever dreamed of."

She dared to look at me with pity. "Because my parents love me and my sisters. We love each other."

And then this smelly, repugnant girl shared with me her miserable story. She told me of her four younger sisters and how they shared the same sleeping mat. How they played together. Searched the shallow rock pools for shellfish. Helped their mother in the field. At night they all sat outside their little house while her father played the ukulele and her mother sang. "We don't care if we're poor. We don't want anything from the Keawe. We just want to be a family. My little sisters will be missing me, crying for me. They need me." She appealed to me then, and the pleading in her eyes was raw and sickening. "Don't you have a family that misses you? A little sister maybe?"

I thought about the days and nights alone while mother was busy with her duties. Lonely hours spent reading the ancient scripts in the frangipani burial grounds because it was the one place I could be sure to evade the taunts and pitying glances of the others. Evenings spent making up stories in my head of a mother who wouldn't leave me all the time. I thought about the real sisters that had been denied to me. A sister who would always defend my back and champion my cause no matter how Ungifted I was. Something twisted inside me. Something hateful. "My family is here with the Keawe. As is yours. You may be sad now but your parent's sadness will not last long. Their bellies will be filled with the Gift price and soon you will not even be missed."

A fresh spate of crying. "They will never be happy. Not now." Before I could contradict her, she blurted it out, "They killed my father. When he tried to stop them from taking me, your Keawe set him on fire and we all had to watch him burn." The rest of her story came unbidden then and I listened even though I didn't want to.

When the Keawe came to Anuhea's house, there were only a handful of them. They were led by Noalani but she allowed another to be the spokeswoman. One of the inner circle ordered the family to bring forth their daughters. "For many tides now, we have felt a burning here from this place. A summons. There is one among you where the Gift is strong. We know you have daughters. The village has told us so."

Anuhea's father was a quiet man, solid and sure. But on this day, Anuhea felt his fear. All the way in their hiding place, she felt it. Her little sisters cried and she shushed them. 'Look after your sisters Anuhea' her mother had told her. She was the eldest. It was her job to take care of the little ones. Always. And so on this day, they hid and Anuhea shushed and soothed her sisters.

She could hear her father's dissent, his attempt to bargain with a Supreme Being. "Please great ones. We are but a humble family. We do not have much. Our most precious possessions are our children. Please don't take them from us. We ask you to bestow that honor upon another family more deserving than us."

Anuhea could barely hear her mother's soft voice as she added her pleadings to that of her husband. "Please leave us be. We don't have much. We beg of you."

"Enough!" The leader took over then. She ignored the man as was Keawe custom. "Woman, we have wasted enough time here. Call your children now. Your Keawe demand it."

Anuhea's father spoke the last words she would ever hear him say, "No, I won't let you take my daughters."

From her hiding place Anuhea heard a hiss and sparking sound like a log snapping in a hungry fire. Her mother screamed. The Keawe woman raised her voice above the terror. "If you are within reach of my voice, hear me now.

Your father burns slow and certain. If you do not make yourselves known by the time he is reduced to ash, I will set your mother alight next."

Anuhea and her sisters were wide-eyed with horror. They could hear the agonized screams of their father. Above it their mother shouted, "Run! Anuhea take your sisters and run."

The little girls struggled against Anuhea's arms. "Mama, Papa!"

Anuehea tried to restrain them, "No, we can't go out there."

Her sister Litalia hit at her. "Let me go. We have to help them."

From far away they heard a new sound. They didn't know it but it came from their mother as the Bone Bearer very slowly dragged a searing dagger of fire down her back, crisscrossing skin with intricate patterns of torture. "How long must your mother suffer before her daughters remember that they love her? Come out children. I know where you are hiding but it would be so much better for you if you came out here and put an end to this."

The sisters listened to their mother's whimpering screams as the Keawe tortured her and Litalia turned eyes full of hatred on Anuhea. "Why don't you do something? You're the one they want. I've seen you play with fire when you think everyone is asleep." She shoved at her big sister. "You're the reason this is happening. Do something!"

But Anuhea could do nothing. Yes she had sparks in her fingers but that was all. She had never unleashed fire's wrath. Never spoken to the heart of earth. Nobody had taught her how. And so she sat there with her little sisters and cried while the Keawe burned their father and tortured their mother. But Litalia was strong and determined. She bit Anuhea's restraining hand and wriggled free. She ran to the clearing in front of their house.

Anuhea shouted and ran after her, "No! Litalia come back."

Both of them stopped at the sight before them. Their father was alight. Their mother was on the ground, arms and legs spread-eagled and pinned face down. Her back razed with a multitude of cuts. She turned her head and saw the girls, whispered, "No. My babies please. Go." Another plea to the audience of Keawe. "Please don't hurt them."

There was no more torture that day. The Keawe had got what they came for. They took Anuhea and left her mother and sisters alive. "We are protectors of women. Even for women as foolish as you." They left the Gift price. Litalia ran to hug Anuhea one last time, whispered in her ear, "One day, I will come for you. I will make them pay for what they have done to us."

The Keawe dragged Litalia away kicking and screaming, throwing her on the ground beside her mother.

The night seemed colder, deader when Anuhea finished telling me her story. It numbed me. I knew Keawe could punish people. I had seen them mete out harsh judgments on those who transgressed against earth. But we were gods after all. Guardians and caretakers of a precious earth that man was always too quick to desecrate. I looked at this heartbroken girl not much older than me and I reminded myself that none of her horrible story would have happened if her parents had given her up freely. Her Gift did not belong just to her after all. Keawe had a sacred responsibility – that's why Earth entrusted us with her power. For them to refuse it and spurn entrance to the Sisterhood – well, that was sacrilegious. And just plain stupid.

I put pictures of burning fathers and mothers out of my mind and made my decision. "I'm going to help you escape from here."

"Thank you. All I want is to go home. My mother will need me more than ever."

Her eagerness only further affirmed for me that this ungrateful wretch did not belong here amongst the gods. I would be doing her a favor. I would be doing us *all* a favor.

"I will come back for you after midnight when everyone is sleeping. We will leave then. Don't speak of this to anyone."

She nodded her head, all tears forgotten. Then a shadow of doubt crossed her face, "How will we escape"?"

I shriveled her with a look. "I've lived here all my life. My mother is the Bone Bearer and I can come and go as I please." I faked a smile. "Wait a few hours. Soon, very soon you will be free."

There was no preconceived plan. It came to me gradually as I left Anuhea's room that night. With Noalani away, I had free rein of her quarters. I knew where the Tangaloa Bone was and how to use it. It welcomed me with a warm glow in my hands that I could feel all the way to my secret places. I wrapped the Bone in soft tapa cloth in case of prying eyes and made my way to Anuhea's room. A whisper and she crept to join me outside, her whole body alight with excitement.

"Follow me. I will take you to a secret exit out of the Citadel."

That girl was so stupid she would have followed me anywhere. How could Mother earth have entrusted so much power to such an imbecile? Anuhea blundered along after me through bushes and trees. I had to slow my pace down because she was huffing and puffing trying to keep up with me. How could one so poor be so fat? I thought food was scarce for poor people? We walked until I was sure we were a safe distance from the Citadel and then paused beneath the soft lilting frangipani trees. She looked around, gasping for breath, "What is this place? It looks scary."

It would. To a cowardly sluggard like her. I smiled secretly to myself in the gentle moonlight. This was my favorite place. Here, we would not be disturbed. Here I could do as I liked.

Anuhea's voice was fearful. "Where are we? I thought you were going to show me how to get away and go home?"

With my back to her, I eased the Bone from its wrappings. Softly it breathed its desires. "I said I would help you go free."

I turned to face the stocky chunk of a girl that quivered wet with perspiration in the humid night. She eyed the staff in my hands, fearful. "What is that?" She took one step back. "You said you would help me. You said."

The Fire in my core, it knew what was coming. It tasted the sweet promise in the air. It hungered. It trembled with longing. "Yes, I did. Anuhea, you are unworthy of the Gift you have been given. As the Bone Bearer, I revoke your rights to it."

The fool only looked confused. But then what did she know about ancient tradition? About Keawe birthright and blood lines? All she cared about was sniveling for lost family. I exhaled and as I did so, the Bone I bore aloft crackled and sparked. The surge of power was painful but it was a pain I wanted. "Tonight you will go free." Anuhea stumbled and fell backward, shrieking garbled prayers and pleas to the gods for help.

I am the only god who can hear you.

The girl shriveled. Her flesh melted into bone and a searing light connected us. Anuhea's Gift hurt way more than Melita's. It brought me to my knees, shuddering with the weight of the agony that ripped through me. But then surging power filled me. It seamed with my very essence in a delicious fluidity. Ecstasy had me in her embrace. I lay back on the wet grass. For a moment I was one with the stars overhead. Flying. Lost in the wonder and awe of the universe that was mine to claim. I don't know how long I lay there for. I knew only that nothing would ever give me as much pleasure, as much joy – as the consuming of another's Gift.

After a long time, I rose a new woman. It seemed my feet did not even touch the earth, so light and graceful did every pore of my skin feel. I was alight and my body, my heart and mind sang to the earth that had made me. The surge of pleasure that this added power gave shocked me. I could not fathom how this girl had carried all this within her and *not* rejoiced in it. I didn't have a shred of guilt for the girl that used to be. How could there be? She had only been a vessel for the Gift that was meant to be mine.

The morning breeze scattered Anuehea's ashes through the frangipani grove. 'Go Anuhea, dance and run wild forever. I promised you would be free.' My laughter ricocheted through the trees and I didn't care if anyone heard me. Every day brought me closer to that which I was meant to be.

There was a mild uproar the next day when Anuhea's absence was noted. She had been a level four red Bone initiate after all. Knowing how she had been an unwilling admission to the Sisterhood, people thought she must have run away. A team was sent to her family. I heard talk of more torture and threats but didn't pay much attention. Why should I? Anuhea was in a better place now and I was busy with Keawe matters.

Ikaika, the elder in charge of training the young ones was excited by my progress. She went to Noalani upon her return to the Citadel. "Covenant Keeper, it is a wondrous, beautiful thing. Your daughter can do things with fire and earth that I have never seen in one so young!"

The assembled sisters hummed and buzzed with curiosity. It wasn't like Ikaika to be excited about anything or anybody. The Elders gazed at me with newfound interest. After so many years of nothing, could it really be true that Pele the Ungifted had finally blossomed?

"Show them Pele." Ikaika instructed.

It was not raw firepower that revealed a Gift worth praising but rather, how well one could summon and manipulate Fire in its smallest forms. I took position in the center of the sand-covered arena facing the target – a circular array of black rocks that barely touched the other. One of them was marked with a scratched X. That was my focal point. The crowd quieted with hushed breath as I tried to settle my rapid pulse. *Calm. Serenity is mine.* I reached with one hand and pointed. I spoke to Fire and she answered, rushing from earth up my spine and down to my fingers eagerly. The single strand of flame whipped out like a coiled spring. Straight and sure. Fire found its mark, barely trembled and the single rock wavered and liquefied into molten ball that seeped along the sand. A direct hit.

There was a scattering of applause. Melting a single rock amidst a pile of many was one of the basic skill tests. But there was more. Ikaika called for three of the intermediate Keawe to come forward. "Pele will undergo a triple attack test now."

The crowd erupted. Chatter, questions, doubts and protests. I was nobody's favorite but none of them wanted to see the Bone Bearer's daughter killed in the circle. Noalani rose from her seat, startled. "Ikaika, what is the meaning of this? Pele is only a first level initiate. A triple attack test so early in her training would be foolish and deadly."

Ikaika moved to stand beside me. She put both arms on my shoulders and stared right into my eyes. "I believe you can face a triple assault. Do you?"

I shook her hands loose. "I don't believe. I know. Don't insult me with doubts." I turned to face the crowd. And my mother. "Bring on the testing. I am ready."

A group of Elders conferred in the corner before they sent out three Intermediate Keawe. I knew them by name only, otherwise they were strangers to me. Luata, Kahula, and Tamua. They stripped to the basics of Olohe warfare – barefoot with a loincloth and a wrapped band across their breasts, skin gleaming with coconut oil. They stood across from me in a triad formation and awaited Ikaika's signal. As soon as she nodded her assent, the lead woman, Luata dropped to her knees and sent a double whip wire of flame searing toward me. The other two waited, hung back. Clearly they thought one could take me alone. I smiled at Luata's position. Like many of the Keawe, she needed to be in close proximity to the earth for full effect – which is why so many Keawe preferred to fight low and to the ground. To identify the most powerful among them, all you had to do is watch and gauge how high they carried themselves. The Inner circle of the Sisterhood all walked tall on the battlefield. My mother was the only Keawe who could summon fire without even touching the earth. I had once seen her raze an entire line of rebelling warriors – while standing on the second floor of her home.

I met the double whip assault without flinching, pushing a shield of dirt and rock to meet it, yanked it from the ground before me. It wasn't a thick wall but it was enough to deflect Luata's fire whip. "Is that all?" I turned to address the Elders. "Perhaps these three do not know the protocol for a triple assault? I know I am new to my Gift, but I have seen the triple test and it is a well-orchestrated team effort. Are these women doing it right?"

I pretended to bow as I spoke, but the insult was clear. Before the Elders could answer, Luata flushed and spat at me, "*Lapuwale, pa'a ka waha!* Worthless, shut your mouth." She motioned for the other two to stand beside her.

The three of them clasped hands, knelt. Kahula and Tamua were on the outskirts. They each sparked the initial fire strike with a fleeting scratch of their fingers through the sand. All three of them blazed into light and separated. Luata advanced. She was angry now. She wielded ropes of fire in each hand, spun them about her body and head with effortless ease. They carved heated pathways through the air between us. For a moment I was mesmerized. The other two Sisters did the same, moving to circle about me so that I was surrounded by swirling patterns of fire. I was locked in a spider web of flame. Or so they thought. Luata was overeager. She broke formation and leaned in to land a blow across my face. I let her, the sting lit up my whole being, set the blood coursing through my veins. Before she could melt back into formation I reached and yanked at her arm, feinted and twisted her arm behind her back.

I paused for a heart's pulse and whispered, "Feel the power of the Broken, *lapuvale*." Power coursed through my veins, one vicious wrench and there was the sound of bone breaking. "Snap."

Luata whimpered but I wasn't done with her. I threw her to the ground at my feet, kneeling to duck a chain swipe of flame from Kahula behind me. I slammed my fist on the earth and it answered with a rending groan and shake. My attackers struggled for balance. Shocked that I had power over the ground beneath their feet.

Luata was trying to stand, biting her lip against the pain of her arm that dangled uselessly by her side. "Not so fast dearest sister," I said.

A vicious motion of my hands and the soil surged to my command, a giant eel of brown coiling itself around Luata's mid-section, pinning her arms and pulling her back towards me. Once at my feet, I planted one foot square on her chest, leant down to grab her head in my hands. *Jerk, twist.* A quick, clean death. The crowd was shocked silent.

I always thought I would be afraid in my first battle. But this? This was exhilarating. This was truly living.

Now for the other two. Kahula tried hitting me with a fire rope again. Instead of ducking, I grabbed it in my bare hands and let it sear into my flesh. Smoke and the stench of burning flesh filled the air before I made the fire my own and turned it against its owner. Her control over it was easily broken because her meager gift was nowhere near as powerful as mine. She screamed as her fire betrayed her.

Tamua went to strike at me with her fire attack. A thought, a feeling and that seething rope of red and orange belonged to me. Without even touching it, I assumed ownership and it obeyed my command and wrapped itself around Tamua's neck. She choked and grabbed at her throat, trying to get free. I had two Keawe in my grasp now, at my mercy.

And I did not feel merciful.

A pause to look around at the shocked expressions that gaped at me. Horror, fear, awe – respect. The things I had longed for all my life, culminated in that moment of decision. There was no hesitation. An expansive gesture, I threw my arms out wide and unleashed the fury within. Whips of fire lashed and both women were decapitated. I didn't even glance down at the heads which rolled to rest at my feet.

There was absolute silence. Every Sister was on her feet. Including Noalani.

I bowed. "I believe that's called a victory?"

I left the arena without waiting for a response. Our battle rules clearly stated a triple assault test was to the death. Except, I had never seen anyone take a literal interpretation of the guidelines. All the test battles I'd ever watched had ended in an opponent humbly ceding defeat and the victor being admitted to the next tier of Sisterhood. Celebrations, music, dancing and singing. Laughter and light. Not anymore. Not now. I scorned such weakness. All those Keawe had not taken the triple assault test to its true ending because they had been weak. Lacking the fortitude and triumphal Gift necessary to be a true warrior of earth's core.

I vowed to change all that.

That night was a somber one amongst the Keawe. I was left alone in my mother's chambers to think about the day's events.

Noalani confronted me. "You did it, didn't you?"

"What?" I didn't need to fake confident ease. I relished in it.

She was pale in the lamp light. "You took the Bone and used it on another. You stole someone's Gift and killed them. Who was it?"

"I don't know what you're talking about. I've been training for a long time to perfect the Gift I've been given. It hurts you would accuse me of such things. Besides, don't you mean *you*, mother? You used the Bone to steal the Gift of that girl ..." I had to reflect for a minute to try and remember her name. "You used your power and position as Covenant Keeper. The only person here, who is a killer, is you."

Noalani flinched. For the first time, she looked old to me. Tired. She looked weak. "No. What I did, I did for you as a gift from mother to a daughter. I did it because I love you, more than anything. All I wanted is for you to be happy. Are you happy Pele?"

I smiled, "Yes I am. Very happy. Out there in the arena today, what I did – I never dreamed that such a thing, such a day could be possible. It was glorious."

She was guarded now. "Was that necessary? Those women were your sisters."

"They have never treated me as one of them. I'm not an equal in their eyes and I have yet to meet any in the Covenant that regard me as a Sister."

Noalani didn't push the issue with me anymore that night. But from then on, she watched me closely. Did she believe me? I don't know. What I do know is that after the triple assault test, the relationship between us changed and not only that – the distance between me and the other Keawe, increased.

Where before people ignored me as worthless – they now spoke of me in hushed tones as I passed by. It's a good thing I didn't want any friends because I surely had not won myself any by killing three Intermediate Keawe.

I was admitted to the Intermediate and then the Senior circle. I stood alongside Keawe many years my senior and they didn't like it. I felt their hatred. It burned into my back in training sessions and scratched at my face in council meetings. For some inexplicable reason, it hurt more than their earlier treatment of me. I had always thought it was only a Fire Gift that separated us, but I saw that I was wrong. They were nothing like me. There was nothing that bound us. There was distrust and there was fear. I had killed three of their own and it drove a wedge into the divide that already separated us. Knowing that made me angry. It made me hate them even more because it was evidence they had turned away from the ancient traditions and did not honor the sacred charge we had been given by Tangaloa.

Noalani saw all these things and her wariness of me only increased. I felt her watching me during classes and fight sessions. One day in particular stood out. One of the sisters, newly covenanted to Noalani had been caught leaving the sanctuary to meet her lover. That she was meeting a boy was not in itself an offense. But there were rules to adhere to and a process to follow before a Sister could allow a man into her life. It could not be secret. And it could not be without the sanction of the Keawe Elders. This Keawe had foolishly allowed herself to become attached to this young man. The girl's name was Tiala and she wept as she knelt before my mother.

"Please, I meant no harm. Forgive me."

Noalani ignored her and motioned for the guardians to bring in the boy. He was pleasant to look at, wearing only a tapa cloth covering at his waist so that his broad chest was on bare display. He had glossy black hair that hung down his back and braided through with a scattering of red feathers. They had his hands tied with liana vine but he did not cower or tremble to be in the presence of the Keawe Covenant Keeper. He must have been afraid – how could he not have been? But he did not show it. It was only when he saw Tiala that his composure snapped. He pulled free and ran to kneel beside her where they whispered words of endearment to each other. It was like the world faded away for them and they were in a cocoon of their own making. Something vicious and poisonous twisted inside me. It was a sinuous green eel that burrowed into places I kept hidden. What was it?

Jealousy.

I watched them hold each other, whispering words of comfort and reassurance that would be meaningless in the hours to come and envy was a crippling thing that took me by surprise. Why did I want that? Why did I long for a boy to hold me that way? Look at me that way? Defy death to be with me?

I hated myself for the weakness, the foolishness. And so when the Elders passed judgment on the lovers, I rejoiced. When Noalani called for one to carry out the sentence, I stepped forward with boldness. Eager to rid myself of the Green Eel.

She didn't like it. "Pele, the task of executioner usually falls on an Elder, one with more experience than you."

There was a quiet murmuring in the assembly which only fuelled my desire to do it. "Our Covenants state that any with a willing heart and a steady hand can serve in this duty. Please, I ask for the honor of serving you and our Sisterhood."

She flushed but hid her anger well. She couldn't deny me. Not when I stood before the Assembly and quoted the Covenants to her face. "Very well then. So be it." She spoke to the offender before her. "Tiala, you have one last chance to redeem yourself. Forsake this boy and his life will be forfeit for yours. You are one of us. Don't turn your back on your birthright and your Sisterhood."

There was no hesitation. Tiala gripped the boy's hand tightly and raised her voice so it spoke to the very back of the Assembly. "I choose him. I choose love."

Perhaps the boy thought they would die together. Perhaps somehow, he thought there would be some guarantee of eternal togetherness in that. What a fanciful notion. Several of the Guardians went to separate the couple. That's when the reality started sinking in. The boy fought against the hands that restrained him. He shouted and struggled but it was useless. Noalani spoke the ritual words that released Tiala from her covenant. A Guardian wrenched the bone pendant from around her throat. Another used a shark tooth knife to hack off her hair.

It was my turn.

Guardians freed Tiala from her bindings and flung her into the circle. Watchers hissed as she stumbled and fell onto the sand. All eyes were on us. The murmuring crowd faded away. I blocked them all out. All I could see and hear – was the trembling girl in front of me.

Tiala spat at me with contempt, "You! It matters not what power you have now, you have never been one of us and you never will. No matter how many of us you kill. You will never be one of the Sisterhood, we all saw you kill your own flesh and blood in the triple test assault. We saw you. You liked it!" Her voice rose to a shriek.

"Yes, I did. Just as I'm going to enjoy killing you." I spoke to Earth and she answered. A single rope of pure fire ruptured from my right hand. I gripped it firmly and swung its coils above me. "First, I will silence you." A deft twist and the crackling rope flashed out at Tiala and whipped around her face. I wrenched it tight around her mouth blocking off her scream of pain with pure flames.

The young man raged, "Tiala!"

She writhed against the constraint, tried to pull at the fire ropes. Then she tried to summon an attack flame but her focus was all off and she couldn't make anything more than a scattering of sparks. She dropped to her knees as the smell of burning flesh choked the air, rolled on the ground in jerky, contortions. It was an odor that turned my stomach. I fought nausea as I looked around the assembly. No-one met my gaze. Instead they huddled in groups, silent. Fearful.

I loved it.

Noalani's command interrupted, "Pele, end this now."

The look on her face was a stone dagger to my chest. It wasn't pride or joy in her daughter's strength. No. It was disgust. Contempt. She rose to her feet and in that moment she wasn't my mother. She was the Covenant Keeper of the Keawe, giver and taker of life. "No matter what offenses Tiala has committed, she is still a Sister. We do not torture our own. Not like this. We give a quick, clean death. Finish this execution now!"

There was a hum of agreement from the assembly. Like mindless bees. Fools. All of them. No matter. What did they know? They hadn't tasted anything more than their pitiful share of Earth's Gifts. Not like I had. I turned back to Tiala and finished her off. Fire can be very incisive when directed with the right precision. It can make dismembering a person a work of art, a thing of beauty.

Blood spatters in the sand like scarlet hibiscus petals.

Beautiful.

Noalani spoke into the hushed silence. "Release the boy."

He ran over to the pieces of the girl's body. Clung to them. Wept over an incomplete corpse. Begged the gods to bring her back to life. "Please, I can't live without you. My love, don't go."

There was nothing precious or sweet or beloved about them now. That which had made me envy them was gone. He was just a blubbering boy, clutching the pieces of a dead girl in his useless arms.

Noalani ordered the Guardians to take him away. Return him to his village. She warned him never to return. The boy cried some more. "Kill me. Let me burn with her."

His pitiful pleas would have incensed everyone, if he wasn't so beneath us. The death ritual for a Keawe – even one who had been excised from the Covenant – was a sacred thing. We returned our bodies to the earth that had made us. The Covenant Keeper herself would summon the funeral fire, releasing the Gift back to she who had entrusted it to us. The thought of a male – any male – being allowed to burn with a Sister was revolting.

Even though he was nothing, *less* than nothing, I wondered why we didn't just kill him and be done with it. Why let him go free?

Late that night, after the funeral ritual was complete, I asked Noalani that same question. Her reply was stiff and cold. "The greater sin lies with the Sister. We are the ones entrusted with the Fire Gift. We are the ones taught to live by a Keawe code. A man is just a man. They are ruled by their baser nature and must be treated as such. In life and in death."

"But surely it's a mistake to let him go. He's going to spend the rest of his life hating the Keawe."

"Exactly. And in doing so, he will be a warning voice for any others who assume that we are like other women. He will be a reminder of who we are and what we stand for. Our ancient laws seem harsh to many, but they are there for a reason. To maintain the sacred guardianship that we hold. They are laws that even I, the Covenant Keeper, am not exempt from."

We were both silent then and I knew she thought of my father. The man she had killed at my birth. The way the law dictated she must. Did she think of him every time a Keawe went rogue?

Every time a Keawe made the mistake of placing a man above her Covenants?

Did she think of him every time she looked at me?

"Pele, why did you volunteer to stand as executioner today?" She spoke softly in the soft shadows.

Carefully Pele. "To serve you. To serve the Sisterhood."

"The Gift of our Earth Mother is a heavy thing we must bear and the weight of it can be too burdensome at times."

I feigned innocence. "What do you mean?"

"There is such a thing as too much fire. The Gift within us must always exist in harmony with those around us. Just as many must be reminded to live in harmony with the earth they walk upon, so too must we nurture the fire within us with gentleness. You have seen what our Mother can do when man abuses her. She is our Mother and like any mother – she can be loving, gentle and kind. She exists to love and nurture her child. But there is another side to every mother. That which must be strong, firm, cruel even – to ensure continuity of life. Think of a wildfire that devours an expanse of forest. Yes it destroys but in so doing, it sows the seeds for new life to begin. Our ocean mother can wipe out an entire village when the earth shakes but that ensures man doesn't take his place here for granted. Mother Earth likes to remind us that she reigns supreme. She must be treated with respect because we are only walkers here. Not masters. Not even us."

I had heard the same words many times before, so often I could recite them. Hearing them from her now, when I had silenced everyone with the strength of my Gift, irritated me. She must have sensed it. "Pele, fire is very persuasive. Don't make the mistake of letting her rule you. Fire will consume you. It is my task as Keeper to watch that such a thing does not happen to any of our Sisters. And if it does, I must do what is necessary."

The unspoken threat slithered into all the spaces between us. "Go now. Sleep. It has been a long and difficult day." She looked tired. "It's always a blow to my soul when a Sister dies. It gave me no pleasure to see one of us die today Pele. Such a thing should never give joy my daughter. Please … remember that."

I left her but inside I was a seething mess. I had been rebuked by the Covenant Keeper.

And I didn't like it. Not one bit.

Weeks went by without incident. I was obedient. Earnest and co-operative. I wanted the Elders to have nothing to hold against me when the time came for admission to the Council. There was a place on it for me and I itched to take it. I wanted Noalani to have no suspicions of me.

Choosing Day came – when young men would present themselves to the Keawe and hope to be chosen as consorts for a day, a week, a month perhaps. Consorts were given wealth. Land. The admiration and honor of their village. There was always the risk of course that a Keawe would find fault with her chosen consort and kill him. But such a thing was frowned upon in general. Men were for our choosing but we were to behave as gods – with benevolence and impassionate care. The Sisterhood had no issues with men per se. They were like children who needed to be guided in all things with a gentle but firm hand. Patience was key.

A Consort was tolerated within our Citadel. He was treated well and allowed to move freely. Within reason. When a Keawe tired of her Consort, he was released from his duties and sent back to his village with a generous tribute. No Consort ever stayed longer than a few months because otherwise that was a sign a Keawe was becoming too attached to him – which was forbidden. If a Sister decided she wanted to have a child, she would seek the permission of the Elders. If granted, she would cease taking the special herbal concoction that rendered her infertile. As soon as new life stirred within her, the Consort was sent away and a Sister was forbidden to tell him he had fathered a child. Such knowledge would seal his death warrant. It rankled at times that we even needed men to procreate. It fostered a reliance that didn't sit well with us. We were gods. We spoke to the stars above and breathed with the fire beneath our feet. Yet we needed a man's seed to make life.

That was an irritation.

I was old enough to choose a Consort. But I didn't want to. Not really. Why would I want a boy following me around everywhere? Hanging on my every word? Getting in the way of my training? But I went to the Games anyway. Just for curiosity's sake.

Noalani smiled when she saw me enter, beckoned for me to sit beside her. "Will you take a Consort this year Pele?"

"I doubt any will be choosing me Mother." I was only half-joking. I had no illusions about where I stood in comparison with the rest of the Sisters gathered there. Unlike the others, I invested no time or effort in my appearance. All around us the Keawe glistened with fragranced coconut oil and the sun danced on the colors of their finery. Feather-crested head pieces. Shell-adorned pandanus shifts. Mulberry stained lips and kohl lined eyes. In full regalia, the Sisters were a beautiful sight to behold. And my mother the fairest of them all. Would she take a consort this month I wondered? She rarely did anymore. Few of the Elders did. A consort was a flippancy they could do without.

The ceremony was beginning. It was the same every year. The young men who came to offer themselves as Consorts would compete in various sports. The winner of each would then "choose" one of the Sisters. The events began with wrestling. One of my least favorite sports – all that grappling around in the sand, hand-to-hand, all that effort and exertion when all I wanted to do was razor fire my opponent's head from their shoulders …

The first pair was two very young boys. I guessed them to be no older than me. Seventeen, perhaps even younger. They were not evenly matched and the more skilled boy quickly subdued the other. The match was over before it had even really begun.

Noalani congratulated the winner and he was beaming with pride at being the first to choose. "Thank you Great Covenant Keeper."

"Now you must choose the Keawe that will take you for her Consort."

His delight was tiresome. Didn't this fool know the choosing was an illusion only, put in place to encourage the random nature of the pairing? If a Sister didn't want a Consort or if she weren't interested, she would refuse and the young man would move on to "choose" another. If none of the Keawe wanted him, he would be thanked for his service and sent home. Tribute-less.

I was bored with the process already. The boy at least wasn't stupid enough to choose one of the Elders which would have been pretentious and potentially dangerous for him. A sure-fire way to buy him a one-way ticket out of here. Instead he went and knelt before a young initiate who had only recently been admitted to the Sisterhood. She was new enough to this that she blushed and smiled way too much as she accepted his offer. I rolled my eyes. I gave them a week before the Elders kicked him out. Silly girls who did not guard their emotions with a Consort quickly found themselves without one and would not be allowed to participate in future Selections.

Several more wrestling bouts and I was getting bored. A whisper to Noalani. "Can I be excused?"

A frown. "No. Stay. You are overdue for a Consort."

"I don't want a consort. I'm too busy with my training."

Her hand on my arm stopped me from leaving. "This is not a request Pele. Sit."

I fought my irritation and sat back down. Fine. Give me a consort then. I didn't have to speak with him or lie with him after all. He could clean my bedding every morning and make my lemon leaf tea. And after a month I would send him away.

"Bring in the next contestants," Noalani said.

Two more boys walked into the arena. No, correction – a boy and a *man* entered the sands. The older was compact and rippled with muscle. Not very tall but he wore his strength and power proudly. I guessed him to be in his mid-twenties and I was surprised. Very few mature men offered themselves as Consort. It was a role befitting the young. Those without a wife, a family or an estate. Someone biddable. Compliant. This man who stood in the center of the ring stamped with bold tattoos was not some half-boy, ready and eager to please. He carried himself like a warrior, one accustomed to battle and I was sure I echoed the sentiments of all the assembled Keawe when I wondered, *what is such a man doing here?*

Noalani recited the ritual words. "Do you offer yourselves freely as Consort to the Keawe? Do you give of your body and will to the serving of your Chosen Keawe? If so, let the fight begin."

The younger boy's voice quavered and he stumbled over the ritual response, "I am Maui and I offer myself freely as Consort to the Keawe. May our Mother Earth smile upon me with favour and give me her strength and warmth."

The older one spoke with confidence, "I am Akamai and I offer myself," a deliberate pause, "freely, as Consort to the Keawe."

"Begin," Noalani said.

I watched Akamai as he unstrapped the bone knife he carried in a sheathe at his back and removed his outer vestments until he wore only his loin cloth. All of his markings were revealed – scars and tattoos – and they shouted a story of warrior hood. Again I wondered, *what is a man like you doing here?*

The two circled each other. The younger boy looked afraid and I didn't fault him that because the other's every move announced his warrior intent. Akamai moved light and liquid on his feet. A surprise for one so bulky, rugged. He took his time. Waited for

Maui to make the first move. When he did, Akamai countered it with lazy ease, using Maui's own impetuousness to overbalance him. A twist of limbs and Maui was face down in the sand with Akamai standing over him. A Guardian declared him the victor. No-one clapped because it was so obviously an ill-match. Maui was lucky to escape with only a bruised arm.

Akamai leant to help the boy up before turning to face us. A sardonic glint in his eye. "How do we proceed?"

The Guardian overseeing the Consort events explained, "As the victor, you now make your choice and if your selected Keawe agrees to your selection, then you will be her consort for as long as she wishes."

Akamai's face darkened and his voice was low and deadly. "Not much of a choice for the lucky man then, is it?"

He didn't wait for an answer but drew himself tall and proud. Pointed at Noalani. "What about that one over there. I choose her."

A hushed gasp of outrage. No-one dared to speak of the Covenant Keeper in such a cavalier manner. I flinched, waited for Noalani to extinguish him with a single flick of her wrist. But she merely shrugged. "I am not for the Choosing. Choose another."

Akamai grinned – and jerked his chin at me. "Fine. I will take your daughter then." His eyes raked over me and dismissed me.

My mother did not like it. "No. She refuses you also. Select another. Better yet, be gone from here. You are not a suitable candidate for Consort," she said.

His eyes laughed at me. "Forgive me. I had not realized she was so much of a child that she needed her mother to speak for her. Perhaps such a baby should not have been allowed entry to the Consort games?" He mocked me. He mocked us all and I didn't like it.

I leapt to my feet, "You are mistaken. I can speak for myself." I threw him a withering look of disdain. But he refused to be withered. I thought of all the things I could subject him to. The torture I could inflict. Someone needed to wipe that mocking smile off his face and teach him to respect the power of a woman. "I accept. You will be my Consort."

Noalani whipped around to face me. "What? No. I won't allow it." She pulled me and whispered harshly in my ear. "He is unsuitable. Dangerous. Too much for you to take on."

Akamai grinned that daring smile at me. The one that was laced with pity as if he could see right in my damaged little-girl soul to all the broken pieces inside. I pulled my arm away from Noalani and raised my voice for all to witness. "According to our laws, I accept this man Akamai for my Consort. As a proven sister of this Covenant with agency and the power to choose, I speak for myself." With my eyes, I dared Noalani to contradict me. Contradict our laws. Contradict our ceremonies.

Her face twisted as she muttered, "Fine. Have him. But be careful."

We both watched as the two men were led away. Akamai did not look back at me but I was sure of his mocking smile anyway. When the ceremony was complete, my mother dismissed us all. She said nothing more to me, only shook her head in warning. I ignored her and went to claim my Consort.

He was sitting apart from the others. Sharpening a bone knife as he sat in the shade of a fruit tree. I came up behind him but he didn't look at me. Just kept working at the rasping edge of the white blade with sure, fierce strokes. It gave me a chance to study him closer. His long black hair was loosely pulled back and tied with sinnet. The day was hot and he wore only the battle loin cloth. His strappings of shark hide and mulberry ribbon lay in a neat pile beside him. Sweat trickled in rivulets through the muscled grooves of his back.

It hit me suddenly. This was it. This would be the first time I had a conversation with a real live boy. *No, a man.*

I couldn't breathe for a moment. A million questions descended upon my mind like a hungry flock of sea birds. Squawking, pecking, and fighting for nuggets of thought. How did one talk to a Consort? How did one treat them? Now that I had a consort, what under the Earth Stars was I supposed to do with one?

He got to his feet and turned to smile at me, "Ahh, here she is. The owner of my heart and will. For as long as she so desires."

I didn't like his mocking tone. Or the dangerous glint in his eye. We were the same height but nowhere near the same size and his nearness made me uncomfortable. It was a reminder that he was heavier, bigger and stronger than I. Physically anyway, I reminded myself. I could take him with a fiery thought – that soothed my troubled mind somewhat. Gave me the composure to respond, "Gather your things. Follow me."

There were many curious eyes on us. I could feel them burning into me. All the Keawe knew that unlike most others my age, this was my first Consort. I walked fast, away from the compound and towards the quarters I occupied. Because I was the favoured daughter of the Covenant Keeper, I had my own rooms attached to my mother's lavish home.

He kept close to me the whole way. Too close. I didn't like it. Having a stranger at my back like that. I gritted my teeth and ground my insides. What had I been thinking? How was I supposed to sleep or ever have any peace with a strange man at my side? I bit down on a scream of frustration. How did other Keawe stand to have Consorts!?

In the dimness of my rooms, I motioned for him to put his things down. "Leave your things there. You will sleep in that room."

He didn't move to my bidding. Only stood there with a raised eyebrow. "Oh? I don't sleep with you?"

My lip curled in disgust at his forwardness. "No. I warn you. Come anywhere near me and I won't hesitate to set you alight. I am Keawe after all."

He laughed. Low and soft. "That you are. Trust me, I'm not going to ever forget that."

He threw his things lightly into the corner and sat down on the loose rushes, pulled one leg up to hook an arm over. "So, now what?"

Exactly. Now what. I fought it but the question burst out anyway. "Why did you pick me?"

He stared across at me and looked me up and down. Again. This time his gaze lingered. At the base of my throat where I wore the Red Bone carving that marked my Gift and my standing amongst the others. Down further to my bare arms, paused at my bare midriff and then continued to my unmarked legs. "You don't have any of their tattoos. Why not?"

He gave me a question for a question? Pride raised my chin, had me meet his stare head-on. "I am late to my Gift. I have not yet taken the full Covenant of Sisterhood. But it will be soon. There is none other who bears as much fire within as I do now."

In the close confined space, I could smell him. The air tasted of sweat, salt, and fresh-cut grass. It was not unpleasant but I didn't like the reminder that there was now a man in my personal space.

"I ask again, why did you choose me?"

"Because you are the daughter of the Covenant Keeper." The words were direct and without guile. They hurt a little. What had I expected? That he would lie and tell me it was because of my beauty? My eyes? The sinuous curves of my body? The rich mystery of my hair? Why else would a man choose me?

"Who told you I was her daughter?"

"No-one."

"You lie."

A shrug of his broad shoulders. "No-one needed to tell me. The likeness is very strong. Impossible to miss."

Perhaps he meant it as an insult. But it was a precious pearl to a daughter who had heard far too many people commiserate, '*Such a pity your daughter is not beautiful like you.*' I flushed as his words sparked a thread of heat within.

He noticed it and smiled. "Why did you accept?"

"Because I needed another set of hands. To cut wood, dig holes and make coconut braid." In that moment, I decided what I would use this Consort for. "Get up. We have a house to build. Follow me."

We walked through halls littered with the giggles and laughter of other Keawe mingling with their Consorts. Sounds that only made me hasten my step. Sounds that had him laughing at me more. So much that I whirled around and hissed, "Stop it."

"Stop what?"

"Mocking me." I took two steps closer so I could whisper, "I don't need or want a Consort. If you want the tribute, if you want me to keep you around – then you will act as my servant and understand that your only tasks will be to carry out my orders … outside the sleeping bed. I don't want you for that, do you understand me? If you can't accept that, then I will send you back to your village. Without a tribute payment."

The mocking light went out of his eyes "I understand. Order and I will obey."

The next few weeks were among the busiest I'd ever had. Akamai and I quickly fell into a routine of hard work that began early before the sun stained the horizon. We worked together to cut down trees with stone adzes and then fashion them into the brace poles for my new house. I had accepted that I would never be truly accepted by the Sisterhood and I was done trying to live among them fully. Noalani didn't like my decision to build my own quarters but she allowed it.

He was a hard worker. Strong and unwavering. Yes, he was in the Warrior class but he explained that his father had been a farmer and so he had a few skills with building tools. We worked on the house in mornings and then when the sun was high in the sky, we would train. I did not want to fall behind in my Lu'a mastery and I was grateful to have a training partner because none of the Keawe would agree to spar with me. Not since the day I had beheaded those women in the Triple Assault test.

"Why are they afraid of you?" Akamai asked.

"Because I have fire within me."

"All of you have fire within. But they – they are afraid of you. I see it in their eyes. In the way they move around you. Why is that?"

"You are mistaking respect for fear. If there is any difference in the way they behave towards me it is because I am the daughter of the Covenant Keeper. That is all."

He asked a lot of questions. About the Keawe. About our Fire. About our beliefs. And most importantly, he asked about my mother. At first I was a stone. I gave him nothing. But as the days wore on, our hands calloused on the same wood logs and our sweat mingled as we strained under the burden of rock baskets. I softened. The only defence I can offer now, is to say, I had been alone and lonely for much of my life. I did not know the meaning of friendship as I had never had any friends.

And that is all Akamai was to me in those first few weeks. A friend. He taught me new tricks with the sling shot. I showed him my special wrestling move- the one I called the *fe'e*, the octopus, because it was so slippery and evasive that no-one could ever hold me. He told me about his battles in the Warrior class. And I shared with him stories of my childhood, my struggles to stand alone and immovable before my gift had spoken. Those days with Akamai stand in my memory as some of the happiest. They were my idyllic time before the chaos that came later. And no matter what happened next, I will hold fast to my memory of the one friend I have ever had in my long life.

I drew the line at some things of course. I did not tell him what my mother had done for me. Or how I had taken the fire of those few who did not deserve it. I knew my mother watched us closely, worried for signs he was more than a Consort should be. But we spent every day working and training. And every night, Akamai slept in the other room. We were friends and I kept a careful distance between us.

Until it all changed. Until the night a black star lodged itself in my brain.

We had labored all day putting the roof on my little house. I was exhausted, every muscle ached and after the evening meal, I went to bed early, sinking into a deep sleep. Late in the night, something woke me. A sound, a presence, a feeling. I will never be certain. I opened my eyes and I knew – I wasn't alone in my room.

The shadows moved. A face in the starlight streaming through the eaves. A girl. A face that was oddly familiar. The bone white glint of a raised knife in her hand as she leapt at me. *No!* I rolled. Too late. A stabbing pain in my shoulder. I was more shocked than hurt though. *How dare she? How dare anyone try to attack me?!*

I struck back with my other arm but didn't connect. She was on me, a hand on my mouth, trying to keep me quiet, a heavy weight pressing on my chest. *Fire, I need fire.* But before I could explode with the rage within me, she raised her arm again and stabbed.

My eye.

A star fell from the heavens and lodged in my brain. Burning, searing, piercing. More stars, so many of them, a haze of light, so bright it blinded me. So hot, hotter than any fire. Screaming. I was screaming. I was pinned to the earth with a lance of pain. *I will never fly, I will never speak to the stars. Not when they are lodged in my brain.* I screamed and the scream filled the world and swallowed it up.

Akamai came. He came and he saved me from the girl who cut the shadows with her knife. He pulled the blade from my eye and carried me to the healer. He held my hand as she cleaned out the mangled mess. He held me down as she cauterized the socket with a fire stick. I could hear Noalani's voice as she gave orders, issued commands, asked questions. Efficient, authoritative, in command. And all the while, Akamai was there holding my hand. "Be strong Pele. I am with you." I clung to his words, to his presence through the throbbing star that had taken root in my brain and would not die.

Feverish days followed. The blade had been poisoned. It took all the skill of the healer, all her medicines – to keep me from falling over the edge of death. When the fever finally left, I was a burnt out husk. Alone in a lonely room.

No, not alone. My Consort was there. My mother was a frequent visitor but she was a Covenant Keeper first and a mother second. As it should be. She had things to do, responsibilities to honor. It was Akamai who fed me. Helped bathe my wounds every day. And it was Akamai who yelled at me and yanked me back to consciousness, out of the dull haze of misery I wallowed in.

"Get up." He jerked my sheet away roughly.

"Why?"

"You can't lie here forever."

"Leave me alone."

"No." He grabbed my hand and forced me to my feet. "You're going for a walk."

"I don't want to. Let go of me."

He threw me over his shoulder effortlessly. Walked with quick sure strides outside towards the distant river. The sunlight hurt my face. The threat of people looking at me, gawking at me, leering at me – hurt me everywhere. "Put me down. I'll kill you."

He didn't listen. He knew I had no will to even slap at a mosquito.

I covered my face with my hands but slivers of light and color still found their way in. It hurt. All of it. A sob, "Please, make it go away. Please let me die."

Akamai took me to the river and threw me in. I spluttered, screamed in outrage, "What are you doing? What's wrong with you?"

"You stink. You need to bathe."

"You don't know anything about what I need."

He waded into the water carrying a coconut shell of white sand mixed with fragranced macadamia oil. He scooped handfuls of the sweet smelling mixture and started bathing me. He started with my hair and then worked his way down to my arms, back and legs. There was nothing sexual about it. I hadn't bathed for days. He was my friend and he was going to make me clean. I was a carved log, immovable and without feeling. His hands were gentle but efficient as he massaged the oil into my skin and scrubbed at stubborn blood stains. I was naked but I didn't care. Nothing mattered anymore. All the fire in the world wouldn't give me my full sight back. I could take the power of every single Keawe sister and still never sleep easy again. Akamai scrubbed away all the hurt that he could reach and rinsed me with splashes of icy river water.

"There, you're clean. You will feel better now."

I snapped then. Sobs came from deep within. Guttural, keening hurt rushed up from my darkest deepest places. "No, I will never feel better. Never." I stood in the rushing river and cried.

Very carefully, he took me in his arms and held me close, soothing me with his voice, his nearness, his calmness. "Yes you will."

It felt good to be held. To be comforted. But he didn't hold me for long. He raised my face to his. "It's time for you to look at it Pele."

I averted my face. "I don't want to. Don't look at me."

"You lost an eye, that's all. This isn't the end of the world."

"How do you know?"

"You're a warrior. You are alive. That is what matters."

He peeled away the leaf bandage from the right side of my face with careful precision. Burning star twisted in its chaotic nest. It hurt. A whimper escaped and he frowned at it. He forced me to look into the water, at my reflection. "Look and see what I see – a warrior who can endure anything."

I looked.

My right eye was gone. There was a gaping hole with twisted edges of raw red and congealed pus. A dead star would rot there forever and always. It hurt still. I had been plain and forgettable before but now I was grotesque. Memorable for the wrong reason. I caught at the sobs that spilled out no matter how hard I tried to contain them. "I'm hideous."

"No, you are beautiful." He raised my face away from its cruel reflection and his fingers gently danced feather soft over my ravaged skin. He didn't flinch from my stare. "You are a warrior. You are alive … and you are beautiful. Very beautiful. "

I didn't believe him. I never would. But I let him hold me in the fading daylight as the green forest around us mocked me with its glorious perfection.

They had kept the would-be assassin alive, waiting for me to decide her fate. Noalani went with me to see her. She was in a pit barred with wood logs. They pulled them aside and the filthy figure below blinked against the harsh sunlight. She bared her lips and snarled like a feral beast. They brought her up and threw her on the ground before me. She had been beaten and starved.

Skin and bone. She was young – barely my age. She did not raise her eyes to us – only stared at the dirt.

"She came in to the Citadel through the sacred burial grounds. It's a mystery how she found her way or how she slipped past the guardians. We don't know where she's from either. She's not speaking in spite of all our efforts." Noalani said. I could guess what kind of efforts she was referring to and I was glad. I only wished I had been there to hear her scream and beg for mercy.

"We don't need her to talk." A flick of my wrist and a familiar ripple of flame coiled around my arm.

At the sound of my voice, the girl's face jerked upwards and her eyes lit up. "You!" She leapt but I was faster. A vicious twist and a rope of crackling fire was around her upper torso, restraining her. Not too tight. Not too hot. I didn't want to kill her. Not yet.

"She knows you?" Noalani was surprised. So was I.

"I've never seen her before in my life." I took a closer look at the girl who had taken my eye. "Wait, there's something familiar about you."

She reared forward and spat in my face. "Murderer."

One of the Guardians backhanded her and she fell to the ground. I pulled on the fire rope and forced her to stand. I was curious now. "I don't know you."

"You killed my sister."

Then, in that moment, I knew her. I knew who she reminded me of. *Anuhea*. That pudgy, undeserving red Bone initiate. Her face melting in a blaze of stars under a jewelled sky. Of course. *Wait, how could she know?*

The girl snarled, "That's right. Anuhea was my sister. You told her you would help her go home, but you lied."

Noalani said, "Why are we even listening to this? Pele, we kept her alive so you could kill her yourself. Do it now before I exact a mother's vengeance." The air rippled with tangled energy and I knew the whole earth wanted to rage with Noalani's anger.

"Leave us. A quick death is too good for her. Let me work on her for a while," I said.

"Are you sure?" Noalani reached to caress my face, careful not to touch the raw flesh, careful not to look at it.

I shrunk away from her. "Yes. Leave us."

They left me with this muddy, skeletal girl with hatred burning in her eyes. "You sucked her Gift dry like a parasite," she said.

"How did you know that?" I let my fingertips blaze with red and raked them across her face, drawing blood, searing trenches of charred flesh. If I was going to live forever grotesque, then that's how she would die. "Who told you this thing?"

"Anuhea. I have seen her. She is a spirit walker. She needed someone to know what happened to her. She won't rest until she has vengeance."

"You're lying."

"I speak truth. She's here now. Can't you feel her?"

I was cold in the sunshine. Spirits. They were the worst kind of enemy. One you could not see. I couldn't stop myself from looking around. Was she telling the truth? Was Anuhea really here? I knew angry deaths became angry spirits. My head ached and the black star pulsed with a white heat. It gave me the resolve I needed. She did this. She took my eye. I was scarred for life. Why should I care about an unresolved spirit? A dead girl with issues? I was Pele the warrior.

"Good." I raised my voice, "Anuhea, are you watching this? You sent this poor fool to find me?" I released the rope that bound my captive. She staggered, weak and weary. I had the bone knife she had used to take my eye. It felt smooth and light in my hands. A firm grip, a quick step forward, one arm on her shoulder as I leaned into her as if we were locked in an embrace. *Upward thrust, twist, rip and slash.*

The girl's eyes widened in frightened surprise. A wet gushing on the sand between us as her innards splashed out. A foul stench in the air. Quickly, before the light died in her eyes, I said it, "Yes, I killed your sister. I took her fire and made it mine. She was a handful of ashes in the wind when I finished with her. It felt good."

I stepped back and let her sink to her knees, still with that startled look on her face, hands grabbing at her disembowelled gut. Fury choked me. It started from the knife point of pain in my head and burned through every part of me. I whirled around, yelled at the empty air. "See what happens when angry spirits talk to the living Anuhea? Be as angry as you like you daughter of pigs, my anger will always burn brighter. Always!"

I turned back to my victim. I wasn't done with her yet. Her two eyes mocked me. A reminder of what she had done. I braced her head with one hand and stabbed the knife first in one eye and then the other. A sickly squelching sound. So satisfying. *A spirit walker with no eyes, ha!*

I slit her throat next. It was pointless but I couldn't resist it. There was blood everywhere now and I relished it. Sometimes, fire was too clean. Sometimes, you just needed to feel the satisfaction of killing with your hands. Flesh, blood and bone.

A deep breath of fetid air before I dropped the knife, gripped her lolling head in my arms and twisted. Sure and quick I snapped her neck and let her drop. The blood on my hands was sticky and thick. I smeared it on my face, down my arms and then finally, my eyes. Or what was left of them.

Blood. It was life. It was red vengeance. It was beautiful. It would hide my grotesque scars and heal my soul.

"I am Pele, I am a warrior. I am alive." Laughter. It bubbled out like foam on a waterfall as I looked down at the girl who had talked to angry spirits. "Look who's angry now Anuhea."

The black star burned in my brain. Would it never stop hurting?

I stumbled back to my little house, with the pain in my head blinding me. It's where Akamai found me as I knelt and swayed.

"Pele, what happened?"

Wild laughter. "Look Akamai, I'm all dirty again. But it's alright because I'm a warrior. I'm alive. I've got angry spirits following me but I'm alive."

"Are you hurt? I'll get the healer."

"No. Don't leave me alone please. Angry spirits. In my head. In the air. All around us. Can't you feel them?"

"Shh, it's alright. You're safe. There's only us here." He hoisted me into his arms and carried me to my sleeping mat. His skin was warm and smooth. Being in his arms was safe.

"Don't let me sleep. She's waiting, she's watching. I killed her sister but she's not going to give up. Don't let me sleep."

"I won't let anyone hurt you."

I looked in his eyes and knew he meant it. But how could even he stand against the spirits? "Don't leave me."

"You've got blood all over you. I'll go get some water to clean you up."

"No please don't go. Stay."

I don't know whether it was the raw panic in my voice, or the way I clutched at his arm but for the first time, Akamai stayed with me through the night. He held me as I battled sleep, even though I was slick with blood and stank of sweat and fear.

Because that's what friends do.

In the morning he was gone, busy with the daily chores that Consorts tended to in the Citadel and the daylight mocked my fears of angry spirits. I was glad. I did not want to talk about my nightmares. I bathed and dressed and went to see my mother. Noalani was happy my attacker had been disposed of. "You must learn how to fight one-eyed Pele. You will have to compensate for your compromised vision. I will allow your Consort to stay on with us for a few months longer. He can train with you." A thoughtful pause, "There is nothing between you, is there?"

"No." And there never would be. Not now. Who would ever love a grotesque creature like me?

"Good. See it stays that way."

We didn't speak of it, but we both knew no-one else would train with me. I had been an outsider amongst my sisters before but now? Keawe were known for their wild beauty. My difference screamed at them on my mangled face.

"I would train with you myself but I must find out how that assassin found her way into our citadel. Who hired her. Why they wanted you dead. Someone amongst us is a traitor and I will not rest until I find her." Noalani said.

My mother was very busy looking for the traitor who didn't exist. Not in this world anyway.

My training sessions with Akamai now had an added intensity. There was an urgent ferocity in everything I did that had not been there before. My nights were filled with fear and every shadow hinted of menace. I had thought I was powerful and untouchable but a skinny girl with a bone knife had proven me wrong. My eye socket slowly healed into a pinched warped mass of sunken flesh but the pain was always there. Sometimes a dull ache but other times it would stab at my brain with a viciousness that left me gasping. A constant reminder that I was not safe. As the black star burrowed deeper every day, I knew what I had to do.

I had to get more power.

It wasn't easy. Security for the Citadel had been tightened since the attack. Movement in and out was strictly monitored. I had to wait until the Choosing time when the Guardians brought in the new recruits. A mass of fresh-faced hopeful young girls, eager to become Keawe. I watched, I waited. I picked my targets carefully. Girls who were quiet and reserved. Shy and friendless. I befriended them. Earned their trust. Took them to the frangipani grove and each time, I returned feeling a little bit safer, a tad more secure. A little less afraid of the whispers in the dark.

Because there were whispers. Pictures. Blood-filled dreams. It always started with the assassin standing over me in my sleep. Watching me. Stabbing me. Then it flickered to the faces of girls whose gifts I had taken. Voices. Of the girls whose gifts I had taken. They were angry. Sad. Soulful. Lost.

Because of you, we cannot move on to the Spirit world. You carry a piece of us and so we are trapped here.

The nights held no peace for me. Sleep was fitful and unsatisfying. I sought excuses to stay awake. Took Akamai with me into the forests to hunt, to fish – anything to keep the nightmares at bay. Anything to soften the ever-present throbbing of the black star in my head. "Can you hear that?" I asked.

"Hear what?" Akamai said.

I leapt to my feet, reaching for my knife, looking around into the shadows. "That. Whispers. In the darkness. They're plotting something."

He joined me to peer into the darkness, weapon ready. "No. I can't hear anything."

You have betrayed our earth mother. Defiled her sacred gift. She will forsake you Pele. Our blood cries from the dirt. Cries to her for vengeance. For peace.

"Go away!" I shouted into the night. "Leave me alone."

"What's wrong?" Akamai asked.

"They think they can drive me insane with their spirit talk, but I won't listen." I raised my voice, "Do you hear me? Be as angry as you like. Send as many vengeful assassins as you want."

My head lanced with pain and it made me even angrier. "Even with only one eye, I will gut you all. I am warrior Keawe." I whirled and threw a fire ball into the trees. They lit up with scarlet and crimson.

"I guess we're not catching any pigeons tonight then," Akamai said.

His wry grin had me relaxing and the crackling glow of the flames around us was a comfort. No angry spirits would get through that. "I don't like to eat pigeon anyway."

"So why are we out here then?"

"The Citadel suffocates me," I replied.

We sat in companionable silence for a while as I tried to escape the ever-present misery in my head and lose myself in the glorious expanse of the stars above.

And then Akamai spoke, "What will you do when your mother dies?"

Stunned. My mother dying? Who could have ever imagined such a thing? "What kind of question is that?"

"Will you become Covenant Keeper?"

"I never thought about it."

"You aren't happy here. Why would you?" Akamai said.

"I'm her daughter. I should be the next Keeper."

"But why would you want to?" Akamai asked. "You live alone from the others. They're afraid of you."

"I don't need them to like me. It's power that rules the Keawe and I have that, no I *am* that power," I argued.

"You don't even like any of them Pele. It's a Sisterhood that you don't belong to."

"These are useless questions because my mother is not going to die. She's the Covenant Keeper and Bone Bearer. She's probably going to live forever!" I said.

"No-one lives forever. Death comes for all of us. What will you do when Noalani dies?"

I was angry then. "What are you trying to say Akamai? Where are these questions coming from?"

He went still. Quiet in the dead of night. Stared out into the flames, shrugged off the tension and stood. "Let's go for a swim."

He stripped off his weapons and waded out into the silver water. "Your fire for repelling angry spirits has made it very hot around here. Come join me."

Grateful he had let the Noalani subject go; I too, laid my weapons on the grass and walked into the pool, savouring the cool chill on my skin. I dived and when I surfaced, it was with a lighter heart. Even the ache in my head had dimmed somewhat. Side by side, we swam to the center of the pool. The moon was a golden orb suspended in a sky soft as a bat's wing. There was a crisp fragrance of mint and orange in the air from the nearby fruit trees. I snuck a look at the figure beside me.

Rivulets of water trickled down the contours of his back from his long black hair. Moonlight drenched his bronzed skin, played on the slashes of white scarring here and there. I liked to look at him. Our time together was drawing to its end and I would probably never see him again. He had been my Consort for a few months now and even though it had been in name only, we shared a closeness that I would miss terribly. Akamai was the brother, the cousin, the friend I'd never had. Perhaps that was worth so much more than being a lover. It seemed almost profane to realize I was closer to this man than I had ever been to any of my Keawe sisters.

He ran his hands through the water and something in me flamed at the sight of his body rippling and glistening with black pearl droplets. *Who am I fooling? Yes, he's my friend but I want him to be so much more.*

On impulse, I leaned over and kissed his cheek, ignoring the way he jumped and moved away from me. "I never said thank you."

"For what?"

"For saving my life. And for making me get out of that sickbed."

"You would have been fine without me. Eventually. You're a survivor," Akamai said.

"Even so, I'm grateful." I took a huge breath and plunged on, "I will miss you when you return to your village." *Please say you'll miss me too. Please say it.*

He didn't. "You never asked me why I came to the Citadel to offer as Consort."

"For the same reason all the others come – because you wanted the tribute price?" I said.

"I would rather slit my own throat then serve the Keawe."

"So why did you come then?" I asked. But not sure I wanted to know the answer.

"I had a brother. Younger than me. But he died."

The conversation had turned to unexpected things. "Oh, I'm sorry."

"Are you really?"

I was blustering now. "Of course I am. Why wouldn't I be?"

"You're Keawe. That means you don't have feelings for commoners. Why would you care about our sadness, our losses or even our love?"

He was glaring at me now and for the first time, I was afraid of my Consort. "I don't want to talk anymore. I'm going back."

He caught at my arm. "No you're not."

"Let go Akamai. Now."

"Or else what?" He gripped my arm even tighter. It hurt. "Will you set me on fire? Melt the skin off my bones? What will you do?"

"Why do you hate us so much? What did we do to you?"

"You don't know? You really don't know?"

"We are Keawe. We make the earth fertile. We safeguard our mother earth that gives you life, gives all of us life. We are worshipped and for good reason."

He laughed at me and my rote words. "Go out there Pele." An expansive gesture at the distant horizon. "Go out of your Keawe Citadel, walk among the people you say are your worshippers and listen to them. Truly listen to them. Feel their hatred. Their fear. Soak it in if you dare."

"You speak nonsense."

"Who do you think sweats and slaves so you can live here in this wealth? Where do you think your food comes from?"

I pulled free from him, hating the revulsion in his face. "The people offer us tribute as is our due. We speak for the gods. The stars, the earth …"

"They hand over the fruit of their fields and harvest because otherwise, the Keawe rain down fire on their crops and burn villages to the ground. You take their daughters and cast aside your brats who don't make the bar. You ensure our people are so poor that we send our young men to service your needs."

"Stop it! It is an honor to be chosen. It is a sacred privilege to serve the Keawe."

"If you truly believe that, then you are more foolish than I thought," he jeered dismissively.

"Don't lie. You're just like the rest of them. You came here wanting power and prestige. Why else did you come here then?"

In that terrible moment of hesitation, pain fractured in his eyes. "I came for revenge."

It all came out then. Akamai had a younger brother, barely on the cusp of manhood. A younger brother who had made the mistake of falling in love with one of the Keawe. Even worse, she had loved him in return and they had been found out. It was such a familiar story, I could have told it myself. But I didn't. I only listened and every word sunk inside me like cold stones. Because I knew how this story was going to end.

"She chose my brother and because of that, your people killed her." His fury leached out of him and choked me. "They killed her slowly and made him watch."

I whispered in the stillness, "What happened next?"

"They let him go free."

"See? We are not so cruel after all? Where is he now?"

"Dead. I'm the one who cut him down from the kukui tree where he hung himself."

"No." An indrawn breath. Suicide is rare among our people, both Keawe and commoner. Spirits of suicides were known to be lonely and reluctant to move on. I cast a fearful glance around in the shadows. Akamai's brother could very well be right here with us now. Why, he could be the reason why Akamai had chosen me for Consort. I didn't like this. Not one bit. A centipede of fire crept up my spine.

"This wasn't supposed to happen Pele. You and I." Anger was replaced with tenderness. It was at odds with his warrior markings and weaponry. Just as we would always be at odds. That made me sad.

"I hadn't planned on being friends with you either," I said.

He slid a hand behind my neck, calloused skin sending a frisson of delight through me and leaned to place his lips against my forehead. A kiss. The smile he gave me was sad. It spoke of all the possibilities that no longer belonged to us. "I'm sorry. I came here to kill the one responsible for my brother's death. I never planned on loving her daughter."

The words didn't delight me the way they should because I knew he couldn't mean them. Not really. Not once I told him the truth anyway. He waited for me to respond, searching my face. I couldn't let him know my true feelings for him. Not now. Not ever. "You can't kill Noalani."

He released his grip and stepped away from me. "It won't be easy."

"You can't kill Noalani." I repeated it louder this time.

"You can't stop me." There was true contrition etched in his face. "I'm sorry Pele. I wish it could have been different for us. The blood debt to my family must be paid." And then, an eagerness that I had never seen in him before, "I have watched you for weeks now. I have seen how you are with her, with all of them. You're not like them. You're not one of them. You don't belong here." He took my hand in his, his voice thick with hope. "Come with me. With Noalani dead, the Keawe will be in disarray. It will be easy for us to slip away. I know these forests like the back of my hand. There is a canoe with supplies in a cove not far from here. We could be gone from this land and never look back. Together."

Every word was a blow. He had given this a lot of thought. He had planned this whole thing from the beginning. "Is that all I was to you? A way to get to my mother?"

"No. I'd hoped Noalani would take me for her Consort."

"So you had to settle for a poor imitation of her then."

"Don't speak that way." He gripped my shoulders and forced me to look into his eyes. "I have worked alongside you, trained, hunted and fished with you. I've never met a girl like you before."

I was affronted, "I am no girl, I am Keawe. Did you truly think I would help you murder my own mother?"

Now he looked offended. "Of course not. I will fulfil my family's blood debt on my own." His hands dropped and he shifted back, "I didn't need to tell you of my plans. I will be gone from this place by the morning. It was foolish of me to share them with you. But our elders say love is foolish, and I want you to go with me."

And then he leaned forward and kissed me. His lips tasted of the ohelo'ai berries we had feasted on earlier, sweet and tangy. I was lost in his kiss – but only for a moment. Because louder than the hungry beating of my heart, were the whisperings in my head. *He does not love you. How can he when he does not know you truly? How long will it be before he finds out all your secrets? How long before he sees your sick, twisted soul for what it truly is? Mother Earth has forsaken you. As long as you walk on her soil, you will never find happiness.*

"Stop it!" I pushed him away from me and clenched at my head that pounded with its never-ending chant of pain. "Shut up. Leave me alone."

"Pele? What is it? Are you alright?" Akamai asked.

I looked at this man who had become what I had never expected, wanting to imprint his countenance one last time before it turned against me once and for all. "The girl your brother loved was named Tiala. She was a junior Keawe sister."

"Yes … wait, how do you know that?"

I remembered how tender his hands had been as they wiped the blood from my face, how soft his voice had felt against my cheek as he urged me to live. I remembered all these things and I knew I could not let this man go to his death at Noalani's hand. I owed him truth. Even if it cost me everything. "Because I was there. Because I'm the one who killed her. My mother passed the sentence according to the Council rules of the Keawe. I volunteered to be the executioner."

"Why?"

"Tiala cast her Keawe sisterhood aside for a boy. It wasn't a worthy sacrifice. She deserved to die."

"You cut her to pieces. You gutted her in the sand and left her to wallow in her own shredded insides and my brother saw it all. Why?"

Even then, I didn't feel bad about it. Ancestral law dictated her death. By spitting on her Keawe heritage, Tiala had relinquished all rights to mercy. No, I didn't feel bad about Tiala. Or her crying lover. But I felt sorrow for Akamai. Love versus family blood debt. Not much of a choice there. "An example needed to be made. A message had to be sent to our Sisters and to your brother. He needed to see and understand the weight of the law Tiala had broken and his part in it. He went free. He was free to love again. He was free to find another." I truly believed the words I had spoken, "He didn't need to die Akamai. His death was his choice – a foolish one but still, his choice. He could have found another."

"A person doesn't just move on after his chosen one has been ripped to pieces in front of him. The people we love aren't like the tide. It's not like picking a new flower every time one fades. That's not how it works. But you wouldn't know that, would you?" Akamai said.

"You're not talking about your brother anymore are you?"

"You're a monster."

"I am a warrior. You said so yourself. There's a difference."

"A warrior kills for honor, for family, for love. You kill for pleasure. I saw you with that young girl who took your eye. I hoped I was wrong. "

"She deserved to die Akamai. Surely you of all people understand blood debt."

"I watched you with her. You savoured every minute of that killing. It wasn't a warrior kill. It was butchery."

"I am Keawe. My ways are beyond your comprehension." I stood there in the water and used my tongue deliberately and cruelly, wanting to cut him as deeply as his words had cut me. "Warrior or no, you are only a commoner. Even less than that, you are only a man. I am beyond your judgement."

Even as I said it, I knew it to be true. He was not my equal. The class difference between us was always going to be a barrier to true friendship. To love. These are all the things I told myself as I planned how I would kill him. "So Akamai, how strong is love?"

He was wary now, eyes assessing my every move and breath. We were no longer a boy and a girl savouring each other in the moonlight. We were opponents. "What do you mean?" he said.

"Is love stronger than vengeance?" I said as I circled him slowly. There was an ominous ripple in the water. Getting out of the pool should have been my immediate goal. Keawe cannot summon fire when they are in water. But I didn't care. Was it because I wanted this to be a fair fight? Or because something deep within me longed for death … longed for it all to be over?

"It could be. Is love stronger than fire?" he asked. "Can you turn against your sisters? Can you forsake who you are?"

We both knew the answers to those questions. I made the first move. A lunge forward which he easily side-stepped. He hooked an arm around my neck which I twisted free from in an instant. The water slowed me down. We had sparred many times before and each of us knew the other's strengths and weaknesses. Akamai was fluid and seamless in his movements while I was staccato bursts of energy and thought. *'You're too impulsive. You need to plan before you strike,'* he always said.

We grappled, weaved, twisted, feinted and lunged. The water was slick and as he slipped from my grasp again he growled, "It doesn't have to be this way Pele. Come with me. Where else will you find love?"

"I have everything I need here."

"Liar. Your own mother can't bear to look at your scarred face."

He baited me. It worked. I rushed him and he caught me in an arm lock that I could not break free from. His breath rasped against my cheek, "I don't want to kill you Pele."

"You won't have to." I turned and sank my teeth into his face. Salt tang of blood.

"Aargh." He let go. I sprang backwards into the shallows, scrabbling on loose rock.

A vice grip on my leg. "No you don't. You will stay and fight fair in the water. No fire for you."

I kicked and his hold on me loosened enough so I could scramble and splash through the water and out onto the shore. Chest heaving in the moonlight as I stared at him. "I don't want to hurt you."

He stood and waded slowly out of the water, eyes never leaving mine. "Then don't."

"What would you have me do? Turn against my sisters?"

"Love me. Come with me. Make a life with me. Away from here. Away from this madness. You do not belong with them. "

It was tempting. The two of us. We were hunters and warriors. We could seek out a quiet place on some distant island. The Keawe would hunt us but we would have a fighting chance. His skills and my fire power. We could have a life together, if only a short one. I wavered and in that moment, I heard them. The spirit whisperers. *No matter where you go, we will walk with you. Gift stealer. Blood taker. Traitor.*

"Get out of my head!" I raged. The familiar pain mocked me and I stumbled as my vision turned hazy. It was the reminder I needed. Me and Akamai could never be. There was too much fire within me. Too many voices. One day, I would be the Covenant Keeper and all who had spurned me would burn. All of them.

He waited. "Come with me?"

I looked at his face one last time, with sadness. Regret for what could have been. "I can't. I'm sorry."

He leapt at me then, knocked me to the ground, had his blade at my throat. But it was too late. I unleashed the fire within and the girl of flesh and blood was no more. He flinched, tried to pull away as the lava churned within my veins, but I wrapped him in my arms and held him close. He did not scream. I flipped us both over and knelt above him, leaned down close and placed a searing kiss on his lips. A kiss of fire that spread and devoured his entire face. Then I leant back and watched as the flesh melted away from his body.

Skin, bones, teeth, love, and vengeance – my fire devoured them all.

And when it was done, when there was nothing left of Akamai but a pile of ash, I walked into the river and stilled my flame. I sank into the water as billowing clouds of steam filled the night and I cried for his death.

Because that's what friends do.

A few days later, Noalani summoned me to her. "Your Consort – what happened to him?" she asked.

"He betrayed me. I had to eliminate him."

"Oh? He seemed very dedicated. I was beginning to worry you two were getting too close."

"Appearances are deceiving. Even those closest to us can be the betrayer," I replied.

"So true." She stood and walked towards me with the Bone held loosely in one hand. "And what about you Pele?"

"What about me?"

"Tell me how you have betrayed me," she said. Her voice was quiet and cold. "Tell me how you have betrayed the Gift our Mother entrusted you with."

"You speak in riddles." The tension between us was a line pulled taut while a big fish fought to break free.

"Stop it. I am no fool," she hissed. "There are initiates missing. People talking. Suspicion is rife. I can't have unrest within my Sisterhood. You have gone too far."

"No, you did." I pointed to the centre of the room. "You stood right there and sucked the power out of that girl. You, not me."

"I told you, what I did, I did for love. I did it for you."

"I never asked you to." The air began to simmer and burn. "I was a child. You were the Covenant Keeper. You started this. All of it."

"You were hurting. A mother who loves her child does not stand by and let her suffer."

"I'm suffering now mother! Can't you tell?" I pushed my face into hers and she shrank back. "Melita … all of them, they won't let me rest. They're in my head, vicious, vengeful, taunting. All of them. My eye – they did this to me."

"What are you talking about?" said Noalani.

"I'm talking about the spirit walkers. They hate me, they plot my death at every turn. Can't you see? That's why I needed to take more power. So I can defend myself. I will never be safe from them until I have more."

"No, Pele you are safe. Here with me, with your Keawe sisters."

Her naïveté angered me. "My sisters? Those women are not my family. Haven't you seen the way they look at me? Don't you hear the whispered hatred they bear for me? I'm not safe here mother." My rising tone matched the haze of sparks that began to light up my clenched fists. "You're safe because you're untouchable. You have the Tangaloa Bone and so you have nothing to fear. Look at me. Look at my face – see what Keawe sisters have done to me!"

"How has it come to this?" She was crying now. "I only wanted to help you belong. But you have taken it too far."

"I just need a little more, please mother." I grabbed at the Bone in her hands, pleading. "Let me use it one more time and I promise you I will never take it again. I can't sleep. I can't find peace. I will never be safe until I have just a little bit more."

"You are enslaved by the Gift. The taste of it, the feel of it. You have broken our law. Don't you understand what you have done? What I must now do?" Noalani said. She pulled against my grip on the Bone. "Oh Pele, I'm sorry."

She was going to take the Bone away from me. She was going to use it against me. My own mother she was going to hurt me. A surge of pain in my head hit me then, so strong so vicious it blinded me for a moment. Followed by the voices, triumphant and laughing. *Finally, we will get the justice we deserve. Die by your own mother's hand!*

"No!" I wouldn't let them win. I wouldn't. I was a warrior. They could take my eye, my peace and even my only friend – but I would not let them win.

I tightened my grip on the Bone and tugged. Noalani and I struggled. She spoke the ceremonial words, called on the Bone to wrench my Gift from me. But I fought her with all the combined fury of the Gifts I had taken from those who did not deserve them. For one piercing moment we gazed into each other's eyes and it was like looking into a mirror. *Liquid pools of moonlight.* At the very end, I saw it – the likeness between us. The beauty, the fire, the strength we shared.

And then Noalani erupted into a night sky of stars and each of them stabbed at my soul. The Bone was a filament of red light between us as I shattered into a thousand pieces. Agony. I died and was reborn.

I never planned to kill my mother. But I suppose it was inevitable. How else could I ascend to godhood and become the Bone Bearer?

Was I sad? Yes. But I also rejoiced because now, I was Pele the Fire Goddess and there was none other as powerful as I.

Unfortunately, it didn't stop the spirit whisperers. If anything, they only intensified as I extended my reach throughout the other islands. There were many foolish enough to think they could challenge my rule but opposition soon died once the Gifted realized that individually, they were no match for me. Some tried to rally together and come against me but they too were unsuccessful and their voices joined the others who hovered at the edges of the darkness. Taunting, hating, crying.

I learned to shut them out. Ignore them. Because I was a warrior, a survivor.

Until the day my body could no longer contain the fierce power within and I was forced to enter the world of endless heat and fire deep below the earth's surface.

But you cannot kill a goddess. I always knew I would rise again. I just needed to find one strong enough to host me and my fire Gifts.

Iolana

There is a secluded property in the green richness of Hawaii Kai that has its privacy guaranteed by great wealth. A white columned building reminiscent of a long-forgotten era stands tall in the golden sunlight and enveloped by lush gardens. The house is fronted on all sides by an expansive terrace of white marble. Fountains ensure the air is always light with the sound of dancing water. The fragrance of plumeria wafts on the constant breeze.

This is the sanctuary of the Keawe, Hawaii's earth guardians. Many generations ago, the Keawe were blessed with the gift of fire. Hand in hand with their elemental gift, the ancient Keawe were prophetesses, revered as royalty and worshipped in temples. They safeguarded the genealogy and communed with earth's voice. Their names were synonymous with deity. But progress has a way of eroding deity. As a people's traditional beliefs and spiritual connection with the land faded, so did they.

Now, there are only six Keawe left and when they are gone, there will be no others.

On this day, the morning sun bathes the Keawe who are seated cross-legged on the cool marble. Each is dressed in forest-green, the very barest of flowing robes draped on their sinuous, lithe forms. They sit with heads bowed, hands loosely clasped, breathing the regulated breaths of meditation. In their midst sits the leader, the focal point that centers their contemplation. She is old, very old. But ageless. Her long black hair is lustrous and thick, pulled away from her unlined face but then left to fall freely down her back. Beauty is etched into olive skin in persuasive yet decisive strokes. Her eyes are sightless. She has been blind since birth.

Her name is Iolana. She is Keeper of the Keawe, as was her mother before her – and on this day, she is very afraid.

The peace of the morning air is ripped by Iolana's scream. Abrupt and harsh. The meditation ceases. All the women leap to their feet, the same fear reflected on all their faces. Iolana asks, "Did you see her? Did you feel what I felt?" Hoping desperately that they will say no. Hoping she only imagined it. But it was not a mistake.

The others speak with hushed voices. "Yes. We saw her. We felt her. But how can this be?"

Iolana walks to the edge of the terrace, raising sightless eyes to the horizon, the distant blue line where heaven meets ocean. "Summon the Olohe."

The Olohe are at their training session on a green lawn that flanks the cliffs. Six women – one for each of the Keawe. Lean, lithe figures that dance and flow in a sinuous symphony of movement as they move through the sequences of their life's craft. They are dressed in white. Loose flowing cotton pants and brief banded tops. Their heads are shaven bare, their bodies gleam with coconut oil. Each has the same marking on her right forearm – the triangular patterns of the Shark tattoo. At the back of their neck, there is another ritual marking stamped on the peak of their spine. The Olohe are masters of the ancient Hawaiian martial art of Ku'ialua. They are as graceful as they are deadly, fluid and worshipful – whether they are dancing the hula or administering a quick, quiet death in the night. In olden times, they were assassins and warfare strategists – leaders on and off the battlefield.

Today, there is one Olohe for each Keawe. Each has been a student of Ku'ialua from early childhood and selected to serve the Keawe as her protector. Olohe have no elemental gifts, no 'special powers' but it is they who ensure the physical safety of 'guardians' who are a mere shadow of what they once were. Because today, the Keawe are mistresses of fire no longer. They are but monitors of a sick earth's vital signs and attuned to earth's elements in all her forms. Which means when an ancient elemental force as powerful as Pele reawakened in the body of a young woman called Leila Folger, far away in Samoa – the Keawe felt it.

And it terrified them.

Iolana's eyes burned white as she addressed the gathering and her voice did not betray the fear she felt within, "We must go to Samoa. Call a gathering of our sisters throughout the Pacific. Pele the Destroyer is reborn. The vessel that carries her must not be allowed to live."

Who am I?

In Samoa, the heat arrives before the fullness of the morning sun. Seeping in softly through the screened windows, wet in its humid embrace. Eight o'clock and sweat was already staining the uniform of the grim-faced nurse as she stood in the doorway, shaking her head at the couple that lay on the bed, entwined in each other's arms. Asleep.

Roughly she shook the boy first. He awoke with a start. "What is it? Leila? Is she alright?"

Calm replaced the panic as he gazed at the girl asleep in his arms. Safe. Alive. And well. The nurse was not happy. "What are you doing in here? This is against hospital policy."

"Shh …" Daniel slowly arose from the bed, gently loosening from Leila's embrace. Still she slept. He gave the angry nurse a grin and walked her away from the bed, out into the hall. "What is? Patients having their family spend the night at the hospital with them?" he asked.

Daniel nodded across the hall where other patients slept in a line of beds. And each of them had family who kept them company.

They slept on mats on the floor because no self-respecting Samoan ever let a family member go into the hospital without someone to stay alongside them.

The nurse frowned even more. "It's not right for you to be here all the time with her. Are you this girl's family? No you're not."

Daniel was about to say, 'Yes I am. She's my fiancé', when a muffled gasp from the room interrupted. He spun around. Leila was sitting up in the bed, looking around with mingled fear and confusion. He smiled. Pale, rumpled, and wearing a dingy hospital gown – she was still the most beautiful girl he had ever seen.

"Hey, you're awake." He went to hug her and she shrank back from his touch.

"Who are you? What is this place?" Her look of fear had him slowly releasing her. He sat beside her on the bed and spoke soft and slow. Calming.

"It's me, Daniel. You're in the hospital. Remember? You've been in a coma and you woke up yesterday. I must have fallen asleep holding you last night." A reassuring smile and a nod at the sour nurse. "This nice lady is here to check on you. Make sure everything is alright." He gave Leila a nudge and leaned in close to whisper with a teasing tone, "She's been giving me a hard time about staying with you because I'm not family. I was about to tell her that we're closer than family. I'm your Vasa Loloa and you're my Fanua Afi."

But there was no answering smile on Leila's face. She shook her head, terror in her voice, "What are you talking about? I don't know you. Where's my Dad? I want my father. I don't know this place. Somebody help me! Get away from me."

Leila pushed against him, eyes wild with fear. Daniel stared in horror as she started thrashing and screaming, pulling at the wires and tubes that connected her to the monitors. The sour-faced nurse shouted for help. Two more nurses came running in, pushing past Daniel, curt and efficient.

"Move. Out of the way." With quick precision two nurses restrained Leila while the other gave her a shot of something in her IV line. They soothed her with professional ease. "There, there. It's alright. We're here to help you. You're in a hospital, you've been sick and you're just a little confused. Calm down. No-one is going to hurt you."

Whatever they had given her worked quickly because in a few minutes Leila's body relaxed and she sank back onto the bed with a weary sigh. Her eyes were glazed and her speech slurred as she asked the nurses, "I want my Dad. Please can you get my Dad?"

"Of course we will. You just rest now and he will be here soon," said one.

The other took Daniel to the side, "Where's her father? You better call him that she's awake and asking for him."

He whispered, "I can't. Her father's dead. He died two years ago. She knows that already." He glanced at the drugged girl on the bed. "Well, she knew that before she got hurt. I don't understand. What's happening? She looked at me like I was a stranger. She didn't know me."

"Shh … we'll talk outside. Come." A nurse took him outside into the hall. "The doctor warned you that she might have compromised brain function when she regained consciousness, didn't he?"

Daniel interrupted, "Yes but he said she might be a little confused. Disoriented. Not this. She has no clue who the hell I am! She looked at me like I was a complete stranger. Last night when she first woke up, she was different. She was fine. She knew me. We talked. She loved me. Dammit, what's going on?" His voice rose to a shout and he was battling for composure.

"Daniel? What is going on here?" The stern voice of disapproval startled him. "Why are you speaking with such disrespect to this nurse?"

It was Salamasina, frowning at him. He wilted with relief. "Oh Mama, I'm so glad you're here."

He swept the old woman into a fierce hug. He was tired, hungry and beaten. "It's Leila." His voice caught and his grandmother instantly assumed the worst.

"Oh no, my son. I'm so sorry." The compassion on her face was genuine.

Daniel rushed to correct her. "No she's okay. Leila's awake."

"That's wonderful news. I don't understand, what's the problem then?"

"She's awake but she doesn't know me. She can't remember anything about what happened and she doesn't recognize me." Shoulders slumped; he sank into a chair in the corridor, face in his hands.

"This is a foolish reaction don't you think?" Her lips pursed in disapproval as she sat beside him. "The important thing is that she's going to be alright. There will be plenty of time for you two to catch up. You must be patient my son. And remember, she will need you more than ever as she recuperates. Now is not the time to be discouraged. Or to be selfish."

A deep breath. "You're right, Mama. As always." A half-smile. "What matters is that Leila is awake. Everything's going to be fine now."

"Yes, so maybe now you will consider getting some rest? You can't keep going like this. I'm going to take you home for a good meal and a sleep. You can come back tonight."

Together they stood and Salamasina hugged him. A rare moment to hold the boy that had always been her reason for living. She felt tears burn her eyes. Daniel pulled away. "Thank you for being here. And supporting me. I know you've never been happy about me and Leila."

"I don't think any mother ever thinks any girl is ever good enough for her son. Don't worry about my feelings. I only want you to be happy." She smiled, seeing him as the little boy that he used to be.

Daniel caught the glint of tears. "What's wrong?"

"Nothing son. I was just remembering … when you were a little boy, you would hug me and promise *I'm never gonna grow up Mama. I'm gonna be your little boy forever.*" Tears broke free. "Sometimes I wish you were that little boy again. And for always."

"Oh Mama, of course I love you. Even if I'm not your little boy anymore." He bent to kiss her forehead. "I'm just going to say goodbye, tell her I'm going."

"Of course. Give me some time to go find her doctors. I want to see what they have to say about this latest development." One last quick hug and Daniel went into Leila's room where a nurse fussed with charts and meds.

She looked up as he walked in. "The drugs have calmed her a bit. We don't want her to be agitated though so please, just a quick visit. She's still trying to process everything, no big revelations or any more information about anything alright? It will only add to the sensory overload. There will be plenty of time for that sort of thing in the days to come." She left him with that last warning.

Leila lay in the bed staring out the window.

"Leila?"

She turned to his voice. Slowly. She was crying and the look in her eyes caught and held him captive. They were the eyes of a child, lost and afraid. "Where's my Dad? Why isn't he here? I need him. He's the only one that loves me. The only one who understands me. I need him."

Three steps and he was kneeling at her bedside, holding her hand in his, choking on emotions. "I'm sorry Leila, he's been delayed. But I'm going to stay with you until he gets here." The lies tasted like broken coral in his mouth. "I'm going to stay right here. Right beside you."

She flinched at his nearness and carefully pulled her hand away from his. A wall shut down between them and her tone was carefully polite. Distant. "Thank you. That's very nice of you." She wiped her face on the sleeve of her hospital gown in a vain attempt to hide the fact that she had been crying. And still wanted to cry buckets more. "I'm sure I will be fine by myself until he gets here. You can go … Daniel. That is your name, right?"

He nodded. To have her speak to him with the neutrality of a stranger hurt more than any pain he had ever experienced. "Yeah, that's right. I'm Daniel."

I'm Daniel Tahi. I know what your lips taste like. I know your favorite snack is Diet Coke and Doritos. I know you're scared of needles but you were brave enough to get a malu tattoo because of all it symbolized for you as tamaitai Samoa, a Samoan woman. I know you roll your eyes when you think someone is an idiot. I know you wish you were six inches shorter so you wouldn't be taller than most of the boys you've ever met. I know I have your fire, your name tattooed across my heart. I am Daniel Tahi. I am telesā vasa loloa. I am yours. And you can't remember who I am.

She seemed troubled by the look in his eyes. They stared at each other for what seemed like an eternity but couldn't have been longer than a few seconds. For one wild moment Daniel considered leaning closer and capturing her mouth with his. Kissing her. Breathing and forcing the memory of their past into her with his kiss.

But before he could do anything so stupid, there was a sound at the doorway.

Keahi. "Can I come in?"

Daniel stood up, his every nerve tingling with the liquid ice of hatred. "No, you can't. I thought we agreed you couldn't come anywhere near Leila." He flexed his fingers, aching to wrench water from all its hiding places and lasso it around Keahi's neck. Resisting, knowing that something like that would definitely be way too much for Leila to handle right now. Heck, she couldn't even remember who he was, let alone the minor detail that he could summon water and talk to fishes.

Daniel and Keahi faced off. The Hawaiian was still bandaged, an open button-down shirt revealing the swathes of white wrapping the full length of his torso. Daniel noted with some satisfaction that he also had a couple of Band-Aids on his neck where he had last marked him with a water coil.

"Well?"

Keahi's response was whispered – for Daniel's ears only. "I heard she was awake. I just wanted to see if she was okay. Can I talk to her? For just a minute?"

"Like hell. No. Get out."

That's when Leila peered from around Daniel's bulk, trying to get a glimpse of whoever he was talking to "Who is that?" She caught sight of the lean, lithe boy in the doorway. "Oh." An abrupt sound, soon followed by a greeting. "Hi. Did you want to see me?"

Keahi's smile was immediate. And laden with relief. "Yeah. I came by to see how you are. It's good to see you awake."

He took several steps inside the room and Daniel's eyes narrowed at him warningly. *Careful, don't push it.* Keahi ignored him, so intent was he on looking Leila up and down. A big smile. "Wow, you look great. You're skinnier and kinda washed out but you do look heaps better than I thought you would. I mean after what happened to you …"

"Shut up, you idiot." Daniel's command was a muttered one but still clear enough for Leila to hear him. She frowned at him and immediately smiled again. At Keahi. A really big smile. *What the f…?*

"Thanks. My head hurts but yeah, I'm fine." Another smile. "Thanks for checking on me." *What's with all the smiling? Why is she so happy to see this freak who almost got her killed? Hello?!*

Daniel interrupted. Brusquely. "I think you gotta go. The nurse said Leila isn't supposed to have visitors. Until she's stronger."

She frowned at him. "But you're in here." She looked back at Keahi. "I'm sorry, what's your name anyway?"

Keahi raised an eyebrow. *Not the bloody Khal Drogo eyebrow again …* He looked back and forth from Leila and then back at Daniel. "Wait a minute. Are you kidding me?" He stopped, looked at Daniel for confirmation and then leaned in to whisper. "She doesn't remember anything?"

Daniel shook his head and Keahi continued, "How about you? She must remember you."

"Not yet." It hurt to even say the words.

Keahi grinned. "Aww man, that bites." He leaned against the doorway and for a minute, he looked sympathetic. "That's gotta hurt dude. How you holding up?" Then the attempt at sympathy faded as a thought ran like wicked fire through him. "Wait, that means, she's technically not even in love with you anymore is she? How could she be? She doesn't even know who in hell you are." He laughed. Long and loud.

Daniel spoke through gritted teeth. Hushed but deadly. "Get out. Before I throw you out that window."

Keahi's laughter ceased abruptly and his expression darkened as he leaned in close. "Yeah? You and what ocean?"

Every nerve, every muscle, every sinew in Daniel tensed taut and wired as he drew himself up to tower over Keahi. "I don't need any special powers to hurt you. Just like I don't need to leech fire off someone else to kick-start my own gifts. You parasite."

Keahi seemed unmoved by Daniel's disdain, his ever ready mocking grin "You just can't stand it, can you?"

"What?"

"You can't stand it that me and Leila share a connection … a bond you'll never have."

Daniel flinched. "You share nothing. You've got no right to be here. Because of you, Sarona almost killed her."

Finally, Keahi lost his smile. "I got every right to be here. Because of me, Sarona's dead."

Leila interrupted, irritation coloring every word. "Would one of you please tell me what's going on? What am I missing?"

"Nothing's going on. I'm just telling Keahi it's not a good idea for strangers to be here bothering you while you're still not well."

"And I'm telling Daniel nicely, at times like this, you need your closest friends around you. Friends who you can relate to and connect with." A sly smile. "In all sorts of explosive ways."

Leila looked confused. "So you and me – we're close? We're friends?"

Keahi side-stepped around Daniel and walked over to stand by Leila's bedside. "Oh yeah. We're best friends." He reached out with one hand and gently tucked a loose strand of her hair behind her ear, and then trailed a whisper soft caress along her cheek.

Daniel's voice was harsh. "Don't touch her!"

Too late.

Red patterns glowed on Keahi's skin, like coils of heated steel wire. Leila's eyes widened in disbelief. She shrunk away from his hand. And then her *taulima* armband seethed with an answering fiery burn. "What's happening?"

The terror on her face spurred Daniel into action. He wrenched Keahi away from the bed, slamming him up against the wall, one forearm jammed at his throat. "I said don't touch her." Rage unlocked power. The tattoo that stamped the full length of his arm, sparked with iridescent blue fire and where it met Keahi's neck markings – it hissed and smoked. As water burned.

Before Keahi could react, Leila made a muffled sob of terror. Both boys turned. She sat bolt upright on the bed, staring at the evidence of their angry Gifts. Horror. "What are you?"

Panic unlocked power. The arterial current of fanua afi lit up her malu and her fingers sparked with cindered light. She held out her hands. Fear. "What am I?"

Keahi shook loose from Daniel's restraint with a triumphant smile. "I told you, we're friends." A sideways glance at Daniel's ice blue fury. "All of us. We're the same. We're telesā." Laughter. "There's a couple more of us out there. We're a team like the X-Men, right Daniel?" His wry grin dared Daniel to contradict him.

But Daniel only had eyes for Leila. As molten tears glistened and ran down her face, a trail of ruby fire. As she looked helplessly at the strange sparks that lingered at the edges of her being. Regret consumed rage. He calmed the ocean within him and went to take her hands in his. With delicate precision he summoned water from the jug on the bedside table so that it rippled through the air with silken ease and lightly entangled about her fingers, stilling the hints of flame. He wiped away her tears with hands of water while she stared at him wide-eyed and questioning, but somewhat soothed.

"I'm sorry we frightened you. Keahi's right. We're your friends. We care about you and we're going to help you get through this. Help you get your memory back. For right now, this fire and water stuff has to be kept under wraps, okay? We don't want to scare people." He placed a delicate kiss on her forehead before backing away. "We're going to leave you to rest now. I'll be back later." To Keahi. "Let's go."

Keahi didn't want to leave but he felt like had won the war, getting Daniel to admit he had been right after all. He threw Leila his careless smile. "Later Leila. We'll work this out." He followed Daniel out into the hallway and together the two of them walked out of the ward and towards the parking lot. Past a line of concrete water tanks.

Keahi shook his head, amazement coloring his words, "I gotta admit, I didn't think you had it in you – agreeing to help Leila together."

Daniel didn't answer and so Keahi kept talking. "I can't believe her memory got wiped. But then, she went through a lot that day. What she did? Taking that plutonium battery out like that – took a lot of courage. She could have died. Wonder how long it will take for her to remember everything …"

And then Keahi wasn't talking anymore because Daniel had turned, grabbed him by the shoulders and threw him against a concrete tank. He gripped the back of Keahi's head and smashed his face into the tank wall. One, two, three times. Blood gushed from Keahi's mouth and nose. He swore. Spat out chipped tooth fragments and then broke free and spun around. Dazed and in pain, Keahi's training kicked in. He struck with a straight-foot thrust kick to Daniel's mid-section, knocking him off balance.

But Daniel had started this with the element of surprise – which goes a long way. So does the element of water. In answer to his command, water ripped through the top of the tank, spraying chunks of concrete into the air. Before Keahi could execute another kick, a thick coil of water encircled him, yanked him off his feet and into the air. He struggled, shouted, "What – are you scared to fight me fair? Let me outta this!"

With outstretched hands, Daniel manipulated water, slamming Keahi into the concrete wall again and again. He watched with impassive eyes and Keahi fought – and failed – to get free. Pain. Ribs cracked and flesh bruised. Blood smears stained the tank wall.

Finally, Daniel forced Keahi to a kneeling position beside him, still bound in ropes of liquid. He was a battered mess but still defiant. He choked on bubbles of redness as he cursed again.

Daniel spoke, "I don't care about fairness. When it comes to the girl I love, I'll do whatever it takes to keep her safe from you."

All of Daniel's tattoos burned with steel blue intensity. "Know this, we're not the same. We're not friends. There's no team. You stay away from her. Or I'll kill you."

And then Daniel Tahi walked away.

Daniel knew he should have felt bad about pummeling Keahi's face into a cement water tank. But he didn't. He kept seeing Keahi's sick, twisted smile and the way he touched Leila. But worse than that, Daniel kept seeing the answering spark in her. Her malu lighting up. The tattoo arm band, *his* tattoo. The one she got for him. For them. Celebrating everything that made them work. The only time he'd seen her light up that way when someone touched her – is when that someone was him. When *he* touched her. When *he* kissed her. But in there today? She lit up for Keahi. Her body spoke to his. And the spark in her eyes as they stared at each other had been all too familiar to him.

So no, Daniel didn't feel bad about hitting Keahi. He left the hospital driven by rage. He didn't care that Mama was probably looking for him. He didn't care that he'd left Leila alone for the first time in weeks. Too many feelings were ripping him up inside. He had to get away from there. Now.

He took to the coastal road, drawn to the blueness yet again. He drove and he couldn't shake Keahi and Leila from his mind. "Dammit!" Being in the truck was suffocating him. He needed air. Vast ocean spaces. He wrenched the steering wheel and turned into the first bare strip of beach he could find. Opened the door and then slammed it so hard, the whole truck rattled. And yes, he swore. Cursed fate. Destiny. Genetics. Ancestral birthright. Airplanes. School. Rugby games. English class debates. Everything and anything else that had brought he and Leila together. "I hate this."

He sank to his knees on the rocks. Head in his hands, he wept. Drowned in a grief so consuming he didn't think he would ever breathe again. *Why is this happening to us? After all that's happened to us, why can't we catch a break? Leila, I need you. Please come back to me.*

After a while he stood and strode down to the water's edge. He shouted out over the sea and let his anger speak to the water. Far out by the white surf of the reef, a roaring sound spoke to his troubled heart and then the ocean surged and reared its massive head. It shouted back with a whirlpool tornado that scythed across the churning surface towards him. It felt good to see something as chaotic and ugly as he felt inside. "Bring it!"

The water obeyed, touching down on the rocky shoreline and ripping up a pathway like a massive power drill. It spat chunks of razed stone and coral. *Yes.* This was more like it. Power – kickass waves of it coursed through him and he loved it. Daniel raged and the ocean shared his hurt and anger. It was a heartbroken Vaniah Toloa song that he didn't want to hear. Not when it was playing his own pathetic symphony. This was Earth's fault. Ocean, air, sky, land, fire – all of it. "I hate you!"

Daniel wanted the ocean to devour everything. Wash it all away. He directed the spinning water back out towards the distant reef and beyond. *Let's see what happens … how far can my control extend?*

And then it happened. He lost it. He felt the moment that his control slipped. Like a cord to his gut snapped. One minute he was riding the wave. The next he was a just a fool standing on a strip of sand watching in horror while a black wave raced towards him. Tsunami. Towards the shoreline. Towards land, villages, houses in the faraway distance behind him.

This can't be happening. Don't panic. Get the connection back. He reached for the blue wire that tied him to surging channels of blue energy. He tried, but he couldn't do it. Seeing that massive wall of water coming straight at him didn't help. *Shut your eyes. Try harder. Pretend there isn't a death wish coming at you.* He took deep, slow breaths.

It didn't work. Nothing. No wired pulse of blue fire. Just blank empty space. A sick hole in the pit of his stomach.

He backed away, stumbling over loose coral. A flashback to a long ago night on a smoldering field when Leila lost control of her flame and he had yelled at her. Is this how she felt? Terrified at what she had created? Choking on revulsion because she had released the chaos she kept hidden inside her where nobody could condemn her for it. *I wish she was here to help me fix this.* He could hear the wave. The churning of heavy duty equipment stuck in third gear. It was a multitude of jet planes taking off. A thousand steel grinders going at full speed. The noise was deafening. He was not too overwhelmed to appreciate the irony of the situation. Vasa Loloa 'son of the Ocean' was going to be obliterated by the very ocean he was supposed to be the master of.

Even though he knew he couldn't outrun a tsunami, he still turned to try. Then he saw her.

It's Mama. No, it was a woman who looked like a younger version of his grandmother. She was dressed in some loose flowing dark blue dress. She walked over the sand dune, her black hair in wild disarray in the rushing wind. She walked with a cane, a slight drag to her left leg.

Her reproof was ice. "Daniel Tahi – what have you done?"

She didn't wait for an answer. Instead her eyes bled white like crashing surf and she turned to look out at the approaching wall of water. *What's she doing?*

Daniel stared at this enigmatic figure who was his grandmother – but wasn't. Who looked like his grandmother – but didn't. She raised one hand, palm outward. *Talk to the hand. Is she nuts?! Does she think she can hold off a tsunami like that?*

He was about to run and grab her to go with him, when coils of water rose from the receding shallows before them. Her lips moved but he couldn't hear what she said. Her left arm swung in a slow arc and as she leant forward into a gentle pushing motion – the wave stopped. Just like that.

Daniel hardly dared to breathe at the sight. A stark grey shoreline, a lone figure with a walking stick by her side, wind whipping at her hair, eyes bleeding white fire as she held the might of the ocean at bay with the barest of gestures.

What is she waiting for?

Then she turned to him with a derisive stare and he understood. *She wants me to see it. See what she can do and I can't …* She wanted there to be no doubt as to her power. For added emphasis she slowly curled her fist shut and yanked with one vicious tug. The wave responded as if tied to her by an invisible string of obeisance. It arced in the center rushing straight at him. He leapt back and fell flat on his butt.

Thanks a lot lady. Alright, I got it. You're a megastar Vasa Loloa and I am just an infant.

A careless flick of her hand and the towering cascade of ebony water dissipated. Just like that. It was gone and the ocean was a smooth silk blanket. It was as if the tsunami had never been.

She waited as he stood up, dusting the sand off his hands. Daniel looked at this stranger who had averted a disaster and in that moment, he knew who she was. "Tavake."

The woman who had trained his birth mother and then drove her to her death on a faraway Tongan island. The woman who had given birth to the only mother he had ever known – his grandmother Salamasina – and then cast her out because she didn't end up with the same genetic stars as her mother.

She gave him the briefest of nods. "Daniel Tahi, son of Moanasina."

He didn't like that and it showed on his face. She raised an eyebrow and amended, "Son of Salamasina." She paused, waiting.

The woman just saved his life and probably the lives of many others. He couldn't *not* say it. "Thank you."

Again with the regal nod. And then censure. "You are a fool. You should never invoke Vasa Loloa unless you have the skill and strength to control what you summon. What if I had not been here? What then?"

"I made a mistake. It won't happen again."

"You have great potential. You always have. Vasa Loloa is strong in you. She always has been. Like your mother before you. You need training. You need to be taught how to use your gift. And not kill anyone. Or yourself."

She shouldn't have mentioned his birth mother. That wasn't smart. A curt nod. "I said thank you. I have to go."

He turned to leave but she wasn't done with him. Not by far. "I've come to Samoa for you Daniel Tahi. I'm here to teach you how to master your gift."

He walked away. "I'm not interested."

"You should be. What happened just now? It's going to happen again. And I won't be there next time to stop you from hurting people. Your gift has manifested late but that doesn't mean it's not very dangerous. You need me."

He paused to face her. "The only thing I need is for you to stay the hell away from me. I know who you are. I know what you did – to my mother. And to my grandmother. You telesā make me sick. All of you. I've seen how you treat your children. You call yourself a sisterhood but you use each other and cast your own children to the side like trash." All the bitterness from the last few weeks, all the heartbreak – his every word was spiked with it.

Tavake called after him, "The girl Leila Folger – she's not what you think. We are all in great danger."

This caught him. Set his gift alight. A geyser of fury burst through the ground beside him as he confronted her, spraying them both with white rage. "Leave her out of this. I'll protect her with everything I've got."

"You misunderstand me." Tavake waved the rushing water away with an effortless impatient sweep of one hand. "You are the one who will need protection from what burns within her. She is no longer the girl you love."

"I'm outta here. We're done." Wet and weary, Daniel walked up the shoreline.

"You can find me at the Tanoa hotel. When you're ready. I'll be waiting."

Tavake didn't try to stop him again. She watched as he got back in his truck and drove away. She could wait. She knew what was coming. She knew he would need her. Soon.

Help Me

The next few weeks passed by in a dizzying blur. Leila's American family came on their first visit to Samoa, using the company jet to bring with them half of Uncle Thomas' administrative staff so he could keep up with work. The Folgers were not happy Leila had been in some mysterious accident on a remote island in Tonga. They were even more upset upon hearing it resulted in the death of an American volcanologist who just happened to be a good friend of Leila's. They were angry at anyone and everyone who had been involved with their niece going to Tonga in the first place. When they first arrived at the hospital, it was to find a rugged, six foot plus, unshaven, tattooed young man asleep in a chair outside Leila's room. Dressed in ragged shorts and a faded Manu Samoa jersey.

Daniel jerked awake to find a disapproving face staring down at him. He jumped to his feet. "You're Leila's family from America."

Thomas didn't smile. He was much shorter than Daniel but he wasn't cowed by the boy that towered over him. "And you are?"

"Daniel Tahi. I'm Leila's ..." he hesitated. Unsure. What was he? Now that Leila didn't know him, what was he to her?

"I love her. She's everything to me." He said it with simple assurance. Unapologetic. *This is me. This is who I am. This is how I feel.*

Thomas was taken aback by Daniel's directness, but only for a moment. "You're the one who was with her in Tonga. When she almost died."

Daniel flinched. "I'm sorry. I tried to keep her safe."

"Yes, and we all see how well that turned out."

With that the older man walked into the hospital room and shut the door.

Daniel sank back into his seat, face in his hands. It had been a very long few weeks and there seemed to be no end in sight. He tried to hold on to the good things, like the fact the girl he loved was alive and well. Never mind that she no longer knew him.

"Daniel?" Again he raised his head and stood. This time it was a petite woman with blonde hair and blue eyes. Sad eyes. She extended her hand. "I'm Annette, Leila's aunt. She stayed with us on her last trip home."

He shook her hand, grateful there was no recrimination in her eyes. Because he was drowning in enough of it all on his own. She sat beside him. "Can you tell me what happened?"

Daniel took a deep breath and relayed the official story. The one he, Lesina, Keahi and Teuila had agreed on. They had gone to Niuatoputapu with Jason because he wanted to study the crater there. It was supposed to be a fun adventure. Something had gone wrong. A freak lightning storm had killed Jason and then the volcano had erupted. They had been trying to escape when

Leila had tripped and fallen. She had hit her head and now, she had woken from her coma with memory loss. The lies tasted like ashes in his mouth.

Annette listened and when he was done, she placed a hand on his. "You care about her very much. I can tell. I'm glad my niece has you." The words were a small comfort but Daniel was glad for them anyway. He was weary with relief that Leila's family had arrived. Yes, he worried they would take her far away but there was also a part of him that hoped lots of money would succeed where pure longing had failed. To make Leila better. To bring her back to him.

The Folgers took over the best suites at Aggie Grey's Hotel and Annette transformed Leila's hospital room into a haven of serenity and fashionable décor. Thomas wielded his financial might and flew in a team of world-class medical specialists including neurologists who subjected Leila to a myriad of tests. They poked and prodded her, gave her memory and reasoning tests, worked her over in physical therapy and even put her on a special diet. Each day it was something new. Every day, Daniel came to the hospital before he started school and again at the end of the day when he had closed the workshop. Each day, Leila got a little stronger. And each day, Daniel died a little more inside. Because no matter how much better she looked, or even how much calmer she seemed – one thing remained the same. Leila could not remember who he was and what they were to each other. She could not remember ever having loved him.

She was caught up on lots of other vital details. She knew she was parentless. She dimly recalled getting on a plane for Samoa but that's where the definites ended. She was hazy on who Matile and Tuala were but seemed content to accept they were her Samoan family. She certainly had no problems with falling in love with Matile's pineapple pie and decadent koko rice. With everyone, she was shy, quiet and impeccably polite. She was diligent about doing the memory exercises with the specialists. "I want to remember everything. I do," she assured them all.

Politeness and earnestness went a long way towards rebuilding friendships and reconnecting with aunts and uncles. But it couldn't make a person light up at the sound of someone's voice. Or reach for their hand. Long for them. It couldn't force a person to be in love again. No matter how much you wished it.

At the end of two weeks' worth of tests and observations, the specialist team was ready to announce their conclusions. Thomas invited Matile and Tuala to be there. Matile insisted that Simone accompany them. And Simone called Daniel who added his brooding presence to the meeting. (Daniel had never been so grateful before for Simone's ninja ways.)

The lead specialist was a woman called Dr. Mitchell. She explained that Leila was physically in good health. Yes she was a little anemic. Needed to gain some weight. A period of rest and 'taking it easy' would be helpful. But otherwise, she had a clean bill of health.

"The good news is Leila has no anatomical damage to the brain," Dr. Mitchell said.

"But she's still not herself. She can't remember HEAPS of stuff," Simone interrupted looking meaningfully at Daniel.

"It's called retrograde amnesia. A type of memory loss where a patient retains their memories up to a certain point in their lives. It's commonly associated with head injury or trauma. In Leila's case, it seems to be more psychogenic where an individual consciously or unconsciously wishes to avoid remembering that trauma. In retrograde amnesia, patients are more likely to lose recent memories that are closer to the traumatic incident than more remote ones, as we see with Leila."

Daniel blurted out before anyone else could, "Will she ever remember the rest? What about the missing pieces?"

Dr. Mitchell gave him a sympathetic smile, "There's no reason why she shouldn't, but we can't give you any definite timeframe. Many patients with retrograde amnesia do go on to regain their lost memories. But a rare few never do. Leila needs time. It's not something that can be rushed or forced. The best hope is for her to return to her old routine, her familiar surroundings and try as much as possible to allow her memory to come back gradually."

Leila joined the conversation. "I want to stay here in Samoa. It feels right." She smiled out the window at the vibrant colors of the tropical garden. "It's so beautiful and serene here. Can I please stay Uncle?"

Thomas didn't like it. He had planned for them all to be on their private jet out of there as soon as Leila was discharged from hospital. He frowned at the doctor. "She should be in Washington D.C with us, where she will have the best medical care. Not here on some third world island."

No, please don't take her from me. How will she ever remember me when she's a thousand miles away?

These were things Daniel wanted to say, but couldn't. He swallowed his selfishness. Because maybe what was best for Leila and helping get her full memory back was taking her back to America. So he was silent and tried not to drown in the question that screamed inside him *How can you make someone fall in love with you all over again – if our love, a love that I always thought would survive anything, wasn't strong enough to make it through retrograde amnesia?*

The specialist nodded encouragingly at Leila's enthusiasm. "Your niece is right Mr. Folger. This is the place she has lived most recently and it seems she has forged very strong ties here.

The fact she wants to remain here is a good sign. It tells us that there is familiarity and recognition – no matter how slight. If you take her back to her childhood home, she may never regain the last two years of her memory because there will be no triggers for those memories. If she has secure and stable surroundings here and good family support," a nod at Matile and Tuala, "then I would strongly recommend Leila stay here in Samoa."

Thomas was oscillating between guilt and impatience to get back to work in D.C. But he was a great believer in relying on the experts and he had brought in the best – and so it was decided. Leila would remain in Samoa. She would move back in with Simone and finish up the academic year at the National University of Samoa and then head to D.C for Christmas. Matile and Tuala didn't like the idea of a sickly Leila going back to her own house, but Dr. Mitchell insisted Leila needed to be back in her own room, her own space. "Familiar surroundings and routines will be the best triggers to ease her memory back."

The day came when Leila was discharged. Annette helped her to the sleek black rental sedan and a chauffeur took them to the little box house that sat peacefully behind its capable chain link fence. Simone greeted them, eager to show off the modern additions to the house that only plenty of Folger money could buy – evidence of Thomas' attempts to assuage the guilt he felt at his incompetence at taking care of his dead brother's daughter. He seemed to be taking it as a personal slight that his headstrong niece lived on an island thousands of miles away from Potomac and even more of an insult that a volcano had dared to erupt on her. Didn't it realize she was a Folger?!

The entire kitchen had been replaced by gleaming silver appliances and the house was now redolent with the coolness of 24hr air conditioning. Solar panels ensured the air would always be cool and the water would always be hot. On Annette's insistence the house had also been fumigated, and a security system installed. The sturdy gate that Daniel had repaired long ago had been replaced by an electronic one that hummed efficiently as Thomas pushed the remote button.

Daniel winced as he surveyed the transformation. The old Leila would not have been happy. The old Leila had been fiercely proud of her house just the way it was, happy that it was *not* a Folger fortress. But then, this was not the old Leila. Who was he to assume he knew what she was thinking or feeling anymore? He was just her friend. Just here to help.

He got out of his truck and went to grab a box from the trunk of the sedan. Thomas grunted. The man was only enduring his presence but Daniel didn't care.

Until Leila loved him again, nothing and no-one else could trouble him.

A buzzing crowd was waiting to welcome Leila home – Simone, Maleko, Sinalei, Rihanna, Mariah and hanging back a little, Lesina. After Thomas and Annette had left and Maleko had been shooed out the front door with the others, protesting the whole time because he wanted to play on the brand new Xbox and gigantic flat screen television – the core group remained and Lesina cornered Daniel outside on the verandah, "We need to talk."

"What?"

"I think we have to tell Simone what Leila is. What we all are. You know, telesā."

Daniel threw a worried glance over his shoulder, "Why?"

"Because he's the one that's closest to Leila right now and he needs to know what she's capable of. So far, her fire hasn't shown up but we both know it's in there somewhere. Do you want her blasting out one day when you and I aren't here? She could hurt Simone. Dammit, she could burn the whole house down."

Daniel didn't like it but he knew she was right. It had taken Leila months of training to assert some kind of control over her powers and none of them knew what state that control would be in when and if her fire started flaring up. "Can't we just take turns to hang out here? Make sure they're never alone, keep an eye out for Leila's Gift to show up?"

"That's not realistic. You've got school and work, so do I. I've already asked Simone if I can stay here for a while, just until I get back on my feet ..." A fleeting look of pain on Lesina's face reminded Daniel she had only recently returned from Jason's funeral in California.

"I'm sorry. I've been so caught up in this whole Leila thing," Daniel said. An awkward silence. "Are you okay?"

"It was brutal. The whole trip there with his parents, meeting his family ... all of them treating me like I was his beloved girlfriend when really, I'm the one who killed him." An abrupt breeze rippled through the trees and the air simmered with electricity.

"Sarona killed him. She did it. All of this," said Daniel, with a wary eye on the flecks of white light that lit the fingertips of the tormented girl before him. "Jason wasn't your fault."

"Yeah, just like Leila's memory lapse isn't your fault," Lesina snapped.

They were at a standoff. Back to topics they could handle. "Fine. We'll tell Simone. But he's going to freak out." Daniel winced. "And be mad we didn't tell him sooner."

They waited until Leila went to take a shower before they broke the news. Daniel was right. Simone wasn't happy. A shriek, "You mean you two KNEW about this and you NEVER told me!?"

Lesina shushed him, "It's not something you go around telling people."

An affronted look. "I'm not 'people' eh. I'm Simone, Leila's best friend." A vicious shove at Daniel's chest. "And yours! I always knew she could do stuff with fire but I knew she knew that I knew and together we were both fine with each other knowing."

Daniel and Lesina exchanged confused glances, "Huh?"

"So let's get this straight. You already knew Leila was fanua afi and it didn't bother you?" Lesina asked.

Simone waved an airy hand at them, "Oh puh-leaze! I saw her the night of the fashion show, remember? I was there, hello! She was on fire. Literally. I don't know anything about fanua afi rubbish and I don't care. Leila's unique with an added unique zing element," he snapped his fingers, the double snap of awesomeness, "and I'm unique with my own added unique zing element. That's what makes us such a great duo. I get her. And she gets me."

"So what's the problem then? Why are you annoyed?" said Daniel.

Simone put one hand on his out-thrust hip, "I'm insulted you two knew and didn't tell me. I'm insulted you two knew and assumed I wouldn't know. Like, how stupid do you think I am, huh? I live with the girl 24-7, hello!" A glare at them both. "I thought I was the only one who knew."

At that moment, the sounds of warbly singing cut through the antagonism. Heads turned to listen. It was Leila singing in the shower. She sounded terrible.

All three of them burst out laughing at the same time, the tension and worry of the past few weeks culminating in a lighthearted release. Leila was healthy and strong. She was out of the hospital. And she was singing really badly in the shower. Everything was going to be alright.

Much later, after a delicious meal sent over by Matile, Simone announced that Lesina would help him with the dishes. "Daniel, can you take the rest of Leila's stuff into the room for her?" He pointed at a cluster of boxes by the door. "I don't know what all of that is. Her aunty Annette brought it all from America."

"It's late. I have to get going," said Daniel. He leaned closer and dropped his voice to a whisper, "What are you doing? I'm not going in her room."

Simone pushed him. Well, he tried to push him but Daniel only raised an eyebrow at his attempt so he gave up. "You two haven't been alone in weeks. Go. Talk to her. If anyone's going to help get her memory back, it's you."

"Simone's right," said Lesina. "Go work your magic."

Daniel was outnumbered. He grabbed one of the boxes and walked down the hall to knock on Leila's door.

"Come in."

He opened the door and hesitated. He'd loved this girl for almost two years now and this was the first time he'd been inside her bedroom. "It's me. Simone asked me to bring in some boxes your Aunt left for you."

"Sure," said Leila. She stood there in the middle of the room as twilight deepened the shadows on the wall.

Daniel went and placed the box on her desk. They hadn't been alone like this in weeks. Not since that last night in the hospital when they had dreamed their perfect beach wedding. That perfect moment which just might have to last Daniel a lifetime. He was suddenly, inextricably shy. What to say to this stranger?

But she spoke first. "I wanted to talk to you anyway. About the fire thing. Remember the day in the hospital when Keahi touched me?"

How could he forget? Daniel nodded.

There was an edge of excitement about her. "What was that? It hasn't happened again since." She held her hands up to the moonlight that streamed in through the window. "I've been waiting, watching, hoping for it. Where is he? I think he sparked it in me. Do you know him?"

This is gonna be harder than I thought … "Yeah. I know him. From school. And other places."

"So why hasn't he come back to see me?" Barely disguised hopefulness.

"I don't know. Busy I guess."

"Hmm, maybe Simone will know how to find him," she said.

"Doubt it." It was a mutter under his breath but still, she heard him.

"You don't want me to see him?"

"I don't think you should be messing around with your fire gift until you get your full memory back. It's dangerous."

She narrowed her eyes at him. "You don't like Keahi."

"I don't trust him. And you shouldn't either. The old Leila didn't."

"So you say."

"What's that supposed to mean?"

"People keep telling me what I'm supposed to think and say and do. How I should behave because you all know me better than I do. Do you know how frustrating that is for me?" Leila asked. "Why should I trust you? Just because you say we were the perfect couple?"

"Go ahead and ask Simone," said Daniel. "Ask anyone out there and they'll tell you why you shouldn't be hanging out with Keahi. Why you shouldn't let him anywhere near you."

She backed away from the anger in him, back into her polite and distant shell. "You're upset. Simone tells me we were very close. Before the accident." Careful regret. "I'm sorry. It must be difficult to be around me. You don't have to keep visiting me. I'm alright now. The doctor said I'm going to be fine."

"I don't mind. I want to be here. Soon, one day you're going to remember and then everything will be alright."

"But what if I don't want you to be here? Don't you understand? I don't know you. I see it in your eyes. You look at me like there's something missing. But there's nothing missing. This *is* me. I can't give you what you want."

Daniel flinched but stood his ground. "You've got it wrong Leila. I don't want anything from you. I'm your friend. I want to be here for you whenever you may need me. That's it. Nothing more, okay? Can you handle being friends?"

Her eyes narrowed at him as she tried to decide if he was sincere. Finally, she relented. "Yes."

He was encouraged. "I can help you remember things. Fill in the gaps. Besides Simone, you and me spent the most amount of time together. Ask me anything you want to know. Just see me as a Leila encyclopedia." He fumbled in his back pocket for his phone, "Hey, I know. Look at these." He went to sit beside her. Cautious. "May I?"

She nodded and made room for him beside her on the bed. He sat, careful not to touch her – this girl who had once craved his touch. He pulled up his message history and all the attached pictures. "You're enrolled at the university with us. You've missed a lot of class but I – I mean *we* all – can help you catch up. This is a pic of everyone at the canteen."

He let her scroll through the photos, trying to keep his tone casual. Light.

No pressure Daniel. Keep it light. It was torture. Excruciating. Holding himself in check when all he wanted to do was take her in his arms and reassure himself with the feel, the taste, the touch of her – that she was alright. She was here, she was back.

She paused at one of the photos. "Where was this taken?"

"A dance club in town. We went out with Jason and Lesina. It was a fun night."

"We look happy." She gave him a guarded look. "Were we happy a lot?"

"I like to think so." He didn't try to stop the grin. "Sure we had our fights sometimes. Mainly because you're so stubborn. Miss Independent who doesn't want to rely on anybody."

"That sounds like me. I don't need anybody."

It was an offhand remark and it hurt him to hear it but she continued, unknowingly ... or was it that she just didn't care? "Who's he? The blonde guy. Jason? Who is he? To me, I mean."

Daniel's shoulders slumped. If he needed any more confirmation that Leila Folger was no longer the girl he knew, then this was it. He took a deep breath before replying. "Jason Williams. He was a scientist who came here to study volcanic activity. Your mother was funding his research. That's how you two met. He was your friend. A very good friend. He was helping you with your fire thing."

Interest sparked in her eyes. "How? What does he know about it?"

"You wanted him to find a kind of cure so you could get rid of it."

She was bewildered. "Why would I want to do that? That makes no sense. I don't believe you." A hostile glare now. "Where can I find him? I want to talk to him myself."

"You can't."

She was angry. "You can't stop me. You don't own me. I don't care what you say or what you think we used to be to each other. I want to talk to this Jason Williams."

"You can't because he's dead. He died on the same island where you were injured. I brought his body back with us."

Silence. He studied her face. Did she care? Did she remember him? Anything at all? Would that kick-start her memory? She was impassive. "Oh. Too bad." Curiosity. "How did he die?"

"One of your mother's sisters killed him. She shot him." Daniel figured it was best to keep it simple. No need to get into Air elemental telesā right now. He hoped she would drop the subject now.

No such luck. "Why? How? What really happened on that island?"

He didn't want to but she would have to hear it eventually. Daniel gave her the condensed version of the nightmare sequence of events that had led to Jason's death. And her accident. She brushed over the recital of Jason's shooting but had questions about what happened to her.

He answered them all as best as he could and when she finally seemed appeased, he felt a burden had been lifted from his shoulders. He didn't want to be Leila's memory-keeper, holding on to even the most painful things because she might need them. She moved away from the bed and went to search through a side drawer. Looking for something.

"Ah, here it is." Leila turned to him, holding the carved Bone shard Lesina had returned to the hospital. "This was in my things. Do you know what it is?"

"No. Sarona wanted it as part of the exchange on Niuatoputapu Island, but I don't know why."

Leila had a puzzled look on her face as she studied the intricate patterns. "It's beautiful. Look, it's not just a single bone piece. There's different materials, all interwoven somehow."

Daniel went to stand beside her. She held the Bone shard up to the light so they could see it more clearly. "Yeah, you're right. That's unusual. Where did you get it from anyway?"

She gave him a wry look that almost looked like the old Leila. "How should I know? I've got retrograde amnesia remember? You're the one with all the answers. You tell me."

"I think your mother gave it to you. But you never showed it to me."

And then Leila laughed. "I thought we were supposed to be eternal lovers?" She was taunting, almost harsh. "I kept secrets from you? That doesn't sound very love-stricken to me."

Daniel was confused. He studied her and Leila stared back with a cold sneer. She preened in his gaze, threw her head back and tossed her hair. "What? Why are you looking at me like that? You and Simone say I'm supposed to love you with a fiery passion but how do I know that? What were we to each other really?"

Daniel shook his head trying to make sense of the shift from frail, polite and distant – to mocking, brazen, confident. She leaned forward slightly and her voice dropped to a whisper. A caress. "So, did we … lie together Daniel Tahi? Tell me, how was I?"

Shocked, Daniel flinched away from her. "No."

She laughed at his discomfort. "If it wasn't earth-shattering then why are you still here waiting for little Leila to remember you?" She moved towards him. Closer, closer. Too close. "Hmm, just what do you want from me Daniel?" There was a sensual mockery in her voice, like she knew something he didn't.

Daniel backed up and met the wall. "Nothing. I told you. I'm here as a friend. I want to help in any way I can to get you better. To get your memory back."

His pulse was racing. But for all the wrong reasons. This girl before him, moved like a snake studying its prey. He had only ever been afraid of Leila once before. That long ago day when a kiss had set fire to the world. Since then, he had seen her wield heat and flames with fury and passion – but never once had he doubted her care for him. But here now, in this quiet room – Daniel Tahi was afraid. Of the manic gleam in her eyes, the inexplicable smile on her lips, the frenetic half-breaths she took as if struggling to contain something. Someone.

"So tell me boy, just how far are you willing to go to help me remember? What are you willing to do?" She whispered into the darkness and it was a dangerous caress. She was still holding the Bone shard tightly in her right hand. With the other she reached for him, "I think this might work."

Then her lips were on his and at first contact, Daniel was almost weak with a sense of coming home. This was Leila, the girl he loved more than life and breath itself. This was Leila, the girl who had given her life for his. He swayed on his feet and gave himself to the kiss. The sweet, perfect melding of two wills, two people in love who had been parted for way too long. But, it was a moment that burnt out as quickly as it had begun.

Because this was not Leila.

Ask yourself this. If you were blindfolded – would you know your heart's choice by the feel of them? The scent of them, the taste of them? Would you know the pattern of their heart beat? The whisper of their breathing? Would you know the way they kiss? The way their pulse answers yours? Worse yet – if another looked and sounded like your heart's choice – would you know them for an imposter?

Daniel kissed a girl in a darkening room and knew. He knew as surely as he knew his own heart.

This was not Leila.

He tried to pull away but she wasn't finished with him. Her grip on his arms tightened and then it burned. She was going into fire mode and she didn't care how it hurt. He wrenched his lips away but they were already blistering and his skin festered as she fought to keep her hold on him. His reaction was instinctive. His *pe'a* and sleeve tattoo glowed blue and steam hissed as she flinched. He shoved her away. "Get off me."

She didn't fight him then. Instead she stood in the center of the room, threw back her head and laughed. "What's the matter lover? I thought you missed me?" An arch look. "Isn't this what you've been dreaming of all these weeks? Hoping for? Me in your arms, kissing you, wanting you?"

He felt suddenly sick. He tried to wipe away the cindered taste of her from his lips with the back of his hand. "You're not Leila."

The light went out of her eyes. And with it, any semblance of the girl he knew. So much that he wondered how he could ever have thought that she was Leila. She spoke low and deadly. "That's what I've been trying to tell you all along. That pathetic weakling you call Leila? She's dead. Gone."

The air between them reeked of burnt things. Very old, dead, burnt things. "Who are you?"

She smiled. "I am Pele. I've been asleep for a very long time. And now, thanks to your playmate's willingness to throw herself into an active volcano, I am awake."

"What are you? A spirit of some kind? An *aitu*?"

A shrug. "I am Keawe. The greatest fire guardian our Mother Earth has ever anointed. I walked this earth as the Bone Bearer a millennia ago. By some mishap of fate, my physical temple was taken from me. I've been waiting for a very long time for another vessel worthy to house me. Your friend Leila is blessed to be the Chosen One. When she gave up her life, our Mother allowed her body to serve me." Pele looked down at herself with a sneer, "Ideally, this is not the body I would have chosen. It's physically far inferior to that which I am accustomed." A faraway look in her eyes, "I was the finest practitioner of Lu'a in all the Sisterhood. This body will struggle to execute the mastery and skill that is within me." She held her arms out to him, "See these? Can these arms wield a shark tooth club in battle? I think not. So insipid, but I will make it strong. Be glad Daniel Tahi, you are in the presence of a god."

Her contempt for the girl he loved made Daniel simmer with liquid energy. "That body doesn't belong to you. I won't let you have it."

The smoky odor of half-burnt rot intensified as she spat at him. "You can't stop me. No-one can. I am the Creator and Destroyer of lands. Of lives. I see, I want, I take. And there is none who can stand in my way."

The Bone shard in her hand glowed a fierce scarlet. She advanced on him and Daniel's breath caught in his chest. What was she going to do? His senses screamed for water- and found it – in the corrugated iron tank outside the back of the house. It strained to respond to his summons, even as he asked himself,

'Can I do it? Can I attack this woman who wears Leila's face, wears her body, breathes and pulses with her heart?' He tensed in anticipation but didn't need to find an answer to that question. Not right then, because even as she moved toward him, she faltered. The surety dimmed in her eyes and the Bone shard slipped from her fingers. A hand went up to her head. "Aaargh, pain. It hurts. What's wrong?"

The glowing embers of her tattoos dimmed and she staggered and swayed. It was like a switch had been flicked, leaving a half-empty, bewildered husk behind. He grabbed her before she could hit the ground, swept her up in his arms and carried her to the bed.

"There you go, careful now." She looked up at him with those bewildered eyes that razed him to the very core. "You're alright. I've got you."

The smell of deadness was gone and he caught a faint whiff of vanilla as he gently laid her back on the pillows. That shield was back as she shifted away from his touch uneasily. "What happened?"

He knew it was futile, but he had to ask it anyway, "Leila? Are you back? Are you … in there?"

She pushed him. "Get off me! What are you doing in here?" She scrambled over to the other side of the bed, "I told you I don't know you. I'm not your girlfriend. Get out."

He backed away, palms upraised. "Hey, calm down. I was only helping you get to the bed. You were dizzy. You would have hit your head if I didn't catch you. That's all it was."

The apprehension on her face seemed to settle as she battled whether or not to believe him. Confusion won out. "What happened? The last thing I remember, you were showing me photos of people, of us and now this …" Hands on her temple as she scrunched her face up in pain. "Aaargh, it hurts. So bad." She locked her arms around her knees and rocked back and forth on the bed, moaning softly.

Daniel ached to go to her. Hold her. But he couldn't. "The doctor said you might get some residual headaches, remember? I'll go get your meds."

He left her then. But not before grabbing the Bone shard from the floor and slipping it into his pocket. He wasn't sure what had just happened, but he knew he didn't want her anywhere near that bone carving. Out in the living room, the others reacted immediately to his expression and the emotion roiling off him in waves.

"What is it? What's wrong?" Simone demanded, looking behind him. "Where's Leila?"

"She needs her meds. Massive headache." He looked at Lesina. "Can you go check on her please? Stay with her? I don't think she should be alone right now."

Simone narrowed his eyes suspiciously. As soon as Lesina had left the room bearing the glass of water and the pills the doctor had prescribed, he pounced, "What happened in there? Did you pressure her?" He intensified his attack, "You heard what the doctors said, don't hassle her or try to force her to remember things. Let it come back slowly."

Daniel held up his hand to block the rapid flow of reprimands. "Calm down. It's not anything I did. We need to talk." He threw a worried glance over his shoulder. "Where no-one can overhear us. Out there."

They moved out onto the verandah. "What is it?" said Simone.

"There's something wrong," said Daniel. "That girl in there? It's not Leila."

Simone rolled his eyes at the drama. "Hello! We know that. It's called amnesia. Until she gets her head back on straight, she's Little Miss Lost and we all have to be patient."

"No. I mean, that's really not Leila. Yes, it's her body. But it's not her inside it."

Simone almost laughed. Almost. But the intense look on Daniel's face stopped him. He muttered, "Kalofa'e. Poor thing." A deep breath. "I know this is tough for you. You're hurting and that *vasti* girl in there isn't making it any easier for you. What did she say now? You shouldn't pay any attention to what comes out of her mouth. She's messed up inside."

"I wish that was it. We were talking and then she switched, She turned into a different person, talking all this crazy stuff about being a spirit guardian called Pele who lived a thousand years ago. I'm telling you, it wasn't just Leila being confused. It wasn't Leila at all. There's a different person living rent-free inside her body."

In any other place it's doubtful whether anyone would have given Daniel's claim more than a raised eyebrow and a jeering laugh. But this was not some Western culture or country. This was Samoa where *aitu* have firm hold on many people's imaginations. Where many whisper of demonic possession and curses after they stop singing their evening hymns. Where many cover their mirrors at night for fear of tempting the jealousy of a *teine Sa*. Where fools who litter in sacred areas can well expect to wake up the next day covered in boils in all their secret places. This was Samoa, where the ancient beliefs still lingered on the edges of Christianity. And so there was no laughter from

Simone. Instead, his voice dropped to a whisper, "She's possessed? By an *aitu*?"

Daniel shook his head tiredly. "I don't know. I don't think that's the right word for it. All I know is that Leila walked into that volcano and something called Pele walked out of it." There was awful grief on his face, "Simone, she says Leila's dead."

"Stop that! She's not dead. She's alive, she's in that body somewhere – do you hear me? My cousin's aunty's friend was possessed by an *aitu* and there's things we can do to cure her. How about a priest? Let's ask Aunty Matile. She'll know what to do with demonic possession. Did you watch that movie, The Exorcist? This is just like that."

"No, it's not. We're not getting Matile and Tuala involved. Or any witch doctors either. Nobody is doing some exorcist chanting over my girlfriend or giving her weird stuff to drink or doing crazy dances around her either."

Simone was affronted. "Don't be like that. My cousin's aunty's grandmother was possessed and the taulasea healed her *mai aitu*. It's legit eh. Don't be mocking it."

"I thought you said it was your cousin's aunty's friend?"

"Whatever. You know what I mean."

Daniel sighed in weary resignation. "This isn't some ghost story like the ones we used to scare each other with when we were kids. This is real Simone. What if she's telling the truth? What if the reason why this girl can't remember anything is because Leila doesn't exist anymore? You weren't there on that island. You didn't see what happened. She died." Tears glistened on his cheeks as Daniel voiced his worst fears. Spoke the terrible truth about what had really happened on that long-ago day. "I held her body in my arms and she was gone. Her skin came off in my hands, she was a bleeding mess of raw tissue. I tried everything to bring her back. She was dead. And then ..."

He stopped, unwilling to name what even he himself couldn't quite comprehend. Simone urged with impatience, hanging on every word, "What? Then what happened?"

Daniel confided the events on that scorched night which would be forever seared in his memory. The day Leila had died. The day his world ended – and then awoke renewed with the healing touch and song from a woman of ocean mystery. His shoulders slumped, "She warned me. I didn't get it at the time, but I do now."

"What did she warn you?"

"She said, one day all of earth's *telesā* would regret Leila's healing. Even me. Especially me."

Simone paced, waving his hands about with wild, jerky movements. "Let me get this straight. Leila gets fried in a nuclear explosion in a volcano. You thought she was dead." He waved away Daniel's interruption. "Alright, alright – so she WAS dead. Then some freaky mermaid woman jumps up out of the ocean, sings a song, 'Under the Sea', works her Circle of Life magic and heals Leila. Then she tells you," a dramatic Darth Vader chant, "Daniel, I am your mother - and oh by the way, your girlfriend might be a different person when she wakes up because I just sold her soul to the Dark Side? And then you let her swim away with her fishy friends? You only think to tell me this now? *E ke valea?!* Are you stupid?"

Daniel cringed. He was regretting his honesty already. *Maybe it wasn't such a great idea to tell Simone the whole truth and nothing but the truth ...*

No, he knew how Simone operated – he was going to have his melt-down and dramatize it with lots of spice – but give Simone a few minutes and he would then calm down and actually be useful.

Daniel walked away from all the exclamation marks and wild hand gestures, down the steps of the verandah and into the yard that hummed with life. Forever hungry mosquitos zoned into him immediately. The quiet coo of a wood pigeon resonated in the soft darkness. It didn't seem right that the world should be so normal. So sane. So quiet and assured, when the one he loved was lost to him. He breathed in deeply of the jasmine scented air, trying to get a grip on the panic and sadness that threatened to suck him.

A quiet step behind him. A much calmer Simone. "Alright, I've finished yelling now. Talk to me. *Fai se ka plan*. What are we going to do?"

Daniel turned with a relieved smile. "I don't know. This isn't something medical. She's been given a clean bill of health by the specialists."

"Maybe if you tell them what really happened? They could run more tests. Check her out better."

"Are you kidding? Hell no. They'd think I was crazy. Just telling you this story sounds crazy. Besides, I don't want them subjecting her to all kinds of lab tests. Leila entrusted her *telesā* secret to me and I can't betray that. She would hate to get locked up in a psychiatric ward somewhere." Daniel appealed to the one friend he had in this nightmare. "Telling the doctors is the last option. I could be wrong. Maybe, Leila's just struggling with amnesia and it will all be okay in a few days … or a few weeks."

Simone responded to the plea in his voice. "Sure. You've been under a lot of stress too. Let's keep close to Leila over the next few days and see whether she acts strangely again, whether she talks like this Pele person. Don't worry. We'll get her back. Leila's in there. I know it. We'll do whatever it takes and get her back."

They walked back into the house with unspoken fears weighing heavily between them.

And what if she's not in there? What if Leila's gone? What if she's dead? What then?

Inside the house, the girl who called herself Pele, was deep in a drug-induced sleep and in the furthest confines of her mind, someone fought against the darkness.

It smells of dark, rotten things. Dead things. When you've been in it long enough, your eyes get used to it. Enough so that you can see the dim outline of where you are. I'm in a cave of some sort. There's a pool of stagnant water in the center and I'm sitting on moss covered rocks. There's rusty shackles on my wrists and ankle, chaining me to the rock wall. There are specks of light in the ceiling.

Where am I? How long have I been here? I am alone. I am afraid.

Daniel.

I scream his name, willing him to hear me, find me, save me. Daniel. His name echoes throughout the cave, bouncing off the walls, mocking me. Laughing at me. I curl up in a tight ball. I scream until his name is but a whimper. A whisper in my mind.

Daniel. Where are you? I need you ... please ...

Daniel, help me.

Guilt

Keahi had lived with guilt for so long that it no longer meant anything. It was like breathing, eating and sleeping. *Wake up. Remember you're a selfish bastard who killed your own twin sister. Feel bad. Go eat breakfast.*

So yeah, Keahi was used to guilt.

Which is why it was irritating him to no end that he couldn't get past the bad feeling every time he thought about Niuatoputapu. Or every time he remembered a sour-faced girl trying to give him fire lessons in an abandoned quarry. A girl whose earnest efforts in a muay thai class transformed her from a brooding, sullen figure – to an awkward, laughing one as she tripped over her own feet and tried – and failed to execute a roundhouse kick. He remembered facing the same girl across a rocky field. The way she had shown no fear, the defiant rise of her chin as she surveyed a line of strange telesā and still called for Sarona to return Teuila. Leila had been brave, fierce and selfless.

While he? He had been a selfish, cowardly prick.

He wanted to make things right but he didn't know how. Making things right wasn't a Keahi forte. He had gone to see Leila as soon as the doctors finished stitching him up, intent on apologizing – but he had only succeeded in making Daniel mad. Which in turn got him riled up and resorting to barbed sarcasm. So yeah, Daniel's surprise attack on the way to the parking lot, perhaps on reflection, wasn't much of a surprise after all. Keahi could even concede, he had (possibly) kind of deserved it.

Now Leila was out of hospital. By all accounts she was fine. Just a few memory issues. Keahi wanted to see her. He wanted to do a very Un-Keahi like thing. Apologize. The tricky part was getting access to her. The part that made him nervous? Wondering whether or not Leila remembered his role in the whole Niuatoputapu mess. Had she forgiven him or was she going to set him alight?

Keahi wasn't the only one struggling with guilt. Teuila was back at the Women's Center. Mrs. Amani had welcomed her back with a warm hug and her weak relief made Teuila feel bad about running away. It was a regret overshadowed by her worry for Leila. Teuila couldn't shake the memories of that bleak day when Leila had confronted Sarona over a leaking reactor battery – for *her*. She had seen Leila on fire as Sarona hovered in the air above, hitting her with lightning strikes. Teuila was having nightmares about knives, blood, fire and fear. Nightmares from which she woke up silently screaming, her sheets soaked with sweat and tears. Teuila was glad that Leila was alright. Relieved that Sarona hadn't succeeded in her mission to destroy her.

But Teuila was also scared. Because the reasons why she'd run away in the first place hadn't changed.

Teuila had a visitor. "She's waiting for you at the front office," the messenger offered helpfully.

Teuila excused herself from class and dragged her feet on the way to the office. She had a horrible suspicion about who was visiting her. A deep breath before entering. She cringed at the gushing welcome.

"There she is! My baby girl."

Suspicions confirmed. It was Siela. She advanced with outstretched arms, *"Auuu, sau ia.* Come here and kiss your mother. Oh how I've missed you!"

Considering that Teuila had been back from Niuatoputapu for over four weeks now and her mother had never once deigned to visit before – Teuila very much doubted it. She allowed herself to be pulled into an embrace that smelled of stale sweat and cheap perfume. Over Siela's shoulder, Teuila could see Mrs. Amani's frown. *I'm sorry,* her eyes seemed to be saying to Teuila, *she's your mother, I couldn't legally keep her out.*

"Let me look at you. *Oka,* you're growing up so fast. Such a beautiful baby girl. Isn't she Toma?" Mother looked at the man sitting in the corner of the office and Teuila realized for the first time that her mother hadn't come alone to visit her.

Toma rose heavily to his feet, wiping sweat off his forehead. *"Oka se vevela.* It's hot in here. Isn't your air-conditioning working properly?" he snapped at the girl at the reception desk, before greeting Teuila with fake cheer. "Good to see you again Teuila. Your mother has been so sad without you around."

Teuila was rooted to the spot. This was the man who had beaten her mother. The man who had tried to rape her. Shock, horror and fear. What was he doing here? How could her mother have brought him to the Center? Mrs. Amani came to her rescue, put a reassuring arm around her shoulders. "You're not welcome here at the Center. You're upsetting Teuila. You'll have to leave."

Toma tried to chase away his immediate ugly look of hate with a smile. "Teuila knows I'm sorry for our differences. When a man gets drunk, he makes mistakes. That's why Jesus said we need to forgive others."

Siela interrupted, "Shh, that's enough of that. The past is in the past. Teuila, I want you to come home. You're my daughter and you belong with me."

"No, I want to stay here." Teuila gave Mrs. Amani a pleading look, "She can't make me go back with her, can she? Please, let me stay here."

"Come inside my office so we can talk about this," Mrs. Amani invited Siela. "Teuila, why don't you wait here?"

The three adults moved into the inner office and snatches of their conversation drifted out. '*She's afraid of what could happen if she goes home with you ... already ran away once ... don't want a repeat of that ... we can keep her safe here where she's happy ...*'

Teuila wanted to bolt from the room and get as far away as possible from Siela and her boyfriend. Where would she go? Who would take her in? Where could she stay? Where would she be safe? Maybe Leila's house? But who knew whether she was still going to want to be friends with her when she got her memory back? After what happened on Niuatoputapu ...

Teuila's nails cut into her palms as she clenched her fists, trying not to panic. Trying not to cry. For a brief moment she wished that Sarona hadn't died because she had promised Teuila a new life, a new start. It was a wish that dissipated as soon as it came though, leaving Teuila with a sour feeling of guilt in her mouth.

Sarona had tried to kill Leila and Daniel. She had shot that nice palagi man and tried to leave Teuila to burn in a nuclear meltdown. Wishing for Sarona was a stupid idea.

The adults came back. Siela didn't look happy. Mrs. Amani explained, "Teuila, your mother has agreed to wait a while because it would be too disruptive to take you away from your classes here at the Center so close to exams."

Exams were in two weeks. That wasn't much of a reprieve. But Teuila said nothing as Siela gushed over her and kissed her goodbye. She shrank away when Toma leaned in to hug her and so he patted her on the back instead. The couple left and Mrs. Amani ushered Teuila into her office.

"Come with me. Sit down and let's talk this through."

Teuila didn't want to talk. But this was a woman who had done so much for her that she couldn't refuse. "I won't go back to her, I won't!"

Mrs. Amani sighed. They had been through this conversation before – the last time it had ended in Teuila running away and joining Sarona and going through God only knew what on some obscure island in Tonga. Her voice was kind. "I don't want you going back there either. I understand how you feel. It makes me very angry that your mother can't see what her actions are doing to you. And that she would come here today with that man! I wanted to call the police but they wouldn't have been much help. No charges were ever laid against him and he didn't do anything violent here today."

Quiet tears rolled down Teuila's cheek. "I don't know why she wants me to live with her anyway. She doesn't care about me, doesn't pay attention to me at all. It makes no sense."

"I'm afraid your mother has heard about your friendship with Leila Folger."

Teuila was bewildered. "So?"

"So, the fact you are friends with an nineteen year old millionaire makes you a very attractive daughter to have around," Mrs. Amani said.

It all made sense then. "We have to tell her that I don't get anything from Leila. She's not going to give me stuff just because my mother wants it. Besides, Leila just got out of hospital. She may not even want to speak to me when she gets her memory back."

"Your mother doesn't care about any of that. She wants to go with you to visit your 'sick friend'. She seemed to know a lot about Leila's condition and even where she lives. I think she's got a connection with one of the nurses at the hospital."

"Please Mrs. Amani, isn't there something we can do? Some kind of legal thing?"

"We can try but as I explained before, the laws here are still very much weighted against us. I'll give the law firm for the Center a call and see what they can do. Whatever you do, please don't run away again, alright? I'm trying to help you – please have faith in me and we will figure this out, together. "

It wasn't the answer Teuila wanted but it would have to do for now. She left the office with a promise not to run away again. At least not right now. But instead of going back to class, Teuila slipped through the gardens to the grove of trees at the back of the Center. There, she sank to her knees in the tangled grass and closed her eyes, hoping it would happen. Several deep breaths and it did.

It was like music. The gently pulsing, lingering sound of life, of earth, breathing in sync with her, soothing her ragged heartbeat. Dozing flower buds awakened and turned their faces towards the girl kneeling in the grass. Vines unfurled from the trees above and leaned in to encircle her, leaves wiped away her tears. From stillness, a feather-light breeze danced its way through her hair, whispered against her cheek. A nearby stream picked up speed and added its refrain. Everything that pulsed and breathed – radiated its message of solace. Nature spoke and Teuila listened. She listened and she knew, she was not alone. People had always let Teuila down. Failed her. Hurt her. Disappointed her. Betrayed her.

But Earth never had and never would.

Butterflies

Daniel didn't go straight home when he left Simone standing guard over a sleeping Leila that night. Instead, he went to the Tanoa Hotel and inquired at the reception desk for the one woman he had never wanted to see again.

Tavake.

She wasn't surprised to see him. "Daniel Tahi. Shall we go somewhere we can talk?"

Without waiting for a reply, she walked to the poolside bar expecting him to follow. Daniel gritted his teeth, hating her self-assurance. Hated knowing that she had been expecting him. Hated that he needed to see her. Hated the suspicion that she was the only person who could make any sense of the miserable mess he found himself in.

The silver pool beckoned to him and he had to bite down on the urge to feel, listen, breathe with the water. He wanted to go swimming. Submerge his mind, body and soul in liquid peace, be anywhere except here.

Tavake sat at a table and beckoned for him to join her. She ordered drinks for both of them and not until the waitress had filled their order did she speak. "How can I help you?"

"You said on the beach there was something coming. Something bad. It had to do with Leila. You talked like you knew what it was. Like you could help."

She nodded encouragingly. "And?"

"And I want to know – what were you talking about?" Hostility radiated from him even as he asked for help. For answers.

Tavake had him right where she wanted him. She knew it and he rankled at that knowledge. She sipped at the chilled *vai tipolo,* savoring the tang of lemon, considering her words. "The answer has its origin many generations ago. So long ago, even we are not sure of the details. It's told in our telesā history but in the centuries of retelling, some essential pieces could be missing."

Daniel tried not to show his impatience. He had been trained well by a woman who believed in courtesy and *fa'aaloalo.* But this was driving him insane. "Could you please just tell me what's wrong with Leila and how I can fix it? She gave her life for me, risked everything for us. I was supposed to do the same for her. Keep her safe," he muttered down at his hands. "Some useless vasa loloa I turned out to be. What's the point of having this water thing if I can't even use it to fight for my girlfriend?"

Tavake leaned forward to place a hand on his. "I can help with that. With training, you could be an invaluable weapon in the battle that is to come."

He tugged his hand away from her. Harsh. "I'm not here for that. I'm here for Leila. What can you tell me about a spirit Keawe called Pele?"

An indrawn breath. Sharpness. The pool beside them began to churn with silver tension. "Where did you hear that name?"

"You recognize it. You know what's going on with Leila, don't you," said Daniel.

The woman opposite him seemed to be lost in a trance, talking to herself. "So it is true. Iolana was right. May Tangaloa help us all."

She straightened and faced him direct. "Tell me what you know."

Daniel threw a glance at the bubbling disturbance of the pool. He had unsettled her. He liked knowing it. "No. You tell me what I want to know. What's wrong with Leila? Who's Pele? What is she?"

"So be it. Our ancient stories tell us that the Telesā gifts were given by Tangaloa herself so we could stand as guardians of the earth."

He interrupted her impatiently. "I already know all that. Mama told me your creation story. And the bit about a Tangaloa Bone. Some story about a prophecy. I don't care about all that. Please tell me what's wrong with Leila?"

She didn't like the interruption. "I can't teach you unless you are willing to listen. The first requirement for one wishing to live and breathe in harmony with their Ocean gift, is to be teachable."

He'd had enough. He shoved his chair back with an angry grating sound and started walking away. She got to her feet, "Where are you going?"

"This is a waste of time."

"Wait!" She walked to face him. "Pele was a *fanua afi*, an earth telesā who lived a very long time ago. She was seduced by the fire, and her Gift wasn't enough for her. Legend tells us she used an ancient artifact called the Tangaloa Bone to take the fire powers of others. In effect, draining them dry and thus killing them."

"Kinda like a vampire?"

Tavake brushed that idea way with impatience. "Nothing like a vampire. What is this fascination with blood sucking creatures that sparkle in the sun? Such an absurd notion. Pele's Gift drove her insane. She stole so much of our Mother's potent power from others that she burnt herself out and destroyed her own body of flesh and blood. But not before a bloody rampage through many of our islands, taking lives and destroying entire villages who tried to stand against her. It was our version of the Dark Ages. She was psychotic. You can be sure, none mourned her passing."

"What does some long dead psycho have to do with Leila? Why is my girlfriend claiming that she's Pele?"

"Because she is. Pele never really died. She was too powerful a force for that. It was only the physical body that housed her spirit, proved too weak to contain it. Her body couldn't handle all of the power she stole. Think of it as energy. Pure energy. It can never truly be destroyed, it just changes forms, moves to different places and conductors. The fire that was Pele's spirit and life force went back to the place that it came from, to its origins. Pele's spirit has been slumbering in the earth's core for centuries. Yes she has appeared throughout history as a spirit, as a ghost – if you will, but only ever in transience. She could never go very far from her volcano temples. When your friend went into that volcano on Niuatoputapu, she would have been in a weakened state and easy prey for Pele. I don't even know how she physically survived the blast."

The look she gave him was searching and Daniel shifted uneasily. Unwilling to share too much with this enigmatic woman. "I told you, Leila's strong."

"So what's happened?" Tavake asked.

"I'm not sure. Leila's just come out of hospital. She was in a coma for a while after Niuatoputapu and when she woke up, she couldn't remember the last two years. The doctor calls it retrograde amnesia. We're supposed to be helping her to remember things. Tonight, I was showing her photos of us, of the past, when something happened and she changed. She started saying all this stuff about being Pele."

"What exactly triggered Pele?"

Daniel lied. That's what you do when you don't trust people. There's no way he was telling this woman about the Bone carving.

"We argued. She was angry about something and that's when her voice changed. Her face, her body – she was a different person. It wasn't Leila. It only lasted a few minutes though. Then she complained her head hurt and she slipped back into being the girl with no memory."

"Pele's hold on her host is still weak. Perhaps strong emotions hasten the transformation. You must try to keep her stable. Happy."

Daniel wasn't buying it. "All of this could be straight up fantasies in your head right now. You realize it sounds like some screwed up movie. Like I stumbled into a twisted legend where nothing makes sense?"

"You don't believe me?"

"You haven't seen her or talked to her. How do you know what's really going on? You're not a doctor. A brain specialist." He scrambled for other possibilities. "Maybe she's just confused."

"You're right, I haven't seen her. All the things I've just told you are not common knowledge. You don't learn them in school books. You can't get them from Google. How could Leila have known any of it? Why would she be talking about people and places she knows nothing about – if what I'm telling you isn't true?"

Daniel's shoulders slumped. Hopelessness. "But why? What does Pele want?"

"What she's always wanted – to rule supreme," Tavake said. "Our time is short. She has not yet fully awakened. She's not in complete control of Leila's body or fully aware of her own cognizance. We have a window of opportunity."

"To save Leila?"

She gave him a pitying glance. "To kill Pele."

Much later that night, after Simone and Lesina had gone to bed – Leila awoke with a dull throbbing pain at the edge of her consciousness. It was a wet, hot sticky night thick with rain. Too hot to sleep. She got out of bed and looked out the window. She wished she could dance in the rain, seek out spaces of coolness between the drops. She was so tired of the pain in her head. It had hummed with the same buzzing ache ever since she first woke up in the hospital. With that boy at her bedside. She frowned. That boy, Daniel. He stared at her with such intensity.

Always searching. Always waiting. Looking for something. Like he was waiting for her to morph into someone else. Be someone else.

She hated it.

Ugh, thinking about him always made her head hurt more. *Enough.* She left her room, walked through the darkness and slipped out the front door. Quietly. She didn't want to wake anyone. She just wanted to be out *there.* In the rain.

The grass was a welcome coolness beneath her feet. Within minutes she was soaked through. Wet hair plastered on her face, her back, clinging to her skin. *That's better.* Still, there was a heat underneath her skin that wouldn't wash away. And the same pain. Would it ever stop? She looked up at the moon, a swollen orb high above. *Do you know me? Do you know who I am?*

The heavens recited the rote words she was trying to imprint. *You are Leila Folger. You came to Samoa two years ago. You made friends. You fell in love.* Why couldn't she remember any of that? She closed her eyes and let the rain beat its rhythm on her skin. *Daniel Tahi. Questioning green eyes. A half-smile, always warily staring at her.* Surely she would remember loving him? Surely she would remember something? He was so big, so imposing, so damn sure of who she was that it infuriated her. His certainty made her resent him. Why did *he* get to know who she was? Why did *he* get to be the one with answers to the pounding ache in her brain? Why did *he* get to know how he felt? About her, about everything?

She clenched her fists. Anger built within in a steady, marching advance. What did it say about her that she couldn't remember? Couldn't choose to be, to think, to say, to feel, to love who the hell she wanted?

It's because you are weak. Leila Folger is a pathetic puny excuse for a telesā. Leila Folger is a waste of earth's fire. She panders to this boy and his expectations of her. She grovels to her family and friends and their demands. She makes excuses for others. She is afraid to unleash the power that is truly hers. Leila Folger is weak.

And I, Pele – I am strong.

A searing pain razed through her temples. She dropped to her knees in the grass. "Aaargh! What's happening?" She raked her nails through the wet soil, clutching at fistfuls of grass. Again the rolling wave of pain. This time it came with the voice that filled her mind with harshness, *Say it! I am Pele. I am strong.*

She raised her head from the ground, swayed. The black malu ink smoldered red, hissed and fizzed as raindrops turned to steam. She stared at the fiery patterns and muttered, "No, I'm Leila." Her voice rose to a scream, "No. I'm Leila. Get away. Leave me alone!"

The voice mocked her. Laughed. *You fool. I will never leave you. I am you. You gave yourself to me. This body is mine. And the sooner you accept that, the better. I have waited a thousand years to walk the earth again. A child like you cannot stop me.*

She buried her face in her hands. "No, I am Leila. My dad's name was Ryan. My mother died when I was a baby …"

That's where you're wrong. Again. Foolish child. Your mother did not die at your birth. She was a powerful telesā matagi, the Covenant Keeper of her sisterhood here in Samoa. Your stupid father stole you from her, took you far away from your home, from your destiny. You are Nafanua's daughter. And when you flame, when you unleash the fire inside you – I will be truly free and in total control.

This time the wave of pain came with searing flashes of light. She clutched at her head and retched as the world around her spun in a torrent of color and sound. Vomit was a burning sourness in her throat. "No, please. Somebody help me."

She threw up until there was nothing left inside her and then she stumbled back inside the house, to search through cupboards for her medication. Big gulps of water as she drank the pills down and then sank to her knees on the floor to wait for sweet relief.

Daniel's night had been restless and fitful, screaming with dreams of faces on fire. A smiling woman who smelled of old, dead things. He was up early the next day and in the workshop, turning to sweat and sparks to dull the fears that choked him. At least here, he worked with certainties and absolutes. Here he was in control, here he knew what to do and did it well. He was behind on several work projects thanks to days spent by Leila's side in the hospital and he worked alongside his team with busy efficiency for the rest of the morning. He didn't see the text from Simone until he broke for lunch. The six missed calls.

Get ovr here. Nw!!!!

He didn't bother changing or cleaning up. Just ran to the truck in heat-splattered overalls and was soon driving up the road, his mind racing with possibilities. None of which were good. The motorbike parked in front of the box-house was the first thing that caught his attention when he arrived. He was out of the truck in a heated flash, fists clenched. The sounds of laughter from the living room baffled him as he opened the front door.

"Simone, what the hell is going on ..." the words died away as he took in the sight before him.

Faces. Lots of faces. Simone. Lesina, Sinalei, Maleko, Rihanna, Mariah. And Keahi and Leila – sitting next to each other on the couch. *Too close*, his brain registered. Loyalty had been a driving force in Daniel all his life. Seeing all his friends gathered here, laughing, with Keahi in the midst of them – was a knifelike betrayal.

Simone looked relieved to see him. "There you are!" He walked quickly over to him, pulling at his hand. "Can I talk to you for a minute in the room?"

Keahi and Daniel had locked eyes. Tension, that everyone else seemed oblivious to. Keahi's face still bore the marks of their last confrontation and the anger coming off him in waves was meeting Daniel's head-on. Before Daniel could act, move, rage, smash – Simone had him moving along the corridor and into the room. Hissing, "Don't you dare. We have to talk."

Once they were alone, Daniel rounded on the traitor. "Why is he here? He's not allowed anywhere near her. And all of you, sitting around laughing, just enjoying the show."

"I called you. Texted you. No reply."

"So? You're tougher than he is. All of you could have forced him outta here."

Simone shook his head. "No, we couldn't."

"Why not?" He moved to the doorway. "I'll throw him out myself."

Again, Simone moved to block his path. "Stop." He planted his hands firmly against Daniel's chest. "Listen to me. Leila woke up this morning with more of that headache. The pain was so bad the meds did nothing for her. All she could do was lie there, shaking."

This revelation did nothing to appease Daniel's mood. He shoved Simone away from him and swore. "Why didn't you take her to the hospital? Or come get me? You're supposed to be looking after her when I can't be here."

Simone bristled right back, waved a finger in his face. "Back off big boy. We were about to take her to the hospital when Keahi pulled up. I wouldn't let him in. Told him to get lost. He didn't like it but he was going to leave when Leila came running out of the room and begged him to stay."

"What?"

"Just like that. Headache gone. No more shakes. No more weird staring into space. No more muttering to herself. She's smiling. Laughing at his stupid jokes. And she hasn't left his side since." He wrung his hands in frustration. "I didn't know what else to do but let him stay. You said she went all demon-possessed on you yesterday when she got upset and I didn't want to risk a repeat of that. What if she blew the place up? Keahi calms her somehow. Settles her. She likes having him around. I've been watching them all day."

Daniel swore. The last forty-eight hours had been like going through a meat shredder for him, puzzling over how to protect the girl he loved. And here everyone was, laughing and having a fabulous time? The chain snapped. He pushed Simone aside, strode out through the center of the living room and collared Keahi. "I told you to stay away from her."

With little effort, he picked up the smaller boy and threw him across the room. Keahi hit the bookcase, sheltering his head from the falling clutter.

Shock. Screams.

Chest heaving, all Daniel could see was blue rage wired with steel. He advanced but this time, Keahi was ready for him. Shaking off his slight daze, he leapt up and bounced on the balls of his feet. Light, agile and ready. His eyes sparked with a dangerous glint. "Is that the best you can do water boy? Bring it."

Daniel swung at his leering smile but Keahi was too quick for him. Duck, weave, spin. A roundhouse kick to the side of his head and it was Daniel's turn to go down. He scrabbled at his surroundings, books and knick-knacks, pulled himself up so he could face Keahi again. A muffled shout as he charged and took Keahi down in a vicious tackle and then both of them were twisting, rolling and punching at each other on the floor.

"Stop it!" Lesina screamed but nobody listened. It was up to the triple tag team of fa'afafine to fix the situation. Under Simone's expert directions, Mariah went for Keahi and he and Rihanna grabbed Daniel.

"Maleko, a little help here." Simone snapped at a jaw-struck Maleko.

And then the two boys were separated, both breathing heavily as they regarded each other across a chaotic room and struggled against those trying to restrain them. Simone was furious. "Animals! Meaola le mafaufau! See what you've done to our house? That does it. Both of you are banned from here. Get out."

Daniel shook himself free, wiping at the blood that tricked from his cut lip. "You're right." He looked at Keahi. "Outside. Let's do this."

Simone interjected with his hands on his hips. "No you won't. You will go home Daniel. Go home and think about what a dumb ass you are. You too Keahi. Get on your bike and don't come back."

And then Leila stepped in. What happened next shocked everyone and would cut Daniel more than anything else thus far. Leila cried out, "No, please don't go." She ran to Keahi, concern marring her face. "I want you to stay." She threw an angry glance over her shoulder at Daniel. "He can go. He started it anyway." Back to Keahi. A soft tone. "Are you alright?" Fingers gently danced along his jaw. "I can't believe he did this to you."

Simone spoke into the stunned silence. "Leila, I don't think that's a good idea. Keahi doesn't belong here."

Leila stiffened, moved closer to Keahi and cast an accusatory stare at Daniel. "No, *he* doesn't belong here. Everyone saw what happened. We were all having a good time when he had to come and ruin it. If anyone should leave, it's him."

Even Keahi didn't know what to make of this. Even he was uncomfortable with the shift. "Umm, Simone's right. It's better if I go."

She clutched at his arm, pleading. "Please stay. I've been in so much pain ever since yesterday and having you near makes me feel better. I don't know why, but it does. Please?"

Keahi shrugged his shoulders helplessly at the others. Panic. Keahi had never liked neediness in women. The look on his face was almost comical. With awkward hesitancy he raised his arm and allowed Leila to press into his side. He patted at her back with awkward hesitation like one would pet a kitten they didn't really want.

Daniel didn't wait to see how the rest played out. It was all too much for him. This girl was a stranger and every word out of her mouth was a cruelty. The group watched as he walked across the room and out the door to his truck.

Leaving Leila in the arms of another.

Keahi didn't stick around for very long after that. He'd been worried about an angry Leila fire-blasting him, but a clingy Leila who couldn't take her eyes off him was far more disturbing. He left Simone and the others cleaning up the trashed living room and took off. Simone made a witchy face and screeched after the departing motorbike. "Le alelo kao i se umu. Ova le fia kama mamafa ae airena. Aincholeek! And daaahling, when we call you a 'major' what we mean is a MAJOR PAIN in the ass!"

Keahi was cruising idly past the produce market in town when a familiar face caught his eye. It was Teuila moving through the crowd, clutching at a plastic bags of shopping. He hadn't seen her since Niuatoputapu. He pulled over and got off the bike, wrinkling his nose at the sickly sweet odor of over-ripe fruit. "Teuila!"

She didn't hear him. He started moving through the market, making an irritated face at the pesky little boys trying to sell him stuff. "Fa'atau se pepa chips?"

"Get lost."

The little boy stopped smiling. "Aikae, meauli!" He leaned in to jab a vicious kick at Keahi's ankle before taking off.

Keahi swore but didn't bother giving chase. He turned his attention back to Teuila. He couldn't see her. *Where is she?* There was a small crowd gathering around a disturbance of some kind. He moved closer. Teuila was at the midst of it. She was staring at the ground, rigid with shame as a woman screamed obscenities at her. The spectators were fascinated.

"I don't know why you can't do this small thing for your mother who has given everything for you ..." On and on it went. "You're ungrateful. Selfish. The Bible said, honor thy father and mother."

Teuila's head flashed upward at that. Defiance. "The Bible also said you have to love your children and don't hurt them."

Siela's face had an ugly twist to it as she drew back her hand and slapped Teuila across the face. "Salapu! Shut your mouth."

The crowd buzzed with censure. Children in Samoa weren't supposed to answer back. Ever. *'She needs discipline ... se fasi ...'* Teuila would get no support from this crowd. She went back to staring at the ground. Then a large man joined the spectacle. He wore a lavalava belted underneath his massive belly which protruded from his unbuttoned shirt. Even from where he was standing, Keahi could smell the stink of stale beer.

The man grabbed a chunk of Teuila's hair in his meaty hand and jerked her head back. "E ke kaukalaikiki? Lou mea moepi! Don't disrespect your mother eh!"

Teuila shut her eyes and trembled, willing everything to go away. The man pulled his other hand back into a fist to hit her.

Rage ripped through Keahi, propelled him forward. "Let go of her."

He grabbed the man's wrist and bent back on his thumb, breaking his grip. Teuila stumbled and fell backwards. It happened so swiftly, her captor barely registered what was happening. Before the man could react, Keahi hit him with an elbow to the face, breaking his jaw. He sank heavily to his knees on the concrete, the perfect position for Keahi to grasp his head in his hands and knee him once, twice. Bone cartilage shattered, blood gushed. Keahi released him and he slumped to the ground where Keahi proceeded to kick him in the gut. "How does that feel?" Keahi shouted. "You're not the man now, are you?"

People shouted, the crowd surged. A woman screamed, begged for Keahi to stop. Teuila looked. It was Siela. Wringing her hands, crying for the man who had once tried to rape her own daughter. In a faraway peaceful place in her head, Teuila mused on the realization that she had never seen her mother cry that way for her.

Someone helped Teuila to stand while others pulled Keahi away from the man on the ground. He pushed them off and backed away. "I'm done with him."

Siela was on her knees crying over the bloody mess Keahi had made. He pointed at her, "You're a sick excuse for a mother." For a moment he struggled with the raging urge to hit her too. "Both of you. Stay away from Teuila, or I'll kill you." He clenched his fists and the guttural sound in his throat sealed his threat.

He looked around for Teuila, found her, took her hand in his. "Come on, we're getting out of here." Chest heaving, he backed away from all the shocked faces. Still wary, still on guard. Teuila didn't argue. Just allowed herself to be taken away. Keahi pulled her to a halt beside his motorbike in the parking lot. "Are you alright?"

She shook her head. Numb. He didn't wait to try and coax anything more from her. He got on the bike and told her to climb on behind him. "Hang on. We're outta here."

He gunned the motor and had the bike weaving expertly through cars, ramshackle buses and impatient taxis. Teuila had never been on a motorbike before but she wasn't scared. She put her arms around his waist and held on.

Teuila was stunned. This was the first time ever, that anyone had ever protected her. Stood up for her. Fought for her.

Keahi drove until the crowded marketplace was far behind them. He didn't think it was a good idea to take Teuila to the Center. Not right now anyway. It would be the first place her mother would go to look for her. So instead he took her up the inland road and then along a grass-covered track into the forested hills. Teuila gave him a wary look. "What are we doing out here?"

Keahi held his hands up. "Just thought you might want some space before you go back to the Center, that's all. You're safe with me, I promise. Hey, if you're not comfortable being here, no worries, I can take you home right away."

Teuila considered him for a moment and then nodded. "Fine. I'll stay for a little bit." She looked around and her eyes widened. "You live here? In that?"

Keahi grinned as they both looked up at the rickety tree house that teetered in the embrace of a massive tree. "What? You don't like it?"

"Like it? I *love* it." Teuila exclaimed. She followed him to the rung ladder that circled the trunk and scrambled up to the wood slat deck. Rotting timbers creaked as she made her way across the decking to look out over the balcony at the sweeping vista of rainforest and distant ocean horizon. "This is awesome." A section of railing broke away in her fingers, crumbling to the forest floor below. Teuila stepped back, "Falling apart and super dangerous – but awesome."

"Yeah well, free awesomeness is hard to come by. So I'm just really careful and I don't ever have house guests." Keahi pushed an upturned crate towards her. "Sit. Thirsty?"

He got three cans of soda from a cooler in the corner and gave her two. "One for your face."

She held the stand-in ice pack to her cheek where Siela had hit her and snapped open the other can. The cool bubbles were a welcome sweetness after the heat and dust of the market and Teuila drank it down thankfully. "How did you find this place?"

"Got lucky. Someone at the gym was talking about a deserted tree house. The owners are a couple from America who tried to start a rainforest resort but their money and patience ran out after building only one room so they abandoned it and went back home. I needed a place to live, so score." Keahi looked around them. "It's not much. But it's free. And it guarantees that I get to be alone."

They sat in companionable silence for a while as the sounds of the forest seeped into the spaces between them. Birdcalls, the whisper of wind through the trees, the constant drone of mosquitoes. Then Keahi asked, "You gonna talk about it?"

"About what?"

"Back there. Was that him? The guy who hurt you? Got you and your mom sent to the Center in the first place?"

Teuila nodded. She crushed the empty can underneath her foot. It was a jarring sound at odds with the green peace of the afternoon. "I don't want to talk about it."

"Me neither." Keahi leaned back against the wall. Nonchalance cloaked his coiled edge of curiosity. "Let's talk about

Niuatoputapu. I know why Sarona took me there. But I want to know why she had you with her."

The girl who had never made the mistake of trusting any males, ever – looked at this boy who had just smashed another man's face to a bloody pulp – and wondered how much she could trust him with. "I do things with the plants and trees around me. I can't control it. I don't know when it's going to happen. It just does. Usually when I'm scared or in danger. Nothing major. It's kinda lame. Not like you and that fire thing."

"Yeah, well Leila's the firepower. I can't even light up without a trigger." He drained his soda and gave her a thoughtful look. "So Sarona didn't teach you anything useful?"

"She didn't have time. Besides, she was only using me as bait anyway." *Nothing special here. Why did I think anyone would want me to join their super cool team anyway? Loser with a capital L.*

Keahi stared at her for a long while, a thoughtful look on his face. Then he got up and started making his way down the ladder. "Let's go see what you got."

She scrambled after him. "I've got nothing. Didn't you hear me? I can't control this thing. I don't even know what this thing is."

Keahi ignored her protests. He chose a spot in the lanky grass. "Leila said you have to listen and feel the earth inside you. Some crap like that. Go on, shut your eyes."

Teuila felt silly doing it but she shut her eyes anyway. "Now what?"

Keahi moved closer but was careful not to touch her. "Listen to all the sounds around you and try to feel them."

That's easy. I've done it heaps of times.' There in the forest, miles away from traffic, crowds and people, it was even easier to feel that perfect peace as it slipped inside her. A slow-building warmth and quiet joy as everything living spoke to her, welcomed her, loved her. She could sense Keahi beside her, a safe, comforting presence. But beyond that there was the soft breeze. Rustling grass. Whispering leaves. A creak of aged wood as trees swayed ever so slightly in the wind. The call of birds. Buzzing insects. She went deeper still. The warm ground beneath her feet. Burrowing, wriggling creatures. An ochre butterfly with powder soft wings. A tired heliconia flower drooping in the late afternoon sun. Teuila felt all this and felt joy. Light and free. So what if she wasn't a flame girl, pretty and confident and strong like Leila? The glory of Earth encircled her and Teuila never wanted it to end.

"Aww heck!" Keahi exclaimed beside her, "Look at that."

She opened her eyes and gaped at the magnificence before her. The air was aflutter with a myriad of butterflies. Feather soft beating wings and tendrils of dancing color. Teuila raised her hand and butterflies alighted. Others speckled Keahi's face and shoulders. She laughed at this battle-scarred boy covered in butterflies and he threw her an unwilling grin. "What? This look doesn't suit me?" He shrugged and gently waved the blanket of butterflies away. "Do something else. Let's see what else you can do."

This time Teuila didn't hesitate. She was buzzing with excitement as she closed her eyes and breathed with the pulsing heart of Mother Earth. This time she focused on the soft grass beneath her feet and down further to the rick, black soil that fed it. The earth that cried for her, the earth that bled for her during those dark times in her short life when it seemed no-one else cared. She remembered those painful, hurtful times and Teuila surged with bitter anger.

Teuila spoke and earth answered. Keahi's shout of alarm jerked her out of her reverie. "What the hell? Teuila!"

She looked. The ground was rippling around them. The waves seemed to emanate from where she stood and Keahi fought to stand. As she stared horrorstruck, the ground surged and coils of earth wrapped around his ankles, yanking him off his feet. He was down and fighting to break free as the soil was a living, breathing thing trying to choke him. It was a losing battle. As fast as he pushed a python-like coil off, another took its place. Panic. "Teuila, quit it."

"I don't know how."

"Whatdoyoumean – you don't know how? Make it stop."

Teuila shut her eyes tight and tried to rid herself of the dark sadness and fear, push away all the bad things that had sparked this attack on Keahi. *Gardenia flowers, sitting in a mango tree eating juicy sweet fruits, picking passionfruit, tart sweetness on her tongue, lying in the grass in the sun. Good thoughts, happy thoughts – please!*

As suddenly as it had begun, the attack ceased. The life slipped away from the soil until Keahi was kicking and flailing at nothing but a pile of dirt. Teuila bent to help him up. "I'm sorry. I didn't mean for that to happen."

But Keahi wasn't mad. He looked at her with new-found wonder. "What are you?"

"I don't know." She asked shyly, "You're not mad at me?"

"Are you kidding me? I'm excited. You should be excited. Leila's fire telesā, Sarona was air and storms and stuff. Those freaky Tongan twins were ocean telesā. But you – you're like some flower power child, tree hugging, wind whipping, grass growing girl."

She had to laugh at that. "Wow, so poetic Keahi, thanks. I always wanted to be a tree hugger, grass grower."

They continued experimenting on into the approaching dusk, alternately laughing and shouting with each new discovery. Until finally Keahi ruffled her hair, "That's enough kid. We gotta get you back to the Center before they send out a search party for you."

Sitting behind Keahi on the motorbike with the wind whipping through her hair on the way back to the Center, Teuila was happier than she had been in a very long time. They still didn't know exactly what she was but it didn't matter. She was no longer alone.

Dravuki

Daniel didn't want to see Leila. Didn't want to talk to her or be anywhere near her – at least not right now. He went to work and checked on Leila throughout the day by texting Simone. No, the Pele demon hadn't reappeared. No, Leila hadn't set anybody or anything on fire. She had spent most of the day sleeping, drugged out on her pain meds.

'Ugly Scar Boy hasn't come over eithr.'

Daniel didn't want to talk about Keahi. *'Thanx. Busy at work. Wil come ovr tomorrow.'*

He worked until the sun had long set and all his team had gone home. Salamasina called him in for dinner but he wasn't hungry. No, there was only one thing Daniel wanted, only one place he hoped to find some peace. The ocean called to his troubled heart and he answered.

There was a full moon over Taumeasina Cove as the green truck pulled up. This was where the Pualele Outrigger Canoe Club kept all their boats. It was deserted. Just what Daniel wanted. He selected a single-man canoe and carried it easily to the water.

The tide was high and the night was silver clear. A perfect night to go paddling. He paddled for about an hour, losing himself in the rhythmic motion of lean-push-stroke. Black diamonds glistened on the water. A light salt-breeze soothed the skin and the soul. Here, he could forget for a moment, everything and everyone. Fire girls and heartache had no place here. It was just him and Vasa Loloa.

In the shimmering distance, something leapt, splashed. He felt no fear. He often saw flying fish, even a dolphin or two when he went paddling. But as he paddled further, the splash came again. Louder. Bigger. There was something moving in the water. Something big. It broke his focus and spiked his curiosity. Hmm … maybe he could sense it? Hear it? Talk to it? Whatever it was?

Perhaps because he'd had such a turbulent few days – make that turbulent few weeks – whatever the reason, Daniel sought distraction. He directed the va'a towards the last splash and opened his mind to the black depths below. Searching. Listening. Feeling. What was down there?

Gleaming, slippery skin. Moving, sinuous weave through the water. Hungry. Lonely. Searching. Sad. Missing home. Missing family. Black moonlight. Missing my mother … Hey, who are you? Get out of my head!

He gasped. Stopped paddling. Shaken. There was something there. Something that felt him, sensed him. Heard him. Something big. He looked wildly about. The ocean surface was still. Too still. A hushed indrawn breath in a silken night.

And then it leapt. "What the hell!?"

Out of the water in a flush of silver droplets, twisting and writhing in the moonlight, it was massively long, thick and heavy. It hung poised for an instant, like a sinuous marionette in the sky, a coiled spring – before it unfurled and dived back down again. Seeking the safety of the anonymous depths. It was an eel.

But unlike any eel Daniel had ever seen before. Longer than he was tall and as wide as his waist span. Dusky grey-green skin, a flash of pearl-shell eyes and then it was gone.

WTF? For a moment Daniel forgot he was Vasa Loloa, forgot he could speak to ocean creatures of all kinds, shapes and sizes. For a heart-stopping moment, he was just an individual alone in a tiny canoe in the middle of a black ocean with a monolith of an eel somewhere in the water below him. An eel big enough to overturn his va'a. All he needed now was the Jaws soundtrack to start playing …

He calmed down. Took a few deep breaths. "You got this."

He sat motionless in the canoe and opened his mind to Vasa Loloa. Again he was swimming then hurtling through the liquid depths, searching, sensing. *There it is!* A glimpse of the weaving, broiling creature. He reached tentatively for its thoughts and fell back in the canoe again. Because the Eel was talking to him. Speaking in distinct words and thought patterns. He had never experienced this before. Usually, when his mind encountered a sea creature, he caught impressions, images, pictures only. Sometimes emotions. Basic stamps of – PANIC. FEAR. HUNGER. Nothing else. But this? This was different. She was thinking streams of sentences. Words running into each other.

Who was that boy? Have to get out of here. He's too close. Must get away. Need to escape.

Daniel opened his eyes and searched the ocean around him. He looked and saw it. The water rippling, surging as the creature swam away – towards the distant cove where the freshwater river met the ocean. He paddled, quick and sure through the water. He couldn't see the Eel anymore but when he paused to breathe with the ocean within him – he heard her. Sensed her heartbeat. Felt her wild emotions as she swam, trying to get away from the one who pursued her. The Eel was afraid because she had never had her mind touched in this way. He muttered under his breath, 'This doesn't make any sense. If she wants to escape, why doesn't she head for the open sea?'

It was a long paddle to the shoreline and Daniel was puffing with exertion by the time he reached the shore. He pulled the canoe lightly up onto the sand and left it there. A quiet breath, a listen to the pounding surf and he caught her thoughts again. *There!* She was close. But she was as aware of him as he was of her. And she was moving fast parallel with the shore. He broke into a run over coral, rocks and driftwood. Unfeeling of the sharp things beneath his bare feet. He had to find her. *Where's she going?* She was on land now. Daniel was baffled. None of this made any sense.

She was ahead of him. A few more steps beyond that cluster of rocks and he would be upon her. He paused, caught his breath. *What's my plan? Hello, do I even have one? What am I gonna do with a monster eel?*

He crept through the shadows to peer over the rocks. It was a sight that would be forever burned on his memory. The giant serpentine creature was right there in the shallows, thrashing and writhing half in the water and half on the sand. What was wrong with it? He opened his mind to Ocean again.

Bad move.

Pain. It knifed him with a vicious stab right to the center of the brain. He dropped to his knees, "Aaargh."

The Eel was in pain. What was causing the hurt? He looked closer and that's when he saw it. The Eel was changing. Her edges morphing, ripping, dividing, rippling into something else.

Into someone else.

As quickly as the pain had begun– it stopped. Because what was splashing in the shallow water was no longer an Eel. But a woman. A girl. With skin the color of gleaming night and a bold mane of wild wiry hair that glistened with silver droplets of water.

Daniel stood there awestruck. The girl sat there half in the shallows with her knees hunched up and hugged close to her body. She took slow, deep breaths with her eyes shut and Daniel knew she was seeing her way through the last remnant of hurt that had wracked her body through the shift. Because that's what it was. He had just seen an Eel shift into a human being. Awareness flooded him. That's why her thought patterns had been so distinct. Because she had not been an ocean creature after all – at least not one that he was accustomed to. He took a few steps forward, hesitant. He knew she had been afraid, startled by his invasion of her thoughts. He didn't want to scare her any more than he already had. He wished he could still sense her mind so he could convey his apology, his message of calming friendship – but the bond was gone. It was an ocean creature bond only.

"Are you alright?" he called out.

She opened her eyes and glared at him. "No I'm not. You mind-raped me."

Daniel was aghast. "I did not!" He walked forward and stopped short when he realized the girl was naked in the water. A mutter, "Oh hell." He turned away, spoke over his shoulder. "I had no idea you were out there in the water. I didn't mean to freak you out."

A snort of derision, "So if you didn't mean to, then what was that?" The sound of her getting up and wading through the water, across the sand until she had come around and faced him head on. Still very naked. She was his height, an Amazonian figure with bold curves and legs as stacked as his. And she didn't give a stuff that she had no clothes on.

Daniel averted his eyes and spun around again, facing his back to her. "It's tough to explain. I do this thing when I go out paddling where I can sense the living things in the water. I do a sweep, it's a routine thing. You know, checking what's out there before I paddle out into it."

She was suspicious. "You go fishing with that mind power? Is that how you catch fish? By mind freaking them?"

"No. I just talk to them, connect with them." A groan of frustration. "I can't explain it. But I'm telling you, I didn't know you were out there. I had no idea you weren't a real eel." Aside, "It's not like I run into shape-shifter eels every other night ..."

She moved to face him. Again. And again he turned away. She was impatient. "What's wrong with you? Why won't you look me in the face? What are you trying to hide?"

This girl was unbelievable. "Apparently *you're* not trying to hide anything. I'm looking away because you're butt-naked. And I'm trying to be respectful of your modesty. Even if you aren't that worried about it."

A loud, rich-bellied laugh. He snuck a sideways glance at her. She had her hands crossed over her chest, head thrown back as she laughed. "I'm Dravuki. My skin is the most comfortable thing for me to be in. I have no shame for it. But if it means I can't have a face to face conversation with you then so be it. Give me your lavalava and I'll protect your modesty by covering up."

She was grinning at him in the moonlight as he loosened his lavalava and handed it over to her. She gave his brief shorts a cheeky whistle which he flushed at and he looked away while she tied the fabric around her chest sarong style. "You can look now."

Daniel heaved a sigh of relief as she teased, "Better now? You know most boys would be excited about stumbling across a naked girl as luscious as me on a lonely beach. I'm hurt you want me to cover up so bad."

Is she for real?!

He stared at her and she rolled her eyes at his intensity, "Oh relax. I'm kidding." She bent and shook her wild mane of wiry hair so that water scattered everywhere. Upright again, she regarded him with her unabashed gaze, and then her eyes widened in shocked recognition. "Your eyes!"

"What about them?"

She leant forward and tugged at his shorts. He jerked back, "Hey! What are you doing?"

"Oh relax. I'm not after your man-parts! I'm looking for – this." His birthmark. She let out a huge breath and stepped back. "It's you. You're the one."

"Are you alright? Like, mentally alright?"

She flashed him a huge grin and offered her hand. "Hi, I'm Talei. Otherwise known as big-ass gorgeous gargantuan eel."

"Daniel. Sometimes accidental brain spy of giant eels." They shook hands. It was a surreal experience. He was on a moonlit beach talking to a girl who had just been an eel only a few minutes before. Just another day in the paradise that he found himself living in and not always happily. He motioned in the direction of his birthmark. "So what was that about?"

She ignored the question. "You were in a canoe. Where is it?"

A jerk of his head, "Back there. You're fast. I had to sprint to catch up to you."

She grinned and he was struck again by her easy assuredness, her relaxed confidence. "Why don't you give me a ride back to the other side and we'll talk?"

She started walking in the direction he had pointed and Daniel followed. Because what else was he supposed to do? The whole night had a dreamlike quality to it and he was just flowing with this strange turn of events. "You're not worried at all about being in a canoe alone with a boy you just met in the middle of the night?"

Talei gave him a look of disbelief. "That's a joke, right? I could ask you the same thing. Aren't you afraid to be on the ocean alone with a girl who can shift into things even more threatening than a giant serpent?" She laughed again. This girl laughed a lot. And it was a rich, throaty sound that made Daniel think of his grandfather's favorite rare treat, coconut rum. She had a direct stare that he couldn't turn away from even if he wanted to. "No, if anyone should be nervous here – it's you, strange boy Daniel."

They didn't talk again until they were settled in the canoe and Daniel was paddling them back across the lagoon. She studied him with open interest. "So what are you?"

He tried evasion. "What do you mean?"

"You were in my head when I was in eel form. Like you were standing right in here." She tapped at her forehead. The smile was gone. "And no matter how hard I tried, or how far away I swam, I couldn't shake you out. What was that? And how come it only stopped when I shifted?"

"I'll give you answers, if you give me some. Fair deal?"

She was defiant but teasing. "I could shark-shift and rip pieces off you bit by bit until you answered me."

"And I could rip into your shark brain and make you bite your own tail off."

They were at a standoff so what did she do? Laugh. Hard enough that she shook the boat and he frowned at her as he tried to stabilize it. "You realize that a shark eating its own dorsal fin is a physical impossibility, don't you?"

He grinned back, her humor infectious. "What can I say, I'm all about defying the impossible."

She gave him a fake regal bow. "Fine, you got me. Let's swap info. And because I'm a lady, I'll let you go first. Ask away."

"You can't really turn into a shark, can you?"

"I'm Dravuki from Fiji. I can shift into just about any sea creature I want to. Some come to me easier than others." Her eyes narrowed at him, "You're pretty relaxed about meeting an eel girl. I never imagined that I would get such a relaxed reaction."

If only you knew ... "I've seen weirder things."

"Interesting," Talei said. "Now my turn. How can you get inside an eel's mind?"

"I've got some ocean connections. It's in my DNA. I can sense animals that live in the sea. Hear them, feel them, and sometimes if I try real hard, I can influence them to do what I want. But I'm new to this so I'm not very good at it."

"Is that it? What else can you do with this ocean connection?"

Daniel kept paddling and mused on how much he wanted to bare his soul to this strange girl. "That's more than one question. It's my turn. Where are you from and are there others like you?"

She didn't seem to have the same reservations he did. "Vaka Levu, one of the Fiji islands. I'm a student at USP university, my first year. As far as I know, I'm the only Dravuki. Just me. Swimming around all by my lonesome." She quipped the last bit but there was a sadness in her eyes which Daniel could relate to. He knew what it felt like to be the only one. "What about you? Are there more Ocean boys out here? And what else can you do besides snoop around in fish heads? That's not a very useful skill is it?"

She plastered an innocent expression on her face and he had to chuckle at her attempts to tease him into revealing more than he was ready to. "Oh, I get by. I've got a few more talents hidden away."

He was getting tired now. All the sleepless nights had taken their toll on him. Without even realizing it, a current surged beneath them, pushing the canoe forward. Enough so he could ease up on his paddling. Talei's eyes widened at the surge of power and she gripped the sides of the canoe tightly. "Hey, what's down there?"

Daniel couldn't resist giving her a teasing grin, "Don't tell me the monster Eel girl is scared of a little water power?"

Her eyes flashed and she scoffed, "You'll have to do more than that to impress me."

They had reached the shore now. Talei jumped out and helped Daniel pull the canoe up over the sand. He didn't need the help, but she didn't hesitate to join him as he hoisted the boat over his shoulder. "I've got this end." Silver light glistened on the muscles rippling in her shoulders and her skin glistened like ebony silk. Coiling down the center line of her spine was a mosaic of darker black patterning, a single lined tattoo that ran from her neck and disappeared into the lavalava.

They worked as a duo to stow the boat in the canoe shelter. "Wait here," said Talei. She dashed away into the shadows, to some trees further along the shoreline. She returned fully clothed and carrying a backpack. She threw Daniel the wet lavalava. "Here you go. Thanks for the borrow. So, you going to give me a ride?"

"Do I have a choice?"

"Not really," she said with that same infectious grin as she got into the passenger side. "I'm not done interrogating you."

Talei lived in the university dorms about a twenty minute drive away. "How did you get here?" Daniel asked.

"Walked. How else?" she said. "I come out here most nights for a swim. I was going to the river by the university but there's not much water there now that it's the dry season. And so filthy. Ugh." She rustled through her backpack. "You want a piece of gum?"

When he refused she popped two pieces in her mouth and immediately started cracking gum and blowing bubbles. The crisp fragrance of peppermint.

Their conversation for most of the drive back, revolved around Talei's Dravuki abilities. She was surprisingly open about herself. Used to all the eerie, doom-filled secrecy of the telesā world, Daniel found it a welcome change. No angst, no double meanings, no secrecy. He asked a question and she answered it. Yes, she could turn into any sea creature she wanted to. No she didn't know if she could be any other kind of animal because she'd never tried it. No, she'd never met any other Dravuki.

"Our legends tell of people who became sharks, turtles, dolphins. Aren't there any Samoan legends like that?"

"Quite a few actually. I never thought there was any truth to them."

"Neither did I."

"So how old were you when it first happened?" Daniel asked.

"My mum threw me off a cliff when I was eight. I turned into an eel so that's how we knew what my spirit shape was."

"Your mother threw you off a cliff?!"

"Yeah, but it was okay. She knew I would turn into something."

"You could have died."

"No. She knew I wouldn't. She was an Oracle. Y'know, she could see pieces of the future." *Snap, crackle, pop.* The very ordinary sounds of gum chewing and bubble blowing were an odd refrain for a conversation about shape shifters and oracles.

"Talei, you are one strange girl."

"I prefer 'unique and intriguing' myself." A grin to show she wasn't offended "Hey, this is me. Pull over here." Daniel parked the truck beside the shrouded buildings. Talei continued, "My mother knew I would be Dravuki before I was born. It was just a matter of forcing it. That's why she threw me off."

"If you say so."

Talei flashed him another huge grin, laughing at his doubts. "I know so." She got out of the truck, blowing one more huge bubble before slamming the door shut. A wrinkle of her nose as the bubble popped and she paused to peel the minty freshness off her face. "Just like I knew I would meet you Daniel ocean-boy." A wink. "Trust me, we are going to be very good friends."

She sauntered off before he could get in a reply, so he only smiled as he drove away, shaking his head. Strange, bubble-blowing, gum-cracking, eel girl or not – he liked her. He didn't believe in her story about a future reading mother, but Samoa was small enough that he was pretty sure he was going to run into her again somewhere.

Talei

I'm in shock. My mother would laugh at me if she were here. If she was alive. She was right. Beyond the grave she has reached out to remind me yet again, that I must not doubt her. I must have faith in her visions, her hopes, her certainties.

Tonight I met the boy with green eyes and the crested wave birthmark. She told me I would and yet, I doubted her. I blamed it on the ramblings of a dying woman. But she spoke true. I wait until the boy drives away and then I let the tears come. I miss her so much and here in this foretold meeting with a stranger, I have found her. I can feel her and the love she has for me.

Mum, I miss you.

I am Talei, daughter of Akanisi. My father's name is inconsequential. He left us when I was still a baby and it was always just my mother and me. Us two and the future that walked alongside us. For as long as I can remember, my mother lived in the future. Sometimes she kept it to herself and only shook her head at my scrapes and scratches, sad but knowing. Other times she took me with her into her visions.

"Don't go to school today Talei. Come with me to the rock pools to search for sea urchins."

I knew better than to question her strange requests, and when my friends were sent home early covered in angry red wasp bites because they had disturbed a nest behind the school hall, my mother winked at me. "See? Always listen to your crazy old mother. She will keep you safe."

I often hear people say they wish they could see the future. People say what a wonderful gift that would be. Sometimes, people are stupid.

My mother could glimpse the future and it was a heavy burden she carried, because if you can see the future, then you can never truly live in the present. My mother foresaw my grandmother's heart attack but she could do nothing to stop it. So instead she watched and waited for the moment when a blue kingfisher would sit in the sugar cane field outside our house. Watching. Waiting, with its head craned to one side. Because that would mark the start of her vision. The vision where grandmother would stop at her weaving, clutch a hand to her chest and then slip to her knees. Softly. Paper thin skin growing cold as her heart gave up.

So I know better. I know the gift of prophecy and revelation is a curse. For of what use is seeing the future without the power to change it? My mother could not avert hurricanes. Heal scarred heart tissue. Stop my father from falling in love with another woman. Make my teacher be a nice person who didn't have a fondness for using a cane on her students. No, my mother could not change the future.

But that didn't mean she gave up trying. So hers was a life spent always running … always trying to change tomorrow. Having to decide what to let be and what to try and influence. If you can glimpse the future, how far do you go to ensure your child doesn't get hurt? How much do you allow your child to experience? To feel? How much do you allow her to hurt? How far do you let her fall? How much do you let her bruise?

My mother was a woman who glimpsed the future. She couldn't change it.

But she always told me – *I could.*

Because I am Dravuki. I swim with the eel, hunt with the shark, dance with the dolphin, sway with the jellyfish.

As one of them.

When I turned eight years old, my mother took me to the edge of the cliff and told me the story of the shark and the turtle. How long ago, a woman and her child were driven from their village and threw themselves into the ocean to what they thought would be their deaths. Instead, they were turned into a shark and a turtle and found refuge in the sea. I remember it was a brilliant blue and gold day, with the salt wind leaving its trace on my skin. It was high tide and the white surf on the distant reef looked like the lace on her Sunday hat. I listened to her tell me the story but I was impatient for her to be done so we could get on with the business of birthdays. I was hoping for a netball. And a proper hoop. So I could stop practicing with a curve of steel wire coiled around the vakalevu tree outside our house and that dry coconut for a ball. Yes, I was hoping for good things on my birthday. I was tall. Strong. Fast. Solid. Immovable in defence. Relentless in offence. I had plans. I was going to be a National netball representative for Fiji. And then get selected for the Silver Ferns. All I needed was a proper netball and hoop to practice with. Yes, I was hoping for good things on this very important of birthdays.

Instead, my mother told me the story of the shark and the turtle. Then she knelt in the dirt on the edge of the windy cliffside and held my face in her hands.

"Talei, you are like them. You are a shark. A turtle. An eel. A stingray. You are one of the ancient ones like your father. I have seen it." She kissed me and smiled with sad eyes. "It is time for a girl to start the journey to being a woman. It is time for you to embrace your true nature."

And then my mother threw me off the cliff into the dark water below.

Shock. I screamed. I fell and I screamed. It must have only been a few breaths before I hit the water, but it felt like a lifetime as I hurtled through the air. I had never doubted my mother's love for me. I was her Precious. Her sweet brown sugar. Her only child. And yet here I was, thrown off a cliff. I hit the water. Pain. It was like falling on a concrete netball court. The impact stunned me. I went under, tossed and turned in the eager current. I could see the light far above me, beckoning with its promise of air and sweet release. But the water wouldn't release me. I panicked. Fear drowned me. I fought but it was futile. I fought and then the unthinkable happened.

Twist. Writhe. Contort. Skin ripped. Bones shifted. Pain. It felt like an eternity. But it was only a moment of redefining. And then I was rippling. Lithe. Lissome. Twisting, Sinuous and slippery. The water was no longer my enemy. It caressed and embraced me. I was free.

I was Eel.

That was the first time I swam in the skin of another creature. The first time I knew I was like the ancient ones spoken of in legend. The Eel was my first change and it would always be my first choice, automatic and instinctive whenever I shifted. For a long time, Eel was the only blend that I ever entered. I loved the way she moved with sinuous grace, weaving in and between currents. Eel is beautiful. She is fast. Fluid. And free. I spent many hours for many days after school, exploring our coastline and coral rock formations as Eel. She showed me the wonders and mysteries of the shoreline. After swimming as Eel for many moons, my mother had to issue me with a warning.

"Talei, you must swim as another creature. You cannot be Eel always."

"But why not?"

She sighed at my stubbornness. "You are Dravuki which means you can walk in the skin of many. Not just of one. You will need to know the heart of more than just Eel." And then the answer that I could never argue against. Ever. "I have seen it."

I muttered. "In that case, the whole world has to do what you say, doesn't it?" I walked away, mimicking her, "I have seen it. It is written. I have seen it ..." Did I mention that sometimes, I was sick of my mother seeing the future?

But when I was done with my grumbling, I did as she instructed. As always. Because she was my mother. And nobody loved me as she did. This I knew. So even though, I couldn't see the things that she did, I would always obey. Because my mother loved me. But more, because I loved her.

From that day on, I tried to wear the skin of other ocean creatures. And it wasn't easy. My mother had been right. I was too used to Eel. She had made me immune to the call of others in the blue depths. I had to study the movement and behavior of another creature for many days before I could shift. I went out alone in my small canoe. I would slip into the water with a ragged pair of goggles and swim with whatever creature I could find. I chose Turtle. She fascinated me. She was cumbersome and heavy on land but fluid and fleet in water. She lived for many years and travelled widely, more so than Eel. Who knew what wisdom she carried? What secrets would speak to me from those bright eyes set in wrinkled skin? I swam with Turtle until at last, I could swim in her skin. With her heart.

The change when it happened, was magical. An exuberant thing. Where Eel twisted and swayed with the currents, Turtle mastered them. Read them and rode them. She saw things that Eel didn't. Felt things that Eel couldn't. Among them was a pull, a longing. An inner need for a place I had never seen. That I knew Turtle had never seen. It was the place of our birthing. A silver beach on a faraway shore where our mother had long ago scrabbled in the sand and carefully placed her eggs. Covering them with warm sand, patting and smoothing it down until she was certain we would be safe. Secure. Hidden from the marauders. The scavengers. The egg-eaters. Yes, I could feel this place. See this beach in my Turtle mind's eye. I knew it like I knew the sound of my heartbeat, I felt it like the pulse of blood in my veins. Even though I had not been there since. The pull was so strong that when I swam as Turtle, I had to be very careful not to give in to it. Not to answer that call and abandon my home village and swim the thousand miles it would take for me to reach that distant shore that had been my birthplace. My mother's birthplace. My grandmother Turtle's birthplace. As Turtle, I swam further distances than I did as Eel. Confident and comfortable in the open ocean, far beyond the safe embrace of our coral reef. Sometimes I swam alone and other times I swam with my sisters. We went in search of the salty seaweed that we loved to eat. As Turtle, I felt like I belonged to an ancient family that was always present with me, even though I had never met them. I felt a connection to the Mother Ocean that was binding and permanent.

After many months as Eel and Turtle, I minded my mother's counsel and chose another creature to swim with. Dolphin. Playful, poised and purposeful. It was easier this time to become a different skin. For many days I swam with a pod of them off the coastline of our village and they were some of the most joyous days of my life. Dolphins are social creatures –more so than I have ever been as a human. They loved to play, dance and were always in search of new delights and fanciful interests. Not only that, but they didn't carry the same fear of humans that Eel and Turtle did. Dolphins went in search of people. As Dolphin I followed behind the boats of fishermen, doing tricks to get their attention, delighting when they responded. The day we came across a group of children playing in the shallow waters who didn't run away from us was my favorite in memory. We let the children touch us – run their hands along our marbled skin, shying away from the ticklishness of their touch. We let the smaller children ride with us, clinging to our dorsal fin for support, preening in their shrieks of delight. Swimming as Dolphin was way more fun than being Eel or Turtle. When my mother began to purse her lips at me in disapproval as she watched my antics from shore, sadly, I knew it was time to choose another ocean creature because Dolphin was taking too much of my time. And so I said goodbye to the pod and chose another.

Thus the rest of my childhood went. Mornings were school at the dusty schoolhouse surrounded by sugar cane fields. Afternoons were for netball practice with the regional team. And early evenings were for swimming as Dravuki, a different skin each week until I knew that creature and its ways like I knew my netball combinations. Jellyfish, shark, lobster, stingray, and blue marlin – I was all of them, and they were me. But no matter how many ocean skins I swam in – Eel remained my twinsoul.

I had to be very careful though. My Eel was not some inconsequential thing lurking in swaying sea-grass. Over six feet long, I was a gigantic serpentine thing and not a sight that inspired happy '*awwww how cute!*' responses in anybody. When I swam as Eel, I did so in the depths of night, seeking out the dark spaces of our lagoon, quietly evading the night fisherman and sand walkers. Despite my best efforts, whispers and rumors began to abound in our village of a mysterious creature that only swam at night. Something big. Monstrous. Scary.

"Eh, I saw it with my own two eyes! It was like a giant snake, or a dragon fish. A spirit demon from the sea. It clutched a whole shark in its gaping jaws. It had teeth like knives!" Sativalu was the most expressive and loudmouthed gossiper of mystical terrifying Eel stories. All the talk had me rolling my eyes, muttering under my breath about the stupidity of people who spoke first before even seeing. I had a good mind to creep up on Sativalu the next time she was swimming in the freshwater pool at the back of the sugar cane fields. That would teach her to make up lies about innocent eels that went about the night, minding their own business, catching little fish for their supper and nothing else!

But Mother listened to the stories with shadowed apprehension. As I feared she would. And berated me with whispered warnings. As I knew she would. "I told you to be careful. No more swimming as Eel. Choose the small creatures. The rainbow fish. Or the star creature. How about the sea urchin?"

She may as well tell me to roll myself in batter and volunteer for the frying pan at the fish and chip shop. "Mother, why would I willingly make myself weak and defenseless so that some stupid hungry human can eat me for their dinner? Is that what you want to happen to your only daughter?"

"Don't be foolish child. You are Dravuki. No one can match your strength or gift. Do as I say, no more Eel."

I didn't like it. But I was obedient. To an extent. No more did I swim as Eel in our lagoon. Instead I was sandfish and swordfish and masimasi – evading nets and hooks until I was far out beyond the reach and prying eyes of our village. Only then would I be Eel.

Life was going pretty good for us. I graduated from our little village school and was accepted to the university in Suva. My selection for the national netball team got me more excited though. The future was bright.

And then my mother got cancer. She knew it before any scans and doctors of course. She was waiting for me one day after training. "Talei, come sit."

"Let me grab a shower first Mum," I said, making a yucky face at my sweaty uniform.

"*Oi lei*, never mind that. Come sit."

"Okay then, you asked for it!"

She took my hand in hers, "You must apply for a transfer to the university campus in Apia."

"In Samoa? Why"

"They have very good programs and you can still play netball there."

"But you'll be so far away!"

"It won't matter. I'll be dead."

Yeah, that's how an oracle talks. No sugar-coating of the future or anything delicate like that. Probably because they've had time to get used to the idea of any impending horrors that they forgot everybody else might need a little warming up first? "Tell me what you've seen Mum."

"I have cancer. It's incurable. We have some time, but not much. I'll be gone by the time the school year begins."

"Have you seen a doctor yet?" Dumb question. My mother thought medical professionals were untrustworthy sharks who liked to cut people up for fun. "Even an oracle can get things wrong sometimes Mum."

"I will, I will. You can go with me. I promise." She waved at me impatiently. "In the meantime, put in your application to transfer to Samoa. Think of it as my dying wish." A piteous look. "Please?"

My mother was a con artist. To the very end. I put the application in and promptly forgot all about it. There were other more pressing things to focus on. Like the cancer that was spreading horribly fast through her little body. She let me take her to the doctor as she had promised. And she gave me a gleeful look of triumph when he told us what she already knew. A loud whisper, "See! I told you."

"Mum, you're not supposed to be happy to get proven right on a death sentence."

She nudged me in the ribs, "Admit it, you were doubting me."

"No, I was hoping you were wrong because you're my mum and I want you to stick around. That's what normal daughters do who love their weird, wacky mothers!"

"Be nice to me eh. Don't you know I'm dying?"

Mum refused the doctor's offer of chemotherapy. "Even with radiation, you can only promise me an extra three months to live? Never mind doctor. I will spend my final days with my daughter. At home." An aggrieved look that only I knew was fake. "I will treasure every breath with my beloved only child. As I waste away like the foam on the ocean waves …"

Mum always fancied herself as an actress. I was used to her various roles but even this one was a bit over the top. "Quit it mum," I muttered furiously.

In the car, she gave me that wide-eyed look, "What? I'm sick, why are you angry with me?"

"While you're busy acting tragic dying woman, could you please stop for a minute to remember this is rough for me? I don't want to sit around and watch my mother die. I'm going to be all alone without you. You're my best friend mum. Please don't joke about this."

"*Oi lei*, I'm sorry baby. Death is a natural part of life. I forget you are young and not ready to accept that yet." She reached to hug me quickly, "We will have fun in these few months left, you'll see."

And we did. We planned her funeral together with lots of laughter. My mother had many friends and they made her every day full. Our little house was a site for lots of bingo, card games, rude stories and jokes, sing-alongs and plenty of food. Food that my mother increasingly ate less and less of. She was beginning to fade and even jokes made her tired.

She woke me in the middle of the night. Her last on earth.

"Talei, you are a good girl. You always make me very happy. I was worried you would take after your father. But no, you are a hardworking, reliable girl. You have his Dravuki spirit but that is all. When I go, always remember, I am proud of you."

I cried. After all the laughter and light-heartedness, I still wasn't ready for my mother to leave. What daughter ever is? I held her fragile body close, "I love you."

"I know. That's why I know you will not disobey me now. When I am gone, you must go to Samoa."

"Oh, not this again," I groaned.

"Shh, this is very important Talei. Of all the things I have seen, none are as crucial as this."

The fierce strength in her face stilled my arguments. "I have seen the end of days Talei. The end of our islands, of our Pacific. It will come with fire. It will come with water. Many will fight it, but it will come." She grabbed my hands tight and her thin fingers were like talons of determination. "Promise me, you will go to Samoa."

I nodded. "But mother, why? What must I do there?"

"Find the boy. The one who speaks to the sea. You will know him by his forest eyes and the wave birthmark on his hip."

I tried to make light of her intensity. "Mum, like I'm going to run around pulling down random boy's pants so I can check out their hips!"

She didn't smile. "Go to him. Help him find what he seeks. Do everything in your power to help him. Stand by his side as he wars against the Fire."

I wondered if she was losing her grip on reality. She had seen so many things in her life, so many that I know she never shared with anyone. Maybe it was finally all too much for her. Maybe this was the cancer talking. I patted her arm and tried to soothe her, "Let's not talk about this now. You should be asleep. You need your rest. Tomorrow we're having a party remember? Lina and Sulita are bringing your favorite lole saina sweets and their karaoke machine."

She shook her head. "Tomorrow I will be gone. Promise me you will do this thing."

"Why me, mother? Why?"

She pulled me close. Held me in a sandalwood-fragranced embrace. This tiny woman dwarfed by the bulk that was me. Warrior princess me. She whispered. "Because I have seen it. There is no other who can do this thing Talei. Only you."

I pulled away. Frowned. Shook my head. "What if I say no? What will happen?"

She gave me that look. Sad. Knowing. Heavy with finality. "You will all die." She turned with an expansive sweep of her arms. "And all this? Our islands. Our waters. They will never be the same again. I have seen it. The red wave comes. Higher than those hills. Taller than the tallest trees. It burns. The red wave, it burns." Silent tears ran down her cheeks. "This is not my will. This is not the wish of my heart. I have battled this vision for a long time. I have tried to dream a different dream. See a different future. For you. For him. For us. But there is no other path."

You don't live as the daughter of a seer for nineteen years without accepting that some arguments are futile. And so, I promised my mother I would go to Samoa in search of a boy with green eyes and a crescent shaped birthmark. A boy who spoke to the sea. Even though such a promise sounded silly. Even though, I had no clue how I was supposed to find such a boy. Or even what I would do to help him.

The only clue she could offer was an enigmatic reminder of my Dravuki power. "You must stand strong and use your Dravuki powers. You will soar with wings my child. You will touch the heavens and hold the star-bringer in your hands. Never forget, you are Dravuki. And I love you."

When she had gotten the oath she wanted, my mother leaned back on her pillows with weary relief. "Thank you." A sad smile. "I only wish I could stay and see you through this. It's wrong for a mother to abandon her child when she will face her greatest challenge." Tears. Finally, after months of laughter and lightheartedness, my mother cried about dying. She cried because she was worried about me. Because she didn't want to leave me alone.

I held her and we cried together for a long while. When we were all cried out, I fell asleep beside her and by morning she was gone.

I said goodbye to my mother. And after the funeral, I said goodbye to the place I called home. To all that I knew and loved. And I came to Samoa.

In search of the boy she called Son of the Ocean.

The Tangaloa Council

A keen observer at the Tusitala Tanoa Hotel that day would have been intrigued by the arrival of a steady stream of arrestingly striking women. All throughout the day, they came to check in at the imposing grandeur of a hotel originally named after the Scottish writer, Robert Louis Stevenson who had made Samoa his home many years ago and who had been gifted the name of 'Tusitala', teller of tales.

Eyes turned to look. Activity stopped to admire. To wonder. These were no ordinary women. They arrived in long, sleek limousines chauffeured by subservient men. They wore the very finest in Pacific couture and dripped with the jewels of the blue continent. Black pearl, pink coral, ocean bone, river rock, rare feathers and oyster shell. They had the ageless faces of those whose looks were carefully preserved either by the most advanced technology money could buy – or the wisest secret elixirs of earth's guardians. Even those who did not know what they were – knew they were not 'like us', knew they were no ordinary women. People stared. People whispered. *Who are they? They must be famous ... celebrities?*

The women said very little. Only checked in with their Gucci luggage and asked to be taken straight to their suites. They kept their eyes hidden with Dior sunglasses and their Manolo Blahniks were a clicking cacophony of sound over the tiled floors. One group in particular, stood out. There were six of them dressed in floor-length robes of the deepest blue and each woman was accompanied by another that walked a foot behind them. Unlike the women they followed, these attendants wore white. Flowing loose linen pants and brief tops. Gone was the jewelry, accessories and stilettoes. These women wore functional sandals and a single torque around their necks fashioned from braided sinnet and flinted with shell. They had identical tattoo markings on their forearms – repeating triangle patterns of the Shark tooth. All six of them stood out in particular because of their shaven smooth heads and the delicate shark tooth patterning behind their right ear. They were lithe and light on their feet and moved with a fluid grace, every movement alert and taut. As they strode through the hotel lobby, their eyes darted everywhere, searching out every onlooker, every corner and turn. They stood back while one of the vibrantly attired women took care of all the necessary check-in details. "We have reservations under the name Keawe."

An over-eager hotel employee rushed up too close to take their bags. A young man with an eager smile, "Let me take your luggage beautiful ladies."

He went to place a hand on the lead woman's bag but before he could even touch her, the white garbed attendant reacted with lightning speed. She grabbed his arm, twisted and pulled, slamming his face into a nearby post, pinning him against the coconut carved wood. Blood bubbled from a broken nose. Shock. Pain. "Aaargh!"

His attacker wasn't even breathing fast, her face expressionless. She leaned in close to whisper in his ear, "No one touches the Keawe. Let this be your only warning."

As swiftly as she had restrained him, she let him go and he slumped against the post with a heaving gasp, wincing and rubbing at his arm. The young woman turned. None of the group had even raised an eyebrow at the altercation but they had a stunned audience in the hotel staff and bystanders who gaped. The lead woman in dark sunglasses merely sighed, "We are tired. Show us to our rooms now please."

The receptionist rushed to comply and the group made their exit, with the six attendants following with careful guardianship. Another guest whispered, "Who are they?"

"A delegation from Hawaii. I hear there's a high-level environmental conference being held at the hotel over the next week."

The truth was so much more than that.

This was an epic meeting, the first of its kind in over five hundred years. Called by Iolana the sensate leader of the Keawe and sanctioned by Tavake the oldest among them – it would bring together all of the Pacific's elemental guardians – to form the Tangaloa Covenant. They came from Tonga, Fiji, Tokelau, Rarotonga, Vanuatu, Niue, Nauru, American Samoa and Hawaii. Their numbers were few, their gifts sorely weakened by the onward march of progress. The Blue Continent had always been the greatest source of strength for them and she was hurting in new unforeseen ways. But the combined force of the Tangaloa Covenant was still a force to be reckoned with, and they would need to be if they were to face the wrath of Pele the Fire Goddess.

The Covenant met later that afternoon for the first of a series of discussions. Tavake came with a straggling few Vasa Loloa. She had been battling treachery in the ranks lately and there were very few sisters left she could trust. Only two in fact. And not very strong sisters either. Tavake had eliminated the traitors who had gone to aid Sarona in her stupid quest for vengeance. She bitterly regretted her decision and not just because Pele was rising. Her leadership seat at the Covenant table would now be in question and she would have to fend off the grasping tentacles of the Ariki – the elemental air guardians from the Rarotongan island of Mangaia.

Unlike the Keawe, the Ariki were vivacious and loud. There were fourteen of them and they came resplendent in the colors of the TAV design label, vibrant birds of paradise. Their leader, Apollonia was a petite woman, barely grazing 5'4, who jangled as she walked with mincing steps – bangles, anklets and necklaces all a jingle. Hair a mass of honey curls, sprinkled with cinnamon strands, thick lashes, pouty lips and generous curves all combined to make her seem almost doll-like. Her cutesy exterior did not fool Tavake for a moment. Apollonia was a lionfish, frilled prettiness hid her deadly venom.

"Come along sisters, this is going to be soooo much fun," Apollonia said as she led the way into the meeting room. She smiled with exaggerated friendliness at Tavake and gave her a lipstick air kiss. "Dearest Tavake, it's been too long!"

Tavake wrinkled her nose at the overpowering scent of Chanel "Yes, the last time was over an ill-fated whaling expedition I believe?"

"How can I forget? Because of your interference, my sisters and I were out by a few dollars."

More like a few million. But hey, who's counting?

In Tavake's eyes, Apollonia and her sisterhood were the worst kind of Earth guardian. They used their gift to manipulate fishing treaties and deals that gave them kickbacks, making them very rich. Tonga was the first South Pacific country to put a conservation program in place with a series of national marine reserves and one of the first to legally ban whale hunting in their waters back in 1978 – things which Tavake had fought for and which Apollonia viewed as incredibly stupid and wasteful. Especially when so much Japanese yen was involved. The two stared at each other with simmering hate.

"Now sisters, let's not bicker. At least not so soon in the meeting."

The opponents turned to the sister who gently reproved them – Lupe, one of the only two telesā from the atoll of Tokelau. A slight woman in pastel lemon with a soft smile and an even softer voice, she was also Vasa Loloa. They greeted her with deference and even Apollonia looked appropriately humble. Lupe was a tireless environmental activist, well-known for her work on behalf of a people for whom global warming was a very real threat. "Tavake, I know our purpose for gathering is to discuss Pele's awakening, but is there any chance we could also put Tokelau on the agenda?"

"Of course Lupe. How have you been? Did you attend the Pacific Forum meeting this year? I couldn't make it due to some domestic strife in my sisterhood …"

The two moved away to discuss their mutual environmental activities and Apollonia watched them go with a sneer. One of her seconds asked quietly, "Do we need to be worried about them?"

"No. There are only two from Tokelau and their Gifts are unimpressive. Let them waste their efforts on a sinking coral atoll while we focus on more pressing concerns, shall we?" The women laughed.

Apollonia moved on to greet the guardians from Fiji – the Sereana who spoke with the voices of Air. "Bula and welcome Adi," she said to a tall woman in majestic red and gold. "How is the state of affairs in your Sisterhood?"

Adi arched an eyebrow and gave her a cool glance, "Abandoning all pretenses at diplomacy Apollonia? You may as well come right out and say it – how many sisters do the Sereana have and how will we sway when the wind changes?"

"Such blunt talk sister," Apollonia laughed gaily. "No, I merely meant to inquire after your beautiful islands. It's been many years since I was last in Fiji."

"A good thing. I could not guarantee your safety if you were to visit," said Adi. A smile belied the dagger of her words. "Let me save you the idle chit-chat. The Sereana stand with the Keawe. We will vote however Iolana wishes us to and we won't be swayed by those who prostitute their Gift to the highest bidder."

Adi moved away before Apollonia could respond, leaving her fuming. The entrance of the Sisters from Niue distracted her. There were five Air guardians from the tiny island and they were an unknown element for Apollonia because they had a new leader who she had yet to meet. She took a guess and addressed the most senior of the group, "You must be Ofa? We are sisters of Air together, welcome."

A young girl who didn't look more than fourteen years old stepped forward. "I'm Ofa. It's an honor to finally meet you. Our Sisterhood is small but determined. We are eager to join forces with the Ariki."

Finally, someone Apollonia could connect with. A gracious smile, "We must speak further, perhaps after today's Council session?"

"Later then," Ofa said.

The group from Niue moved to find their seats at the table, but not before Apollonia took one of them aside. "What happened to Ololini? I thought she was next in line for Covenant Keeper?"

The woman grimaced. "Ofa killed her in one-on-one combat. She also took out two others who tried to oppose her ascension."

"Well, well … it seems the little one is feisty," Apollonia said to her second. "She will make the perfect ally." Apollonia liked ambition in others. It was something she could understand.

She continued on, greeting the Sisters from Vanuatu, American Samoa and Nauru, sending out feelers of invitation and threat. She wanted there to be no doubt in anyone's mind of the place of the Ariki at this council. They were the largest, most powerful Covenant Sisterhood left in the Pacific and as such, they deserved the leadership seat and when the time came, it was she Apollonia, who must wield the Tangaloa Bone.

It was time for the Council to begin. Iolana relayed the vision her Keawe had seen and described the surge of red power which marked the awakening of Pele the ancient one in the body of a nineteen year old girl, Leila Folger. Her second took over, summarizing the research they had done into the Niuatoputapu eruption, their conclusions about what had happened there.

When the Keawe were done, the floor was opened for discussion. Tavake sat in leadership at the Council table. If Nafanua had lived, that would have been her place. But the Matagi Sisterhood of Samoa were no more and that alone was a matter for much dark muttering and discussion. What had truly happened? How had the matagi sisterhood been destroyed? As far as they knew, there were no survivors, no witnesses —only the stranger from America.

"I'd heard whisperings but I didn't believe them. If this girl did kill Nafanua and her Sisters then she wielded incredible power even before Pele occupied her body," said Lupe. "I find it difficult to believe that one girl could wipe out an entire Covenant. Even if she is fanua afi."

A murmur of assent. "Isn't there anyone we can speak with who might know more?" asked Adi. "Tavake, you were close to Nafanua. You must have a source here in Apia?"

"I have an offspring that lives here, yes. Ungifted, works as a healer," said Tavake. "But you know our laws. We do not involve ourselves in the domain of our other Sisters. They are their own law in their islands."

"Oh come on, we all spy on each other though. There's no shame in admitting it. How else are we to stay up to date on everyone's business?" laughed Apollonia. "Surely this daughter of yours must have done some poking around for you?"

Tavake flushed. "Not all of us operate under suspicion and mistrust. I had no interest in Nafanua's affairs. We were friendly neighbors, that is all."

Ofa spoke up, "Do you expect us to believe that a daughter of the great Vasa Loloa Tavake really had no knowledge of the leading telesā in Samoa and her Covenant? Even an Ungifted would have been aware of the local Guardians."

Apollonia was triumphant. "Yes, my esteemed Sister from Niue is right." She appealed to the Council, "We're desperate here. We need as much information as we can get about this girl who hosts Pele. I say, we summon Tavake's daughter so the Council may question her."

"I disagree," said Tavake. "The woman knows nothing. We have not seen each other for a long time."

"Oh, but our Sisters from Tutuila mentioned you had been sighted here in Apia only a few months ago? Didn't you visit your daughter then?" asked Apollonia with feigned innocence.

"I'm sorry. I could be wrong. I only repeated what I heard from some of our family here in Apia. They thought they had seen you Tavake," said Gau. She was a quiet, shy telesā, easily flustered and eager to avoid confrontation.

"I was here but I did not visit her. Who among us is close to our Ungifted?" Tavake asked. It was a question that needed no answering. Almost all of them had felt the shame of bearing a child without a Gift – and the loss.

All except Ofa. She spoke into the uneasy silence with the unfeelingness of youth. "In that case, all the more reason to bring your daughter here. She might have valuable information that you don't know about."

Iolana spoke, "The Keawe must side with Apollonia on this. We know of no others in Samoa with telesā links. The present danger requires we speak with your daughter Tavake. If she knows nothing, then no matter, we will keep searching for information about this girl. She must have friends, some family connections here that we can bring before the Council."

Tavake didn't like it but she had no choice. "It is agreed then. The woman called Salamasina Tahi will be brought before the Council in its next session."

"While we are on the topic of Nafanua," Apollonia said, "Someone needs to take control of telesā activity here in these islands. Nafanua had vast holdings and business interests that profited our cause throughout the Pacific. What are we doing to get those back?"

"Trust you to be thinking of money at a time like this," said Tavake.

Iolana spoke through the tension. "Sisters, this Council was not called to fuss over paltry things like money and land." She turned sightless eyes on Apollonia. "It's not about jostling for power either. We are here because Pele has awakened. We must band together in true sisterhood and stop her."

"Well spoken Iolana. An important reminder for us all." Adi said. "What else do we know about the incident in Tonga which allowed Pele to escape her confines?"

"This happened in your territory Tavake," said Anaoero, leader of the Sisters from Nauru. "There must be more you can tell us?"

All eyes turned to the Tongan Covenant Keeper. "The key players from that day are dead. Some were killed by the girl's hand. Others had to be dealt with. They were of my Sisterhood and issues of trust were breached."

"Oh, so that explains your much weakened presence at this Council!" Apollonia was gleeful and the three Tongan telesā gave her dagger looks.

"Hmm, it's a pity they're dead. It would have been helpful to hear their stories," Adi said.

The Council adjourned their session then. Many of the Sisters were travel-weary. "We will meet again tomorrow morning," said Tavake.

"Yes, then we can talk to this daughter of yours,' said Apollonia. "Do you want my Sisters to go get her? Encourage her to speak truthfully?"

Tavake's eyes narrowed. "That won't be necessary. You have no hold over my children Apollonia, not even the Ungifted."

"Hmm, if I didn't have great faith in your loyalty Tavake, I would think you were protecting this woman from the Council, sheltering her? What are you hiding from us?" Apollonia said.

"You go too far, Ariki bitch," snapped Tavake. She leapt to her feet, inked patterns aflame with sapphire anger, "I would see you choke on your words."

Iolana interjected then, "Enough. Two of our Olohe will bring this woman to the Council. Is that acceptable Tavake?"

Every Council member was watching the exchange with keen eyes. The Tongan Sister gave the sensate the barest of nods, "Yes, thank you Iolana."

Apollonia smiled with triumph as Tavake and her two Sisters left the Council room. *Enjoy your last days as Tangaloa Council leader Tavake. I know I'll savor every minute of taking you down.*

The missive was delivered to the house by two women dressed in white. Salamasina greeted them with polite deference, "Can I help you?"

"You are Salamasina Tahi." It was not a question.

"Yes, what's going on?" asked Salamasina.

"We have a message for you from Tavake."

Salamasina took the sealed envelope they handed her. "Would you like to come in?"

"No thank you. We will wait."

The old lady read through the note quickly. It was brief and to the point. Tavake could not risk Ariki eyes getting their hands on her message and so she hoped Salamasina would understand all she could not write.

The Tangaloa Council want to question you about Leila Folger. You will not be harmed. Speak the truth as you know it. We will not speak of a young ocean. Leave the past where it belongs.

Salamasina read between the lines and she was afraid. For Daniel and for herself. But she hid it well. "I am to go with you?"

"Yes. We have a vehicle, parked out of sight. Please travel with us."

Their words were graciously offered but all three of them knew they were not making a request. Salamasina nodded. "Of course. Let me change into something more presentable."

The two Olohe went to sit on the verandah chairs. "We will wait for you."

It took only a few minutes for Salamasina to change out of her gardening clothes. She needed to be quick. Daniel was out but he could be home any moment. She did not want him anywhere near these women with bald heads, strange attire and unusual tattoos. She whispered a prayer for strength to get through whatever was coming and then she was ready. She walked out on the verandah with her handbag. "Shall we go?"

Too late.

Daniel's truck pulled up in the driveway. He surveyed the visitors with careful interest. "Mama, you going somewhere?"

He went up the steps and gave Salamasina a quick kiss on the cheek. She smiled up at him and tried to disguise her apprehension. "I missed you this morning. You left before breakfast."

"Sorry. Lots of work on-site to catch up on. I'm here now though," he said as he put a protective arm around her shoulders and eyed the two women. They were both young – he guessed them to be barely twenty. It was difficult to tell them apart. Similar build and height, and with distinctive shaven heads. The one distinguishing feature between them was their eyes. One with dark brown, the other with brilliant blue. They did not smile as he greeted them. "Hi, I'm Daniel."

They didn't respond and Salamasina rushed to fill the awkward gap. "I'm just going to town with these nice girls. To a meeting, a conference," said Salamasina. She wasn't a very good liar and Daniel quirked an eyebrow at her.

"What kind of conference?" he asked.

"One on traditional healing methods in the Pacific. There are healers from lots of different islands. It's going to be fascinating," said Salamasina. She appealed to the Olohe. "Right ladies?"

They exchanged a look and then the dark-eyed one answered. "Yes. Fascinating." She turned to leave. "We have to go Mrs. Tahi. You don't want to be late."

"You heard her. We don't want to be late," said Salamasina. She patted Daniel on the cheek, making a face at the two days growth he'd been too busy to shave. "There's food in the fridge for you. Why don't you go shower and shave and eat."

The blue-eyed girl smirked at that. *Yes, why don't you listen to your mummy ...* her look said.

Daniel ignored her. "How about I come with you?" he said to Salamasina. "I feel bad I haven't been around much. I miss you." He was only half-joking as he faked an aggrieved look.

"I'm fine," said Salamasina. Love for her child gave her the strength she needed. "We each have our responsibilities to tend to." A gentle nudge. "Go on. I'll be alright. We will meet later."

Daniel frowned as the women walked down the steps. He was about to go in the house when he saw the car they were walking towards, parked on the other side of the house. A blue Porsche Panamera. It wasn't a car that regular people or traditional healers drove. It was a car that set him on edge and had him vaulting over the railing to go to his grandmother.

"Wait. I'll drive you in my truck," he said.

His grandmother's escorts were irritated now. The girl with blue eyes snapped at him. "She said she was fine. Why don't you go back in the house?"

Daniel took Salamasina aside, "What's going on Mama? Who are these women?"

"I told you, we're going to a meeting. I'll be fine," said Salamasina.

"We're wasting time. The Council won't like it if you're late," said one of the women. She pushed past Daniel and tried to take the old woman's arm. "Please get in the car."

That was all it took for Daniel to shift into taut, cold defensive mode. He stepped forward and sheltered Salamasina behind him. "I don't like this. My grandmother isn't going anywhere with you two." Low, deadly, dangerous.

The blue-eyed visitor raised an eyebrow in disdain. "Boy, you don't know who you're dealing with. Step aside and let the woman come with us."

He gave a wry grin – at this girl who didn't look much older than him, this girl who was smaller, shorter and lighter than he was. "Boy? Excuse me?"

The two women tensed. Salamasina knew she had to do something. "Daniel, you're right. I'm not going to a health conference. Tavake wants to see me. I didn't want you to worry, I'm sorry."

"Mama, no. You can't trust her," said Daniel.

"She won't harm me." Salamasina took his face in her hands. "I'll be alright. There are things she and I need to discuss."

They exchanged a long, tense look which spoke volumes. Every instinct in Daniel screamed for him to intervene but Salamasina's will was strong and finally he backed off. "Fine." He turned to the women in white. "Where is this meeting with Tavake?"

"The Tanoa Tusitala Hotel," said the dark-eyed woman. She nodded at Salamasina. "We will bring you home when the meeting is done."

Daniel stepped back and the three women got into the Panamera. The woman with blue eyes was driving. She reversed the car and then paused. "Don't worry, your mummy is safe with us, *boy*." The added emphasis had him clenching his fists. But he did nothing else as the sleek car drove away.

Salamasina's interview with the Council didn't take long. She answered every question with openness. Yes, she knew of Nafanua and her Covenant but she had kept a careful distance from them. "I knew enough about telesā to keep a low profile and stay far away from the local Sisterhood. I am only a village healer. Nafanua was a rich businesswoman. We moved in … different circles."

The Council wanted to know as much as possible about Leila. "I first met the girl through my son. When I discovered she was Nafanua's daughter, I tried to discourage their friendship but my son was determined," said Salamasina.

There were piteous looks from the kinder members of the Council. "Young love is difficult to dissuade," said Lupe. "Especially when telesā are involved."

The Council asked more questions and Salamasina answered them all. The one thing she kept back, was the fact Daniel was Vasa Loloa.

"Since the girl woke from her coma, does she know your son?" asked Apollonia.

"No. She can't remember anything about her life from the time she first moved here," said Salamasina. "It gives my son great heartache."

"But not you?" said Apollonia, with a knowing smile.

"I hope she never remembers," Salamasina said with harshness. "A mother must place her child's safety and happiness first.

Leila Folger is a pleasant enough young woman but she has brought nothing but pain to my son. I have lived many years apart from the telesā world and never shared my past with Daniel. Until Leila, he knew nothing of telesā and the less he knows the better. I mean no disrespect when I say, that I don't want your world to play any part in my son's future."

"We understand," said Iolana. "Thank you for speaking with us."

Apollonia spoke first as soon as Salamasina had left the room. "Well, we didn't find out much that we didn't already know. I'm not sure how much we can trust her. I got the feeling she was holding something back. Should we bring in the son?"

"No," said Adi. "The fewer outsiders who know about us the better. Besides, I don't see how a lovesick teenage boy could be helpful."

"We know where the girl lives. Let's have the Olohe watch her. What do you think Tavake?" asked Iolana.

There wasn't much Tavake could do except agree. "Yes, if you can spare them. But discreetly. We don't want to do anything to alarm Pele. Not until we are ready."

"Why can't we just kill the girl now? Before Pele is unleashed?" Ofa asked the question which many of them had been thinking.

"It's too late for that," Iolana said. "Pele is already awake and there is only a thin thread of consciousness remaining from the host, keeping her at bay. I don't know how that girl is still even alive in there. Pele's power signature pulses stronger every day. She doesn't have complete clarity yet, this I can sense, but it's only a matter of time. Extreme emotion will be a trigger. Threaten her, frighten her and we risk pushing Pele over the edge."

Tavake agreed. "Yes, if the girl was powerful enough to kill Nafanua and her Sisters with her own firepower, then it's too dangerous to approach her unless we are united by the Tangaloa Bone." She glared at the young woman from Niue. "No-one should try to take Pele on her own."

Iolana added, "It would have been different if the host were Ungifted, just some random teenager. But then, it's doubtful if an ordinary woman could have survived Pele's immersion in her body."

"We must proceed based on the facts that we have. The Keawe monitor the earth's elemental energies and if they say Pele has awakened, that is enough for our Sisterhood to act," said the Covenant Keeper from Vanuatu.

There was a heavy pause. All had come to this place knowing what needed to be done, knowing there was little choice in the matter. But even though this was a time foretold in prophecy, it didn't make it any easier to handle. Who wanted to go down in history for launching cataclysmic destruction?

"We must proceed with caution," said Lupe. "What if we make the situation worse by gathering the Tangaloa Bone? What if we're playing right into Pele's hands?"

"She's right," said Gau. "The only reason why Pele was able to cause so much destruction in the first place was because she had the Bone. We shouldn't do anything to help her ascend to that kind of power again."

"We won't," Apollonia said. "It's simple, we make sure Pele doesn't get her hands on the Bone."

"But there's no guarantee she won't get it," argued Lupe. "There's a reason why our Elders separated the Bone. The power it gives the Bearer is too great, too dangerous."

"And there's a reason why they left directions on how to put the damn thing back together, precisely for a time like this," said Ofa.

Back and forth it went as the women debated the future until all arguments for and against had been exhausted. "We don't have any other choice. It's time for the gathering of the Tangaloa Bone," Iolana said. "Is the Council agreed? We must be united in the decision."

Silence. Apollonia slid smoothly into the spaces. "We of the Ariki agree. It's time for the location of each piece to be divulged. We offer to retrieve the pieces on behalf of the Council. The Ariki have the greatest number of telesā present and so it's only logical we go get the pieces."

"Logical? I think not," Tavake said.

"Oh? Are you offering your Vasa Loloa then?" A frown. "Hmm, that's right, there's only three of you. And let's be honest, shall we? Your sisters are not quite up to par, not like they used to be. You yourself are getting on in years. As the wisest and eldest amongst us, you are a treasure. I would hate for some unfortunate accident to befall you if you went out in search of the Bone pieces."

"Your concern for me is touching but misguided. I assure you, we Vasa Loloa are more than capable of retrieving the pieces. As leader of this Tangaloa Covenant, it is only right I be in charge of the search. Especially as I will be the one who wields the Bone when the time comes," Tavake said.

"Yes, about that ... The Ariki are the strongest in numbers and in Gift power on this Council which means the position of Bone Bearer comes to me. I don't want such a grievous burden on my little shoulders, but I know my duty." Apollonia said. The wire of tension in the room threatened to snap.

"Enough!" Iolana said. "There can be no room for discord amongst us. Do you not understand what we are facing? Once Pele fully awakens to her Gift, there will be no need for scraps like this because we will all be dead. Along with countless others that are meant to be under our protection."

There was a rueful silence at the rebuke. Then Ofa jumped in, "It's a question of numbers. The Ariki are the most powerful group. Send them to get the Bone. The rest of us can watch out for Pele, some of us can go help the Ariki or whatever. But we need to decide and get moving. I'm not going to sit here and squabble over stupid things while every minute Pele gets stronger. All of this delaying makes me wonder, is it because you're all afraid? I'd rather take my chances on going to slit her throat one night in her sleep. If I'm going to die, I'd rather die fighting on my feet."

To have the youngest accuse you of cowardice is a surefire way to get you to act – and so the decision was made. Apollonia would lead the expedition to retrieve the Bone pieces. The others would assist as needed. Tavake and Iolana would monitor the Pele situation here in town.

It was a relief to have the choice made. There would be no going back now. Everyone turned expectant eyes on Iolana. "Bring the tapa," she ordered the Olohe.

The room quieted as two Olohe carried in an ornate carved wooden box. They placed it on the table and brought forth the tapa pieces, unfolding them with reverent hands. The ancient peoples of the Pacific had no written languages, at least not in the way those in the Western world would define a 'written language'. The tapa were imprinted not with words, but with symbols and markings, similar to those of the ancient tattoos many of the Sisters wore. There were few among them who could decipher the markings but Iolana had them inscribed in her memory, her heart and soul, as was necessary for the Keawe Covenant Keeper. Bringing the Sacred Tapa here today was a formality only, so that none could doubt the authenticity of her words. Her voice rang out strong and clear in the conference room.

First, she recited the creation story of the Telesā, the origins of the Tangaloa Bone, a legend they all knew well and then she moved to the story of Pele and the Dark Times. Then on to the words which only she knew. The decree of the Guardians who first separated the Bone a millennia ago.

The Tangaloa Bone, fashioned by the hand of a god and washed in her blood – is too dangerous to remain amongst us. Let it be broken in pieces and hidden away. Let there be ageless guardians appointed to watch over them, safeguard them from the hungry grasp of the power-seekers. The elements of Air, Fire and Water shall hide them.

Water. In ocean's darkness where spirits walk, guarded by Saveasi'uleo. Enter at Pulotu's gate but be wary of he who watches over Vasa Loloa with eyes that do not see.

Air. Sacred bone of storms and wind and rain. Let it always be in flight. Let it have its home in the sky, the heavens, the trees. Seek the white pe'a and there you will find the Matagi Bone.

Fire. Let it rest in earth's black heart, a space where once fire burned. The aitu shall guard it.

Let the Tangaloa Bone come forth when the earth bleeds from every pore and cries for relief. Let the unifying power of Tangaloa then be used to bring together all telesā as one heart and one mind. Fatu ma le ele ele. Let it be done.

When she was finished, Iolana's shoulders crumpled. In that moment she looked very tired and very old. "Sisters, my part is done. I entrust you now with the sacred knowledge I am guardian of and may Tangaloa guide you to use it wisely."

"Don't worry Sister. The Ariki will not rest until we have found all the pieces. We will take care of Pele," Apollonia said with barely disguised triumph. She stood, "Please excuse us. We have much to do."

The Council dispersed then, with excited chatter and plans as Apollonia led the way out.

Until it was only Tavake and Iolana remaining. And the Keawe's Olohe guardian of course. "I know that was difficult for you, but it was the best option," Iolana said.

"I'm not worried. Apollonia is young. She has much to learn," Tavake said with a grim smile. She tightened her grip on the walking stick as she moved with her awkward gait across the room. "We need the Tangaloa Bone restored and the Ariki are the strongest combined force among us. It was the logical choice."

"That is true," Iolana said. "I am afraid Tavake. With each day, Pele's Gift grows more powerful. I can feel it. Power of such magnitude I do not think any one soul can contain it."

"What are you saying?"

"We are concerned that Pele will be the Destroyer she once was. That she will knowingly, *willingly* wreak havoc on all that she surveys. But there is another possibility. What if the host cannot cope with both her own and Pele's combined Gift? When Pele self-destructed a thousand years ago, the eruption she caused set off a cataclysmic event in the Pacific. The evidence is there in your own islands of Tonga."

"The monolithic boulder field inland on Tongatapu?"

"Yes, relics of Pele's destructive fury. The ancient stories of peau kula, the red wave, mega-tsunami that wiped out entire islands."

"I know them."

"Pele's legacy." Iolana's step faltered and her Olohe was beside her in a flash, steadying her. "We cannot allow it to happen again."

"We won't let it. Pele will be stopped. At all costs," Tavake said.

"Even if it means ceding the position of Bone Bearer to another," Iolana said. It was a statement, not a question.

"You have given this a lot of thought," Tavake said, tight lipped and cold.

"Sacrifices must be made. I don't want Apollonia at the helm of our Tangaloa Covenant any more than you do. But I'm a sensate. I can read your Gift and it has weakened considerably since the last time we met. Based on today's power readings alone, the Ariki must lead the battle against Pele." Her face softened. "I'm sorry. But you yourself said it – Pele must be stopped at all costs."

Late that night, long after his grandmother had gone to bed, Daniel was beating up the bag at the back of the workshop. He was spending a lot of late nights this way. It was better than lying awake thinking about a girl who didn't even remember his existence, puzzling over ways to fix the mess he had made of everything. *Why did I let her heal Leila? I should have stopped her. I should have taken her to the hospital and let proper doctors fix her. Why did I let a strange ocean spirit touch her?*

These were the thoughts he tortured himself with. Because that's what you do when you're a boy like Daniel in love with a girl like Leila.

Wind cooled the sweat on his torso as he pounded the bag with his fists. Stripped down to just a pair of rugby shorts, he was a very angry, very powerful figure in the moonlight as he hit and kicked at demons only he could see. He didn't hear the car glide into the driveway, or hear her walk up.

"Daniel."

He spun around, fists at the ready, chest heaving from the exertion of his workout. It was Tavake standing there in the shadows. "You." He stilled the violent swinging of the bag and started taking off his gloves. "Just the person I want to see. Why did you call my grandmother in to your Council meeting?"

Quiet, restrained rage.

"I had no choice," Tavake said.

"Don't lie," said Daniel. "You're sitting in the head chair at that table. You didn't have to take her in there. Now those other telesā know about her."

Tavake flinched at his attack and then steadied, gripped her walking stick tightly. "They would have found out about her eventually. They're checking out all Leila's friends. That includes you. They would have come here, possibly taken you before the Council. They would have been suspicious I hadn't said anything about my Ungifted Daughter. The Keawe would have discovered you're Vasa Loloa."

"I can handle them," Daniel said. "I won't have you putting Mama at risk like that."

"Don't be foolish," Tavake scoffed. "There are forty-three elemental guardians and six Olohe warriors gathered here in Apia. They won't hesitate to kill you the minute they hear you're Vasa Loloa. And Salamasina would be next as punishment for keeping you hidden all these years."

He wasn't buying it. "Maybe I should tell them myself. Aren't you the one who let Salamasina have me? What's the punishment for a Covenant Keeper who breaks the rules?"

"Threats won't work with me."

"I don't make threats, I make promises. I'll do whatever it takes to protect my family. You probably can't understand that."

A smile touched her lips. "Oh, I understand only too well. A man's strength can also be his greatest weakness …" She walked closer with her lilting gait. "Look, we're on the same side here."

"I find that hard to believe," said Daniel.

"We want the same things, you and I. I'd rather the Council didn't find out Salamasina has a Gifted son, at least not right now. And you want to keep her safe. So we work together to make sure the Council has no reason to harm her."

"I'm listening."

"We both want Pele destroyed."

"No, I want Leila back. Safe and unharmed. There's a difference."

Tavake continued speaking, as if his words were but a buzzing mosquito of nuisance in the hot, wet night. "She's out of your reach. The demon who inhabits Leila's body will never release her. Pele's power is legendary. The girl you love is as good as dead."

"You don't know that. Leila's the strongest person I know. She's in there somewhere fighting to get free. I won't give up on her."

"Then hear me now. There is only one way to drive Pele out of Leila's body and force her to release her mind and soul – get enough telesā to join their Gifts and work together as a team so we can stand as a mightier force than the Fire Goddess. There is a weapon, the Tangaloa Bone. Whoever uses it and unites enough telesā as one – could possibly have enough power to defeat Pele."

"So where is this weapon?" said Daniel. Doubt and mistrust.

"In pieces, hidden in different locations. The Council has begun to gather them already."

"Can it get Pele out of Leila's body?"

"It's the only thing that can kill her. If your girlfriend is still alive in there somewhere, then yes, she gets her body back."

"What's the big deal about this Tangaloa Bone anyway?" asked Daniel. "Why can't all forty-something of you take on Pele without it?" He winced even as he said it, imagining the face of the girl he loved as she faced off against the fury of so many telesā.

"The Tangaloa Bone is the one thing that makes it possible for the three different elements to be covenanted to one person, effectively making the Bearer, all-powerful over Earth's gifts. Once I have the Tangaloa Bone complete, I will use it to defeat Pele. And if Leila is still in there, I'll do my best to save her." There was an eager glint in her eyes. "The others won't let you fight alongside us, but you can Covenant your Gift with me."

"It all comes back to that. Again." Daniel's eyes narrowed. "Why are you so hooked on getting me signed up to your Covenant?"

Tavake shifted uneasily on her feet and Daniel's Samoan hospitality finally kicked in. He flushed with embarrassment as he went to grab two plastic chairs from the workshop office. "I'm sorry. Please sit down. Umm, can I get you something to drink?"

"No thank you," Tavake said as she sat down, placing her cane across her legs. She ran her fingers lightly across its carved patterns for a moment as she considered her words. "I'll be honest with you. My Sisterhood is down to only three. I sit in leadership at the Council for now only because of my age. There are others who want to take it from me. They would use the Tangaloa Bone for other things … more than just eliminating Pele. That's why I need the power your Gift can give me."

"Why am I not surprised," said Daniel. "I've never met a telesā who didn't have a power-hungry agenda. Well, except for one …" His words trailed away.

"This is not about me," argued Tavake. "This is about saving the girl you love. It's about stopping a megalomaniac from running wild again. You have no idea what Pele is capable of."

"I've been fried by enough of you telesā to have a pretty good idea," Daniel said.

"That's why you need me. Your Vasa Loloa Gift is very strong but raw and unpredictable. Let me be your teacher. You'll have a better chance of saving Leila."

And there it was, the truth he couldn't argue with – and she knew it. Daniel hated that she was right. "How does a Covenant work? Is it permanent?"

"It's a simple ceremony, a few words. A Covenant is a two-way promise. I will be able to draw on your Gift for as long as we are bound and in return, I can never use Vasa Loloa against you. If ever either of us attempts to attack the other, the Covenant is ended."

Daniel knew enough about telesā from Leila and his grandmother to know Tavake's summary wasn't a lie, yet still he wavered. He didn't trust this woman who talked to him with his grandmother's eyes and the resolute edge of her voice. He couldn't shake the feeling Tavake was keeping something essential from him. But what choice did he have?

He would do whatever it took to protect the ones he loved and Tavake knew it.

It is your greatest strength – and weakness.

"Fine. I'll do it," he said.

Tavake smiled in triumph. "A wise decision." She rose to her feet. "Come, we can seal our Covenant now. Let us go to the sea where we will speak the ritual words."

Daniel followed as she walked out of the workshop and into the windswept night. Together they crossed the road and went down to the beach where black water moved with restless abandon.

Neither of them saw the figure watching them from the shadows. A girl with blue eyes and the markings of the Olohe.

X-Men

Daniel couldn't stay away from Leila forever. He lasted a week before terse text message updates from Simone were not enough. Before the ache inside had him driving to the box house up the hill. He approached with caution though. Simone had been furious the day he'd ordered Daniel out – and for good reason.

Which was why Daniel came bearing gifts. Simone made him wait outside the new electronic gate for *aaaages* before it finally slid open with a grating noise. Daniel had to wait another long time at the front door before Simone opened it with a terse, "What do you want?"

"I was a jerk and I'm sorry," said Daniel. He smiled his most winning of smiles. One designed to melt even the toughest of an offended fa'afafine.

Simone was unimpressed. "Yeah? Talk is cheap. What else you got?"

"Thought you might like something sweet," said Daniel. From behind his back he brought out a bag of *lolesaina*, the tangy sweets he knew Simone loved.

A snort of disdain. "Hmmph, I'm not that cheap. You better have more."

"Always," grinned Daniel. He stepped to the side and showed Simone the tray of *keke pua'a* he'd placed on a verandah chair. Faint trails of steam were still rising from the hot pork buns. "Put in a special order to Taro King for them."

Simone's eyes lit up at the delicious aroma. A light he tried to hide immediately. "No more stupid boy-tantrums, eh."

Daniel held up his hands in surrender. "Got it."

"Fine. Bring those inside."

Simone stepped aside so Daniel could enter. There was no more feisty fire in his eyes as he put a hand on his arm. "Don't lose it again. I can't look after her on my own. We're supposed to be doing this as a team."

Guilt stabbed at Daniel. "I'm back. We got this." A deep breath. "How is she?"

"Go see for yourself," said Simone. His eyes were sad. "She's out the back."

Daniel put the tray of food on the kitchen table and walked through to the back yard. His breath caught in his chest at the sight of her. Leila stood in the center of the lawn with her back to him. She wore only a black bikini top and a brief piece of elei fabric tied sarong style on her hips so the bold patterns of her malu were on full display. Her hair was pulled up in a messy bun and the lines, dips and contours of her back glistened with sweat in the sunlight. There was music playing from some unseen stereo and a Common Kings melody danced on her wind-kissed skin. She was so beautiful. So vibrant. So beloved that it hurt for him to look at her.

How could such perfection ever be mine? How could she ever be happy with me?
He drank her in with a thirst borne from the blazing heat of a sun-bleached day. But it wasn't only her beauty that shocked him into stillness.

Leila was playing with fire. Tendrils of orange and scarlet danced and rippled to the sway and lilt of her fingers as she manipulated the flames in the air above and around her. She laughed as she spun around with the fire dancing in perfect harmony with her. It was a joyous delight of sound. She sang words in a language Daniel couldn't understand and then she began to weave the flames into intricate patterns in the air – painting a faultless rendition of her malu markings. He had never seen her manipulate her Gift with such complexity. It was exquisite.

It wasn't Leila.

He felt sick. A sudden thrust of sour nausea at the realization.

She turned then and saw him. A flash of dark anger on her face quickly chased away with bland welcome. She snapped her fingers and the fire went out. "Hello." She walked across the grass toward him, eyes narrowed as if puzzling her memory for his name, "It's … Daniel, right?" She even sounded different. Older? The reminder of a peanut-butter American accent was gone. It was as if the other day between them in the bedroom had never happened.

He automatically shook her outstretched hand, still staring. She was oiled skin, raw energy and sultry beauty.

Leila would never stand up straight and tall like that. She'd be slouching. Her shoulders hunched a bit because she'd be kinda embarrassed about being half-naked in the daylight. Even in front of me. Especially in front of me. She would use her hair to cover her chest and tell me off for staring.

He was out of it for a moment or two, as he struggled to breathe through the whirlwind thoughts and the girl frowned. "Are you alright?" she asked.

"Yeah. All good," said Daniel. *No. I'm not alright. Who are you? What's happening?!*

A cool smile. "You're a friend of Simone's." Her gaze raked over him with frank assessment, lingering in places that made him uncomfortable. She reached up with her free hand to shake her hair free from its knot, letting its waves tumble down her back as she licked her lips and gave him a heavy-lidded stare. A confident smile at his unease. "I'm Pele."

No you're not.

He still wasn't moving, wasn't responding to her the way she wanted him to. She pulled her hand away from his with irritation. "Excuse me, I'm a mess. I must go bathe." She walked past him to go inside and his eyes followed her because he couldn't help himself.

This isn't happening. Leila, I know you're in there. Why are you letting her win?

Daniel turned to Simone, swore. "What is going on!?"

Simone shushed him. "Quiet down. She might hear you."

"I don't give a damn if she does. I leave you alone with her for a few days and this is what I come back to?" demanded Daniel.

But Simone refused to be cowed. A raging six foot, two hundred pound plus rugby player didn't scare him. "The keywords there are – you LEFT us for seven days. We've been coping the best we can. You can't just show up now and tell me you don't like what you find. Too bad." He pointed wildly to the house. "That, in there is Leila. My best friend and the girl you're supposed to be in love with. You were supposed to be here, thinking of ways to fix her. But you haven't been. So deal with it."

They were truths he couldn't argue with and no amount of hurt outrage was going to change them. "You're right." He held his hands up in surrender. "Sorry. But why didn't you say anything?"

"You needed space to deal with this. I was giving you that," said Simone. Then compassion was replaced with accusation. "But you sure took your time about it. If you didn't show up this week I was going to head over to that workshop and knock some sense into you myself. That Keahi incident sucked big-time for you, I get that. But this is Leila we're talking about here. No matter what happens, we don't give up on her." His voice dropped to a fierce whisper. "Not until that woman gives Leila back or …" Hesitation. "Or until they're both dead."

Daniel thought about a girl giving her life for his and he was ashamed. "I'm here now. Tell me what's been happening."

The two of them walked across the grass. "I see she's got her fire," said Daniel.

"It showed up a few days ago. After the Keahi thing, she was knocked out with headaches. She didn't want to go to the doctor though, just wanted to sleep all day. We were getting worried. Then she surprised us. Just walked out one morning and announced she was Pele. She hasn't stopped asking questions ever since."

"About what?"

"This place. Me. Lesina. Leila's family." Simone paused and gave him a careful look. "You. And Keahi."

"So she has Leila's memories?"

"I'm not sure." Simone had a pensive look. "She already knew our names and lots of other details but there's still some stuff she's not clear on. And it varies. One minute she'll be sure of herself and then the next minute she spaces out and looks … lost. Confused."

Daniel seized on this small fragment of hope. "So Pele isn't in total control then? Leila's still there?"

"I don't know," said Simone. "She hasn't had a spaced out moment since she got her fire going. It looks like Pele's in charge now."

They were not words Daniel wanted to hear. "Then we're going to have to change that."

"But how?" asked Simone. "What are we going to do?"

"I've been working on something," said Daniel. "I signed up to the crazy Tongan telesā team."

"What?" Simone shrieked. "Have you lost it?"

"Calm down," said Daniel. He briefly described his meeting with Tavake and everything his grandmother had told him about the Tangaloa Covenant.

Simone looked ill. "Wait up. There's a kickass army of women in town, here to take out Leila? And all of them have freaky nature powers?"

"That's why I'm taking lessons with Tavake."

"You think your water boy sparkle is going to protect us?" demanded Simone.

"Hey, a bit of faith would be nice," said Daniel.

Simone looked Daniel up and down and then up again, shaking his head. "No. You're hot, but you're not that hot. We are so screwed."

"No." Daniel pointed at the house. "We can do this. That's Leila. We're not giving up on her. I know my girlfriend. She's fighting for her life in there. We're going to do whatever it takes to get her back. Even if …" Daniel hesitated, turned away from Simone and cursed under his breath.

"If what?"

Daniel spat the hateful words. "Even if I have to ask Keahi for help. Maybe he was right. We need the X-Men."

Simone was mystified. "Huh?! What are you talking about?" He threw his hands up in the air. "Hey, I would like Wolverine's fine ass here too but I think the X-Men are otherwise occupied. Y'know, like maybe Hugh Jackman's working on the next Hollywood blockbuster?" He stamped his foot with impatience. "Newsflash Daniel, the X-Men are fantasy and we're stuck in reality." A dramatic wail. "We're all gonna die!" He started pacing, talking to himself. "Just breathe baby, breathe … I should never have moved in with Bushy-Eyebrows …"

Daniel ignored the dramatic meltdown. "That's it. That's what we have to do." He snapped at Simone. "Where's Lesina? We need her, Keahi and Teuila. Come on."

Leila

The woman smiled at the shivering girl on the ground in front of her. "I've been getting to know you better. Getting comfortable in your life." She tapped at the side of her head. "And going through your memories."

Leila looked up at the woman who held her captive in her own mind. She wasn't as tall as Leila but they had similar coloring and the same long dark hair. She moved with an agile grace and her body was a tribute to the warrior life she had lived – all compact muscle and taut strength. In one hand she held a piece of carved bone. She wore a brief red shift dress that showed her Keawe tattoos and a scattering of battle scars. Her long hair was pulled up on one side and braided through with scarlet feathers. Through the dim shadows, Leila could see the twisted scar tissue where one eye used to be.

"Who are you?" Leila whispered.

The woman ignored her question. "So your mother died for you. How quaint." A long pause that confused Leila as much as it frightened her. "I killed mine. It was very … liberating. Everyone should try it. Killing a parent is truly setting yourself free from them. A most emphatic statement that yes, I can live, I can BE without you."

There was an edge of something in the air between them. Like long-ago charred bones. Death.

"Why am I here? What do you want from me?" Leila asked.

Laughter. "Want from you? You have nothing I want. You're dead. You are nothing. You have nothing. I have your body. I don't even know why this fragment of you is still here." She gave Leila a pensive stare. "What is it that's keeping this piece of you alive, Leila Folger? Nobody even knows you're gone. I've done such a good job replacing you." She mimicked a classic Simone move with her hands on her hips, "Daaahling, I've even improved you!"

Leila bit at her lip to stop the chattering. "You're lying. He wouldn't forget me. I know it. You can't fool him."

"Who? You mean that nice boy who's been hanging around like a puppy dog at my heels all this time? He is so very devoted, isn't he?" She reached down and took Leila's face in her hand, forced her to look up at her. Whispered with satisfied defiance, "He adores me. Worships the very ground I walk on, the air I breathe." A frown, "It's rather annoying actually. I may have to kill him first."

Pele pulled back as Leila leapt against her chains. The harsh rattle of metal resounded in the weary cave. "No! Don't you dare touch him."

"Or what? Just what will you do here in this prison of my mind? Have a tantrum?"

Leila's anguished sob barely rippled the surface of the stagnant pool. "Please, spare him. He's been through so much already because of me." Pleading turned to fury as Pele started to fade away into the darkness again. "Wait, come back! Let me out of here."

Pele's form was hazing at the edges. "Scream all you like. No-one will hear you. No-one will come for you. You're dead Leila. You're nothing."

"Noooooo …"

Leila's scream echoed through the cave and then died to a whisper as she sunk her face into her hands. "Daniel. Please. I love you."

Pele opened her eyes and relished the feel of sunshine on her skin. The sweet flavor of roasting coconut wafting on the breeze from the neighbor's outdoor cookhouse. It was so good to feel. To see. To hear and taste. She looked around at the explosion of colors in the sheltered garden, the ripple of light and the burn of blue sky overhead. A body was such a wondrous thing.

Pele was as close as she had ever been to happy. If only she could shake the disquiet. The question that ate at the edges of her contentment.

Why was Leila still alive? What was keeping her light a glow?

A rattle and a roar behind her as a green truck pulled out of the driveway. Pele's frown faded. Maybe it wasn't a question of what?

But who.

Frustration

Pele was fascinated with the television. Even though Samoa only had a measly four channels worth of programs, she could be glued to the screen for a couple of hours, puzzling over the strange sights. So Simone and Lesina were able to leave her alone for an hour while they met up with Daniel at a nearby park. Keahi arrived with Teuila on his motorbike. Simone had expected there to be tension between the two boys and was ready with lighthearted quips to defuse the situation. But they were surprisingly civil to each other. It was the two girls who nearly hijacked the meeting.

From the moment she got off the bike, Teuila stared daggers at Lesina. "What's she doing here?" she asked Simone.

"Excuse me?" asked Lesina. She tried to glare at Teuila but her outraged stance wasn't very impressive because she was so much shorter than the younger girl.

Teuila turned to Daniel. "You know what she did. How can you stand to be around her?"

The air was charged with electric hostility.

"I asked Lesina to be here. We're going to need help to get Leila back," said Daniel.

"But she's a traitor. She was working for Sarona the whole time," said Teuila.

"Listen here brat," said Lesina, "who are you to throw stones? You were right there with me on that island."

"Sarona tricked me. I didn't know anything about her plans," said Teuila. "While you on the other hand were stabbing Leila in the back from the very start."

The two girls were up in each other's faces now. "I made a mistake," said Lesina, "and now I'm here trying to help fix things."

"Your help gets people killed," said Teuila.

Lesina flinched as if she'd been struck, then she went on the attack, and leapt at Teuila, clawing, scratching and cursing. Daniel and Keahi stepped in and separated the two.

"Hey, quit it," said Daniel. He drew Lesina to the side and looked down at her tear-stained face. "We can't save Leila like this."

"Everyone hates me," Lesina whispered fiercely. "And for good reason. I shouldn't be here."

"She's just a kid. She's hurt and angry. We all are about something. You're letting her tap into your own private guilt-fest," Daniel said with astute assessment. "But you need to get over it, both of you," said Daniel. "That's the only way we're going to make things right."

Lesina glared at Teuila who glowered right back from where Keahi was trying to calm her down. "Yeah, well just keep that little bitch away from me."

With an uneasy truce called, the meeting resumed. Daniel brought everyone up to speed with the Leila-Pele situation.

"That sure explains a lot," said Keahi with his lazy drawl.

"What are you talking about?" asked Daniel. He was cool, calm and collected. A stranger would never guess that he had been trying to smash the pulp out of Keahi only a few weeks prior.

"Leila's hotness for me the other day," said Keahi. "What can I say, even a centuries old Fire Goddess finds me irresistible." His wicked smile had Simone making a gagging noise.

"Oh please, like we needed any more evidence Pele's crazy," snapped Simone. "*Salapu.* Just shut up."

Daniel spoke before Keahi could snap back at Simone. "People, can we not get sidetracked?" He looked at the Hawaiian who was grinning at his own cleverness. "Keahi, Leila's body getting possessed by a psychotic serial killer is nothing to laugh about. Until we get rid of Pele, Leila is off-limits."

Keahi feigned innocence. "What? Why you all looking at me like that?"

"Because you're a man-whore who will have sex with anything female," said Simone.

Keahi was angry but Teuila leapt to his defense before he could respond. "That's not true!" she said hotly. "He's Leila's friend. He would never do anything to hurt her. How can you say such a thing? Keahi's here, ready to fight for Leila, ready to help you."

"Well, somebody has a sweet weakness for you Keahi," drawled Lesina with a smile. "How cute."

"Shut up blondie," growled Keahi.

Teuila was ready to take on Lesina again and this time, Simone looked like he wanted to join in on the action. Daniel quickly jumped in. Frustration had him shouting. "Stop it, all of you. Look at us. We can't even have a meeting to plan what to do without fighting. How are we ever going to take on fifty telesā and Pele?!"

Everyone looked at him. "Wait up – what fifty telesā?" asked Keahi. "The only ones around here were Sarona and her gang of nutjobs. We got rid of them last time."

Simone sighed, "Oh no, it's so much worse than that."

Daniel proceeded to tell the others about the Pacific Covenant and their reason for gathering in Apia. He filled them in on everything he knew from what Tavake and Salamasina had relayed to him. Including the fact that he was taking Vasa Loloa lessons from the Tongan Covenant Keeper.

Lesina looked like she wanted to throw up. "Alright, this just got so much worse than it was before. How are we supposed to take on that many telesā?" She shook her head as she surveyed the group. "I'll be honest. My matagi gift is nothing spectacular on its own." She made a face of distaste at Teuila. "I don't know what she does, but I doubt it's anything impressive. Simone can kick ass if you make him mad enough but great nails and a mean right hook can only go so far against elemental powers." A pause as she got to Keahi and Daniel. "And you two? Fire and water? You aren't supposed to be telesā anyway. As soon as those women find out what you are, they're going to kill you both."

"Way to boost our confidence, thanks," muttered Keahi.

"She's right," said Simone. "It's not looking too good for us. Not when you put it like that."

"That's why we need to get the Tangaloa Bone," said Daniel.

"The what?" everyone else chorused.

Daniel had their complete attention as he told them what Tavake had said about the possible weapon. "They don't have all the pieces together yet. If we can get the Bone complete before they do, then we might have a chance."

"What are we going to do with it?" demanded Keahi.

"Either use it as a bargaining chip – or figure out how it works so we can take out Pele ourselves. And any of the Tangaloa Covenant who come after us," said Daniel.

"So how do we get it?" asked Lesina. "Where are these bone pieces anyway?"

Daniel smiled. "I think we've already got one of the pieces. Lesina, you remember that bone carving of Leila's you returned to her at the hospital?"

"Of course!" Lesina exclaimed. "That must be why Sarona wanted it so bad. Where is it now?"

"I've got it. Somewhere safe," said Daniel. He quickly explained what had happened with Pele that day, skipping over the more embarrassing bits. "The Council doesn't know we've already got one of the pieces. We just need to figure out where the rest of them are."

"How are we going to do that?" asked Keahi with a frown.

"I don't know yet," Daniel admitted. "I'm working on it."

"I wanna know what we do with freaky Pele-Leila in the meantime," interrupted Simone. "I'm the one who has to live with her 24-7. Now that she's better, she wants to go places, get out, look at stuff. I'm running out of excuses to stay at home … plus, I'm bored out of my mind."

"Right now, she's on our side and the Tangaloa Covenant are her enemies. Simone, she thinks you and Lesina are her friends. She thinks we're all accepting of this Pele identity. We need to make the most of that. All of us, let's try to keep her happy, keep her convinced we're harmless and friendly."

Teuila was hopeful. "Maybe if we're her friends then we can convince her to go away and let the real Leila out."

The others exchanged cynical looks. "Doubt it," said Daniel. "The only way Pele's going anywhere is if we make her go. Let's just keep her happy until we're ready to get rid of her."

The meeting came to an end then as everyone knew they couldn't leave Pele on her own for too long. They couldn't afford to have her getting suspicious. Not when their lives were at stake.

Sparks

Simone was right about Pele's itch to get out, to go places. The next day, she announced she wanted to go shopping. "For clothes that a real woman would wear." She pointed with a curled lip of distaste at Leila's wardrobe. "I'm going to burn all these ugly things – except for these." Leila's Louboutin shoes.

Simone had to concede then that Pele had some measure of good fashion sense. He allowed himself to be persuaded into taking Pele to town – with Leila's credit card – for an all-day shopping expedition. "What?" he said to Lesina's questioning face. "*Sass*, I have to go with her." His voice dropped to a dramatic whisper. "You heard what Daniel said, we have to be friends with her. Make her happy."

"Yeah right," said Lesina. She frowned as she watched them drive off.

The pair returned late in the afternoon, with the Wrangler overflowing with shopping bags. Both of them dressed in new outfits. "Did you buy everything at TAV and MENA?" asked Lesina as she struggled to help carry the bags inside.

"Just about," said Pele with a gleeful smile. "And then Simone took me to Plantation House where we had High Tea. Oh, the lemon curd and cream puffs were to die for."

"Yes, then Pele browsed through their Pacific Design Homeware section and decided we should give this house a makeover," said Simone. Lesina wasn't sure if the dazzling smile on his face was genuine or not. "Look at all the stuff she bought."

Lesina's mouth gaped as Pele proceeded to unpack lengths of vibrantly patterned fabric, "New curtains!" Matching throw cushions and linen of every kind for the kitchen, bathroom and bedroom followed until the entire house was aflame with the colors of a Samoan sunrise.

"What do you think?" asked Pele.

Lesina conceded, "It's beautiful. Wow."

Pele laughed. "Isn't it? So much more befitting of me. I can't wait to show off the jewelry I bought from there as well." She inspected the transformation once more. "Perfect. I'm going to shower and get ready for tonight."

Lesina smiled with plastic happiness until Pele left the room. Then she turned to Simone and hissed, "What are you doing? Leila would never buy all those clothes and waste so much money on stuff like this."

"Hey, it wasn't me. I dragged her to Plantation House so I could make her stop buying TAV dresses. How was I to know she would go all Kardashian and buy the whole store?" He sank onto the sofa with a weary sigh. "I never thought there could come a day when I would be sick and tired of shopping."

"What did she mean about tonight? Where's she going?" asked Lesina.

"I have a netball game tonight. She wants to go with me."

"Is that a good idea? There's going to be a lot of people there." Lesina looked nervous. "What if something … unexpected happens?"

"I'm not missing my game. This is for the championship," snapped Simone. "You'll just have to sit with her and be extra nice. Keep her entertained."

Lesina was doubtful of her ability to keep a Fire Goddess 'entertained' for two hours straight. As soon as Simone went to shower, she texted for reinforcements and hoped nothing awful would happen.

Daniel arrived at the gym after the game had already begun.

"Excuse me," he said as pushed through the throng. It was a steaming hot night and the closed confines of the gym only made it worse. The place smelled contradictorily of sweat and soap. And too much Rexona deodorant. The noise of the brisk game and the catcalls of the crowd aggravated his throbbing headache and he tried not to grimace. It had been a long day at work and he'd been up most of the night before doing a Vasa Loloa training session with Tavake because she didn't think it was safe to meet him in daylight hours. *I need to sleep. Bad.*

He was already regretting his decision to come and 'check on' Simone and Pele – but then, he couldn't really have ignored Lesina's slightly panicked text either. He looked around, searching for familiar faces.

Where are they?

He found Simone first. Not difficult seeing as how he was the Goal Shoot and lining up for a perfect shot in the wire hoop. A trio of defenders tried vainly to ruin his aim and when the ball went in, Simone rewarded them with a preening smile and mocking choice of curse word. His supporters screamed in elation. "Go sass, pulili rulezzz!"

Daniel had to laugh at Simone's 'sports gear' – sparkling underneath the regulation pleated skirt was a sequined pair of tights which was only out-glittered by the purple sports bra shining through the white uniform top. And of course accessorized with the right nails and makeup. He wasn't alone though. Simone's team of predominantly fa'afafine were a ferocious force of athleticism and skill on the court – and all while pushing the limits of netball uniform rules. They were defending their championship title against a team from the University of the South Pacific. The two sides were evenly matched and all the players were being pushed to their limits.

But it wasn't the on court action which was causing most of the buzz. There was music playing and something happening at the far end of the gym in the spectator stand, something which had many in the crowd around Daniel, whispering and pointing.

"Check it out. I'd like to get me some of that …" one boy said. His friend laughed and said something rude in return. "Come on, let's go over there …"

The boys walked off and Daniel looked to where they had been pointing. The crowd shifted and he saw her through the gap.

Leila. *No, Pele.*

She was up in the stand, on her feet in the midst of an admiring, excited crowd – dancing. Someone was blasting a stereo and she was center stage and loving it. Her hair fell in thick waves down her back as she swayed and moved in sinuous time to the beat. Her two piece red outfit was skin-tight and as Daniel stared in shock, she languorously stripped her top off over her head and threw it at a boy in the crowd. She was wearing a banded bra top underneath, but still, it was a blatantly sexual thing to do. And, in Daniel's horrified opinion, totally unacceptable.

What the hell? Where's Lesina?

Daniel started making his way towards the dancing girl in red, all while searching the stand for Lesina. *There she is.* Lesina's blonde hair caught his eye. The petite figure was sitting along from Leila's performance, looking as sick as Daniel felt. *Oh great. Some useless babysitter she turned out to be...*

Daniel leapt over the railing and started climbing the stairs, two at a time. Leila – because even though he knew it wasn't her, he couldn't stop calling her that in his mind – was dancing up against a strange boy now, pulling at his hand to join her. He went gladly. Of course. What idiot is going to say no to the chance to gyrate and rub skin with a beautiful girl? The two of them were dirty dancing now and the spectators urged them on with raucous shouts and whistles. Pele's dance partner had one hand on her lower back and another slid to graze the bare skin of her thigh as she hooked one leg around him.

I'm going to kill him ...

Daniel broke through the circle, all his promises to – 'Be calm. Stay in control. Don't regress to caveman behavior no matter what ...' – out the window, as every wired edge of him longed to explode in cobalt flames. Before he could yank the boy away from Pele, someone caught at his arm and an electric charge of energy stopped him in his tracks. It was Lesina.

"Don't do it, Daniel," she said.

He pulled free of her, more annoyed than physically hurt. "Let go," he said through clenched teeth. "I need to get that guy away from Leila."

Lesina threw a glance over her shoulder, back at the pair locked in seamless swaying. The boy's face was mere inches away from Pele's as he leaned closer with his gaze firmly locked on her inviting lips.

Don't you dare kiss her. I'm going to rip your face off.

Daniel tried to shove past Lesina but she wouldn't release his arm. She bit her lip and let another ripple of lightning-edged power zap him, this one stronger than the first. Daniel flinched.

"That's not Leila," said Lesina. Her plea was urgent. "Don't do anything stupid, please. Look at her tattoo, can't you see what's happening? What's about to happen?"

Daniel looked. Pele had her back to him now but her malu was clearly visible, especially as now the patterns were lighting up with ruby red fire. In all the excitement, no-one else had noticed yet. Just then, the boy ran his hand down her thigh again, pulling her body closer to him. His eyes widened though as his fingers encountered way more heat than he was expecting. "Oww! What is that?" He released Pele and stared at her, blowing on his fingers. Over the music, they heard him say, "You're hot."

Pele laughed delightedly. "I know."

Daniel's rage faded and worry replaced it. "Oh no, she's going to flame. We've got to get her out of here."

Lesina wilted with relief. "Yes, but how?" She pointed at Pele who had resumed dancing with wild abandon. "She's happy now but she won't be if you try to make her leave."

Just then Pele caught sight of Daniel. "Hey look, itsh my boyfriend. The one who adorshh meee." She lurched towards him with a leer. "Are you following me?"

"She's drunk!" Daniel muttered at Lesina. "How did that happen?" He gave Pele a tight smile. "I came to check out the game."

"Ssho you're not here for me then?" Pele said with a frown. She swayed as she stood there with her hands on her hips.

You're wasted. Just great. What are we gonna do with a drunk fire goddess? "I might be here for you too," he said lightly.

Pele responded to his teasing tone. "Oh good, I wasshh getting bored wif thesh boys anyway." A pout as she looked around at the others. "They don't want to dance wif me anymore. Will you dance wif me?"

She took two steps forward and tripped. Quick and agile, Daniel caught her in his arms. "Got you."

Pele looked up at him with hazy eyes, "Yessh you do. Sssho what you gonna do wif me?"

Daniel stared down into her eyes, feeling the hot crush of her body against his and the wish for this girl to be Leila was so strong it was like a knife in his heart. In that moment, everything around him faded away. The noise, the shouts from the game, the blatant stares of the crowd, it all disappeared and it was just the two of them in a hot web of longing. He wanted her to be Leila so bad that it hurt. So bad he couldn't breathe. His grip tightened as she looked up at him with open challenge. *What do you want to do with me?*

He needed to get some space between them. He loosened his grip and let his hands slip away from around her waist. She was still unsteady though and it only made her lean into him even more. She was right where he always wanted her to be. Every part of her fit him perfectly. Her hair was mussed and he gently brushed loose strands away from her eyes. She had smudges of mascara on her cheeks and he wiped at them with his thumbs as he cradled her face then leaned to kiss her on the forehead.

I love you Leila. Wherever you are. I'm not going to stop fighting for you.

"Whatever you want me to," Daniel whispered against her hair. In that hot, taut moment he meant every word. He didn't care if there were hundreds of people around them. Whatever she asked of him, he would give her.

Anything and everything Leila. Always.

And then the moment was gone. Pele's eyes closed and she sagged against him as she finally gave in to her very first dalliance with Vailima beer. She was out. Daniel swung her easily into his arms. "Let's get out of here," he said to Lesina.

"Finally," she said.

She followed behind Daniel as he navigated the narrow walkway with a prone figure in his arms. The boy who had been dancing with Pele didn't like losing his hook-up. He blocked their path. "Hey, where you taking her? We were having a good time here." His drunken friends murmured their agreement.

Daniel didn't even hesitate. He barreled past the boy. "Lesina, can you take care of that?"

"My pleasure," said Lesina.

She placed a finger on the belligerent boy's chest. A cold smile. "My friend doesn't want to play with you anymore. She's drunk and we're taking her home." A quick flash – so quick no-one could guarantee they had even seen it – and the boy's eyes rolled up in his head. His body spasmed and then he collapsed on the ground.

His friends clustered around him, buzzing with shock. "*Sole* man, are you alright? What happened?"

"Coming through," said Lesina as she carefully stepped past them in her platform heels. "Give him some air boys. He'll be fine in a few hours."

Daniel had just reached the door out to the parking lot when a massive cheer erupted. Someone had just won the game. Judging by the screaming fa'afafine on the sidelines, he guessed it was Simone's team. Lesina confirmed it much later when she joined him by the Wrangler jeep.

"They were at a draw and the game went into overtime. It was sooo close!" she exclaimed. "You should have seen Simone, he was on fire. The USP team wouldn't have had a chance if not for their goal shooter, some big girl from Fiji. She was huge. But she couldn't win the game all by herself."

"That's interesting Lesina but could you hurry up and open the door please? I've been standing here for twenty minutes now …" Daniel grimaced with Leila in his arms still passed out.

"Oh, my bad. I'm sorry," said Lesina. She opened the car door and helped Daniel settle Leila on the back seat. "Is she going to be alright?"

"I hope so." With Leila safe in the jeep, Daniel turned on Lesina. "How did this happen?"

"When we arrived at the game, those boys next to us were already drinking," Lesina explained, "but I didn't know it was alcohol. They snuck it in past security in regular soda cups. Pele was flirting with them and they offered her a drink. It all went to hell after that."

"So when you figured it out, why didn't you stop her? Get her out of there?" asked Daniel. "You're supposed to be looking after her." He paced up and down as he vented at her. "I don't think Leila's ever even tried alcohol. Did you see the way she was dancing in there? What was that? You can't let Pele treat Leila's body this way."

"And just how was I supposed to stop her?" snapped Lesina. "She could have fried me. What Pele wants, Pele gets. How are any of us going to stop her from doing whatever the hell she wants? You're just mad because she was getting it on with that boy. Accept it Daniel. That is not Leila in the truck. It's a woman called Pele and if she wants to get it on with someone, then too bad." She was yelling now in the dimly lit parking lot. "What Pele wants, Pele gets."

Daniel was going to shout some choice words right back at her but the big double doors to the gymnasium opened and people started streaming out. Laughter and excited conversation about the game filled the air. This wasn't the time or the place to settle this.

"We need to get Leila – I mean Pele – home. Can you go find Simone?" he said, suddenly weary of the whole day. He wanted out of his life.

Lesina looked at his disheartened face and her outrage dissolved. "Sure … this whole thing sucks. I'm sorry."

"Me too," he said simply. "Better go get Simone. Before he leads a naked victory dance party through the gym."

A familiar voice exploded from the shadows. "Did I hear my name being used and abused?"

Lesina turned with a relieved smile. "There you are. Congratulations *sass!* You were fierce out there!" She went to hug Simone who waved her away.

"No, stay away. I stink. The gym showers aren't working. You may worship me from afar daahling," said Simone. He executed a spin, shimmy and shake. "I was fierce though, wasn't I?"

Daniel leant back against the car with a tired half-smile. "You always are."

Simone narrowed his eyes at him. "Liar. You weren't even watching the game. But I forgive you." He blew Daniel a kiss. "Just keep telling me how *shamaahzing* I am." He paused then and looked around. "Where's Pele?"

"Asleep in the car," said Lesina. In answer to Simone's questioning eyebrow, she added, "Long story."

"Which we don't have time for," said Simone. "I need a ride home so I can shower and get dressed. Me and the team are going out to celebrate. I'd invite you but somebody has to stay and babysit the fire girl." He looked over his shoulder. "Oh, and my new friend is coming home with us. She needs a place nearby to shower." A yell. "Talei! Over here."

Talei? It can't be …

It was. The girl from the beach. She was walking with a group of USP players and bid them goodbye with a grin before jogging lightly across the parking lot to join them. "Thanks again," she said to Simone. "I don't want to go all the way back to the hostel before we go out. I warn you, I don't have any party clothes in this bag. Will a nightclub let me in wearing an outfit like this?" She glanced down at her shorts and T-shirt.

"Don't worry, you can borrow something of mine," said Simone with an airy wave of his hand.

Talei was an Amazonian figure next to Simone. She laughed out loud and long at his ridiculous offer of clothes. "Yes, I'm sure I can fit my right leg into one of your dresses."

Even Daniel and Lesina had to smile at that. Talei turned to them and her eyes lit up when she saw Daniel. "Ahhh, it's you."

"It is," Daniel bowed his head at her. "We meet again."

"You have to admit it now," said Talei with a grin.

"You were right," said Daniel. "But telling me we're going to meet up again and we do – is much less impressive when we're on a small island. It was inevitable we were going to bump into each other sooner or later."

Talei laughed again. "No, it's because my mum was an oracle. Wait till I tell you all the other exciting things she predicted about you and me," she teased as she struck a seductress pose. Which she then promptly ruined by blowing a green gum bubble.

"Wait up," said Simone. "You two know each other?"

"We've met," said Daniel.

"We share a weakness for long walks on the beach and swimming with the fishes in the moonlight," added Talei. She made it sound highly illicit.

"*Awolla!*" said Simone. "You've been a naughty boy Daniel."

"Oh, he tried," said Talei airily. "Took his clothes off and everything but he's not my type."

"Yeah, I'm not slimy or scaly enough for her," said Daniel as he and the tall Fijian exchanged a grin.

Simone looked back and forth at the both of them, doubtful if they were joking or not. "Good. Daniel's girlfriends have a habit of causing us all lots of trouble." A dramatic sigh. "We don't need any more scary girls around here."

"Trust me, there's nothing scary about Talei, we've got nothing to worry about," laughed Daniel. Talei responded with a silent '*kiss my butt*' look.

"Well, she's plenty scary on the court," said Simone. "Lesina, did you see her in action? She's almost as good as me."

The girls launched into a bout of good-natured teasing with Simone and everyone moved to the cars. Daniel checked on Pele who was still fast asleep. Simone wanted to continue his netball conversation with Talei so they took the Wrangler while Daniel and Lesina brought up the rear in his truck.

They were almost to the house when the Wrangler suddenly swerved.

"What's going on with them?" asked Daniel. Worried.

"I don't know," said Lesina. She leaned forward in her seat to peer at the Jeep ahead of them. "It looks like they're fighting in there."

The next instant, the Wrangler veered to one side of the road and came to an abrupt halt beside a thicket of trees. Daniel jammed his foot on the brake and pulled the truck over.

"Call Keahi. Tell him to get over here, now!" he snapped at Lesina as he leapt out and ran towards the Wrangler. "Leila! Simone, are you alright?"

There was a flash of orange light from inside the jeep and a shriek of outrage from Simone. "Stop it!"

One door opened and Talei stumbled out and backed away from the Wrangler. Daniel grabbed her arm, "Are you okay?"

She nodded. "Fine. But your girlfriend isn't."

Daniel ran around the jeep which was undamaged except for a few scratches in the paintwork. Simone opened the door before he could and jumped out. "You are one crazy beeatch, you know that?" he yelled back into the car. "You could have gotten us all killed."

"No, when I give you an order, I expect it to be obeyed," Pele shouted as she alighted from the back seat, slamming the door behind her with venom. All signs of alcoholic confusion were gone and she was one very angry woman. Her eyes flashed menacingly and her tattoos simmered with outrage.

But Simone wasn't backing down. Hands on his hips he stamped his foot as he snapped, "I am not your servant. I'm your friend and there's no way I'm going to let you drive when you've been drinking. Especially not when you want to go chasing after some slutty boys you hooked up with at my netball game."

"How dare you," said Pele. "Don't you know who I am? You're just a commoner. I am Keawe. You do what I tell you to." She snapped her fingers and flames leapt to her summons. Before anyone could react, she threw a wire of flame in a loop over and around Simone so that he stood within a circle of fire.

Beside Daniel, Talei reared back with a gasp of shock and Lesina groaned. "Oh no, we're in trouble now."

It couldn't have been comfortable in his ring of fire but it would take more than that for Simone to shut up. "Commoner? Excuse me? Trust me, you don't know who I am. Get me out of here and I'll show you what I am." A string of expletives followed.

Daniel called out to the angry fire girl, "Pele, why don't we take it easy and calm down?"

Pele turned to him. "Not until this insolent creature learns some respect."

"Hey, we're all your friends here," Daniel said. He held his hands out appeasingly as he walked slowly towards her. "We care about you."

Pele shook her hair back and wiped sweat off her forehead. She was breathing heavily in the hot night. "Not true. I don't have any friends."

"Sure you do," said Daniel. "I care about you. So does Simone. Talei's a friend. And nobody's got your back like Simone." His voice dropped to a soothing tone. "Let him out of there."

Pele turned back to contemplate her captive. She and Simone carried on with their verbal battle of insults. Daniel's voice dropped to an urgent whisper. "Lesina, did you call Keahi?"

She nodded. "He's on his way."

"You freaking out there?" Daniel asked Talei.

A shaky grin. "A little. Simone was right." A nod towards Pele. "You sure know how to pick them."

"That's not my girlfriend," Daniel said grimly. "That's a demonic body snatcher who chose the wrong girl to mess with." He focused back on the argument taking place in front of them.

"Pele, let's all go back to the house. You'll feel better after you've had some rest. You don't want to do this."

Pele whirled to face him, her face twisted and ugly. "Why not?" She was giving in to the flame edge now. As they watched, her red skirt began to fragment with the searing heat and tendrils of smoke surrounded her. "Why should I trust any of you? I've been surrounded by lies my whole life." She threw her head back and yelled into the shadows. "I can hear you. The whispers, the laughing. I know you're out there. You have followed me here into this life but you won't defeat me, you hear? This body is mine! I won't let you take my eyes …"

"Who's she talking to?" Lesina hissed at Daniel. "And what the hell is she talking about?"

"I have no idea," he said.

Daniel tried to stay outwardly calm but he was frantically searching for water, sending his inner Gift outward in unseen waves. *Nothing, dammit!* Simone, Lesina and now Talei – all of them were in this danger because of him. All of them were his personal responsibility. He'd already failed Leila. He didn't want to fail anyone else. He took a deep steadying breath, knowing he was taking a great risk now. "Pele. You're in Leila's body but that doesn't make us enemies. From what we know about your past, you weren't fairly treated. We want to help you. You need to know – there's a group of telesā gathered in town. A Tangaloa council meeting. They're here to kill Leila because she's a fire telesā. We – I – love Leila. That means we want to protect you too."

"What?" said Pele. Her eyes widened in shock and the flame wall around Simone disappeared. She stalked toward Daniel, all anger at Simone forgotten. "Who are these telesā? Where are they? Are they Keawe?" Impatient, she grabbed at him with two hands and threw him to the side with the strength of Earth. "Answer me!" Her hands burst into flame again.

Daniel picked himself up, brushing dirt and leaves from his clothing. He fought to contain his anger as he confronted the woman who shouted at him with Leila's face and voice. "Let's calm down and go back to the house. We'll talk about this. I'll tell you what I know and we'll come up with a plan how to fix everything."

"I don't need you. I'll hunt down these women myself, I'll set this whole island on fire," Pele raged. She snapped then and sent a ball of flame shooting towards Daniel.

Everyone shouted, "No!"

Daniel threw his hands up in front of his face but the flames never found their target. Instead something slammed into Daniel, pushing him out of the way and taking the attack meant for him. Not something – someone.

Keahi. He took the direct hit and relished it. An instant of poised crimson outline and then he burst into flame. A whoop of glee. "Yeah!"

Pele was stunned. "What are you?" She slowly walked towards him with her eyes alight, hand outstretched.

"You like?" Keahi asked as he flexed, sending ripples of orange and gold racing up and down his body.

"But, it's impossible," breathed Pele. "You are a man."

"Yes ahh am," drawled Keahi.

"Oh don't make me vomit," said Simone. He came up beside Daniel. "You alright?"

"Yeah," said Daniel. He was trying to hide it but Simone could tell how shaken he was that Leila had tried to attack him. He looked over at Keahi. "Thanks."

The boy on fire shrugged, "Now we're even." He turned back to Pele. "You shouldn't flame at your friends like that. They're not indestructible. Not like me."

Pele was entranced. "Never in all my many lifetimes did I ever imagine there could be a boy Keawe. Our Mother Earth never entrusted her sacred power to males. But, it makes perfect sense. How much better it would be to have a mating of two fire gods!"

Keahi immediately lost all his swagger. There was an awkward silence as the others exchanged stunned looks. *WTF?!*

Pele was oblivious. She reached to caress Keahi's face with fingers of fire. "Have you ever tried it?"

"Umm, tried what?" said Keahi as he took a step back.

Pele was impatient. "Have you ever loved another fire god?"

"No, can't say that I have," he replied with an embarrassed laugh.

"It all makes sense now," Pele said. "The sense of peace and connection I feel when I'm with you, why you made my pain go away. It's because we're the same. We're meant to be together." She took his hands in hers and announced with triumph, "This is why I have been reborn at this time and in this place. So we could find each other."

It was their second meeting. Same place, same agenda but this time the stakes were higher and this time there was an addition –

Talei. After being a witness to the fiery mess after the netball game, there was no point keeping anything else a secret from her. Especially not after she had shrugged off the night's events, "*Oi lei*, I turn into a giant eel in my spare time. You all don't have the monopoly on weird and fantastical."

Daniel had given her a ride home afterwards and for the first time, he opened up about what he was going through. They sat in the truck late into the night as he poured out all his anger and hurt. It felt good to talk to someone that wasn't bogged in the same mire of emotions that he was. Talei listened until he was done. Then she had given him her last piece of spearmint gum. "Go on, blow bubbles."

"What?"

"Do it."

And so he chewed on his gum and tried to blow bubbles. It had been a long time so he wasn't very good at it. Talei thought his pitiful efforts were hilarious. "Stop trying and just chew it," she said finally.

"What are we doing? What's with the gum?" he asked.

"Gum helps me think. Focus. I can't play a decent game of netball unless I've got gum. Chew and feel better."

"Okaaaay sensei," said Daniel. "Whatever you say." He had to admit that after a long few minutes of doing nothing but contemplate the process of chewing gum, he felt marginally better.

Talei got out of the truck and leaned down against the door to look in at him. There was no more laughter or teasing in her eyes. Just calm surety. "It's all going to work out Daniel Tahi. My mother was never wrong. She sent me here to find you because she said you'd need my help to make everything right. I don't know how we're supposed to fix this, but I have faith we will. I have faith in my mother's vision." She repeated one more time before she walked away. "She was never wrong."

Daniel remembered that as he addressed the group. "The other night should never have happened. We can't let it happen again."

"Damn straight," snapped Simone as he glared at Keahi. "You have to stay far away from Leila."

"No," said Daniel, "Keahi has to take over as Leila's security." He looked at the Hawaiian who was just as surprised as the others. "You can't leave her side. From now on, wherever she goes, you go."

A rush of outbursts as everyone except Talei tried to add their heated opinion on this announcement. Simone's exclamation was the most piercing. "No way Daniel. Pele's a skank, we've all seen it. Leila would be sick to her stomach if Pele used her body to get with this …"

Daniel stopped him before he could get creative with Keahi descriptors. "Keahi's the only person on this island – probably the only person alive on the planet – who Pele can't hurt. We use that," he said curtly. "It's too dangerous for anyone else. Keahi, can you handle her?"

For once, Keahi looked straight up scared. Hounded. He shifted uneasily on his feet. "I don't think this is a good idea. Lesina's got matagi powers. How about her?"

"She couldn't even stop Pele from getting drunk at a netball game. We're lucky Pele didn't kill someone that night. She's old school, from an age where women like her were treated like gods. She's got no problem with using her Fire in public or blasting people who annoy her. She's unpredictable and that makes her very dangerous," argued Daniel. His next words were an effort to put out there. "She likes you. Thinks you two are made for each other. Keep her occupied, give us time to find the Bone pieces. I'm working on Tavake. Getting her to trust me. We need time."

There was an uncomfortable silence as everyone avoided Daniel's eyes. Then Talei asked, "Maybe you could use the Bone piece you've already got to get the locations of the others? Use it as a bargaining chip with this Tavake person?"

Grateful for the change in topic, Simone leapt in. "Fabulous idea. They can't do anything without that piece."

Daniel nodded. "I'll talk to Tavake."

The meeting was over but Daniel wasn't done. He called out to Keahi as he walked to his bike with Teuila. "Got a minute?"

"No," said Keahi. The two stared at each other for a long, taut moment. A moment which had Teuila worried. And then Keahi relented. "Fine. What?"

"Pele stole that body. Don't let her win you over too. Leila's fighting for her life in there and we're fighting for her," said Daniel. There was no hostility in him, only quiet certainty and steel resolve. "Leila's mine. Never forget that."

Endure

Time meant nothing in Leila's prison. She drifted in and out of awareness and always, her surroundings were the same. A dark cave, a pool of water and chains. She knew she was losing her battle to stay alive, stay present. Sometimes, when she looked down at her hands, she seemed to be fading at the edges of her fingertips. Sometimes, the cave seemed to be shrinking, closing in on her. But perhaps that was just her mind playing tricks on her?

HER *mind, ha*. This wasn't her mind anymore. She knew that much. Somewhere out there, Pele was laughing, living and loving, occupying the life that used to be hers. The stronger Pele became, the less sure Leila was. Of her memories. Of her life. Of herself. She was waning. She was afraid. Soon, very soon – she would forget who she was, Pele would own her mind completely and Leila would cease to exist.

"No, I won't let that happen," Leila said into the silence. She hoarded fragments of sweet memory with fierce intensity. Running in a 5K with her Dad. Listening to music with Simone. Dancing the siva under a star-filled sky while Daniel sang to her.

She traced the patterns of her taulima arm band tattoo, chanting over and over again, the meaning, the memory of each marking. Her promise to Daniel on that long ago night. *'I'm ready to be that girl. To walk by your side, no more secrets, no more lies. You already had my heart but I'm ready to entrust you with my fears. I don't know what the future holds for us … I'm afraid … but I know that as long as we are together, I can endure anything.'*

She huddled against the wall, hugging her legs close and her *malu* gave her strength. It was a reminder of her telesā ancestry, the sacred lineage of Nafanua the war goddess. She held fast to the days spent in blurred pain as she received her malu, as her mother sang to her of the women who walked before her, the lives they led, the battles they fought, the men they loved and the children they bore. The words resounded in her anguished soul.

Endure. We are with you. Endure.

She tasted still, the nourishment her mother gave her as they waited for the open wounds to heal – sweet *vaisalo*, succulent baked crab, salty *limu* seaweed, raw fish in rich coconut cream. Food for healing, food for strength. She felt her mother's gentle care as she carried her to a silken sea in the moonlight to bathe her new malu in the salt-sting of the healing ocean. She could see her mother's fierce love as she defied her telesā covenant and died for her.

Leila's malu spoke to her of all these things and gave her strength.

Endure. We are with you. Endure.

No

Discovering that Keahi burned with Keawe fire changed everything for Pele. Even the voices that lived inside her were quiet as she mused upon this revelation. A male Keawe was a sacrilegious thing – wasn't it? How could the Earth Mother allow it? There had never been such a thing when she was growing up and Noalani hadn't ever spoken of a boy Keawe. Pele withdrew from everyone around her and went into the meditative state that had been such an intrinsic part of her learning as a child. She searched back in her millennia of memory for the ancient stories she had been taught and called on her substantial Gift to speak to the Earth which sustained them all. She spent several days like this. She spoke to no-one, barely ate or slept. And when she finally got her answer, she was jubilant.

Simone and Lesina were having breakfast when Pele walked in and announced, "It's how Tangaloa always meant for it to be."

The two exchanged glances. *What is she on?*

"Hi Pele," said Simone cautiously. "You hungry? Lesina made pancakes."

Pele ignored him and pointed at Lesina. "You are telesā, are you not?"

"Umm, yes," said Lesina trying not to cringe. *Is this where she torches me? Cuts my head off with a flame whip?*

"Of what?" demanded Pele. "Air or ocean?"

"I'm telesā matagi, air," said Lesina. A nervous breeze rustled through the room.

"Then you must know the story of our origins? Our creation." Pele paced the floor. "Fatu ma le ele ele, heart and earth. That's what we were supposed to be." She stood in the center of the room and chanted the timeless words. "Let Earth give nourishment to Man and let him always treasure her as his heart beats with the red blood of life. Let Earth be the rock man stands on to give him strength, the trees that shelter him, the waters that sustain him. Let Earth's fire be the heat that warms him and in return, let Man be the protector. The guardian."

Simone raised his eyebrow and muttered, "And where's fa'afafine in this story, hmmm? Typical."

But Pele was too buzzed to pay attention. "When man proved himself to be a cruel overlord instead of a guardian, Tangaloa created us, gifted us with our Mother Earth's strength and power. It was necessary to keep us apart from man then. He could not be trusted to walk alongside us, to share in our Gifts. If a Keawe birthed a boy child, he was sent away to live with the commoners. That is the way things were for a very long time. No boy child was ever born Gifted during our time. Yet it seems Tangaloa has had a change of heart on the matter. " She paused and a fleeting look of sadness crossed her face as she put a hand to her head. "Tell me Lesina, what would telesā today do to Keahi if they knew of his Fire?"

"They'd kill him. It's against our laws for any males to be telesā."

"That is where your laws are wrong. They are not the laws of Tangaloa." Pele pointed to the television. "I have been watching, listening, learning. The world is a much bigger place than it was when I walked as Keawe. Our Gifts almost pale in comparison to the technology and power that is out there." A knowing smile. "Well, your gifts anyway. There are so few of you left. I have spoken to our Earth Mother and she is sick. Hurting. Weary of the damage done to her. That is why she is Gifting her power to chosen men as well as women."

"What are you saying?" asked Lesina.

"I'm saying telesā shouldn't be killing off their boy children. Instead they should see if they are Gifted and keep them. Give the others away. Tangaloa means for male and female telesā to stand together and fight for what is meant to be ours."

"And what's that?" said Simone with a wary stare.

Pele waved a hand at the spectacular view from their window, of the Apia township. "Possession of the whole of it. Samoa, the Pacific and beyond. We will take much better care of our Earth Mother than what mere humans are doing."

Pele's audience was at a loss for words. Lesina looked like she wanted to vomit. Or cry. Or both. She jumped when Pele grabbed her by the shoulders. "Surely you can see it? The earth needs our guardianship and we cannot stand by and continue to let her suffer." A shrewd look. "Keahi isn't the only one, is he? That boy Daniel, he's vasa loloa?"

There was no point trying to lie and Pele was triumphant. "I knew it. How many other male telesā are out there I wonder? It's a sign man has evolved. But it's also a response to the dire situation our Mother Earth is in." She turned to Simone. "Call

Daniel. Tell him I need to speak with him. I must know more about this gathering of telesā in town. I will need Keahi here too."

Simone rolled his eyes after Pele as she left the room. "Since when am I her secretary?" he muttered darkly.

"Don't forget, you're the one who said, you have to do everything to make her happy," said Lesina. She was only half-joking.

But before Simone could text anyone, there was the roar of a motorbike. Keahi had arrived for official bodyguard duty.

Pele watched from the bedroom as Keahi pulled up to the house. There was a giddy edge of excitement in the air as she raced to change her clothes and do her hair. She could hear the conversation from the living room as the others greeted Keahi. One last look in the mirror and that's when the familiar voice chastised her.

'*Daughter, what are you doing?*'

Pele's breath caught in her chest. Hot and searing. "What do you want?" she whispered fiercely to her reflection. "Go away Noalani."

'*Yes, can't you see your daughter is busy?*' A different voice. This time mocking and cold. Pele knew it well. Litalia, the girl who had taken her eye. '*She has found herself a Keawe lover. When she's finished with him, she can steal his Gift too.*'

A chorus of voices then. '*Will it never be enough for you Pele? … How many more do you need? … Your hunger knows no bounds … you are sick … evil … Release us.*'

It was a harsh cacophony of accusing sound and Pele hated them all. She had been trapped in lava rivers and volcanoes with the spirits of all those she had killed and she would not let them ruin the splendid wonder of her newfound life, her vibrant young body. She cursed, grabbed a hairbrush and flung it at the mirror.

The sound of breaking glass brought people to her door. Knocking. "Pele, are you alright in there?"

Pele forced calm authority into her voice. "I am fine. Leave me."

A murmur of voices and then silence as they went away.

Pele turned back to the mess before her. The mirror was destroyed but at least the angry spirits were gone. All except one.

'Pele, you have taken so much from so many. But this? Tangaloa will not stand by and let you steal this girl's body.

"This world needs me," argued Pele. "There's so much of our land, our waters, even our air – suffering. Our Earth Mother gave me this body for a purpose."

'You lie to yourself but you cannot lie to me.'

"Maybe Tangaloa has given me this chance so I can atone for my wrongdoings? Make everything right?"

The fragrance of tangy orange and cinnamon intensified so it was a strident rush. Noalani's presence was so strong that Pele could almost see her standing there.

'You dare lay claim to the name and authority of Tangaloa to justify your actions? The killings. The destruction. The breaking of your Keawe oath. Have you learned nothing from your time in exile? This is not your time, not your place. That is not your body and these people are not your family! I am.'

A recrimination which cut Pele to the core. She sank to her knees and her tears hurt more than the broken glass. "Don't I deserve a chance at happiness? A place to belong? Someone to love me?"

'I loved you. I gave you everything. But it wasn't enough.'

Pele's face twisted with rage as she clawed at the cruel shards around her. "No! Because of you, *I* was never enough. Not for the Keawe. Not for the Sisterhood. And not for Akamai."

'You made your choices. As did he.'

Pele wanted to scream and burn to be free of her mother's censure. The air around her was so very hot as she hovered on the edge of reason and an inferno of emotions cried out to be released. A sharp pain brought her back from the precipice, reminded her she needed to stay in control. She had cut herself. Red wetness stained her hands. She took a deep breath and rose to her feet. "You're dead Noalani. Over a thousand years dead and gone. But I'm not. I am young, strong and alive. You can't hurt me."

A few moments more to compose herself and then Pele unlocked the door and rejoined her new life.

"You're hurt," said Keahi. There was concern in his eyes as he reached for her hands. "We need to fix that."

Pele allowed him to walk her to the kitchen sink and wash her cuts. His hands were strong and sure on hers. He smelled of the outdoors. Green forest. Baked black rock. Sweat and sunshine. She breathed him in and she remembered another, from long ago, who she had allowed to hold her hand, care for her. She remembered and something sharp and sorrowful razed at her. *Is this what regret feels like?*

This close to him, she could see the scar patterning on his arms and peering from inside his shirt. *He is a fighter who has suffered much … as am I.* She welcomed his closeness. It had been so long since anyone had cared for her this way. She was quiet as he searched through drawers for a First Aid kit.

"Simone," he called out, "have you got any bandages in here? Leila …" he stumbled over the words, "… Pele's cut herself."

"The cupboard over the sink," said Simone from the next room. He joined them in the kitchen. "*Auoi*, what happened?"

They were waiting for her to answer. "It was an accident. The mirror broke and I was trying to clean up the glass," she explained.

"The cuts are deep," said Keahi with a frown. He worked to clean and bandage both her hands with a tenderness that was at odds with his rough exterior. Simone hovered over him, giving unnecessary instructions like the medical professional he wasn't.

"You have to raise her hands up. Elevate! And ice the injury," he said to Keahi. To Pele he added soothingly, "Don't you worry *sass*, I'll take care of everything."

"No," said Keahi. "That's for sprains and muscle injuries. This isn't netball."

"Elevate is for stopping the bleeding you *vasti*," snapped Simone. "Ice is for the pain. What do you know? You're just a boy. An *ugly* boy."

"I'm an ugly boy who's been in lots of fights and dealt with cuts like this all the time. I got this. You're just a fa'afafine whose biggest drama is a broken nail."

Simone had been virtuously holding Pele's right arm up in the air (for elevation purposes) but at Keahi's jibe, he immediately let her hand go and leapt to the defensive-offensive. "You want my fist in your face? I'll show you drama." Pele's wince of pain as her arm hit the kitchen table distracted him and he switched back to kind, caring Nurse Simone. "Awww, I'm sorry *sass.*" He patted her shoulder and then paled at the sight of the bloody cotton wool Keahi was cleaning her cuts with. "We need a drink. And some air. Keahi, she looks faint."

"She does not."

"She does," Simone insisted. He went to the fridge, grabbed a can of Diet Coke and walked to open the back door. He stood there gulping in big breaths of fresh air, pointedly averting his eyes now from Keahi's First Aid efforts.

"I thought you said Pele needed air," Keahi snapped as he finished applying disinfectant cream to the cuts.

"Yeah. That's why I'm over here. So she can have plenty of air. It's obvious." Simone rolled his eyes and snapped open the can, taking a long sip. "Now I'm drinking so I don't faint. Otherwise you finally get the chance to have your wicked way with me."

Pele watched them both squabble and fuss over her and it was an alien experience. She was accustomed to people's fear, awe, admiration, dread and even worship. She welcomed it all as her due. But genuine care? Camaraderie? Affection and friendship? No, Pele wasn't used to those things.

It's because you look like Leila. They don't really care about you. The demon voices crept in when she wasn't looking. Would she never be free of them? But were they right? Did these people truly like her? Were they her friends? Was her place with them secure? Could she trust? Could she love?

Finally Keahi was done. "I've fixed it up best I can, but you still might need stitches." He had her hands in his, still frowning at them, worried.

She leaned forward with a soft smile. "Thank you. You're very kind." They were words Pele had never uttered before. She meant them.

Keahi smiled without his usual mockery. "You're welcome."

The sound of a truck in the driveway broke their connection. It was Daniel's green bomb. Keahi moved away from Pele. "I'll clean up this mess," he said as he gathered up the medical supplies.

Pele watched him walk away and she was uneasy. Her brain was a jumbled mess of splintered memories and half-forgotten things as Leila's past fought to stay separate, to stand strong against her. Sometimes, she could see everything so clearly. Keahi was an angry boy that had chaotic history with Leila. Daniel was the opposite. A strong, steadying presence, he was love, desire and joy. But just when she felt sure where everyone fit in this new world, it would all haze into a wild conflagration of sparks and crossed wires. Then, nothing was certain and everything and everyone was an unknown to be feared and strategized against. Then, that boy with green eyes and an impossible beauty was a foreboding stranger who looked at her with questioning eyes and always found her wanting. Always found her incomplete. Not good enough. It reminded her of living with the Keawe before she had a Gift. She hated that feeling. She hated that boy for making her feel it.

At those times, the scarred boy who carried darkness inside him, was the one she wanted to be close to. He was tempestuous fire and the serrated edge of a shark's tooth blade. He was like her – all the damaged parts she kept hidden. She knew him like she knew herself. Finding out that he was Gifted with earth's Fire sealed the bond between them. She wanted to do so many things together with him. Burn in a sunset, sear the night sky of stars and set the horizon on fire at dawn.

She only wished she could hold fast to memories and certainties. When you're sharing a body with a girl who is fighting you every minute of the day – moments of clarity don't last very long.

Just give up and die already, Leila Folger!

Pele thought upon all these things as Daniel came into the house. He saw her bandaged hands and he couldn't hide the tenderness, the love in his eyes, in his voice. "What happened? Are you alright?"

"Yes, I'm fine thank you. A careless accident with my mirror," she smiled ruefully. "Simone and Keahi took care of them for me."

He wants to hold me. Touch me. Kiss me. I can see it in his eyes. I can feel it.

The thought made her step back. Throw up her walls. "It's good you're here. We must speak about these telesā women you say are gathered to plot an attack. Tell me everything you know."

She moved to sit at the table and motioned for him to join her. Daniel sat down and the others slipped into the room quietly while he was speaking. "No-one outside of Samoa knew about Leila being fanua afi until Niuatoputapu happened."

"What happened there?" asked Pele.

He gave her a quick summary of events, ending with Leila's time in hospital. "When she finally woke up, you were here."

"Yes, and I am here to stay," said Pele. She looked around at the others. "Leila and I are one now. I know you care for her deeply and I hope you can accept that she has agreed to join our Gifts and spirits. We will all be friends, allies."

Daniel clenched his fists tightly together but stayed in control. So much depended on it. "Niuatoputapu set off alarm bells for the telesā groups in the other island countries. They found out about Leila and they're here to kill her. They think she's too powerful and it's too dangerous to let her live. My grandmother is an Ungifted daughter of the Covenant Keeper from Tonga …"

"Interesting. That explains how you are Vasa Loloa. Your Gift skipped a generation," mused Pele.

Daniel didn't bother correcting her. This conversation wasn't about truth. It was about appeasing a fire goddess and luring her into a trap of trust. "Grandmother says the gathered Council are afraid. They have not yet decided on the best plan of action for killing Leila." The lies came easily. "None of them have fought a fire telesā before. They've heard how Leila killed an entire Covenant all by herself and it worries them. We're not going to let anyone hurt Leila … hurt you. We will stand with you against these others if the time comes. We are your friends."

There was only the hum of the refrigerator as Pele considered his words. The group hardly dared breathe as they waited to see what her conclusion would be.

"I appreciate your offer but I'm sure I can take them on my own. Anytime. I should strike while they are fishing for words and strategy. The element of surprise can win a battle."

The tension in the room pulled even tighter.

"That shouldn't be necessary," Daniel said. "My grandmother and I are working to solve this … peacefully."

Pele raised an eyebrow in disdain. "Peaceful is not a word in the vocabulary of a Keawe Fire Goddess."

"All the same, we'd like to avoid a fight if we can help it," said Daniel. "You're not at full strength yet, are you? Still getting used to this new body." He shot Keahi a glance heavy with meaning.

"Yeah and I thought maybe you and I could hang out today. Simone said you wanted a tour of the island," said Keahi.

Pele leapt to her feet. "Yes! Enough talking, enough sitting in this house." Her smile and lighthearted tone had everyone relaxing a little.

Keahi grinned. "Ever been on a bike before?"

"No, but I'm sure I'll love it," Pele said.

Daniel had an inscrutable look on his face as he watched them leave. Simone came to stand beside him. "You lied to her."

"And I'll keep lying to her. We all will," Daniel said. "She can't know that we're out to find the Tangaloa Bone."

"Do you trust him with her?" asked Simone.

"I don't have a choice."

The week that followed was quieter than anyone expected it to be. Pele was in a good mood which resulted in less diva behavior. She was polite and friendly – which her housemates greatly appreciated. But then, she wasn't around them very much because each morning, Keahi would show up at breakfast time, consume indecent amounts of Lesina's cooking and then go roaring off with Pele on his bike.

They wouldn't come back to the house until late afternoon, laughing and flushed from the sun and wind. Simone was riddled with suspicion. He cornered Keahi one morning. "I hope you know what you're doing."

"Sure I do. Today I'm taking Pele to the Sua Ocean Trench at Lotofaga village. She read about it on some tourist website and wants to check it out. You wanna go? We can all take the Wrangler."

Simone's desire to supervise Keahi warred with his aversion to spending an entire day with him in a thirty meter deep hole in the ground located in an isolated spot. He made a *bleugh* face. "No thanks. I've got a design to work on. Just remember Pele is meant to be an assignment. Nothing else. No funny business, eh!"

Keahi held his hands up in fake submission. "Yes boss, I got it." He laughed as Simone flounced out of the room but his jeering quickly turned into unease because if he was being perfectly honest – Keahi had no idea what he was doing.

Another day, another outing. Keahi could hear Pele singing to herself as she packed a bag for their day trip to the other island of Savaii. She wanted to go see the lava fields. She was excited and he?

He was nervous.

Not because of the enigmatic woman he was spending so much time with, but because of the way he felt around her. She was changing. He didn't know if anyone else noticed, but he sure did. It was as if she was softening, melding into a kinder, gentler version of the imperious Pele who used to think everyone was a 'commoner' placed on earth to serve her. They had gone snorkeling the day before at a secluded beach on the southern coast. Suspended in crystal clear water, surrounded by a myriad of colorful fish, Pele had been in heaven. Back on land, she had hugged him with unabashed delight. "That was amazing! I never knew the ocean was so beautiful. Earth has always been my safety, my comfort. When I was a little girl, the ocean seemed such an ominous unknown domain." She waved a hand out at the blue cloth that sparkled with diamond tipped ripples. "But to see it using these goggles and to be out there with the creatures of the sea trusting me like that? I loved it. Will you bring me here again?"

He looked at her face so alive, so eager – and something twisted inside him. It felt good. Happy. "Sure, whenever you want."

She hadn't touched him again but the memory of her ocean-kissed body pressed against his, stayed with him all day.

He was still thinking about it now. He wondered if she would wear that red bikini again today. Probably not since they weren't going swimming … *too bad.*

"I'm ready." Her voice startled him. He swung around to look at her and his jaw dropped. He looked and then he remembered to breathe and then he looked some more. She was wearing a two-piece again, this time a brilliant fuchsia. Two brief pieces of fabric that barely contained her curves. There was a white sarong tied at her hips. It fell to her ankles but it was so sheer it hid nothing and accentuated everything. Her hair was swept up into a knot and she had dotted it with flowers that complemented her bikini and the jewelry she wore. She frowned at his stunned silence. "Too much for a ferry trip to Savaii? I have a shirt." She pulled a tank top from her bag and pulled it on. "Better?"

Keahi stared at the wall behind her. It was the best way to slow down the crazy tempo of his heart. A deep breath. "Yeah. All good. Let's go."

Keahi was conscious of her sitting beside him the whole way through the ferry ride and then the drive to the lava fields. She talked a lot while he said nothing because he couldn't string together a legible sentence in his brain, let alone out into the open air. It was like every one of his nerve endings was doing some wild dance, celebrating her scent, her voice, her laugh. There was a huge goofy grin inside him and it was a battle not to let it out. To borrow one of Leila's words – it was *ridiculous*. Keahi had never had this problem around a girl before. He had never been at a loss for words. Nobody ever rocked his blasé shields. Not ever.

Until now.

Every so often, she would reach over and touch his arm, ask, "Are you alright?"

He wanted to yell, '*Don't touch me!*' Because every one of his thoughts was stampeding in a gleeful frenzy, shouting '*Don't let go. Stay right here.*'

Even before they reached the lava fields, Keahi wanted to leave. There was something wrong with him and he had to get away from Pele. Quick. So he could go back to being his regular self.

Pele jumped out of the truck first, exclaiming at the desolate majesty of the lava fields. The black waves, frozen in time, rolled onward and outward for as far as the eye could see. She had packed them a picnic lunch and she called over her shoulder for him to follow as she set out to find a spot for them to eat. He caught up with her and at some point, she almost tripped and fell because she was so busy staring at the expanse before them. So he took her hand in his to steady her and then simply forgot to let it go. It felt right there anyway.

They walked for a long while before they came to the edge where lava flowed and became ocean. They stood there hand in hand for a moment, looking out over the sea as it whispered unintelligible secrets. It seemed they were the only two people in the whole world. Pele, Keahi – and earth, ocean and sky.

"I'm hungry. Shall we eat?" Pele asked.

His thoughts, his words were still stampeding and he couldn't catch any. So he just nodded.

Pele spread out a lavalava for them to sit on and then he helped her put out the lunch. Fresh fruit, sandwiches and some of Lesina's koko Samoa pie. Everything was delicious but it all tasted like sawdust to Keahi. *What do your lips taste like?*

She told him stories of her long-ago childhood. Richly fascinating tales of a faraway time and place where women like her were warriors and gods. She talked about her mother who loved her. Sisters who scorned her. She was vulnerable then. Her face lost that hard edge and she looked like Leila. A fragile, bittersweet version of Leila. He wanted to hold her hand again. Comfort her, reassure her. But he had made a promise and so he kept his reassurances to himself.

And then she kissed him. On the cheek. Only a light, fleeting kiss but he jerked away as if she had hit him.

She looked hurt. Sad. "Are you afraid of me?"

He shook his head.

"What's wrong then?

He could taste her on the ragged air between them. Sweet koko, brown sugar and a razor edge of red chili. "Nothing." Without meaning to, his hand went up to trace the armband tattoo. The markings glowed red and she caught her breath. Bit at her lip. His gaze was caught there. Lips, lush, soft, a hint of wetness. He wanted to kiss her. But he couldn't. Shouldn't. She reached to caress his face and then ran her fingers down across his chest. Lower. *This is Leila. She belongs to Daniel. She tried to be your friend, tried to help you, remember? It doesn't matter what she does or says, she is NOT for the taking.*

He pushed her hand away. "Stop it."

"Why? Don't you want me?"

"You don't own that body you're offering me. It's not yours to give."

She moved to him, pressed her warmth against his, took his face in her hands so he couldn't look away. "I'm not offering you this body. I'm giving you me. The outside doesn't matter. I'm Pele. I have feelings. This is me." She grasped at his right hand and brought it to her chest. "In here, I want you in here. I look at you and I can see past the outside. I can claw my way through your walls to what's inside."

A rough movement and she had ripped open his shirt, baring his scarred chest. She placed a single kiss on his scars, then looked up at him. "I want what's in here." Her hands cupped his face, drew him down to her. "Let me in Keahi. There's pain and rage inside you. Let me drown in it. I want to see what's inside."

And then she was kissing him.

She was hesitant at first but her lips on his were enough to destroy his resolve. He crushed her to him, fierce in his desire to have her and she matched him in every way. As they drowned in each other, it happened.

Fire.

It sparked in her first, rippling along her spine, snaking a delicious pathway down to her toes. As their kiss deepened, the fire burned brighter. A gossamer web of scarlet veins lit up all over Pele's skin, incinerating the thin fabric of her sarong. Keahi's gift answered. His tattoos burned from charcoal to red, spilt wine running the full length of his body. Heat charred his clothing to ashes that scattered on the wind. Pele fell back onto the volcanic rock bed and it softened and melted about her, pillowed her in its soft embrace. He was poised above her for an instant, gazing down at this woman of fire and lava beneath him. She was beautiful, like nothing else he had ever seen. Scarlet waves of hair arrayed about her face. She smiled up at him and half-sat up, resting on her elbows. A quick look to the side, an exultant smile. "See what we've made together?"

Keahi turned his head. All about them the rock had seamed with rivulets of molten lava that glowed in searing approval. White clouds of steam billowed in the air. Pele caressed his cheek, "Have you ever seen anything so magnificent? That's us. You and I were meant for each other."

He almost believed her, almost drowned in the possibilities of what they could be – when he saw it. Her arm band *taulima*. The one that spoke of love for another. Keahi stopped. Shook his head and slowly pulled away from the woman that lay there waiting for him. "No, we're not."

Pele reached out to him, "Yes we are. Keahi please. Is there anyone in the world that you can be yourself with? Anyone that can unleash what's inside you?"

He sat back, shoulders slumped in defeat. "I'm sorry Pele. You have no idea how bad I want this. I can't."

A scarlet tear burned a path down her cheek as she clasped her knees in close. "Do you know how many boys I've loved Keahi? None. I'm more than a thousand years old and you're the first boy I've ever been with." A bitter laugh. "Trust me, it wasn't from want of trying. A side effect from overloading on Keawe fire meant I could never be with anyone. No matter how much I wanted to. No matter how hard I tried."

She closed her eyes as the memories rushed her. Of the boy with fair skin and sand-flecked brown eyes. His cocky grin at being chosen as Consort for the Bone Bearer. He was a sailor and she could still taste the salt on his lips as they kissed that night underneath the plumeria trees. The wave of excitement that had ripped through her, the fire that had leached from her and razed him where he stood. His agonized scream. The way the night wind had sent his ashes dancing. He had been the first but not the last. It had driven her near mad that with all her power, there was one thing she couldn't have. One thing she couldn't control. She longed for it. She lusted for it. She wept for it. But she could never have it.

She cried molten tears and each one ate at him. "Keahi, please. We could rule the world together, you and I. Gods of earth and mud and fire. We could be happy together. Please?"

He stood there with empty hands of fire. "No, I can't. Not now, not ever."

Pele watched as the boy of scars and hate walked away. The further he got from her, the quieter his fire burned until he was but a boy of flesh and bone. Naked and striding alone along the desolate lava field. She wanted to hate him. She wanted to set him ablaze, make the ground chasm beneath his feet, devour him in a raging abyss of hurt.

But she couldn't.

Pele loved him. And in loving him – she was that long-ago broken girl still.

The sun had already set by the time they got back to Apia. Daniel's truck was parked in the driveway when they pulled up. Keahi turned off the car and spoke into the dark silence between them. "I'm sorry about today."

"Your decision makes no sense," said Pele. "I know you want me. You feel something for me, I know it."

"Leila was – is – my friend. I betrayed her once before and people died." A sad smile. "I'm part of the reason why you ended up living in her body."

There was eagerness in Pele as she reached across the seat to take his hand in hers. "So you helped bring us together. Leila doesn't care for you, not like this. I am the last of my kind. Reject me and you condemn your only chance to love another whose soul burns with the Earth Mother's Fire. Don't you want to be happy?"

"I gave up on happiness a long time ago." He pulled his hand away from hers and got out of the car.

"Then you're a fool Keahi," Pele snapped at him as she exited the Jeep, slamming the door with way too much force. "What we had back there today was real. It was explosive and earth-shattering. You will never have another woman like me."

With that final announcement, Pele stalked into the house. Keahi groaned and banged his head on the hood of the Jeep, letting loose with a few choice curse words. *That was so stupid!*

A voice from the shadows startled him. It was Daniel, sitting on the verandah. He unfurled from the seat to his full height and moved with deadly precision. "So what was that about?"

Alarm bells were going off in Keahi's head. *Warning, warning!*

What did he see? How much did he hear? "Nothing." He went to get the bags from the Jeep.

"Sounded like a whole lot of something to me," said Daniel. He folded his arms across his broad chest and Keahi was clearly reminded of how much bigger, broader and stronger Daniel was than he.

"Pele came on to me. I said no. She's mad. That about covers it."

A bitter laugh. "So what else is new," said Daniel. A long silence. "I'm outta here. Tell Simone I've gone to pick up the pizza."

Keahi kept a wary eye on Daniel as he got in his truck and drove away. He had to admit that as crappy as his day had turned out to be, things were so much worse for Daniel. "Sucks to be you," he muttered as he went inside the house.

Daniel was thinking pretty much the same thing as he picked up the pizza order. How much more could he take? What if Leila never regained control of her body? Would he stand on the sidelines and be Pele's "friend" anyway? If she survived a Tangaloa Council hit? Could he watch her be someone else? Love someone else?

Those were the thoughts that tortured him as he drove along with the truck steeped in the aroma of hot pizza. He almost missed seeing the confrontation taking place on the side of the road. A jogger surrounded by a pack of about fifteen dogs. She was yelling back at the animals as they circled her and darted in every now and again to snap at her legs. The woman was obviously a tourist running on the seawall at this time of the night. Locals knew enough about the local dogs not to go running in this area — at least not without a handful of rocks. The family who owned this infamous pack of feral creatures had a roadside store and their dogs were nighttime security watch. Nobody ever made the mistake of running past this store at night. Nobody, that is, but clueless tourists in skimpy clothing. Daniel was tempted to keep driving, pretend he hadn't seen her. But he couldn't.

"Nuisance runners," Daniel muttered under his breath as he slowed the truck.

The jogger had her back to the road. She wore a red baseball cap and skintight Lycra that was torn in one leg where the dogs had bitten at her clothing. She stood in the center of the pack, slightly hunched over and waving her hands at the snarling dogs and shouting for them to go away. Across the road, a group of village boys sat under a tree and watched the spectacle with great interest. Laughing. Because that's what Samoans do. Laugh at tourists when they get into trouble.

Daniel got out of the truck. "*Halu*, get out of here!" he called out, bending to pick up a few stones as he walked towards the woman.

A couple of well-aimed throws and the pack dispersed, yelping and barking. "Are you alright?"

She gave him an unfriendly glare. "You didn't need to do that. I was fine."

"Yeah? It didn't look that way from where I was" he said.

"I had it." She was ice in the sweltering evening, with her arms folded across her chest and brilliant blue eyes searing right through him. She looked familiar ...

"Hey, I know you. You're that security guard girl who took my grandmother to her meeting."

"Didn't recognize me with my bald head covered up?" she said.

"No. I was too busy doing a good deed and saving you from those dogs," Daniel said wryly.

"What are you? A Boy Scout?"

He ignored her hostility. "You shouldn't be out running by yourself in this area. Not at night. This is when the dogs are out."

She looked at the sniggering group of boys who were staring at them both with avid curiosity. "Yes I see lots of two-legged dogs. They need to be afraid of *me*."

"*Riiiight.* Lighten up. Tourists out running in skimpy Lycra are their only entertainment. They don't mean any harm," Daniel said. The pizza in the truck was getting cold. "Get in. I'll give you a ride to your hotel."

"Like I would get in a car with a total stranger. That sounds like something only a dumb tourist in skimpy Lycra would do." Now she was mocking him. "Good night, **boy**."

She started walking away. He watched her go with irritation, torn between a hot double cheese pizza and the good manners his grandmother had drilled into him. An unmistakable sickly sweet scent wafted across the road. The village boys were smoking something happy. It was enough to make him lock the truck and stride after her. "Wait up. I'll walk you back."

"I don't need a security detail," she said.

"But I need to make sure you get back okay. Mama would knock me out if I let a girl walk home by herself at night. With four legged *and* two legged dogs around."

"What are you? A mummy's boy?" she asked.

He grinned. "Always."

She broke into a light run and he kept pace alongside her. "Don't you have somewhere to be?" she snapped.

"Yeah. But they can wait. Simone hates cold pizza but I'll just blame it on you."

"Your new girlfriend?"

Daniel laughed, "No. In an alternate reality maybe. Simone's fa'afafine. We go way back and he rooms with some other friends of mine."

"Pizza night with friends. Must be nice." Was that a hint of wistfulness?

"Gets a little lively with a bit too much arguing, but yeah, we like it," replied Daniel. "So now that I've rescued you from a pack of killer canines, are you going to tell me your name?"

"It's not important," she said. She ran with a brisk, efficient running style and was clearly very fit – not the slightest sign of tiredness.

"Sure it is. It's good manners to tell people your name. Especially after they save your life."

A *haarumph* snort of derision, which he ignored. "I'm going to sing really loud until you tell me your name." He started singing with overly loud gusto, the Enrique Iglesias' song, Hero. "I can be your hero baby … I can take away the pain … I will stand by you when the dogs come to rip your leg off …"

The girl stopped running and glared at him with her hands on her hips. "Why are you singing that song?"

Daniel kept jogging on the spot. He mimicked a caveman voice. "You – helpless female, me – big, strong rugby player hero who sings part-time." He started running again and launched into another song, the Script's 'Hall of Fame', adapting the lyrics for maximum impact. "Be a champion … Do it for your country, tell me your name … the world's gonna know your name …"

The Olohe watched after him, singing and weaving along the seawall and there may have been a small smile on her face as she ran to keep up with him.

By the time they reached her hotel, Daniel had sung several more songs with adapted lyrics and was a little out of breath – but trying to hide it. They came to a halt at the hotel entrance. "This is me," she said curtly. "You can stop harassing me now."

"It was my dubious honor to escort you Ms. Killer Assassin," said Daniel. "Gotta go. I hope the dogs haven't broken into my truck and eaten the pizza."

She frowned even more. *Would it kill you to smile? Just once? I bet you'd be stunning if you lost the assassin frown.* Thinking about her like that – as a girl who may or may not be even more beautiful if she smiled – made Daniel feel uncomfortable. *Leave now. You ran her back to her hotel because it was the polite and proper thing to do. That's it. Go.*

"No more running with dogs," he said.

"I won't," she replied, with a hint of a grin. "Especially not with six foot tall rugby player dogs."

Did you just crack a joke? Of course, it would be one at my expense … Go home Daniel. Back to your crazy life and your girlfriend who keeps trying to get it on with everybody except you. What a sobering thought. He was about to leave when she called out to him, "Noa." In response to his questioning face, she added, "My name. It's Noa."

A slow smile lit up his face as Daniel walked back to shake her hand. She was a petite figure next to his bulk and her hand seemed very small in his. The bold stamp of shark tooth tattoos on her arm and her taut, muscular build reminded him of who she was, what she was. "You're not really an assassin are you?"

She gave him a quizzical smile. "I'm Olohe. We serve the Keawe."

"So if they tell you to kill someone, then you go do it?"

She shook her head at him. "So dramatic."

"You didn't answer my question," said Daniel. He was still holding her hand and it suddenly seemed very important to establish just what this girl was capable of. He wanted to know more about her.

He wanted her to cease being a stranger.

Noa loosened her fingers from his so she could turn her wrist over. "Each of these triangle markings represents a different skill level we attain in our study of the Olohe art." The shark's tooth tattoos went all the way up past her elbow. "We're taught many things, how to defend and how to attack. I'm the Olohe for Iolana, the sensate leader of the Keawe Sisterhood. Only the best can serve Iolana."

"How long have you been the best?"

"Since I was fifteen. It will be my honor to serve Iolana until I turn twenty-five."

"What happens then?"

"In theory, we are released from our Olohe Covenant. We're free to go, work, marry, raise families – do whatever we like."

Daniel was puzzled. "Why only in theory?" He didn't do it knowingly, but his hand slipped from its clasp of her wrist, to gently threading his fingers through hers so they stood there in the glow of the streetlight – a couple. Holding hands.

Noa took a while to answer. She studied their linked hands and bit at her lip. It seemed she was trying to decide whether to speak truth. "We usually don't make it that far."

"What?" Daniel was incredulous. "That's crazy. You mean Olohe don't live that long? What the hell kind of job is that?"

She flushed at his strident tone and pulled her hand away from his. "It's not safe for the Keawe. They have no elemental Gifts, not like the others, not like you. They're truth-seekers and sensates, not fighters. Other telesā target them because they want to exploit their powers usually for things to do with money. It's our calling to protect them." She stepped back and took her red cap off as if wanting him to have that visual reminder of who and what she was. "You asked if I'm an assassin. The answer is no. But would I kill to protect my Keawe? Yes. I've done it before and I won't hesitate to do it again." She turned and started walking away.

"Wait, where are you going?"

"Go home Daniel," she shouted over her shoulder. "This was a mistake."

He watched her disappear into the hotel and then anger had him pounding the pavement, sprinting back along the seawall.

What the hell was that? This is what happens when you try to be nice to people … no more being nice to anybody dammit. Especially not to strange girls with shaved heads.

There was guilt teasing at the edge of Daniel's frustration too. Guilt because he'd been talking, laughing and holding hands with a girl who wasn't Leila. For a little while there he'd actually been almost happy. Carefree. He ran back to the truck thinking about brilliant blue eyes, honey skin and shark tooth tattoos.

It wasn't until he was half-way to Leila's house that it hit him.

Noa knows about me being Vasa Loloa … how?

Hope

Late that night, Daniel went to meet Tavake for his training session. The woman was paranoid about being discovered and so she chose a different beach to meet at every time. There was a light rain falling as he parked the truck beside her sleek black vehicle. He could see her waiting for him on the white sand.

But Daniel wasn't there to train. He had come ready to negotiate.

"You're late," said Tavake as he walked across the beach. Wet tendrils of her hair were plastered to her face and her dress billowed in the wind as she leaned lightly on her cane.

"You're early," corrected Daniel. "We said ten o'clock. It's nine fifty-nine."

The ghost of a smile. "Alright. Shall we begin?"

"I've got something to show you."

"What is it?"

He took his phone out of his pocket and pulled up the photograph, showed it to her.

A harsh, indrawn breath. "Where did you get that?" She grabbed the phone off him and studied the picture closely.

"Nafanua. She gave it to Leila."

"Of course …" Tavake breathed, her eyes alight and a strange smile on her face. "I should have known. There was no trust shared between us but we were still sisters who thought alike."

"It's a piece of the Tangaloa Bone, isn't it?" asked Daniel.

She turned cold and imperious. "Where is it now?"

"I have it. Somewhere safe."

"What do you want, Daniel Tahi?"

"Has your Council found the other pieces yet?"

An unwilling reply. "No. There have been some … delays. A few casualties. But it won't be much longer. Apollonia is a very determined woman." A grimace of distaste.

"Give me a chance to go after them, find them before your teams do."

"And then what?"

"I'll give you all three pieces. You said you were worried about power plays in your Council. Promise me you'll use the Bone to exorcise Pele from Leila's body. Promise me you won't kill her. We unite the three pieces and we fight together as a team."

"Why should I trust you?"

The wind and rain had picked up and Daniel had to shout over the surge and crash of the waves. "You can trust me more than the telesā in your Council. Even if I get all three pieces, I don't know how to use them. I need you. And you need me."

"You are mistaken. I don't need you and I won't negotiate with a child," Tavake said with chilling ferocity. "You bring me that Bone piece or you will be painfully sorry. This lesson is over." She pushed past him and began walking with her uneven gait back to the car.

"What about our Covenant?"

"What about it?" Tavake replied. "It only protects you against my Gift, not the ones you love. Don't cross me. It will be your friends and family who pay for your stubbornness. Starting with Salamasina."

"But you're her mother."

"Have you learned nothing of us Telesā? The day we were sure Salamasina was Ungifted, is the day she stopped being my daughter." Tavake paused to look back at him. "Bring me the Bone piece or I start hurting people."

Daniel's attempt at negotiation had been a miserable failure. *Now what?*

Back at the house, Simone noticed Pele wasn't in her room. Lesina was asleep and Keahi had gone. "Where is she?" he muttered to himself.

There was a hazy orange glow from the back yard. He opened the door and Pele's name died on his lips at the sight before him. She was sitting in the garden, cross-legged on the grass with her back to him, doing that meditating thing she liked. Only this time, her entire body was lit up in an elaborate spider web of crimson lines. The fiery patterns seamed the ground around her so the grass was criss-crossed with ruby red veins. It was both beautiful and frightening.

"Pele, everything alright?"

She turned at his voice, startled and the fire designs simmered and faded, leaving burnt black paths in the grass. "Please leave me."

Her words were muffled, like she'd been crying and Simone caught a glimpse of her face. Tear-streaked cheeks and a soulful sadness made him ignore her request. Carefully he picked his way through the smouldering lines. "Hey, what happened?"

The smell of charred earth was strong as he sat beside her. He made a face as he looked around. "Eww, you know there's centipedes and slugs out here?"

She snapped her fingers and a perfect sphere of flame appeared which she then began to manipulate idly. They both watched its flickering light as she had it dance between her hands and hover in the air. "You take your body for granted. All that it can do, all that it can feel. It's a wonderful thing," she said. "Until someone hurts you."

Simone still hadn't forgiven her for the flame fight the other night but he couldn't ignore the sadness in her voice. "What happened? It was Keahi, wasn't it? That worthless man-skank."

"He doesn't want me," Pele whispered.

It wasn't what Simone had expected and he was momentarily at a loss for words. "Oh. Of course he wants you."

Pele stood up and threw the sphere of fire into the air with vehement force. It soared high above them and then exploded at her command, lighting up the sky with a wild beauty. She didn't look at Simone. "I offered. He refused. He said it wouldn't be right." She was getting angry now. "I don't understand. I've seen Leila's memories. I know Keahi wanted her. I know he wants me now. This is his chance to have it all. It makes no sense."

"Men are dogs," said Simone soothingly. But inside he was agreeing with her. *It **doesn't** make any sense. Keahi the Man-Whore, you surprise me …*

The next day, Daniel was turning into the driveway to Leila and Simone's place when he saw Pele standing in the front yard. Keahi's bike was parked by the verandah but he was nowhere to be seen. Pele – dressed in a flame colored dress and wearing stiletto heels – was clearly not out for a power-walk.

He got out of the truck. "What you doing out here?"

"Choosing not to be around certain people," she said with an angry frown.

He didn't know what she was talking about and he was too tired to try and decipher it. He ran a hand over his hair in a worrying gesture that Leila would have recognized. It sparked something in her. A chord of familiarity. For the first time, Pele asked herself, why? *Why does Leila have an ocean of feeling for you?*

She took a moment to *really* look at him. She conceded there was no denying he was pleasant to look at. A strong, kind face and one could get lost in the green ocean of his eyes. He was dressed in a faded T-shirt and an equally faded pair of cargo shorts. It was another sticky hot day and the thin fabric of his shirt clung to his skin so that the contours of his arms and chest were clearly visible. Running his fingers through his tousled hair like that – the movement raised the edge of his shirt, revealing the skin at his waist, a hint of chiseled abdominal wall. His shorts hung low on his hips so she caught a glimpse of the tattoo stamped there. He was fine-tuned muscle and bronzed power – and today he was clearly on edge.

"There's something wrong with you," she stated flatly. "What is it?"

"Nothing," was his brusque response. Immediately followed by, "Everything."

"Don't tell me – you're angry with me again. What have I done this time?"

He gave her a look of surprise. "It's not you. It's my grandmother. She's so stubborn." He paced beside the truck, looking like he wanted to shove a fist through the window. "I bought a ticket for her to fly out to New Zealand today. A surprise holiday so I can get her away from all this but she won't go. How am I supposed to keep her safe if she won't listen to me?" Daniel grimaced as he remembered his frustrating conversation with Salamasina that morning. Even after telling her about Tavake's threats, she refused to leave. *Tavake won't hurt me Daniel. She's my mother.*

"You care about her a great deal, don't you?" said Pele. "You have feelings of responsibility for many people. That must be very tiring."

"Don't you?" asked Daniel.

Before she could answer, there were sounds of loud conversation and bustling activity. They both looked around. The noise was coming from down the road. Pele walked out the gate and Daniel followed. "There's something happening over there," she said. "What is it?"

Several houses down, there was a crowd gathered by the roadside, watching lines of people sitting cross-legged in front of a large open Samoan *fale* house. "It looks like an *ifoga*," said Daniel.

"What's an *ifoga*?" she asked, moving closer to where the spectators stood, pointing and whispering.

He followed her, keeping a close eye on their surroundings, mindful of the possibility that an *ifoga* could quickly turn ugly. "It's an apology done Samoan style."

She stared wide-eyed. The sun was a relentless burn but those seated on the hot ground were immovable with heads bowed and half-covered with finely woven mats of pandanus. "So they're just sitting there like that because they're saying sorry?"

"Yes. Someone from their family has done something bad and wronged another person from the other family. It's a shameful thing that reflects on all of them, so everyone comes to show they *really* regret what was done," Daniel said.

There were people sitting inside the raised *fale*. Eating their lunch with backs turned to the contrite crowd sitting outside. "But they're ignoring them," Pele pointed out.

"That's probably a good thing," Daniel said. "If the family refuses their apology, they can come out and attack the people outside. Hit them, abuse them – even use a bush knife on them in extreme cases."

"How can that be? You're lying," exclaimed Pele.

"No," said Daniel, "the wronged family has every right to do what they will with the apologizers."

"Does that happen?" asked Pele.

"It has in the past. But usually, an *ifoga* will lead to a family publicly giving the wrongdoers their forgiveness. A few years back, I saw the family of a convicted murderer do an *ifoga* for the wife of the victim. She could have sent the men in her family out to shame and abuse them but instead she went out and hugged them, invited them inside her home."

Pele couldn't take her eyes off the assembled crowd. "I could never do that. Be so vulnerable. So weak."

"That's what an *ifoga* means. By sitting there in plain sight for hours if necessary, you are publicly acknowledging that you're in the wrong and you'll accept whatever comes. No matter what. It's the ultimate act of humility. Together with your family, your *aiga*, you're an offering of vulnerability. But at the same time, if you think of it – it's an act of courage and strength. Sacrifice. And love. Because you're ready and willing to die for what you believe in. You'll risk death so as to atone for another's wrongdoing."

They were both quiet as they looked out at the *ifoga*. Elderly men, faces lined with age and sorrow. Young mothers, shushing their little ones as they huddled under the *ie toga* mat of humility. Old women, swaying in the heat but with unmoving commitment to the communal act of apology. Young men with sweat trickling down their bare backs, their *pe'a* an anthem of their shared heritage. All of them with bowed heads under an unfeeling sky.

"It's strangely beautiful," said Pele with a pensive look in her dark eyes. "There's been so much blood, so much vengeance in my millennia that I can't comprehend such a thing. What must it be like, I wonder, to have someone do such a thing for you?"

He didn't move, didn't touch her, didn't even look at her. But in that moment, Daniel felt the closest he ever had to this strange, new woman ever since she had first woken up on that confused morning. In that moment as they pondered upon an *ifoga* of strangers, Daniel felt the stirrings of a dangerous, alien emotion.

Hope.

That spark of hope was fuelled a little more when Daniel had an unexpected visitor at the workshop later that day. She was waiting for him, leaning against a Panamera when he drove up.

"Noa? What are you doing here?"

She was in Olohe mode today. Loose-fit white linen pants and fitted bustier top. On one arm she wore an ornate gauntlet of *siona* wood and burnished bone that ended in pincer sharp talons. On another woman, it would have seemed only ornamental, some chic modern adornment. On Noa it was a stark reminder of what she was. She gave him a sealed envelope. "This is from Iolana. Directions to the Bone piece locations. She said to tell you, that you won't be able to access them alone. Get your Gifted friends to help you. Move fast. The others will soon turn to these locations and it's imperative you get there first."

He was mystified. "Why are you helping us?"

"I'm not. I act and speak for Iolana. She wants you to have that."

He wasn't convinced. "How do you know about my friends? And who told you I was Vasa Loloa?"

A careless shrug. "I've been watching you for weeks. Iolana wanted you monitored."

"Who else knows about me? About us and our Gifts?"

"No-one. Besides Tavake of course," Noa said. "Don't worry, she's not going to hurt your grandmother. If she was capable of that, Salamasina would have been eliminated a long time ago and you would never have been allowed to live."

"I don't get it. Why hasn't Iolana turned me in? Why is she doing all this?"

"She's a sensate and sometimes, she sees things people don't want her to. It's vital Apollonia doesn't get the Tangaloa Bone." Noa opened her car door and then paused, "Oh, one more piece of advice from Iolana – when the time comes, let the youngest one among you take the lead."

"That's it? You're leaving? Offload cryptic words of wisdom and then leave? How do I know I can trust you?" demanded Daniel.

"You don't," snapped Noa. "And you shouldn't. Trust no-one. It might save your life."

Daniel wanted to snap back at her with a few choice words of his own – but instead he stood there and watched her drive away. Leaving him with an envelope of secrets.

Pulotu

The early morning had a slight drizzle to it that promised muggy humidity later in the day. Daniel picked up Talei from the dorm first before driving to Leila's house. Simone, Lesina and Teuila were waiting for them at the gate. They got in the back seat with hushed hellos.

"She's still asleep. Keahi just arrived to look after her. He brought Teuila," Simone told Daniel. Then he snapped, "Lesina your butt's getting too big. I can hardly fit in the middle here. What have you been eating?"

A dark shape moved from the shadowed verandah and walked to the car. Keahi. He kept his voice low. "You sure about this?" he asked Daniel.

"No. But it's all we've got to go on. If Iolana's instructions are correct and it's down there, then we'll get it," said Daniel. "Don't let Pele know what we're up to."

"I got this," said Keahi. A wry wince, "She's not gonna be happy to wake up and find she's stuck here with me."

"Yeah, well just don't burn our house down, eh!" interrupted Simone from the back seat. The others shushed him as Daniel reversed the truck. Simone blew the Hawaiian a kiss. Keahi gave him the finger. All was as it should be. Daniel drove down the hill and towards town.

"So tell me, where are we going?" asked Teuila.

Simone turned on the light in the back seat so he could read the directions from the paper Daniel had been given.

"It makes no sense. Pulotu isn't a real place, is it?" Teuila turned doubtful eyes at the others. "It's just a legend. A story they tell."

Talei interrupted the hesitant silence with impatience. "What kind of legend? What's Pulotu? I'm not Samoan, will someone please tell me what we're talking about here?"

"Pulotu is the Samoan spirit world. A place of darkness." Lesina volunteered the information with casual frankness. "My grandma would tell stories about it when we were kids. To scare us to sleep. It isn't real."

"We read about Pulotu at school when we studied Samoan mythology," said Teuila. "It's guarded by Saveasi'uleo the god of Pulotu who's supposed to be half-man, half-eel sometimes. Or Eel all the time. Or something like that. The legends say only people with royal standing like high chiefs and their families could go to Pulotu because they were the only ones with spirits. All the rest of us regular people didn't have spirits so when we die, that's it. We just die."

Simone scoffed, "Well, if Pulotu is a nasty world of darkness where you get to hang out with a slimy eel, then forget it. I'd rather be a peasant and not go there when I die." A quick glance at Talei who had confided in Simone on that fire-filled night when Pele attacked them in the car. "Oops, sorry no eel offence meant."

Talei gave her a half-smile, "None taken. I wouldn't want to be stuck in a cave with an eel-man either."

Simone nudged her shoulder and wriggled his eyebrows suggestively. "I don't know daaahling. It depends on the size of the eel."

The two of them burst out laughing until Daniel announced, "I don't care if it's just a story. It's where the Bone is, so that's where we have to go. According to the instructions from Iolana, we can find the entrance to Pulotu at Falealupo village in Savaii. That's where we're going."

"I still don't get it," interrupted Lesina. "Because of some old stories and a few clues from strangers we've never met, we're going all the way to Savaii looking for a bone piece that we aren't sure is even there. We don't even know what it looks like. What are we going to do when we get to Falealupo? Wander around hoping somebody drops a bone on our head?"

Teuila protested hotly. "You don't have to come if you don't like it Lesina. As I recall, you aren't even Leila's friend so why are we taking you with us anyway? We all know what happens to people who make the mistake of trusting you."

"You little bitch," hissed Lesina, "show some respect."

"Or what?" Teuila challenged from the opposite side of Simone, "Are you going to shoot me through the heart with a lightning dagger too?"

In answer the horizon ahead of them roiled with dark clouds and a massive jolt of thunder parted the sky. Who knows where the conversation would have led if Simone hadn't shut them both up with a flick of his wrists. "Girls please, *salapu*. You're ruining my day which I had such high hopes for. Look at it this way – we're going on a day trip to one of the most beautiful islands in the entire Pacific. Sightseeing with a gorgeous chauffeur. It doesn't get much better than this. If you're going to *beeatch* at each other then we'll leave you all behind. Me and Daniel would have sooo much more fun without you, wouldn't we baby?"

Against his will, Daniel had the hint of a smile, "I won't even try to argue with that." The mood in the truck lightened considerably as Simone preened, smoothing his hair back and touching up his lipstick. Teuila and Lesina both stared out of their separate windows, reining in their simmering hostility while Talei turned in her seat to mouth a silent "Thank You" at Simone. To which he simply huffed and rolled his eyes, *Am I the only one with any common sense in this car?!*

The rest of the trip was uneventful. Lesina and Teuila had unfinished business with each other but Simone was a successful buffer between them for the entire ferry ride and the long drive through rainforest lined roads to the village of Falealupo. They drove through the quiet settlement and continued on through lush rainforest. There were no more houses to be seen, just green bush and the occasional pig lumbering along.

"What are we looking for?" Talei asked Daniel.

"There's supposed to be a dirt road along here somewhere that will take us to the sea," answered Daniel, "ah, there it is."

He turned the truck down the rocky, bumpy road and everyone fell quiet. They could see hints of blue through the trees and the closer they got to the ocean, the more somber they felt. This was really happening. They were really going to do this.

The road opened up to a desolate shoreline with hungry waves beating against a line of rocks. Daniel stopped the truck and everyone got out, happy to finally stretch after the long drive. Daniel walked a short distance along the rocks and then pointed out to sea. "That must be it." He had to raise his voice to be heard over the crashing waves. He pointed to a cluster of black lava rock that jutted from a restless ocean, about two hundred meters away.

The wind had picked up now and Simone flailed his hands against the wind's fury. "Lesina, do you mind?"

"It's not me," she replied. "There's a storm brewing, didn't you listen to the weather forecast this morning?" She looked out at the darkening horizon. "It's a rough front and it's moving in fast." She raised her voice at Daniel, "Whatever we're here to do, we better do it quick before the storm hits."

Teuila was derisive. "Aren't you telesā *matagi*? Can't you make it go away?"

Stupid little girl Lesina's return gaze said. "We're attuned to the air elements. We can influence them but we can't just cancel them out. Only a Covenant Keeper with the full strength of a Sisterhood can summon and repel storms this big." She turned to Daniel. "I can try to soften it a bit, delay the full storm but it will only be temporary. It's a good sized storm and my Gift isn't strong enough to calm it, I'm sorry. We didn't pick the best day for bone hunting."

Daniel was grim. "We don't have a choice. We're doing this today." He started unbuckling the belt on his cargo shorts — which had Simone faking a flush.

"*Awolla*, it's getting a little hot out here. Daniel please, not now. Everyone's looking at us," he said.

He'd been trying to break the tension and it worked. Everyone smiled – except for Talei who snapped at Daniel, "What do you think you're doing?"

"Getting ready to go in. What does it look like?" He grabbed a fishing spear from the back of the truck and started walking towards the edge of the promontory. "Pulotu is supposed to be off the edge of those rocks. It's an underwater cave of some sort."

Talei stopped him with two hands firmly placed against his chest. "No. This is where I come in, remember? We talked about this."

Daniel shook his head, and gently but firmly moved her hands away. "Yes we did. And yes, you're going in but I'm coming with you."

"You're being foolish. I'm the only one who can swim underwater that far and if the Eel-God story is right, then I'm probably the only one who can make it past the guardian. You should stay here and let me check it out first," said Talei in a whispered undertone.

"No I'm not. This is my idea, my plan. Leila is my responsibility. I'm doing this," argued Daniel.

The others were confused. Lesina confronted them both. "What's this about? Why are you two fighting?"

Talei and Daniel exchanged looks before Daniel replied. "It's nothing. I'm Vasa Loloa so water isn't a threat to me. And I can hold my breath longer than anybody else here."

Talei disagreed with hands folded defiantly across her chest. With the wind blowing at her back, she was a striking figure.

"That's a lie. I can hold my breath longer than anybody else here."

Simone struck a pose, hands on his hips. "In that case, why don't you both go in and check out the nasty cave? And hurry up so we can go?"

The group continued moving towards the edge of the rocks while Daniel and Talei carried on with their muttered argument. 'No ... dammit. I won't let you do this alone ... well I won't allow you to do it at all ...'

Teuila stopped abruptly and raised her voice over the rushing wind. "Wait, what are you two not telling us? And why does Daniel have a fishing spear?"

Before he could shush her, Talei explained. "Daniel's grandmother told him some very important things about Pulotu, didn't she Daniel? Go on, they deserve to know the truth. You dragged them all out here. They're willing to take risks and put their own lives in danger for Leila. Tell them what you told me."

"Dammit Talei!" He turned to face the team. "Mama said that every legend has its roots in truth and not to take the Saveasi'uleo *aitu* story lightly. In Telesā history, there have been those who have given their spirit, their elemental essence to their Mother Earth like what my mother Moanasina did. If the Earth accepts them, they become one with either Ocean, Earth or Air. But sometimes, the Earth rejects their gift. And sometimes a Covenant will punish a telesā who breaks their rules by condemning their spirit to Mother Earth."

"So then what happens to them?" said Simone with raised eyebrows.

"Instead of accepting those telesā as one of her own, they're cursed. They become these ... creatures that have to hang around in creepy places, unable to have their spirit blend with their Mother Earth. Mama believes that the legends of the Eel *aitu* grew up around one such creature," said Daniel.

"There's more," said Talei. "Tell them the rest."

"The Olohe girl, Noa — she said the Council already sent two groups out there to get the Bone and they had to turn back. They had some trouble."

"Trouble?" exploded Talei. "He means, one woman died and two others ended up in the hospital."

"This is exactly the kind of stuff I hate," exclaimed Simone. "Daniel Tahi, I'm gonna *fuki-slam* you myself! This is supposed to be a team. We can't work together if you're going to keep secrets from us. Communication!"

Talei interjected, "That's why I'm the only one who should be going into that Pulotu cave. If there is some kind of eel down there, then she and I will get along famously. I'll be in and out in no time."

Talei peeled her top off and unhooked the clasp on her shorts, stepping out of them with practiced ease. Wearing only a two piece, hers was a bold beauty of generous proportions, with skin glistening like ebony silk. Coiling down the center line of her back was a mosaic of darker black patterning. "We'll do this together then. Try to keep up with me." And then she ran lightly across the rocks and jumped into the rough water. Surfacing she waved at them before diving. Before her skin rippled and her Dravuki twin-soul spoke as Eel.

Daniel was the only one who had seen her in Eel form before. Everyone else gaped. Simone smothered a yelp. "Ohmifreakingosh, look at that! She's huge." His voice was accusing as he turned to Daniel. "You told me she was an eel.

That is not an eel. That is a freakin Loch Ness monster." He waved his hands about his face for air, muttering. "She could eat us all."

Daniel cursed under his breath as Talei slipped under the waves. She had a head start on him. "If we're not back by sundown, then go ahead and take the truck. Catch the ferry and go home." He didn't wait for Simone to reply. Instead he executed a flawed dive into the choppy waters.

Simone threw his arms up in exasperation. "Fine. Go ahead. We'll just stand here like idiots." He stalked across the rocks back to the shore. "Come on girls, no point getting wet out here."

Talei moved through the water, undulating with the rippled current, eyes searching. This close to shore and it was unusually deep here. Strange. She still hadn't reached the bottom yet. She surged onward, moving along the rock face and downward, seeking for some kind of opening. Anything. It grew darker, the deeper she swam. She could see Daniel's shape far above her now as he tread water, waiting for her to find the cave entrance. Talei had never been afraid in the ocean before. At least not until today. Until now. As she made her way along the rock face, she noticed something else unusual. There were no fish anywhere. No other sea life. Nothing. The water was completely vacant of life. Where were the fish? Something, anything familiar? She shook the feeling of unease and continued on, crisscrossing the rock face for what seemed like hours. She was dispirited. This was hopeless. They were on a wild goose chase. There was nothing down here. Literally. These Telesā had rubbish prophecies, she decided.

That's when she saw it. Just as she was about to give up and head for the surface. A yawning hole in the craggy black wall of rock. Enough for a very short person to stand up straight and tall. And definitely enough room for a giant eel. Or a boy to swim through. For a moment she was tempted to enter the opening alone. But she had made Daniel a promise they would do this together. Not only that, she was scared. In that moment, entering a creepy chasm in an underwater rock wall was not something she wanted to do alone. *Hell no.*

She made note of the location, turned and swam back to the surface, sinuous and sure. She broke the surface right beside Daniel and she could tell he was startled by the way he leapt away from her in the water. He swore. "Talei, don't creep up on me like that."

She coiled around him in the water. Not touching him, just swimming in a lazy circle, hoping he would get the message to follow. "You found it," Daniel said, "Good work. Let's go."

He took a huge breath of air and followed after her down through the dark water. Talei wasn't sure how long he could hold his breath for. *I hope you weren't exaggerating, Ocean Boy …*

She kept a close eye on him all the same, watching for signs that he could be struggling, ready to nudge him back to the surface if he needed rescuing. But she needn't have worried. He swam with strong sure movements, aided by an invisible current. So quick that he was faster than she was.

He's cheating! She realized belatedly, that he was summoning a wave surge to carry him along while she on the other hand had to really exert herself to keep up. Just wait till she got him on land …

He saw the gaping hole and made for it. They both hovered at the opening for a moment and peered inside but it was too dark for them to make out anything. Even Talei's eel vision couldn't see anything. Daniel went in first and pushed forward with a mighty kick. Talei followed.

They were in a passageway. Rock above, below and around them. The walls were smooth and Talei could feel Daniel's surge current pushing them both along, helping them on their way. There was enough room for them both to swim side by side. At first it went straight ahead and then it began to slope downwards so they were swimming almost perpendicular. Talei began to worry. They were headed downwards. Deeper into the bowels of the earth. She could feel the pressure building in her gills, a tightness in her chest. She didn't like this. What impact was this having on Daniel? How would she get him out of here if he passed out?

But Daniel showed no sign of slowing. Onward he swam and so Talei kept going, following his lead. The walls glowed dimly with an eerie green luminescence which kept it from being a suffocating blackness. It felt like they had been swimming endlessly and then the tunnel leveled out and they broke through the surface of the water. Air. There was air. What was this place? Where were they?

They were in a massive vaulted cavern of some sort. A ceiling of more slime luminescence towered far above them. There was a narrow rock shelf running the full circle of the cavern and far off in the distance, the cavern narrowed and then opened again into another. So huge they couldn't see the end. Daniel breathed in huge gasps of air. It tasted stale. But it was air. He swam to the rock side and pulled himself up. "Talei, look at this place."

She shivered in the water, stretched and buckled, skin rippled and tore. Cartilage morphed. Pain. Daniel felt it with her and tried to put up a mental block so he wouldn't cripple against the onslaught. "Aaargh." He was dazed for only a moment though and by the time he raised his head again, his vision had cleared. Talei was sitting on the rock face beside him, shaking, legs curled in tightly in her arms embrace. He knelt beside her, "Hey, are you alright?"

In answer, she jerked away from him and vomited to the side. "Awww gross." She wiped at her mouth. "Yes, I'm fine now. There's just something about this place which is making my shift so much more difficult. That hurt."

He stood and stripped off his shirt. "Here. Wear this."

She looked up at him and smiled weakly at his briefs. "Poor Simone would have loved to be here for this. Lucky me."

He acknowledged her lame attempt at a joke with an understanding grin and then helped her to stand. "This place is massive."

"What are we supposed to be looking for?" she asked.

"I'm not sure. Iolana only gave directions on how to get here," said Daniel.

"Let's look around then. The sooner we find it the sooner we can get out of here."

The two of them started making their way along the narrow rock ledge, holding on to the green glowing wall for support. "Eww, this stuff is nasty," Talei groaned. "It's getting in my hair."

Daniel had to laugh at her wild mane that was now edged with glowing green slime. What he didn't laugh at was her continued nausea. Every few steps, she had to pause and retch. He patted her back. "What's wrong?"

She shook her head. "I don't know. It's this place. The air in here is making me feel sick. Or something is."

Finally, they reached the gaping entrance to the second cavern and ducked through, shuffling carefully along the narrow ledge. Once inside, they straightened up and stood in shocked amazement at the sight before them.

This cavern was even bigger than the first cave. The ledge widened so they could walk comfortably on a flat rocky landing. Before them was a vast lake and in its center a raised outcropping of rock. It jutted up out of the water in the shape of a huge stone kava bowl with bold tapa patterns chiseled into its sides. It was an imposing structure and definitely not a natural formation. "That must be it," said Daniel. "All that mumbo jumbo about the Tangaloa Bone and Pulotu was real. The Bone piece must be inside that thing."

Talei laughed delightedly. "Awesome. I'll go get it so we can get the hell outta here. I'll shift."

He stopped her. "No, I'll get it. You don't look too good right now." Unspoken between them was the question, what if she didn't recover enough to shift again. How would she make it back through the tunnel and up to the surface again? There was no way she could do it in human form. "Wait here."

Daniel carefully felt his way down into the water. It was clammy and slimy to the touch. A thick, black substance and not at all like the welcome embrace of the blue ocean he was used to. The clingy feel of it sent a shiver up his spine but he didn't say anything to Talei. She had enough to worry about as she stood there shivering and turning every so often to dry retch. He was in the water up to his waist now. Time to start swimming. He pushed off and began making for the stone altar in the center of the lake.

Talei tried to quell the nausea as she watched him swim with powerful strokes towards the altar. She was impatient. "Hurry up! Use your water boy trick to push you over there faster."

He tried. Nothing. He tried again. Reaching with his mind, his heart, his thoughts for the ocean within and its link to the ocean without. Nothing. It unsettled him but he kept swimming. Now *he* was feeling sick as the water tried to force its way into his mouth and nose.

He was halfway across when she saw it. A swell in the water. A rippling glow from far below. And then a gleaming of skin as a shape broke through the surface and just as quickly, submerged again. Talei shouted, "There's something in the water. Get out. Quick!"

Daniel jerked to a halt mid-stroke, trod water and looked around. "Where? I don't see anything."

Talei knew it from the pale luminescence in the water. She pointed, "There! To your right. Look to your right."

That's when it reared from the depths. It was a gargantuan thing that gleamed with a moth-like whiteness. A quick glimpse of a snake-like head and body that towered above him, a high pitched screech emanated from fanged jaws, and then the creature dived again, sending a rush of water towards Daniel. The water picked him up, tumbled him and hit him against the stone outcrop and then pushed him back into the lake again.

Talei screamed, "Daniel!"

She started moving along the rock ledge, while her eyes searched for the creature. Where was it? *Oh Lord help us, where is it?* Daniel was moving, swimming, climbing up onto the rock. She breathed a sigh of relief. He was alright. There was no sign of the creature. "Quick, get out of the water."

Daniel pulled himself up onto the rocks, chest heaving with exertion and looked around. "What was that? Where did it go?"

"I can't see anything from here. I'll shift and come over there." Talei started taking off the shirt he'd given her.

"No! Stay there. There's no point both of us getting caught." He waved her away and then slowly walked around the rock platform, peering intently into the water. Talei held her breath, poised at the water's edge, fighting to calm the stampede of panic inside her. The black water was completely still, the cavern eerily quiet.

Daniel was on the opposite side of the altar, with his back to Talei when she saw it. It started as a slow-moving current moving in a circular motion around the altar and then intensified to a whirlpool of churning madness. The black water became a mass of writhing coils moving over each other as the creature unfurled. She began to comprehend now the full length of it as the coiled layers kept sliding and rippling over each other as it swam around the center platform. It raised its head up out of the water and swayed as it peered down at the boy on the stone altar, presenting Talei with a clear view of it. A row of scaly spines ran down its back, and she guessed its width to be at least four feet in diameter.

'Saveasi'uleo watches over his kingdom with jealous eyes that see nothing. Guardian of Pulotu, he is one of the Ancient Ones cursed by Tangaloa to live forever, brooding on the error of his ways, festering in solitude. The Great Eel Saveasi'uleo.'

"Behind you!" Talei yelled.

Daniel swung around. At the same moment, the creature reared and struck at him. Gaping jaws revealed razor sharp teeth that dripped with silver saliva. Daniel leapt to one side but the serpent hooked onto his right leg, ripping into the flesh. He pulled free and fell backwards, stumbling over loose rock and half-falling. Again the serpent reared its head and bit at him. This time Daniel was quicker at getting out of the way and the serpent was frustrated. An eerie screech that had both Daniel and Talei covering their ears. Wincing.

Quickly, he took cover behind the altar, back pressed against the rock while the serpent swayed back and forth, frustrated, searching. Talei yelled across the water, "It can't see you. Stay still."

Daniel shouted back over the rock altar. "What?"

The serpent was moving with a sinuous grace around the center islet, searching for its prey while Daniel inched his way along, still in cover of the rock altar.

"It's blind." She recited from the information Iolana had sent them. "*Saveasi'uleo, guardian of Pulotu, watches over his kingdom with jealous eyes that see nothing.* It can't see you."

Daniel bobbed his head up over the rampart, "Yeah?" A screech and the serpent attacked again, moving its bulk with a sinuous speed that belied its size. "Aaargh! Get off." He arched his shoulder and side-stepped, narrowly avoiding getting his head ripped off. Instead the serpent's twelve inch fangs razed his back. A screech of frustration and the coils started moving as the serpent curved around the other side of the island. Daniel yelled at Talei, "Thanks a lot. It's got pretty good aim for something that's supposed to be blind."

Talei ran lightly along the rock ledge, along the edges of the lake, trying to get a better vantage point. Pulse pounding, heart thumping, breath panting. Furiously wishing, *Please don't let us die here. Please don't let a giant eel kill us.* She paused to shout back at him, "Movement. Keep still. It's sensing your movements."

With a quick jerk, the serpent turned its sightless eyes to stare right at her, poised. *Oh no.* "And sound. It can hear us."

That gave her an idea. Talei raised her voice and shouted even louder. She picked up Daniel's spear and started hitting it against the side of the rock wall. "Yeah, that's right Eel monster. I'm talking to you. Come on. Bring it."

The Serpent paused for only a moment and then it withdrew from its attack point over the boy crouched behind the rocks. It slithered over the floor with wet, slopping sounds as it wriggled its massive bulk back into the water. It sank beneath the dark liquid, leaving only a froth of bubbles. It was coming for her now.

Shift, shift, shift – dammit, shift! Talei muttered madly under her breath as she kept running sideways along the ledge, skirting the water, eyes trained on the blackness. It was coming. She could feel it. Daniel pulled himself up with hands clenched on the altar, used it as a support so he could stand and look across at her. Angry. "Talei! Get out of here. Go."

She ignored him. Shut her eyes and took trembling steps into the water, trying to focus, trying to breathe, trying to shift into something, anything. A prayer to the Ocean Goddess. 'Help me please …'

A few feet away from her the blackness churned and the head rose from the water. A silent snarl and Talei confronted a creature of darkest nightmares. Green moss was encrusted in its skin creases and as it leaned closer, Talei choked on its rank foulness. She tripped backwards before its wavering leer and landed hard on her butt in the shallows. The pain jolted her out of her daze and she knew what she had to do. *Focus, shift!* The serpent swayed and then lunged at the girl who lay sprawled before her.

Too late.

Skin rippled, flesh contorted, bone melted. The spear fell on the rocks. Talei was gone and in her place was a giant torpedo ray. With a six foot span and a long barbed tail, she was a fearsome sight. Grey skin mottled with white, her feather edges rippled as she skated away from the lashing eel. It emitted the same high pitched screech as it looped over itself, vainly trying to pin down the flat ray. But now its sheer size was a disadvantage, its massive coils all a tangle as it struck at the black water, again and again. Waves coursed across the lake and the surface churned with the beast's anger.

Daniel watched in horror. He couldn't see the ray now. He couldn't tell if Talei had been injured, where she was now or what she was doing. The creature dived with a resounding splash, waves lapping right up to where Daniel stood so that he was waist deep in water. He clambered on top of the kava bowl for a better view. Where was she?

As a torpedo ray, Talei's vision was pitiful but her other senses more than made up for it. Besides the water was so thick and dark she wouldn't have been able to see much anyway. No, Talei had shifted to this form for a very specific reason and she needed to put it to use. Rays are sluggish and slow-moving – she couldn't outswim the Eel. Talei sank to the bottom of the lake, felt her way along, and sent out her perceptors. It wasn't difficult to sense the Eel. Such a behemoth was the major disruptor force in the water and it was moving with such agitation that she immediately knew its position. It was almost right above her and she got a true sense of how big the Eel really was. It gave her no comfort. Her idea no longer seemed like a good one.

Oh well, here goes nothing.

The ray began to ascend at a sloping angle, moved its feathered edges along the belly of the eel, searching for a vulnerable spot. She couldn't find one. Unlike an ordinary Eel, this did not have the smooth leathery skin she was used to. Instead it was ridged with crusted mollusc plates, almost like armor. There were short spikes along its ridged centre line. The Eel felt her delicate investigations and it didn't like it. A swirl, a ferocious twining movement and the head was only a few feet away from her, gaping jaws of disapproval. The ray's envelope shape made it perfect for evading the biting, chomping teeth and she skittled along and around the eel's girth. *That was close!*

She kept searching for a weak spot. *There!*

A thrill of excitement as she saw a gaping flash of skin. A missing plate in its mollusc armor. She waved her dorsal fins and urged herself along towards it, attached and released the first jolt of electricity that she was named for. A regular sized ray can zap its prey with up to two hundred volts of sheer power. But Talei was not a regular sized ray. She was a four hundred pound, twelve foot long Dravuki shifter with the heart of a warrior and the courage of the ocean goddess. She had internal 'batteries' made of over half a million gelatinous plates and she hit the eel with everything she had.

The eel's reaction was immediate. It began to thrash and shake uncontrollably. The water churned with a mad ferocity and Daniel flinched and covered his ears against the bitter screeching noises. But it was over as quickly as it had begun. Yes, Talei's power was strong but the Eel was too large a mass for her to incapacitate for very long. Torpedo rays can stun fish much bigger than them – but this was – if the legend was to be believed – the Ancient Guardian. Perhaps even Saveasi'uleo himself? Ageless, cursed and confined to his personal hell of solitude to watch over the Tangaloa Bone. No, Talei's electricity wasn't going to knock him out. The giant eel writhed and contorted, trying to dislodge the source of the biting pain.

Talei's electricity was enough to distract the Eel though. Enough to make him very angry. A ray has a sunken mouth opening underneath its belly, with a line of pincer like teeth. Talei sank them deeper into the unprotected piece of skin on the Eel, continued releasing intermittent blasts of her voltage and hung on for the wild ride. Again and again the Eel shuddered and convulsed – then shook its head and intensified its wild snapping and jerking trying to dislodge the ray.

Daniel knew she couldn't keep this up for very long. Her batteries were going to run down soon. *Think, fast!* What to do? He needed a weapon. Something to attack the creature with. Without his ocean powers, he was useless, just a boy.

A boy with a traditional Samoan fishing spear. He peered through the dimness, excited. Where was it? He caught sight of the steel length on the distant rocks where Talei had dropped it. He dived into the black water without hesitation. This time, the Eel paid him no attention – still caught up in its frenzied madness of electricity. Daniel swam with quick, sure strokes to the shoreline. He grabbed the spear and pulled the thick rubber band tight, biceps straining with the pressure. "Now, let's do this."

He turned back to the melee, in time to see the Eel finally succeed in scoring its target. The Ray skittled away too late and the vicious jaws of the beast bit into her pectoral disc. It reared up triumphant, shaking the ray like a dog shakes a kitten. Daniel shouted, "No!" He dived into the water.

The Ray's soft, loose skin tore with the Eel's fury and she flapped loose, falling back into the water. The serpentine thing dived after the ray, coils twisting in a roller coaster of madness and then surfaced again, head twisting back and forth searching for its prey. Daniel paused, yelled and smacked at the water, "Over here. Come and get me. "

The huge head turned to the sound. Daniel swam the few remaining feet to the altar and found his footing in the shallows, wading backwards through the waist deep water with his eyes trained on the advancing Eel, drawing it to him. "That's right. Come here."

A piercing screech and the enraged Eel leapt for him, gaping jaws with a span of at least six feet. Daniel braced himself, dug his heels into the rocky ground, aimed and jabbed the spear up into the creature's mouth. A quick thrust upwards, an enraged screech and then he leaned in over the row of knife like teeth and anchored the other end of the spear into the mouth floor. The Eel flinched backwards, and in that instant, Daniel made a terrible error of judgement. He forgot to loosen his hand from the piece of rubber strapping attached to the spear handle and then it was too late. He was caught.

The Eel reared up out of the water taking Daniel with it, trying to dislodge the spear but it was firmly entrenched. It tried to shut its mouth – big mistake. The bottom of the spear got stuck further in its lower jaw and the Eel was well and truly wide mouthed. It looked like it had a giant sized toothpick propping its cavernous mouth open. And of course, there was a six foot rugby player still hanging off the side of its face. Daniel's arm was being yanked out of its socket as the Eel shook its head back and forth, screeching and groaning.

"Aaargh." He reached with his other hand and tried to loosen the band but his own weight now had it cutting into his wrist. He was going to either have his arm ripped off or the Eel was going to succeed in breaking every bone in his body as it swung him around, relishing in the cracking impact every time he collided with its armoured body. "Taleeeei, I really hope you can hear me. Help."

Far below, a Dravuki Shifter struggled to morph into her human shape while waves of agony threatened to drown her. The giant ray flapped weakly in the shallows. Her batteries were depleted and a huge chunk of her shoulder fin was missing. All she wanted to do was swim away into the shadows, find a soft corner of sand and burrow into it to lick her wounds. Block out this nightmare with giant Eels and Pulotu hell caves.

But she had made a promise to her dead mother. And so Talei summoned all her reserves and shifted. It hurt so bad that when it was complete, she just lay there in the shallows in a foetal position, sobbing. Her left arm and a section of upper torso were bitten almost all the way through. You could see the white of bone through the pulped red mess of tissue. Blood stained the rocks as she pulled herself up with her right arm. She had to hold onto her left shoulder because she was afraid it would separate completely from her body. She had a bloody vision of her arm falling off and being left to rot in this cave. No, she refused to let that be. She refused to let that happen. She refused to let this be the way it ended. She stood, leaning against the side of the stone bowl, drawing in huge gasping breaths. Daniel was stuck, trapped. How to help him? How to free him?

If only they had a knife so she could cut him loose. She caught sight of a length of bone carving lying on the kava bowl altar. It just looked like a piece of stick with a pointed end. This was what they were risking their lives for? She tried not to slip on the blood soaked rocks and reached to take the Shard in her hands. It was as long as her forearm and covered in etched markings but still, a very obscure thing in exchange for all this. She almost wanted to chuck it as far away as possible. Stupid thing. It was long, carved – and sharp. Very sharp.

Talei knew what she had to do. She took the Shard in her right hand and climbed awkwardly on top of the altar.

"Daniel, catch!" Talei aimed and threw the Shard like a javelin. Then she slumped to her knees and prayed it would find its target.

He saw it arching in the air towards him. It was an impossible throw to make. But her aim was sure and true because it was powered by prophecy. It was an impossible catch to make. But Daniel was guided by destiny. The Eel had paused in its mad threshing at the sound of her voice and was poised now, trying to identify her location. It was still enough that Daniel could reach with his free hand – and catch the Shard in mid-air. "Yes!"

He raised the Shard and slashed at the banding, severed it. Then he fell to the black water below. Freed of its pesky attachment, the Eel resumed its maddened thrashing and Daniel was in danger of being crushed. He surfaced and quickly swam towards Talei, still gripping the Shard tightly in one hand. His face paled at the sight of all the blood on the rocks.

"Come on, we have to get out of here." He flinched to see the state she was in. Her eyes were closed, her breathing was shallow. Daniel hoisted himself up over the rim and then carefully lifted her in his arms. "I got you. Let's go."

She moved with him, weak but still responsive. Together they entered the water. He gave her the Shard, "Here you hold this. I'll get us across to the other side." She was shaking her head and muttering in dissent but he ignored her.

Daniel swam with her in the rescue position. The swim seemed to take forever. It wasn't an easy task because Talei was no lightweight and the frenzied thrashing of the Eel had the entire lake awash with waves. At the other side, Daniel half-carried her out of the water. "Just hold on. We're almost out of here. I need you to stay with me, okay? Can you shift?"

She clutched at his arm and whispered, "You go. Leave me. I can't make it."

"No. I'm not leaving you," he said, angry she would even suggest it.

Behind them there was a crashing sound as the Eel's girth slammed into the stone altar. They looked back. The kava bowl had crumbled under the creature's weight and now it was swimming towards the outer edges of the lake. "Uh oh, I think it knows the Bone is gone," Daniel said.

The sightless beast reached the cave wall across from them and started ramming it. Mouth still pinned open wide. The cavern shook and loose rocks fell into the water around them. "It's trying to find us," Talei said. "You have to go."

The enraged beast was getting closer. The walls were crumbling around them. Roaring, crashing, groaning sounds. Daniel sheltered Talei and yelled over the din, "Try to shift."

She shook her head at him. "I can't. I tried. Go."

He picked her up and slung her over his shoulder. She tried to fight him but she was too weak. "If you can't shift, I'll take you like this."

He carried her over the rocks and to the water way where they had first entered the cavern. Behind them was chaos as boulders fell from the ceiling. The entire place was caving in. Soon it would be too late. Daniel slipped into the water and steadied Talei in his arms, looked into her eyes. "Take a deep breath. Swim with me for as long as you can and then I'll take you the rest of the way."

"It's too far. I won't make it. I'm only going to slow you down. Just go."

He was angry then. Shook her. "I'm not leaving you. Look at me. Whatever happens on the way back, know this – I won't leave you. Do you understand me? Now take a deep breath."

She did as she was told and then with the world falling down around them and the angry scream of an Ancient Guardian in their ears – they dived together.

Daniel made Talei go ahead of him through the murky water. She could only use one arm, the other dangled uselessly at her side. She swam and alternately pulled herself along on the tunnel wall. Talei was strong and her will to live was even stronger. For a moment there, she even thought she would make it and that gave her an extra spurt of energy as hope lent added fire to her veins.

Ahead of them she could see the growing light of the familiar ocean. But hope can only power one so far before the burning fire for oxygen takes over. Talei faltered and then halted. Panic choked her. She fought it hard, kicking and writhing. Daniel came up beside her and took her hand in his. Held it with firm resolve. *I will not leave you.* His eyes spoke to her. *I will take you home. Trust me.*

She looked into his eyes, stopped struggling. And let go. Bubbles of surrender rushed from her mouth as water rushed into her lungs. She went limp.

Daniel knew he didn't have much time. He gripped her under the arms and kicked, propelled them both forward, out of the tunnel and into the welcoming outer ocean. Here, he was master. Here, he was home. He felt the tingling rush of awareness as Vasa Loloa welcomed her son of the ocean. There was still so far to go and every minute was one that took Talei further and further away. Daniel called for ocean's might and she answered with a surging current that propelled them upwards with elemental speed. Several heartbeats later and Daniel broke the surface of the water with Talei in his arms.

They exited to the storm Lesina had warned them of. The water was choppy and windswept. The current took Daniel and his precious cargo to the shallows and he walked the last few steps to the sand, carrying Talei in his arms. Speed was of the essence. *Quick, quick, quick.* He lay her body down the sand, threw the Bone piece to the side and ignored the pelting rain as he carried out CPR. *Breathe, pump, pause, breathe, pump, pause.*

Daniel saw nothing, felt nothing, heard nothing else as he worked over Talei's body. There was an eerie familiarity to the scene. Not so long ago he had been on another faraway beach, trying to bring another back to life. Somehow he doubted an ocean spirit was going to appear and heal Talei.

Daniel knew she had a good chance of surviving. She had only been in the water without oxygen for a bare few minutes. She was strong and healthy. She was a fighter. She would make it. He refused to give up.

And was rewarded with her cough and start. "Yes!" he exclaimed. She stirred and coughed some more and he helped her turn over so she could cough and spew up what seemed like half the ocean.

When she had caught her breath, she looked up at his triumphant smile and said, "You did it. You promised you would get me out – and you did it."

"You're not the only one who keeps promises," Daniel said. His smile faded in the rain as he studied her wounds. "We've got to get you to the hospital. Fast. Come on. Can you walk?"

"I think so," she said.

He helped her stand, grabbed the Bone and together they walked up the beach to where he had parked the truck. "I wonder where the others are?" Daniel said. "Knowing Simone, they probably took off to the nearest resort bar to party through the rainstorm."

He was wrong. So very wrong.

They came over the rise of lava rock and that's when they saw them. A group of women walking toward them uncaring of the rain. Daniel counted six of them. Three walked ahead, dressed in green shifts that swirled about them in the tempest. Another three brought up the rear. They wore white and had the familiar shaved heads of the Olohe. The rain was coming down so fast and thick it was hard to see clearly. Daniel and Talei stopped as one of the green clad women – the leader? – called out to them, "Ahh, there you are. We've been waiting for you."

Daniel raised his voice, "What do you want?" He was afraid he already knew the answer.

"The Bone," the leader said. She shaded her eyes against the biting rain. "Thank you for getting it for us."

"I'm not giving it to you," he said.

She laughed. "Oh I think you will." She called over her shoulder. "Olohe, show him."

The three figures in the white of the Keawe assassins, came forward. Each of them pushed a captive ahead of them, hands bound behind them and around their necks – a deceptively thin rope – the Ka'ane strangulation cord. Simone, Teuila and Lesina. "Your friends, I believe?" said the lead figure. She indicated Simone who was the only one gagged. "This one wouldn't shut up. Got quite a mouth on him."

In response, Simone made some muffled sounds and struggled against his restraints. Until his Olohe guard tripped him with one deft movement and shoved a foot against his back, holding him face down on the black rock.

"Stop it," Daniel said. Low and deadly. The rough surf crashing on the rocks beside them, roared even louder but he fought to control his ocean heart and still the blue fire that threatened to erupt. He thought of Tavake's warning and urged his Gift to be still.

The lead telesā snapped back. "No. I'm not here to play games words with you boy. This is an exchange. Give us the Bone and you get your friends back. Alive. Defy us and they will be the first to die."

She raised one hand to the sky and a dagger of lightning and a roll of thunder complied. Then she seared a line of fire down the rock face between them, marking a path of deadly intent. A torrent of wind raised her up several feet above the ground. "We are Ariki from Rarotonga. We speak to the heavens and they answer. We speak with the voice of thunder and rage with the light against all who defy us."

If she was hoping for awe and terror – she was disappointed. This wasn't Daniel's first time facing off against Air guardians. *Been there, done that. Lady, I've seen way worse.* Yeah, when you're the covenant lover of a *Fanua Afi*, it takes a whole lot more than big noise and flashing lights to impress you …

Daniel had a choice to make. It would have been so much easier if it had been only him on that rocky plain by the ocean. But it wasn't. Beside him, Talei swayed, weak from blood loss and going in to shock. He had a responsibility to get her to safety. Simone, Teuila and Lesina were only here today because they were helping him to save Leila. The ghost of a grin flickered across his weary face as he remembered Keahi's words, '*We're a team. Like the X-Men …*' There was only one choice he could make.

He brandished the Bone in one hand and said, "Let them go first."

She laughed and the sound was swallowed up by the storm. "You're not giving the orders here." She turned to one of the Olohe, "Go get the Bone."

The figure in white handed her captive over to another and came toward Daniel. It was Noa. She was a stranger and Daniel hurt and raged inside at her indifference. She stood in front of him and put out her hand. Her fingers were clothed in barbed shark tooth claws. "Give it to me," she said.

"You betrayed us," he said quietly.

Her eyes flashed with anger. "No," she hissed under her breath. "Iolana under-estimated how quickly Apollonia would send out another team to try getting into the Pulotu cave."

The lead telesā woman called out, "Hurry up Olohe. What's taking you so long?"

"So this is what you do? You're their guard dog?" Daniel asked urgently, low enough for only her to hear. "They say jump, they say stab and you do it, no questions asked?"

For a moment something flickered in her eyes. Something real and tender. But then it was gone. She pointed at Teuila and said, "Give me the Bone or I'll start breaking her fingers. One by one."

Daniel handed it over. She walked away to give it to the leader. The woman took it with a reverent beatific smile and gave the order. "Release them."

The Olohe untied their captives and then followed after the Ariki as they left the beach. Lesina went to help Simone up. As soon as the gag was loosened, he let rip with a stream of insults and curse words – confirming that he was indeed – alright. Daniel ignored him. His main concern was for Talei. With the immediate threat gone, she let go of her thread of reserves and crumpled.

Daniel grabbed her and called to the others for help.

They bundled her to the truck, lay her down on the back seat and covered her with a lavalava. Lesina grabbed the keys, "I'll drive." A glance at Daniel. "You look awful."

Daniel didn't argue. He just pulled himself into the open tray of the truck and slumped there as Lesina reversed with precision. The rain was a thousand needles of disappointment. He was beaten. Exhausted. They had been through hell and Talei still wasn't in the clear.

But it had all been for nothing because they were returning to Upolu without the Bone piece and they were no closer to a weapon for saving Leila.

Flying Fox

There was no time to waste. Daniel wanted them to go after the second Bone piece the very next day. "We have to get that Bone before they do," he said to the others.

Talei wasn't happy about being left behind for this one. But with her injuries, Daniel was insistent. "No. Don't be stupid. It took two hours for the surgeon to stitch your shoulder up. They didn't even want to let you out of the hospital this morning."

"My arm's fine. I can help. You need me," she argued.

Simone jumped in, "Yeah, how? You going to shift into a three-legged dog and sniff out the next Bone piece for them?"

Talei mouthed '*beeatch*' at him and turned back to Daniel. "You shouldn't be going at all. After what happened yesterday? You need more back-up."

"He's got me," said Keahi.

Simone jumped in. Again. Dismissive. "You're even more useless than Talei would be. Without Leila to suck fire off, you're nothing."

Daniel asserted his peacemaker powers. "Hey, calm down. Keahi's got martial arts skills that will be helpful if the Olohe show up. And if necessary, Lesina's lightning can spark Keahi. My worry is for you Simone. You going to be okay with Pele?"

"Don't worry. She has no clue what you're all up to. I'm taking her for a girl's spa day. Three hours for massage, manicure and all over body treatments. She's intrigued. I told her it's the perfect cure for an encounter with a jerk," said Simone with a dark look at Keahi. "Just make sure you come back."

Iolana's instructions for the second Bone piece had been a bit more vague than those for Pulotu. They were to go to Lalomata village and have a guide take them to the valley of the Pe'a. Once there, Iolana's note said, 'Search the valley for star mounds.' That was it.

After packing a few supplies, the group of four set out with Daniel at the wheel. They took the inland mountain road and drove for what seemed like hours. It wasn't a pleasant drive. Daniel sorely missed Simone's banter which was always a strategic buffer for tension. What was he supposed to say to a boy who only a few days before, had been making out with the girl he loved? Uncomfortable didn't even begin to sum it up. Lesina in particular didn't like being stuck in a small space with Keahi and Teuila, two of her least favorite people. She ignored them both and instead stared out the window at the passing rainforest.

Everyone was relieved when they reached the mountain village of Lalomata. Daniel parked beside a dingy roadside store and went to inquire about a guide to the valley of the Pe'a. He came back to the truck with a strange look on his face.

"What's wrong?" asked Lesina.

"Shopkeeper said we'll have a hard time finding anyone willing to take us to the valley," answered Daniel.

"Why?" asked Keahi. He got out of the truck and walked around to join Daniel.

Daniel shaded his eyes from the glaring sun as he looked up to the looming mountains. "He says it's a long hike through the bush and the valley is forbidden anyway."

"You offered to pay, right?" said Lesina.

"Yeah. He's calling around, seeing if anyone wants some cash. We have to wait," said Daniel.

The four moved to sit in the shade of a nearby mango tree. They didn't have to wait long. A young man showed up on a rickety bicycle and introduced himself as Paulo. "The valley is far from here. We can go some of the way in your truck but then we'll have to walk," he said.

Once Daniel had negotiated payment with him, everyone piled into the truck and they continued up along a winding mountain road until Paulo pointed for Daniel to turn down a grassy track. They drove into looming forest and the old vehicle groaned in protest as it tried to churn over rocks and uneven ground. Teuila marveled at the stately old trees that closed in on them. "It's beautiful." She reached out to touch leaves as they went past and trees softly bent their heads to oblige. A rustling, soothing sound.

Lesina snapped at her. "Quit it. We don't want the whole damn forest coming after us." She didn't know for sure what Teuila's Gift was, but she knew it had something to do with plants.

"You're the only one in this car it would rip to pieces," Teuila said sweetly.

Daniel wished for the hundredth time that he wasn't stuck with two telesā girls that could still have the energy to stab at each other even while they were all supposed to be in the middle of a war. His grip tightened on the wheel. "We're here, the end of the track. We have to park and hike the rest of the way."

The girls shared an unhappy look. Here was one thing they agreed on. Hiking through a steaming rainforest, slapping at mosquitoes was not their idea of a good time. Everyone got out and the boys grabbed the packs. Daniel handed Keahi a bush knife and took one for himself. "Let's go. Follow Paulo."

The bush knives made Lesina nervous but she relaxed a bit when she realized they were for hacking a path through the thick bush. Keahi and Daniel took turns with their guide to blaze a trail while the girls followed behind them. The deeper they went into the forest, the more Teuila soaked in the green, the breathing, humming life all around them. It spoke to her Gift and she relished in it. Lesina hated the outdoors and her grumbling got louder as the hour wore on, especially as the terrain began to incline. "Owww! Freakin' bugs. How much further?"

"There," Paulo answered. He pointed further up the ridge. "There's a shortcut through the mountain there."

Lesina groaned. "That's so steep though! I can't walk up there." She slumped against a fallen tree stump.

"You could have stayed in the truck," Teuila snapped. "Then we wouldn't have to put up with your whining."

The boys exchanged pained looks. At least on this they were in agreement. *Girls and their issues. Get over it already ...*

"We could stop for a little while and rest," said Keahi loudly at Daniel. "But I'd hate to sit down around here. You know, because of the snakes."

Lesina leapt to her feet, eyes wide and searching everywhere all around her. "Snakes? What? Where?" She scurried over to stand beside Paulo. "I thought there were no snakes in Samoa?"

The others shrugged at her. She grabbed the bush knife from the guide and started moving. "Hurry up, we need to get out of here."

"Nice one Keahi," muttered Daniel with a half-smile as he walked after Lesina. There was no more tiredness or complaining from her now.

"Anything to keep her moving," said Keahi. Together, he and Teuila brought up the rear.

With everyone moving at a brisk pace, they were soon halfway up the ridge. Paulo pointed to a cavernous opening in the hillside. He spoke in Samoan and Daniel translated for Keahi's benefit. "He said the shortcut is through there. Not far. On the other side is the valley of the Pe'a."

"Finally," said Lesina. "Come on, let's get this over with."

There was a renewed burst of energy as they walked up to the cavern. It was bright and airy, nothing like the underwater cave of horrors that Daniel and Talei had gone through. It was huge with smooth lined walls of sand colored stone and the air was fresh and clean. Paulo hung back though and indicated. "Go in that way. Tunnel connects to the valley. You walk straight through there."

"Aren't you coming with us?" asked Keahi.

"No. *Ua sa.* It's forbidden," said Paulo. "I'll wait for you outside."

The group walked a few feet into the tunnel and then stopped short. There must have been a rockslide some time ago and the path was blocked by boulders and dirt.

"Dammit! Now what?" said Keahi.

"Paulo!" Daniel called out.

The young man cautiously made his way inside the tunnel. "Yes?"

"Is there any other way into the valley?" Daniel asked him.

"You can go over the mountain. There is a track on the other end of this ridge. Very far. Very high to climb. It will take you a long time," said Paulo.

"I don't believe this," said Lesina. "We came all this way for nothing." She glared at Daniel like it was his fault.

"Maybe we can dig through this?" said Keahi. The boys tried to shift a few of the rocks but quickly gave up. They were far too heavy to be lifted.

"No, not gonna happen," said Daniel. "We're going to have to go back and take the long route."

"But that's going to take hours! It'll be dark soon," Teuila said.

"We don't have a choice," said Daniel.

Just then, they heard a hum overhead. "What is that?" said Lesina. They all ran back outside to look heavenward. In time to see the red chopper approaching the forested hilltop.

"It's headed this way," said Keahi.

They watched as the helicopter neared and then hovered for a moment before continuing its ascent up and over the mountainside. They caught sight of a few familiar faces looking down at them before the aircraft flew away. The Air leader from the beach and the Olohe.

"It's them!" said Lesina. "Just great. We hike all day and they zoom in on a chopper? We may as well go home now. There's no way we're getting through there."

"No way … unless, Teuila?" said Keahi with a piercing look at the younger girl.

"Unless what?" she said.

He pulled her to the side, whispered conversation. "Unless you move it."

She pulled away from him, gave the others a furtive glance. "Shh … move what? With what?"

"I don't know why it's such a big deal. So what if they know? In case you haven't noticed, we're all a travelling freak show."

She muttered, "I can't. I've never used it on purpose. I don't really control anything. It just pops out when I need it."

"Yeah? Well, we need it. Now. Come on."

Keahi put a stop to her excuses and walked back to the others. "Teuila's going to have a go at it."

He didn't wait for a response, didn't say anything more to clear up the confusion on their faces. Just stalked into the cave with Teuila dragging her feet behind him. Daniel and Lesina followed until they were all once again, faced with the blocked path. Teuila gave Keahi a desperate look. Hissed, "I can't do this."

He put both arms on her shoulders and looked in her eyes for a long moment. Everything else, everyone else faded away as he spoke with surety and unusual tenderness. "You've got this. I know you do. I'm right here beside you."

Lesina arched a knowing eyebrow at them but kept quiet. Especially when Keahi walked back to stand beside her. "Don't even say it."

"I didn't say a word," said Lesina with a fake aggrieved expression.

"Don't even think it then," growled Keahi.

Lesina just folded her arms and smiled. It was annoying. But there was no time to get into it because Teuila was trying to do the impossible. Make earth move simply because she asked it to and not because she was mad. Or in danger. Just because she asked it nicely.

Teuila moved forward and placed her hands on the rock barrier. Breathed deeply. Relaxed. Unlike the other telesā, Teuila didn't feel a wire of connection with her element. She didn't focus on it to hear its pulsing essence or feel it breathe. No, Teuila was unlike any telesā who had ever walked this earth because in her, all three elements flowed. She was a conduit for the most basic and essential life force of earth itself. So she didn't think of water, fire or air. She didn't try to talk to an element or bend it to her will. She just shut her eyes and thought about random things. Her favorite flowers. The way they smelled. The way leaves felt on her face. The way sun kissed her skin and grass tickled at the backs of her legs when she was lying under a blue sky. And behind all that, Teuila had a little wish. A longing.

If only these rocks would move and let me through. It would be so nice.

And so they did.

A rumbling, groaning sound, a scattering of dust and a narrow passageway opened up before them. Through it they could see an almost identical cavern to the one they stood in. Sun-filled, clean and airy. Golden light and soft-swaying greenery beckoned from beyond it.

Keahi whooped, "You did it!" He lifted Teuila up and swung her around in the air. She fought free with an embarrassed smile.

"Put me down," she said.

"What was that?" Lesina asked. Incredulous, she looked at the younger girl with new-found respect in her eyes.

"Oh, just a little something that useless people like me do when the real powerhouses in the room can't manage," Teuila said.

"Not bad," said Lesina, "for a kid."

Daniel gathered up their gear. "Come on. Let's go find that Bone piece." He put down the bush knife he was carrying and checked the water bottles in his backpack were full before he walked out of the cave.

Keahi called after him, "Hey, aren't you going to take the knife?" He gave Daniel a look heavy with meaning.

Daniel shook his head. "I don't need it."

"Okay Mr. Badass, whatever you say," said Keahi under his breath. He strapped his bush knife to his back and followed after the other boy.

They exited the cavern and stood there for a moment, blinking to adjust to the light. The Valley of the Sacred *Pe'a* was not very big. Nestled in the crook of three intersecting mountains, it was only a bare few miles across. A patch of dense greenery with a glint of water in the center. A little lake that probably ran dry during the dry season.

"Look! It's leaving," said Lesina. The chopper rose up over the trees and veered away. "They must have found it already."

"No, see there?" Keahi pointed down by the water where they could make out a small group of people. "There's nowhere for it to land. It must have gone down as low as it could and they bailed over the lake. We've still got a chance."

"We're looking for a star mound," said Daniel as he scanned the valley below. "A stone platform, kinda like the floor of a house in a five sided formation, built up above the ground. It will be covered in bush and look like a small hill from a distance. Iolana's directions say the taulaga pe'a is close to a star mound."

"Like that thing?" Teuila pointed to a rise of green in the tangled forest below.

"Must be," said Daniel. "Come on. We have to get to it before the Council does." He took off at a halting run down the side of the hill, skidding on loose rock and grabbing onto liana vines to steady him.

Keahi and Teuila followed close behind while Lesina moved in a more sedate fashion, cursing the sun, the dirt, the bugs and everything else that seemed to be conspiring to make her life hell. At the bottom of the hill, Daniel continued to lead the way, running through dense bush with a fierce intensity that the others tried and failed miserably to imitate.

It didn't take them long to reach the odd rise in the green foliage which Lesina had seen from far above, but they were still too slow. They heard them before they saw them. Women's voices shouting, snapping out orders and over it all the high pitched chittering of agitated flying foxes. "So much for sneaking up on the flying foxes," Keahi muttered.

Lesina skidded to a halt beside them, her face paled, "What is that? I've never heard flying foxes sound like that before."

There was a scream and then a rip of lightning startled them all. Someone was shooting with sky fire. A cloud of seething creatures raised up in the sky above them, so many flying foxes they blocked out the sun for just a moment before they sank back down. "Doesn't make any sense," Daniel said, "they'll take off at the slightest sign of danger. What's making them stay?"

He was the first to push through the trees and break free into the clearing. They all stood and stared at the chaotic scene. The tree before them was easily the largest one in the forest. It towered above all else and its outspread branches were a labyrinth of foliage and vines. But what made it even more awe-inspiring were the flying foxes. They clung to every branch in thick bunches like layer upon layer of overlapping scales, ticks on a dog. The air around the tree was also thick with the flying creatures wildly doing battle with the band of telesā and Olohe women. Daniel counted three telesā and one Olohe on the ground struggling against the seething mass of creatures with intermittent flashes of white lightning while another two were climbing up the tree.

"What are they trying to do?" Teuila said.

"Whatever it is, they've pissed off hundreds of *pe'a*," Keahi said, grimly. "Get down!" He pulled Teuila down to huddle beside him, in time to evade a stray *pe'a* that had targeted her face. He looked over at Daniel with a grimace of distaste, "It's like a Dracula horror movie. What are we looking for?"

"There!" Daniel said. He pointed towards the top of the tree. Everyone gaped.

"No way ..." Lesina whispered.

It stood out from all the others. A *pe'a* that was double the size of the rest, fur bleached white with age. It was pinned to the trunk by a long spear and it struggled against it with jerky, heavy movements.

"It's trapped. That's why the other *pe'a* aren't leaving," Teuila said.

"Look, it's holding something," Keahi said.

The white *pe'a* clutched in its claws a length of carved bone.

Flying foxes chittered and squawked as they descended in droves on the women that were vainly fighting them off with every weapon at their disposal. The Olohe on the ground had a spear and worked with a calm intensity to stab at the *pe'a*, while two of the telesā were using flashes of lightning to deflect and in some cases – incinerate the creatures. The other was just screaming and batting wildly at the claws that were tormenting her.

"Why isn't she using lightning to zap them?" Teuila said.

"She must have run out of juice. These telesā are nowhere near as strong as my mother and her Sisterhood were," Lesina said.

"We have to get to that white pe'a before it frees itself," said Daniel. As they all looked, the ancient flying fox lunged against its confines, enough to tear through its wing a little, but not enough to break free of the spear that staked it to the tree. It made a horrific shrieking sound which had them covering their ears and spurred the anger of the swarm of flying creatures. "I'm going up there. Keahi, can you and Lesina take care of the women on the ground?"

He took off running towards the tree without waiting for a reply. Lesina glared after him. "Fabulous, I get stuck with the bratty rock girl and the Man-Whore," she muttered. "How do you want to do this?" she asked Keahi.

He couldn't answer because just then the Olohe girl caught sight of them. She took one last swipe with her spear at the pe'a hovering over her and then hurled it with sudden swiftness at Keahi's. He saw it coming and with a deft move to the side – the spear missed its target and embedded in the trunk of a tree behind him instead.

The Olohe didn't hesitate though. As soon as the weapon had left her hand, she followed it with a sprinting leap towards Keahi. He caught a glimpse of her attack from the corner of his eye as he twisted to avoid the spear and so he was ready with a grappling move. He caught her and brought his knee up to her mid-section. It barely fazed her. He felt her hand reaching for the knife at his back. *No!*

He could not let her get that knife. An elbow to her face, once, twice. But still she grabbed the handle of the machete and pulled it from the holster. A step back and then she swiped at him. He side-blocked the blade but she hit him in the face with her other hand and he was caught off guard for an instant. She spun around and hacked at him with the machete again. This time, he took a glancing cut into his upper arm. Ignoring the flash of pain, he ducked into a sweeper kick that took her off feet.

For a moment she was on her back on the ground and their eyes met. A spark of awareness as two warriors recognized the deadly skill of the other. And then she rolled and sprang lightly to her feet. The fight continued. Anyone watching would have marveled at their grace and agility. They were like two dancers in a well-choreographed symphony of movement. Feint, twist, lunge, parry, thrust, leap, spin. On it went as they skirted the edges of the clearing, back and forth, using the natural arena around them as it came in handy. Keahi was good. But the Olohe was better. A shout from Teuila had Keahi turning his head and that moment of distraction was all the Olohe needed. A quick movement and she had a ka'ane strangulation cord around his neck.

"Now, you die," she whispered in his ear.

While Keahi was in the fight of his life, Lesina was busy with her own kind of drama. The Council telesā had turned their attention to the newcomers and targeted Lesina with wind and lightning strikes. She fired back at them with shots of her own but her Gift that wasn't very strong to begin with, was in panic mode and not much of a threat. She huddled behind a rock as the two women called out to her, "You're outnumbered! Come out so we can show you what a real lightning kill-strike looks like." Laughter.

Fear ran wild inside Lesina as she tried – and failed – to spark the fragile Gift inside her. But she had nothing left. A long time ago, Lesina's mother had sent her away because her Gift was not strong enough to join Nafanua's Covenant. She hadn't wanted her to ever become a target for other stronger telesā. She'd paid for her to go to university in America,

'I want you to be successful. The best in your field. I don't want anyone to ever put you down, you hear me?' You can be more than I was. You can be more than your Gift ...'

And now, here she was groveling in the dirt while Air telesā mocked her, while they dragged out her death by lightning strike. She thought of Jason. The one who had loved her and thought she could be more and love more. The Lesina he had loved wouldn't cower in the mud crying. She heaved in a huge gasping breath. If this was going to be the end, she would face it standing up, with her face to the wind. Lesina stood, stepped out from the rock cluster and shouted, "Take that bitches." She threw everything she had left into the blaze of wired energy that ricocheted across the clearing towards the other telesā.

It was a noble effort but one they easily deflected. "Is that all?" one asked. The two women linked hands and powered up.

Lesina winced at the fiery sight of two matagi telesā poised to attack. The next instant, the earth moved beneath her feet and she fell backwards. She lay there stunned for a moment. The earth shifted again and rolled her so she was once again sheltered behind the rocks, this time covered in a confection of dirt and rotting foliage. It was everywhere. In her hair, eyes, mouth and even her nose. "Yuck!" Lesina screeched, all thoughts of lightning attacks forgotten. She tried to wipe muck out of her eyes as she struggled to stand up, slipping and sliding. *What happened?*

Someone stood over her and yelled, "Stay down! What were you thinking?"

It was Teuila. Before the Council telesā could react to this new addition to the fray, Teuila did a sweeping motion with her outstretched hands. The mudscape responded and the earth slid underneath the Ariki's feet. Shrieks of panic as they clung to each other. "What's happening?"

They slipped and fell with the moving torrent until they were a tangled mess of dirt and rocks, trying to stand, slipping and falling. More shrieks and curse words. Teuila smiled with satisfaction. "You just got slimed," she said.

She left them fighting to free themselves and went to help Lesina stand.

"Look what you did to me!" shrieked Lesina. "How am I ever going to get this stuff out of my hair?"

"You can thank me later for saving your artificially enhanced self," snapped Teuila. "Get up. Keahi needs you to spark him."

"What?" said Lesina.

Teuila shoved her forward and pointed at Keahi who was locked in a stranglehold by the Olohe. "Quick, help him."

"I can't," said Lesina. "I don't have any power left."

A noise of disgust. "Useless." Teuila took a deep breath and closed her eyes. Wishing. Hoping. Wanting for earth to help her.

It answered. A jagged line lit up the sky and scissored through Keahi. A direct hit. The Olohe was blasted backwards as Keahi burst into flame. He staggered forward as the chokehold was released and shook his head to clear his vision. "Where'd that come from?"

Both Lesina and Teuila stood there wide-eyed with shock. Teuila looked at the sky, to Keahi and then back at the sky again. "Was that me?"

"What *are* you?" demanded Lesina. "How did you do that?"

Teuila shrugged helplessly. "I don't know."

What was happening with Daniel?

At the base of the giant tree, Daniel paused to open the two water bottles he carried with him in the backpack. It was time to put his lessons with Tavake into practice. A thought, a focus of the blue fire that lived within him and he had water coiled in the palm of his hands, taut and ready. He looked up. One of the Olohe had reached the white *pe'a*. She sidled along the branch towards it with a blade in her hands, reaching for the Bone piece.

No you don't.

Daniel hurled a cobalt missile towards her. Water obeyed its master with vicious force. It knocked the blade out of the Olohe's hand and almost toppled her from the branch. Before she could steady herself, the water returned as a liquid battering ram and knocked her from her perch. She shouted in angry defiance as she fell several meters to a lower branch.

The second Olohe whirled around to see where the attack on her sister had come from. She saw Daniel and threw a *matakana* at him – a circular throwing weapon made of wood, sharks teeth and cordage. It narrowly missed his shoulder and he retaliated with a volley of water shrapnel that shredded through foliage and wood as it flew towards her. A cry as some of them found their target. First blood to Daniel.

But the Olohe wasn't done. Not by far. She ignored her wounds and leapt to the branch above her with the ease of a gymnast. A circular flip and she was up and standing across from the mammoth white *pe'a* that was easily the same height as she was. An angry screech as it saw her. She smiled at its frustration as she slipped a knife from her ankle sheathe. She easily evaded the wild flapping of its unimpeded wing, and then stabbed overhand. With two hands firmly on the blade, the Olohe ripped a line down the flying fox's exposed abdomen. Gutted it. Silenced it.

Entrails spilled. A biting stench soured the air. And the swarm of pe'a took flight.

The Olohe woman reached down and tried to take the Bone piece but it was solidly encrusted in the claws of the pe'a. It had guarded it there for so long that the Bone was now a part of its body. No matter. She used her blade to sever its leg and free the Bone. Once in her grasp, she turned a triumphant smile at her sister several branches below. "We've got what we came for. Tell the others we can leave," she said.

The Council had already taken one Bone piece away from their reach and Daniel was determined they wouldn't get this one. He drew all the water to him and focused the full force of his Gift for a poised moment before he sent water blasting. This time, he aimed – not at the Olohe – but at the thick tree branch she stood upon. Water is used in the engineering industry to cut through steel beams. Wood disintegrated under its force and the Olohe came crashing to the ground in a jumbled heap of greenery and broken branches. She lay there, knocked out with the Bone piece in her hand.

Daniel told his guilty conscience to shut up as he grabbed the Bone from the fallen Olohe's hand. *She's breathing. She'll be fine.* Then he ran to join the others.

Keahi was loving his moment as the Human Torch in the middle of a show-down against Air telesā. The three women were in shock. They had never seen a fanua-afi before and the fact he was a *male* Gifted with fire stunned them even further. They threw lightning at him and he stood there laughing as he absorbed it all. Unfortunately, his control over his Gift was much less impressive. He sent a flame burst at them which knocked them both backwards but it also set fire to the dry grass around them.

"What are you doing?" yelled Lesina. She and Teuila leapt back as hungry flames danced through the clearing. "Do something!"

"I'm trying," Keahi yelled back as he strode through the flames, hoping the fire would somehow follow him like a loyal dog. No such luck. A wall of red and orange heat now separated them from the Council telesā and the flames threatened to leap into the forest around them.

"Daaaaaniel!" shouted Teuila as she backed away, looking frantically over her shoulder. "Help."

Lesina was still blasting Keahi. "How stupid are you? No – don't answer that – you just keep trying to surpass all my expectations on the stupidity frontier."

Keahi was waving his arms and trying to make the flames pay attention to him. "Oh just shut up."

"He's right, Lesina," said Daniel as he came up behind them.

Both girls turned to him with relief. "He's going to set the whole forest on fire," cried Teuila, "please make him stop."

"Lesina, stop screaming," said Daniel. The calm authority in his voice shut her up immediately. "You need to make it rain."

She shook her head. "I can't. I'm all powered out. And summoning rain is beyond me anyway," said Lesina.

"Not you then," said Daniel. He looked at Teuila. "You."

"What?" both girls chorused.

"Quickly. We don't have much time. You made lightning, that means you can make it rain. Just do it the same way you did the other stuff," instructed Daniel.

Teuila didn't think it would work but Daniel was the leader here. She took a deep breath and shut her eyes. It was difficult to think of peaceful, beautiful green things when all around her was chaos and destruction but she forged ahead, trying to reach that calmness, that faraway place of hope. *It's such a hot day. I wish it would rain. Please?*

She waited. Nothing. "It's no use, I'm sorry," said Teuila.

Then she felt a raindrop on her face. Then another. A cooling breeze whispered through her hair. A gentle happiness as earth assured her, *I am here. Always.*

And then the heavens opened and the rain poured.

Fire hissed and spit as water asserted its power and authority. Lesina was gleeful, "Yes!" She raised a taunting eyebrow at Keahi who stood there naked in the rainstorm. "Awww, has your fire gone out? Just can't keep it up, can you?"

Teuila's face was alight with wonder. "It worked. It really worked. I don't get it." She turned to Daniel. "You were right. Now what?"

He gripped the Bone piece tightly in his hand. "Now, we get out of here."

Betrayal

Apollonia was livid with rage. A raging mini-windblast sent a chair flying against the wall as her Ariki ducked. "You had a simple mission. Get a piece of Bone from a feeble old flying rodent. I send three Ariki with three Olohe who are supposed to be the most amazing warriors in the Pacific. All you had to do is fly around the country climbing trees. You take weeks to track this creature. You promise me you're going to catch it. I give you more time. I am patient. And now, you dare to return and tell me you let a few mere infants take the Bone from you? Don't they know who I am?!"

Matalasi had been the unfortunate leader of the expedition. "They were telesā. Unlike any we've seen before."

"Excuses," said Apollonia. "Let me show you telesā power unlike any you've seen before." She snapped her fingers and sent a whip wire of lightning at the woman who quaked before her. Matalasi dropped to her knees as the bolt ripped through her but she bore her suffering without a sound. The rest of the room avoided looking at their sister.

Matalasi's second spoke up. "They were boys with Gifts. One was Water and the other, he spoke with Fire."

Apollonia stopped the torture. "Impossible."

"No, we saw it. We felt their power. They were led by the Vasa Loloa boy," argued the second.

There was a daggered silence in the room for a long while before Apollonia addressed them again. "Go. Find out who he is. Who they all are. I want that Bone piece and I want those children punished for daring to steal from me."

Iolana came to Tavake's room in the quiet of the night. Noa walked with her and they stood together in the shadows and waited for Tavake to answer their knock. She was surprised but not unwelcoming. Once inside, Iolana got straight to the point of her visit.

"The Keawe are leaving," she said. "I have sent the others on ahead. Noa and I will leave tomorrow."

Tavake was mystified. "But why so soon?" Concern. "Do you know something about Pele that you need to tell the Council?"

"Our part here at this Council is done and for better or worse, there is nothing else we can do to influence the future. The safety of the Keawe is my ultimate responsibility. My sisters and I have no elemental power. It's best we are gone from this place," explained Iolana.

"I understand," said Tavake. "Your presence will be missed, especially in the battle ahead. Your wisdom and guidance is of great value to me."

Iolana raised her hand for her Olohe. Noa took her hand. "Yes Iolana?" she said quietly.

"Please leave us. I wish to speak with Tavake alone."

"Of course. I'll wait outside." Noa bowed and slipped out of the room.

Iolana waited until she heard the door latch. "You're stronger, Tavake. You have strengthened your Covenant with a very powerful addition. A boy. Your grandson?"

Tavake didn't bother trying to lie. Iolana was a Sensate and there was very little she did not know. "Yes. I did it to prepare for the challenges to come." A half-smile. "He's good, Iolana. Very good. I have not seen such a Gift since … well, for a very long time."

"You care for this boy," said Iolana.

"I am invested in him and his future," corrected Tavake. At Iolana's raised eyebrow, she added, "Alright, yes, I care for him. I trained another child once, that I hoped great things for. This boy is even mightier than she. He's strong and he has courage. His love for Pele's host is misguided but noble and it powers him to do great things. Our Covenant, our Earth needs a leader like him. I know our laws state there can be no male telesā. Yet, our kind is weakening and our Earth needs every telesā she can get to work on her behalf. Perhaps it's a mistake to kill our boy children."

"Perhaps. But there are those who would fight such a move every step of the way. They see *more* telesā as a threat to their own power and position, rather than a vital reinforcement in the work to conserve our Earth."

"That's why I will be the Bone Bearer when the time comes," said Tavake.

"No, you won't," Iolana said. Her conviction was tinged with sadness. "Even with the Gift of the boy tied to yours, you'll be no match for Apollonia. She has too many on her side. I'm afraid for you Tavake."

Tavake's face softened as she accepted the other woman's concern. "You don't need to be. I have something Apollonia doesn't. The Water Bone piece." She tightened her fingers around the handle of her walking stick. "The one she has is a fake. I recovered the real Bone piece from Pulotu many decades ago and replaced it with an imitation. I keep the true one close to me at all times."

Iolana shook her head. "I fear even with a trump card like that, you will not survive Apollonia. I came here tonight to ask you to go away from here. Give up your seat on the Council and go somewhere where Apollonia can never find you. You're not safe in the Council. Neither of us are. It may even now be too late."

Long after Iolana had left, Tavake pondered over her words. She had never known the Sensate to be wrong about anything, but surely she was mistaken now? She clasped her walking staff loosely in both hands and closed her eyes, reaching for the Gift within. She thought back to the day when her mother had first told her where the Water Bone piece rested. "It's guarded by a fierce demon fish, my child. None can enter the Pulotu Cave and live."

A smile to herself in the darkness. She had entered there. She had spoken to the Ancient Guardian and beguiled its mind with her Vasa Loloa Gift, enough so she could switch the Bone piece with another. Only she could have done such a thing because only she wielded such a powerful Gift. *Not Apollonia. She could never have done it.* The Bone piece had been her constant companion ever since, a physical reminder of the ocean power she carried within. As her Gift spoke, the Bone Piece emanated a sapphire glow – a reassurance that yes, she was the greatest Vasa Loloa in the Pacific and yes, one day soon, she would be the Bone Bearer.

A sharp rap at the door startled Tavake's meditation. *Another visitor?* Perhaps Iolana had returned?

It was Apollonia. She was alone and she was angry. She pushed past the older woman into the room. "Did you think I wouldn't find out?"

Her honey curls were massed into an elaborate style with an obscenely huge fake flower pinned to the top. Snakelike tendrils trailed down the sides of her immaculately made-up face. She was dressed to go out somewhere equally elaborate no doubt – in a pink strapless sheathe that flounced into a fishtail train. Her fuchsia heels made an indignant clicking sound as she took mincing steps across the room. She looked like she was going to the Prom or somewhere else just as adolescent. And as she stamped her foot and waved her fake nails in the air, Tavake wondered yet again, how such a juvenile could have become Covenant Keeper of the Ariki. She mentally rolled her eyes and tried to contain her irritation at being disturbed.

That was Tavake's mistake. Underestimating her opponent.

"Samoa is way too small to keep anything hidden for very long. You should know that," hissed Apollonia.

"What are you talking about?" said Tavake wearily.

"Your treachery on so many levels," said Apollonia. She counted off on her fingers. "Let's see, you have a grandson who is telesā Vasa Loloa. He's friends with a nasty group of elementals. One of them is another boy telesā who happens to be fanua afi. All of them are out hunting for Bone pieces. The first time one of my teams bumped into them, we didn't know they were telesā. We assumed they were just overeager little friends of that American girl, Leila Folger. You told us not to question any of her friends. You told us your daughter Salamasina knew nothing useful. You lied!"

Tavake gripped her staff and drew herself up tall so she towered over the petite woman. "How dare you speak to me this way. What's going on?"

"I'll tell you what's going on. Your grandson and his friends got into a spat with my Ariki. He stole the *Matagi* Bone," said Apollonia. She advanced on the Tongan. "You've been working against the Council all along, haven't you? You've got your family hunting the Bone pieces for you. Male telesā are an abomination. You broke our laws. Filthy traitor."

"Your thirst for power has got you imagining things," snapped Tavake. "Take this to the Council, challenge my leadership seat – I welcome it. There are others who will see you for what you truly are."

"No. I'm not going to challenge you for anything," said Apollonia. She reached up to primp at her hair – or so Tavake thought. Instead, with one fluid motion, she pulled the flower from her bun and it was more than just a hairpiece. It was attached to a thin blade. She swung it in a vicious arc and slashed through Tavake's throat. Blood spurted. Apollonia stepped back to avoid the crimson mess as Tavake clutched at her neck and crumpled to the ground. A gurgling sound as a life bled out.

Apollonia delicately picked her way over to stand in front of the mirror. She had her head to one side as she studied her reflection and then glanced back at the twitching, dying woman on the floor behind her. A smile. "You know what your problem was Tavake? You didn't expect the worst of people." She brought the blood splattered knife to her mouth, closed her eyes and inhaled at the rust odor. Then she flicked her tongue along the blade to clean it before carefully replacing it in her hair.

The Covenant Keeper of the Ariki waited there in the room until she was sure Tavake was dead. Until the floor was thick with blood and the room reeked of new death.

And then she let herself out and went dancing.

Rage

Early the next morning, Iolana and her Olohe stopped by Tavake's room to say goodbye. And so the Keawe could ask her one more time to please consider leaving Samoa. When Tavake didn't answer their knocking, Noa picked the lock and got the door open. Iolana couldn't see the bloody carnage inside the room, but Noa's indrawn breath and tensed protective stance told her all she needed to know.

"She's dead, isn't she?" said Iolana softly.

"Yes, we must get you away from here," said Noa. She backed them both up and instinctively started scanning their surroundings, assessing their fastest route out of the hotel.

Iolana grabbed at her arm. "No. We can't leave. Not yet. Tavake's walking staff. Can you see it?"

"There's no time for that. We have to go," insisted Noa. "I'm responsible for your safety."

"You are my Olohe. That means you do what I say. Must I remind you of your Oath?"

Noa didn't like the chastening but accepted it as her due. "No. Forgive me. I'll go see if the staff is there."

Iolana waited outside until Noa returned. "It was beside her body. I've cleaned the blood off. What would you like to do with it?"

The older woman stepped closer and gripped Noa's arm. She spoke with fierce intensity. "Take the Staff to Tavake's grandson. Tell him it's the Water Bone piece and he must act quickly before Apollonia seeks to retrieve it. He must use it to destroy Pele. Tell him the answer to the Tangaloa Bone lies within him and he should trust his heart. Love will guide him. "

"I don't want to leave your side. It's not safe," argued Noa. "Tavake is dead. I think we should get you out of the country, right now."

Iolana's rebuke was harsh. "Silence! It isn't the Olohe's job to think or to question. It's her job to obey. To give her life if necessary for her Keawe. Take the staff to Daniel Tahi. From now on, we do everything in our power to see him succeed in his goal to exorcise Pele. It's more important than ever that we don't allow Apollonia to get the Tangaloa Bone. If she ascends to Bone Bearer than we are all lost. When you return, we will address the Council and try to convince them to join with the boy and his team. Go now."

Noa went with an unwilling heart, with all her senses screaming that to leave was a bad idea. But such is the lot of an Olohe. Not to question but to obey. To give her life for her Keawe.

Noa found Daniel at Leila's house as she knew she would. He was there with Keahi, Talei, Lesina and Teuila. Simone and Pele were nowhere to be seen. Daniel came out to the front verandah to see her. "What are you doing here?" Suspicion and distrust warred with politeness. He looked at this emotionless girl with all her Olohe trappings and found it difficult to connect her with a stolen hour of running, laughter and song.

She gave him the Bone along with Iolana's message. He was confused at this turn of events but hid it well. It was only when she told him of Tavake's death that he reacted. Shock and genuine sadness flickered across his face. "Who killed her?" He thought of his grandmother and how she would react at the news.

"We don't know. There's any number of telesā in that Council who could have wanted her leadership seat. The Covenant Keeper of the Ariki from Rarotonga is the most likely guess." She turned to leave. "I have to get back to Iolana. The Council will be in an uproar over Tavake's death."

Lesina came out to the verandah as he stood there and watched Noa drive away. "Isn't that one of those Council fighters who grabbed us the other day? What did she want?"

"Special delivery." He held up the staff and the sunlight danced on its intricate blend of carved materials.

"Is that …"

"Yes it is," he said. "Tell the others. We've got all three pieces now."

Lesina let out a whoop of celebration and dashed inside with the news. Daniel stood outside a bit longer as he looked out to the blue line where the ocean met the sky. Sadness tempered his relief at having the restored Tangaloa Bone so close to their reach. Tavake had been a powerful influence on the mothers in his life – the woman who had birthed him and given her life so he could live. And the woman who had spent her life raising him and loving him. She had spent many hours teaching him how to master his Gift and for that he was grateful.

Back at the hotel, Apollonia had called an emergency Council meeting – but without the Sereana of Fiji. A stunned silence as Apollonia informed them of Tavake's death. "We don't know who killed her but it wasn't done by elemental means. Her throat was cut." She gave a delicate shudder and covered her mouth as if she might be ill. "Our poor sister. I have my Ariki taking care of the body. No-one outside our Council must know of this. We don't want the local authorities getting involved in our affairs."

A murmur of assent. All of them had a deep-seated loathing for police and local governments. They were, at best, bumbling incompetents and at worst, dangerous obstacles to the work of the Sisterhood.

With everyone reeling at the horrific loss of the Tongan Covenant Keeper, it was easy for Apollonia to take charge of the Council. She had the numbers, she had the desire and to cement her claim, she had the power and the Water Bone piece.

Or so she thought.

She told the Council of her suspicions. Tavake's grandson was working with a team of assorted telesā to steal the Tangaloa Bone. One of them was a male *fanua afi*. More shock and horror ensued at the news there were Gifted male telesā walking around out there in the world right that minute. Apollonia was hinting at the possibility that it was these abominations who had killed Tavake – when Iolana entered the Council room.

"Why was I not told about this meeting?" she said as she felt her way to the front of the room with quiet confidence.

Apollonia smiled with icy welcome. "My apologies. We were told all the Keawe had returned to Hawaii. Your work here in the Council is done, dear sister. Why do you linger?"

"Tavake's death changes everything. The Council needs to take a different plan of action," said Iolana.

"The Council agrees. We've chosen a new leader and she's laying out our course now," said Ofa. "Apollonia has discovered there are male telesā here in Samoa. They're working against us. Not only do they have one of the Tangaloa Bone pieces, but they killed Tavake. Before we can face Pele, we must deal with these men who dare to think they can be one of us!"

The assembly of women were riled up now and erupted into heated conversation. The mere thought of a boy with elemental Gifts made them sick to their stomachs with rage. Iolana had to repeat herself several times before anyone paid attention to her. "No. We should be reaching out the hand of friendship to this boy and his team. They are our best hope of destroying Pele. Not only do they have the only other fanua afi on the planet that we know of, but they also have two pieces of the Tangaloa Bone."

Apollonia leapt to her feet. "That's a lie. They have the Air bone piece and we have the Water piece. As yet, no-one knows where to find the third piece. Your Keawe directions were too cryptic," she scoffed. "We've been to every extinct volcano in the region – nothing. How can this boy and his friends have the Fire piece?"

"He doesn't. Not that I know of," said Iolana. "I speak of the Water piece."

"You mean this?" mocked Apollonia as she brandished the Bone shard they had taken from Daniel at Falealupo beach. "Oh, I'm sorry, you can't see it, can you?" A simpering laugh.

"I'm holding the *Vasa Loloa* Bone piece in my hands Iolana. All we have to do is get the Air piece back from the boy."

"Give it to Lupe, please," said Iolana. "Just for a moment."

Apollonia frowned. "Why?" She made a '*she's crazy*' sign at the blind woman and several of the Council laughed.

"The Tangaloa Bone was created to speak to the Gifts of our Mother Earth and unite them as one. If that truly is the Water piece, then when it's held by a telesā vasa loloa, the Bone will glow with blue fire," Iolana explained with quiet certainty. "Give it to Lupe, Covenant Keeper from Tokelau."

There was silence in the room as Apollonia obeyed the Keawe. A hushed breath of anticipation. Lupe took the Bone shard in her hands.

Nothing happened.

An uproar ensued and Apollonia was the loudest of them all. She snatched the Bone shard back from Lupe. "No! How can this be?" The diminutive woman screamed as she hacked at the table with the imitation. A wild wind swept through the room. It sent papers flying and vases toppling. She spun around to face Iolana and her eyes burned with a dangerous golden light. "Why didn't you tell us about this before? You knew all along, didn't you? You were working together with Tavake! Traitor." A torrent of air picked Iolana up, threw her across the room and slammed her up against the wall.

"Stop it. How dare you hurt one of your sisters!" said Lupe with horror.

"Shut up," said Apollonia. Without even turning her head, she sent a deadly spray of lightning shrapnel hurtling sideways towards the Tokelauan. It ripped into her and she fell where she stood, her body riddled with what looked like bullet wounds. "Anybody else have a comment to make?"

No-one spoke. "Good." Apollonia turned her attention back to the woman pinned to the wall. "Where's the real Water Bone piece Iolana?"

The Keawe leader was dazed. Her head lolled to one side. Apollonia walked across the room and her heels made impatient clicking noises. She peered up at the Hawaiian. "Where is it?" she repeated.

Iolana's answer was faint. "It's out of your reach now. You will never be the Bone Bearer. Even a boy is more worthy than you."

"I never liked you," said Apollonia. "The blind and the crippled have no place as earth guardians. It's bad for our image." She paused to check her reflection in the decorative wall mirror before she sent Iolana flying. The Hawaiian crashed into the opposite wall and then to the side and back again, as Apollonia shook her like a rag doll with the force of *matagi*. Finally she let her drop to the ground in a crumpled heap. "Ofa, get a team to the Tahi boy's house. It's possible Tavake gave the Bone to her daughter." She stepped over Iolana's body with a look of distaste and kept walking, barking out orders to the assembly. "Do whatever you need to but get me that Bone. Matalasi, take the Ariki and find out where Leila Folger is. I've had enough of this tip-toeing around one fire girl. The Keawe say she can't be destroyed, but today we see the Keawe cannot be trusted."

At the door, Apollonia paused with her Ariki and then turned back to face the others. "We didn't actually vote on the Council leadership seat, did we? Is there anyone here who wishes to oppose my nomination?" The tips of her fingers sparked with energy and that is where everyone's eyes were glued. "Good. It's settled then. Let's go kill us a fire goddess."

By the time Noa returned to the hotel, there were no telesā to be seen and Iolana wasn't in her room. Noa's foreboding grew with every step she took closer to the Council meeting room. It was locked and a blaring Do Not Disturb sign warned away all nosey hotel staff. A few quick glances to check she wasn't being watched and then Noa got the door open. She was unprepared for the sight that greeted her.

It looked like a storm had swept through the place. There was overturned furniture and broken glass everywhere. And in a desolate heap in the corner was a beaten, broken figure.

"Iolana."

Noa ran to kneel beside her Keawe and took her in her arms. "No, please."

Iolana's eyes opened and her smile was a tremulous, fragile thing. A whisper. "I hoped you would come in time. Did you find the boy?"

Noa's *yes* was a sob. A single hot tear ran down her cheek. "I'm taking you to the hospital."

"Too late for that," said Iolana and every word was a halting effort. She clutched at Noa's arm. "You must go, protect the boy."

"No," said Noa. "I took an oath to the death. I failed you and I must pay the price."

Iolana's eyes flew open at that and she raised a frail hand to Noa's cheek. "You took an oath to obey. Help the boy defeat

Pele. Tell him, love is the only answer ..." Her voice trailed away and her fingers slipped to the ground. They left blood marks on Noa's skin and they mirrored the marks on her honor, on her soul, as her oath Keawe died.

Keahi interrupted Daniel's thoughts. "Hey, you coming inside? We got a lot to plan in here. Sure we got all three pieces, but now what?" He couldn't hide his nervous unease as he looked up the driveway. "We have to be careful. Don't want Pele finding out what we're up to."

Daniel agreed. Quickly he went to his truck and burrowed underneath the passenger seat for a tin box. Back inside the house, he took out the Bone piece he had taken from Leila's room. "Keahi, keep watch of the road for Leila's car," he ordered. He placed each of the Bone pieces on the kitchen table. Leila's piece given to her by her mother was the smallest. It fit neatly in the palm of your hand and could easily be worn on a chain as a necklace – the filigree carving was that delicate and beautiful. Earth.

The second piece was Air. Hacked from the body of a flying fox, it had spent many years exposed to the elements, flown from one island to another as the Ancient Guardian always kept on the move with its precious cargo. This piece was longer than the first and showed signs of wear and tear. Sections of the patterning had worn away. "It looks like a beat up old piece of stick," Teuila had announced with disgust when they first brought it back from the Valley of the Sacred *Pe'a*.

The third piece was even longer still. Tavake had used it as a walking staff for many years but kept it in pristine condition and every inch was a work of art as patterns told their story of Ocean telesā ancestry.

There was silence as everyone looked at the Tangaloa pieces lying there in a row. It seemed strange that so much hope could be invested in such seemingly ordinary items. "Now what do we do?" asked Lesina as she voiced what all of them were thinking.

"Now we fit them together," said Daniel.

The girls exchanged worried looks. "Umm, what if that sets off a freaky chemical reaction and the whole place blows up?" asked Talei.

"You better go wait outside then," replied Daniel. "We're not just going to stand here and stare at them."

It was an easy thing to fit each piece into one seamless line. A click and twist and it was as if the Tangaloa Bone had never been divided. Daniel took it in both hands. It was surprisingly light and emanated a strange tingling warmth in his fingers. As the others stared, the patterns lit up with a cobalt glow. Daniel jerked back and dropped the Bone back on the table, "What is that?!" Once out of his hands, the light faded and the staff was just a carved stick once again.

"Did it hurt?" asked Teuila.

"No. It just caught me off guard."

Keahi walked over to the table. "Let me try." He picked up the Bone and then smiled as the carved patterns simmered with a crimson light. "Awesome." He handed it to Lesina. "You try. See what color you make it."

She took it gingerly but then relaxed as nothing dreadful happened. Instead, the staff sparked with shimmering sun-yellow. "Wow, it picks up on our Gifts." A questioning glance at Teuila. "How about you?"

Teuila took the staff and it was as if all the Christmas winter wonderland lights went on at once. A searing white light lit up the entire room and the others had to shade their eyes.

"Shut it off!" yelled Keahi.

Teuila threw the Tangaloa Bone onto the table with a guilty expression. "Sorry."

The others stared at her. "What the hell was that?" asked Lesina.

Teuila snapped back. "How should I know? It was your stupid idea, not mine." She gave the older girl a lethal look and then stomped out of the room.

An awkward silence – in which everyone heard the sound of a Jeep turning into the driveway. "They're back," said Keahi.

"Quick, let's cover it up," said Daniel.

Lesina grabbed some sheets from the linen closet and helped him wrap the Tangaloa Bone. The car door opened and shut and Simone's laughter could be heard as Daniel shoved the bulky package at Lesina. "Hide it somewhere. I'll take it out to my truck later."

Lesina slipped out the back door with the covered staff – just as Pele and Simone walked in the front. "Daahlings we're baaack," said Simone. He looked at them all standing there in surprise. "What's happening? I didn't know we were having a party."

Pele's smile faded at the sight of Keahi. She looked at Daniel. "Can I speak with you? In private?" She continued walking down the hall, clearly expecting him to follow.

Simone shrugged his shoulders at Daniel's questioning glance. "I don't know. We've been at the internet café all afternoon. Pele wanted to research some things and I told her the net would be the quickest way. I showed her how to use it and her mind was blown."

Just great. Daniel went after Pele but stopped in the doorway of her room.

"Come in," she said.

"No thanks. I'll just stand right here," he said. He tried to look everywhere except at the girl in front of him. He knew she wasn't Leila. She didn't dress like Leila, talk like Leila or even move like Leila. But still, looking at her was like setting fire to his soul. A rush of wind on the edge of an ocean-side cliff. Falling. Would he ever stop falling for her?

"Fine. Stay there. I'm not going to jump you Daniel Tahi. No matter how badly you want me to." She smiled to show him she meant no harm with her words. "I just want to talk. I've given the current situation a lot of thought. Me being here and the threat of the Tangaloa Council. These are strange times I've been reborn to. One where a select few males have our Mother Earth's Gifts. Rather than seeing them as a threat, I believe it heralds a new era when Gifted male and female will stand together and fight against all that threatens the sanctity of the Earth which gives us all life."

"What are you saying?" said Daniel. This was a new side to Pele. She spoke with calm sincerity and the haughty pride was missing. Could this new Pele be trusted?

"I'm saying, I want to work together with you and your friends. We can go address the Council, offer them a peaceful resolution. Convince them I'm not a danger. Tell them telesā everywhere must stop killing their boy children. They will listen to me. And if they don't, no matter, I will eliminate them." An arched eyebrow and a hint of the old Pele. "My Gift is very convincing. We can assume leadership of their Council, make new laws, establish a new order for telesā in the Pacific." She started pacing and there was a sparkled edge of excitement in the air. "I've seen so many horrors on this internet that Simone showed me. The extent of the damage humankind has wrought on this world is epic. It's time for true power and vision to be at the helm of all telesā. We could all be that." She came to a stop in front of him and reached for his hands. "I'm not looking for a lover Daniel. I already made that mistake with Keahi. No, I'm looking for a friend. You and the others have all been kind to me. You've shown me a humanity I never thought was possible. What a team we all would make! We could do great things for this earth."

In that moment, she was a young girl alight with enthusiasm and hope – not an age old goddess weary of heartache and betrayal, with hands forever drenched in blood. In that moment, Daniel gazed into her eyes, thought of the Tangaloa Bone hidden somewhere nearby, ready to be used against this girl – and guilt was a knife that twisted inside him.

He was about to speak when suddenly Pele let go of his hands with a cry of pain. "Aaargh." She stumbled back with a hand to her eye. "It burns."

Daniel moved to put an arm around her. "What's wrong?"

She pushed him away, shaking her head. "Nothing. Just an old war wound acting up." She spun around and screamed at the air above her. "Go away."

"Hey, are you alright?" said Daniel.

Pele took a few deep breaths to compose herself but with one hand still to her forehead and covering her eye. "I'm fine. Sorry." She shook her head and walked to the window. "Can you hear that? Can you feel it?"

"What? I can't hear anything," said Daniel. He hated seeing her rattled like this. Fearful, wary and suspicious. Even if she wasn't Leila, it hurt to see her in pain.

But Pele wasn't listening to him. "It's coming from outside," she muttered to herself. She pushed past him, down the hall and out the back door. The garden was a colorful celebration of life but all she could hear, was the call of the dead. The laughter. The taunts. And surging behind them all, driving them forward – the quiet song of the Tangaloa Bone. "Where is it …" She went to the garden shed and threw open the door.

"No! Daniel, don't let her go in there." It was Lesina. She ran out to the garden and there was fear in her eyes. She grabbed at his arm. "It's in there. That's where I hid the staff."

Too late.

Pele emerged holding the Tangaloa Bone in her hands, a look of stunned wonder on her face. "How did this get here?" She ran her fingers lightly along the carved markings, each one so familiar and laden with meaning for her. "I never thought I'd see this again."

The others joined Daniel outside in the yard, all looking as worried as he felt. Especially when Pele whirled around to confront them. "The Tangaloa Bone was fragmented and hidden away after my death. What's it doing here? Who recovered all the pieces? When? Why?"

No-one answered. And in that moment, Pele's initial excitement faded. Her eyes narrowed as the truth dawned. "You wanted to destroy me and you thought you could do it with this." Her gaze travelled the line of each one of them and stopped at Daniel. "You did this. You lied to me." Her voice rose to a wild shout. "All of you." Her hands around the Tangaloa Bone exploded into flame and she threw a fiery orb of rage at Daniel.

Shouts and panic. From everyone except Daniel. An instinctive thought thanks to his hours of training – and a shield of compressed water drawn from the thick humidity, repelled the attack. Pele's tattoos burned with hurt and rage. "I trusted you," she said. The fire dimmed and then went out. Daniel's wall of water dissipated into the greenness.

Everyone watched as Pele walked away, out of the garden and out of sight. The next minute they heard the Jeep roar out the driveway. Pele was gone.

Ifoga

There was chaos after Pele left. Simone was yelling, demanding that "somebody tell me what the hell just happened and tell me right now before I lose it!"

Keahi was blasting Lesina for putting the Tangaloa Bone in the garden shed. "Of all the dumb blonde things to do! He gives you a telesā weapon of mass destruction to hide from a psychotic fire goddess and what do you do? You chuck it in a shed in the backyard!"

Lesina was firing back on offensive-defensive and Teuila was itching to slap her. (As usual.) In the midst of it all, Daniel got a phone call from his grandmother. Or at least it was her phone number that flashed on his screen. But a strange girl's voice spoke to him.

'Daniel Tahi? You need to come home right now. Your mother needs you.'

Before the phone cut off, he heard Salamasina cry out, "No!"

That was all it took. He sprinted for his truck. Keahi called after him. "Hey, where are you going?"

"Home" was his curt response. He slammed the door and revved the engine.

"What about Pele?"

"Later. My grandmother's in trouble."

Daniel cursed at himself all the way home. *So what if she didn't want to take that trip to New Zealand? You should have forced her. You should have made it impossible for her not to go. You should never have left her side.* He had arranged for his welders to take rotating shifts at the workshop so his grandmother would never be alone. He'd told them there were people out there who might want to hurt him through her. All the welding team had assured him they would look after her but he knew they would be no match for any telesā with dangerous intentions.

When he reached the house he was relieved to see nothing out of the ordinary. Salamasina's little truck was the only vehicle in the yard. He ran up the steps, calling for her. "Mama? Where are you?"

She wasn't in the house. He shouted louder. "Mama!"

A voice answered. It came from the garden at the back and it wasn't his grandmother. "She's out here," the same strange girl called gaily.

Daniel threw open the back door and went out to the place that had always been Salamasina's haven of green peace and harmony. He still couldn't see anyone in the abundance of native foliage that his grandmother used to make her medicines. There was a little pond with a waterfall towards the back of the garden and Daniel followed the sound of running water. Salamasina had a garden bench and table there where she liked to read. His feet crunched on gravel as he came around a curve in the path. *There she is.*

Salamasina sat reclined on the bench with her back to him. Her woven laufala hat was low on her forehead and she was dressed in her usual gardening clothes – baggy pants and a button down shirt that used to belong to his grandfather. Sweet relief to see her. "Mama, there you are. I was worried."

He went to her and that's when he saw it. The mottled purple bruising on her face and throat. The glassy stare.

Salamasina was dead.

In that instant, vice-like coils of water snapped around him, binding his arms to his sides and a child walked out from behind the bushes. Two other telesā followed her. "Surprise," she said. She came right up to him, close enough that he could see his first impression was off by a few years. She wasn't a kid, but she was a very young teenager. "You're rather yummy to look at, aren't you?" she said with appreciation. "My name's Ofa. Yes, like the cyclone. I'm Covenant Keeper for the ocean telesā in Niue. Youngest Covenant Keeper in the Pacific ever!"

She spoke very fast, with her words tripping out over each other. She looked at him and then back to his grandmother with an artless regret. "Oh, I'm sorry. I should have called back to tell you. We killed her. But it was an accident. You see, I was doing the water ropes thing, trying to shake her up a little, trying to get her to talk. But she kept saying, *I'll never tell you where he is … I'll never help you find the Bone piece …* blah blah blah." She rolled her eyes. "It was so tiresome. I couldn't stand it. I may have snapped just a teensy bit and gone overboard with the chokehold. But then, she was very old, what was she, like eighty? She's positively ancient. Hey, maybe she had a heart attack. Or an embolism.

You know, when your body just up and quits because life sucks so bad and you're too tired to keep going?"

On and on she went. The words were a meaningless babble to Daniel as he stood there in his grandmother's peaceful haven and stared at the woman who had made him who he was. Her thick braid was grey now but he remembered how the light would catch on the rich mahogany waves of her hair as she sat in the garden and brushed it – while he would play on the grass with his toys. His Papa would come from the workshop and her eyes would light up for him. They would kiss and then she would watch and cheer while he and his grandfather played with the rugby ball. Memories flooded. Emotions drowned.

The kiss she always gave him on his forehead before he went to sleep every night. The quiet way she would say his name when she wished to reprove him. How much he hated to see the look of disappointment in her eyes like the times when he said a bad word, stole a candy bar from the corner store, or pushed a little girl into a puddle in second grade because she made fun of his ears. Her joy when he won a game, scored a try, got yet another trophy at school prize-giving, made her breakfast, gave her an unexpected hug.

Told her he loved her.

All these things and a million more raced through Daniel's mind and he was caught in their ferocity of meaning, so much, that Ofa and her two accomplices faded to nothingness. It was just him and his grandmother – and a slow building chant in his ears, in his mind, in his heart, in his soul.

We killed her ... we killed her ... we killed her ...

Rage, guilt, revenge and unspeakable grief combined. The cord that bound Daniel to reason snapped and his Gift was unleashed in all its savagery. The human body is approximately sixty percent water. It's in our cells, our blood plasma, everything from our eyes to our intestines is awash with it. Even the spine is lined with it. Water truly is the liquid of life.

Or, in the hands of an enraged Vasa Loloa – it's the liquid of death.

Daniel didn't plan it or even understand what was happening. It only took a hearts breadth of homicidal madness. Ofa and her friends never had a chance. Their blood boiled, internal organs exploded and spines ruptured, all in excruciating agony. It was over in a few minutes.

The three women were a sickening, gelatinous mess on the ground and Daniel had his grandmother in his arms. He lifted her easily and carried her out of the garden which would never again be a place of refuge and peace. He took her down to the beach and gently laid her at the water's edge where he knelt and appealed to Vasa Loloa. "Please heal her. Please bring my grandmother back."

Sea creatures felt his pain and swam close to shore, speaking their companionship. The sea currents washed the dried blood and caked dirt from Salamasina's body –a small offer of condolence. But there was no miraculous healing and Daniel wept alone on a lonely shore for the woman who had loved him as only a mother could.

That's where the others found him.

"Oh no, not Mama Tahi," said Simone. He ran down the beach and sank to his knees beside Daniel. A hand on his shoulder. "I'm sorry Daniel. So sorry."

Many years ago, an unlikely friendship was first forged when a little boy who lived and breathed rugby came across another little boy with too much sparkly flair and a missing Hannah Montana lunchbox – crying in a corner of the playground. That boy with rugby dreams had used his fists to right an injustice that day and their friendship had endured. Simone couldn't do anything to right the horror Daniel found himself in, but he could mourn with him and so that's what he did. For a moment the two boys cried together.

Then Simone said, "We came to get you because there's reports on the radio of fire all along the coastal road. They're calling it arson. Someone is throwing fire balls all over the place. The radio says Molotov cocktails but you and I know better."

Daniel put his head in his hands. "It's Pele. This is never going to get any better, is it?" He gave Simone a hopeless look. "I don't think we're getting out of this. I can't see how. Leila's gone. And now, Mama's dead. There's nobody left. I can't do this Simone."

Simone shook him. "Look at me. You can't quit now. Too many people are counting on you. There's too much at stake. If you don't pull yourself together, Pele could blow up this whole island and a lot more people will die. You have to go after her. You're the only person who can get through to her. You and Keahi. Appeal to Leila or Pele. Just stop her from killing us all. Please."

"What about Mama? I can't leave her like this," said Daniel.

"Bring her up to the house and I'll stay with her. I won't leave her alone. I promise."

A short while later, Salamasina's body was safely inside the house and Simone was on the phone to his family and to Matile and Tuala to tell them the sad news. Daniel knew that once

Matile arrived, she would kick start all the necessary arrangements for Mama. At least until he got back.

If he came back.

Everyone was piling into the truck when a familiar Panamera drove up and Noa got out. She was dressed in full Olohe gear and the others tensed at the sight of her weaponry and traditional armor pieces. Teuila wanted to get out and beat her up but Keahi held her back and indicated at Daniel. "Let him handle it," he said with quiet urgency.

"Have you come to gloat? You get off on visiting kill-sites?" said Daniel.

"What are you talking about?" asked Noa.

"I'm talking about your Council members butchering my grandmother. You gonna stand there and tell me you didn't know about it?"

"I didn't know, I swear to you on the spilt blood of my Keawe." Noa's voice caught on the words and she struggled to contain her emotions. "I had nothing to do with it."

"Why are you here then?" demanded Daniel.

"Because the Council killed my Keawe. Before she died, Iolana entrusted me with one final task."

Crammed between Teuila and Talei in the back seat of the truck, Lesina muttered darkly, "Don't tell me she's going with us." A sound of disgust.

"I'm here to help you defeat Pele," Noa said to Daniel.

He still wasn't ready to trust her. "Why?"

"Because I'm Olohe and it's my duty to obey my Keawe." She went to the truck and climbed in without waiting for an answer. "Oh, one more thing – I'm going to kill Apollonia. So don't get in my way and we'll be fine."

It wasn't difficult to find Pele. All they had to do was listen to the radio and follow the fire reports. It's as if she were driving along the coastal road shooting fire spheres at trees, bushes, and abandoned *fale* houses. Nothing major, just marking her path as she went.

Talei spoke up from the back seat. "It's like she wants to be found. She wants us to follow her."

A moment of taut silence as they all digested her observation. Then Keahi paled. "It's not just that. The places she's leaving fire markers at are all spots that I took her to when she wanted to play tourist."

"Great," said Lesina with acid, "she's a spurned lover *and* a demented fire goddess. Way to go man-whore."

Daniel broke in before they could all start arguing again, "In that case, you should be able to guess where she's headed Keahi. Any ideas? Might give us the element of surprise if we can beat her to it."

"The lava fields in Saleaula," said Keahi. He shifted uncomfortably in his seat and tried not to look at Daniel as he remembered just what had happened between him and Pele at the lava field. "Yeah, I'm pretty sure that's where she's going. And for whatever reason, she wants us to follow her."

Pele may have had twisted semi-romantic plans that involved the lava field on Savaii Island but she never got there because Daniel and his friends weren't the only ones tracking her via the radio fire reports. She was driving through the rugged coastal area of Satamai when three large helicopters appeared and proceeded to run her off the road. Pele wasn't upset though. She was itching for a fight and Apollonia and the Council had shown up at the exact right time. She turned off the engine and took her time getting out of the car. Ahead of her, the choppers landed on a sandy plain beside the ocean and telesā poured out.

The more she counted of her opponents, the more delighted Pele became. She clapped her hands with glee and then reached into the car for the Tangaloa Bone. She welcomed the familiar warmth of it in her hands and the red burn as it lit up for her immeasurable Gift. There was a chasm of hurt inside her and she wanted to drown it in the suffering of others.

She called out to the gathering formation of women. "The Tangaloa Council, at last we meet. Do you have a leader? Someone who wants to die first? My staff is hungry and so am I. We have not fed on telesā Gifts for *sooooo* long!" she taunted. "Let the games begin."

By the time Daniel and the others arrived on the scene, the battle was already raging in earnest. Pele held center stage on a raised platform of molten earth as she brandished the Tangaloa Bone high above her. She spoke in turn to each of the Gifts within – Gifts she had stolen from long ago *matagi telesā* and *vasa loloa* – and she relished the opportunity to take on each of the Council telesā on their own terms, eliminating them with their own Gift.

Everyone got out of the truck, and there was horrified awe. The earth trembled beneath their feet as Pele called to it. Springs of bubbling lava burst from scattered pressure points all over the battle field. Daniel was grateful there was no village in the area, no innocent people to get dragged into this war between the elements. The air was thick with smoke and screams. The odor of cindered flesh was strong on the wind. People were burning, people were dying and Pele, she was laughing.

"Is that all you can do?" she said. "Is there no more? Please, give me more. I want more."

Three Ariki swooped forward, borne on raging winds. They were led by Matalasi in a determined attack of lightning bolts and whip wires of energy. Daniel recognized them from their confrontation in the Valley of the Sacred *Pe'a*. It was a recognition that lasted only a moment. The three women were nothing in the face of the Destroyer. Pele obliterated them with a flick of her fingers. "Begone, mosquito!" A dying shriek lingered even after they disappeared in a scatter of ash.

The Council vasa loloa were next. They hit Pele with a tidal wave of fury. It rocked her. Knocked her back and she fell from her perch to the ground below. Perhaps, water would be greater than fire on this horror-filled day?

No.

Pele was mistress of earth and she'd had a millennia of practice to play with the many variations of her power. She knelt and dragged her fingers through the rock at her feet, wrenching at ribbons of ore and seams of stone. She was an earth mover and shaker and she wrenched at it with vicious ease and shook the ground's surface like one shakes a blanket. The earth rippled, sending lines of unbalance all across the wide plain on which they stood. Keahi grabbed Teuila as she fell and he rolled with her, sheltered her safe in his arms. Lesina and Talei ended up flat on their backs while Daniel kept a firm grip on the truck door for balance. Noa was nowhere to be seen.

But Pele wasn't done. Not by far.

"I say unto this earth – be split open," she intoned, reciting the godly words with a joyous anticipation. She paused and then ripped the earth apart before her. It cracked and then a gaping chasm opened. Two unfortunate Vanuatu telesā were swallowed up in its depths. Another was pulled to safety by one of the Ariki who used the winds to avoid plunging into the flaming canyon that Pele had created.

The Council army – if that is what it can be called – was in disarray. Where was Apollonia? Who was going to steady the madness, calm the confusion and lead them to safety?

That was the question paramount in Noa's mind as she ran across a volcanic minefield toward the helicopters. *Where are you Apollonia? Murderer of the blind and betrayer of sisters.* As she had suspected, the brave leader of the Council was sheltering in one of the helicopters, waiting out the battle with her speedy escape readily at hand. Noa pulled herself up into the chopper. "The fights out there, Apollonia."

Apollonia made looking helpless an art-form. She wore a purple bustier and skin-tight black shorts with threaded sandals that wrapped up to the thigh. She was painting her nails, pausing every so often to fan herself impatiently with a pink feather-edged woven fan. "What do you want Olohe?"

"I want your heart on a stick," said Noa as she leapt.

The Ariki was just as quick with a defensive rush of wind that pushed the Olohe out of the helicopter. She hit the ground and rolled to evade a spray of lightning bullets, then threw her own sharks-tooth matakana. It lodged in Apollonia's shoulder and she cursed loudly. She climbed down out of the chopper and Noa was waiting. She hit her with a combination of punches and clawed strikes and every one of them came from that dark place where vengeance and guilt co-exist.

"How dare you lay your hands on me," screamed Apollonia. She threw a lightning strike but Noa was too quick to drop and twist out of its path. Noa pulled out the blade she kept in her ankle holster, spun and stepped in close to the Ariki, so close she could smell her Chanel perfume and underneath it something else – the sour bite of fear. Noa hooked one arm over Apollonia's head and brought her down low, whispered in her ear, "For my Keawe." Then she stabbed her in the stomach, pulled out the blade and stabbed again overhand. In the heart. Noa let the body drop. It was time for her to rejoin the battle and fulfill the rest of her duty to Iolana.

Help the boy defeat Pele. Protect him. Tell him the key to using the Tangaloa Bone is within. Tell him the answer is love.

Someone shouted Pele's name through the smoke.

It was Keahi. "Stop! Don't do this." He walked out on what was left of the plain so she could see him.

Her eyes lit up, "Ahhh, my friends have arrived. Now the party can truly begin," she said.

There was an Ariki attempting to fly up behind her unawares. Pele spun around and used the Tangaloa Bone as a staff to hit her across the face. The woman tumbled to the ground in front of her. Without hesitation, Pele stepped forward and stabbed one point of the staff directly into the woman's chest. A flash of searing light that originated from the Tangaloa Bone, seemed to rip the woman down the center. She screamed as an exuberant light spilled forth and Pele absorbed it. When it was done, she pirouetted back to her conversation with Keahi. "So what were you saying again?"

"You don't want to do this. Haven't you been here before? Remember what happened to you the last time you were a power addict? Is that what you want? To be condemned to burn forever? All over again?"

"Yes," Pele said. "That's exactly what I want. And why not? I have nothing to live for here." She threw a spinning tornado of fire at him, knowing full well what it would do. He lit up in a crescendo of red, orange and yellow.

"Me. You have me," Keahi said.

"You liar!" Once again she raised herself up on a platform of lava so she could gaze down at the apocalypse she had created. "I loved you. I offered you the world. I could have given you eternity. And you rejected me." She pulled water from the boiling blue ocean and began to weave a web of sapphire strands, humming a little tune to herself as she did so. "Isn't it pretty?" she asked. "Why Keahi, what beautiful eyes you have," Pele mocked, "All the better to lie to you with my dear. Why Keahi, what beautiful sensuous lips you have … all the better to kiss you with my dear." A girlish giggle and then she flexed and threw the net over the boy who stood below her. "Why Pele, what a beautiful net you've made. All the better to catch you with."

Before Keahi could burn free she looped the net and pulled so he was suspended like a fish. A quick twist of her wrist and she sent him hurtling out towards the sea. A splash, fizz and hiss as he hit the water.

"Keahi!" shouted Teuila. She leapt out from the safety of the rocks and was reassured to see him swimming towards the shore. She turned and yelled at Pele. "Why do you have to be such a bitch for?" She didn't think it, she didn't plan it but the Earth heard her cry and responded with a maelstrom of boulders torn from the ground and sent hurtling towards the fire woman.

Pele was startled. She threw up a defensive flame wall and skipped back on her lava shield but one of the rocks still clipped her side. Again, she fell to the ground and this time she fell hard. She was not happy as she got to her feet nursing her shoulder. "What was that, little girl?"

She stalked towards Teuila with deadly intent and took her in a chokehold. "You have an interesting Gift. It's a little bit of everything, isn't it? I wonder what it will taste like when I rip it from your soul."

Teuila kicked and fought against the constriction at her throat but she couldn't get free. Not until Daniel's water jet blasted into Pele and knocked her a few hundred meters away.

Daniel helped Teuila stand. "Get out of here. Now."

He turned back to where Pele was rising to her feet. "Enough play time. Daniel Tahi, do you know what happened the last time I walked this earth?" Her scream was like the rushing wind and the blazing inferno all mingled as one vortex of fury. "See how a *real* fire goddess does it."

Everyone looked and horror was birthed. Pele turned to the blanket of blue ocean. It began to churn, bubble and boil. A groaning, rending sound as the earth's crust surged to her command. The waters parted, pierced by a colossal up-thrust of earth. She had summoned a volcano that stretched for miles upward and outward. Smoke and sulphur choked the air as the peak vomited scarlet bile. It ran in eager streams down the sides of the black monolith and into the boiling ocean. Steam hissed and spat. Pele gazed upon that which she had made and saw that it was good. She was the creator. She laughed.

But she wasn't finished. "The goddess gives and she takes away …"

"What's she doing?" the onlookers muttered.

Pele soared above the flaming mountain. They couldn't hear the words she spoke but her intent was unmistakable. She raised both hands high overhead, poised in anticipation. A violent sweeping motion as she parted the air. In answer, an entire section of the volcano sheared away. A deafening crash as it collapsed into the sea. She was the destroyer.

"No!" Talei shouted. "Daniel, she's created a mega-tsunami."

I have seen the end of days. The end of our islands, of our Pacific. It will come with fire. It will come with water. Many will fight it, but it will come … You will die. Our islands, our waters, they will never be the same again. I have seen it. The red wave comes. Higher than those hills. Taller than the tallest trees. It burns. The red wave, it burns …

There were two Vasa Loloa left from Tonga and they immediately knew what had happened. "Peau kula," they said, "Red wave."

It was true. Seismic waves resonated from the herculean landslide, a massive disruption of water as many thousands of tons of rock and earth collapsed into the water, generating a tsunami unparalleled by any other in history.

Unless they could stop it.

The two Vasa Loloa raced to the waterfront with Daniel in the lead. On the sand, they acted separately but in union, reaching out with all of their Gifts to pull back the deadly wave, to contain its mega force. At first it seemed as if the ocean paid them no mind. A deep rumbling roar grew as the Red Wave gathered force, as it went about doing whatever it pleased. Daniel felt the force within as it fought to assert some measure of control over an uncontrollable ocean. His *pe'a* and arm band tattoos burned with a dreadful sapphire energy, so violently that it was as if he were being tattooed all over again. A vessel in his brain burst with the pressure and blood seeped from his nose, but still he wouldn't give up. "It's not enough," he cried out. "We need more telesā." He asked the two Tongans beside him, "Are there any more Vasa Loloa on your Council?"

There were two remaining from the Vanuatu Covenant and they ran over to add their will to theirs. "Still not enough," said Daniel. Then he had an idea. "Teuila," he shouted over his shoulder. "Come here."

"Yes?" she was afraid. She looked at his haggard face and the blood that ran now from his eyes and nose and she was afraid. "How can I help?"

"Take my hand. All of you, join hands. Keahi, Lesina you too. Every telesā we've got." Women came running from out of the smoke and devastation. The Sereana from Fiji joined the line. The remaining telesā from Nauru and Niue. A handful of Ariki. Even Talei the shape shifter. All of them clasped hands in an unbroken circle of telesā unity. Daniel glanced over at Teuila. "You've got all three elements in you. You can be our Tangaloa Bone. I want you to channel everyone's Gift through to me so we can get even the non-water telesā to be a part of this."

She gave him a freaked out look. "I don't know how to do that."

"Don't worry. Just do what you did before every time you've used your Gift. I believe in you. We all do," said Daniel. He swayed on his feet then which made Teuila even more panicked. But she did as he asked. Shut her eyes, searched for her happy place and spoke her hopes and wishes out loud there. A surge of energy went through her and then another. It was working.

"What are you doing? Stop that," shouted Pele. She whirled a fire whip over her head and sent it coiling towards Teuila, the connecting link in the circle.

Lesina saw it coming. She broke out of the formation and deflected Pele's attack with a lightning blast. The others sealed up the gap and continued to focus, sending Daniel the strength of their Gifts via the youngest among them. Again Pele targeted Teuila and again Lesina successfully rebutted.

Daniel felt the additional boost of power and he welcomed it and focused it. It almost slipped away from them but finally, the mega tsunami was harnessed and its force quenched. A cheer of celebration from all those on the beach. Teuila gave Lesina an unwilling grin. "Thanks for keeping me out of her kill-shot." In the midst of a battle for their lives, the two shared a rare moment of unity.

A lazy drawl from above them. "How lovely. All of you holding hands and being best friends. So precious!" Pele sneered "How does it go again? United we stand, divided we fall …" She lashed out with a blitz of flame that scattered everyone. The slow and the unlucky were incinerated. More laughter from the fire goddess. "Now Daniel, it's time for you and I to have a heart to heart conversation." Blood rubies of fiery joy danced on her skin as she preened before him. "Do you like what you see Daniel Tahi?"

"No," he answered, "I don't."

"Aww …" she faked disappointment, "and why not? This is your beloved Leila at her very finest. Her most ferocious." A mutter to herself, "That's the problem with you men. You don't like it when your woman blossoms and unleashes her true self.

Can't handle the heat. You only love a woman when she's weak."

"This isn't you Pele," Daniel said. "I know there's a girl inside who just wants to find a place to belong. Who just wants to be loved."

"Silence! I trusted you. I believed you when you said you would help me. You offered me something I'd never had." She looked sadly at the ball of fire that danced in her hands and then caught at her eye as she winced in pain and shouted at spirits only she could hear, "Aaargh, stop hurting me!" She looked around her with a feral blood thirst. "Leave me be demons."

"You're hurt, suffering. Come home. We're your friends, your family."

"I have no friends and my family is dead." She muttered into the wind, "All the fire, all the fury, I held it all in my hands. But it couldn't quench the deadness inside me. The loneliness. I was alone. I was Broken. You took that brokenness and used it against me. You lied to me." She was earth fire incarnate as she screamed. An unspeakable light issued from her core that bled with all the broken hurts of a millennia. It seeped out of her eyes, ripped from her fingertips and toes. An incandescent wave of energy razed across the beach and everything it touched, it turned to ash.

Daniel used his Gift to throw up a protective wall of water that shielded him and the bedraggled team that stood beside him. The force of Pele's blast had the wall buckling and everyone covered their eyes. When they opened them, they stood in the midst of a scorched wasteland that bled with red rivulets of lava.

"Death is my friend. Vengeance is my family," said Pele.

She was poised for her final strike and Daniel knew none of them would survive it. He steeled himself for the extinguishing flame that would come.

"No, this can't be the end. This wasn't my mother's vision. She would not send her daughter here to die," Talei said. She refused to die without a fight, but what she could she do? That's when she heard it, a whispered memory in her heart and soul.

You will soar with wings my child. You will touch the heavens and hold the star-bringer in your hands. Never forget, you are Dravuki. And I love you.

Awareness flooded her. "My mother was right," whispered Talei. "I am Dravuki, the shifter. Not of Ocean. But of all." She closed her eyes, listened to the whisperings of the wind and ran towards where Pele towered above them on her fiery throne.

Pele saw her coming and laughed. "Oh look, here comes the netball girl."

She raised the Tangaloa Bone but before she could wield its power, Talei leapt into the air – and shifted into a bird. The manu sina, wood pigeon and native bird of Samoa. Glossy dark green plumage and ruffled black, she was beautiful. And in true Talei style, she was huge with a generously proportioned wingspan and reaching clawed feet. Pele was startled and stumbled backwards, raising the staff to cover her face, thinking the bird was trying to scratch at her.

She was wrong. Talei was after the Tangaloa Bone. She grabbed it from Pele's hands and swooped into the air in a graceful arc.

"Give that back!" Pele shouted. She lashed out with a whip wire of flame but Talei easily skimmed out of its deadly path. Daniel and the few left on the ground smiled. Even amidst the death and devastation, it was a glorious sight to behold the giant bird escaping from Pele's clutches with her precious Bone.

Pele whirled on them. "Fools. I don't need the Bone to destroy you all. I'm powerful enough to make this entire land sink beneath the waves."

Daniel ignored her. He looked up at the circling manu sina and wished it well. *Fly far away Talei. Don't let her ever get the Tangaloa Bone again. Go to safety. Live well.*

He should have known better. Since when did Talei ever turn her back on her friends? Instead of flying away into the distant horizon, she swooped down low and dropped the Tangaloa Bone at Daniel's feet. He picked it up and it sparked blue at his touch. Pele sent immediate retribution. A direct fire-lash designed to incinerate him and retrieve the Bone.

But at the last instant, Noa stepped into the direct line of attack. She staggered and crumpled. Daniel tried to hold her, support her as she fell but her blistered flesh came away in his hands. He sank to his knees beside her and as he looked at the bubbling seared mess that was her body, he knew she would not survive. "Why, Noa?"

She tried to speak and he leaned in closer to catch the words. "An Olohe lives and dies to obey. Iolana said … must tell you. The key to the Tangaloa Bone is within you. Is … love."

A fragile breath and then she was gone.

In that moment he knew what he must do. It was the only thing left he could do. He knelt for a moment and clasped the Bone in both hands. He didn't know if it would work. He wasn't even sure quite how to do it. But he knew he had to try. If the Bone could take the Gift of any telesā, then surely it could take the Gift of its bearer? He closed his eyes and called forth the Ocean that pulsed within him. The patterned markings on the staff burned blue and his fingers stung with the fire of it. He clenched it tighter.

"What are you doing, Daniel?" asked Teuila fearfully. When he didn't answer, she shook at Keahi's arm, "We have to stop him. I think he's siphoning out his own Gift. He's going to die."

Too late. A serrated edge of cobalt fire knifed down the center of Daniel's chest. His *pe'a*, his sleeve, all his tattoos were ablaze – so much they could barely look at him. "Stop it!" shouted Teuila. She went to grab the staff from his grip but a shield of cerulean energy blocked her path. It burnt and she leapt back with a cry.

Daniel's every nerve ending was aflame. It was both ecstasy and agony at once. There was a direct line from his core to the staff, pulling, tugging, eating away at everything that made him whole, everything that gave him life. He didn't have much time. He stood and walked out onto the wasteland. Knelt in the still warm ashes, with head bowed and offered himself in supplication with the Bone staff before him.

"What's this?" Pele asked in confusion as she gazed down at him. "What are you doing?"

It hurt to talk now. Every word was a supreme effort. "You're right Pele. I wronged you and I'm sorry. As evidence of my regret, I offer you everything I have. My Gift. My life. Take them, but please, let my friends go free and let this land live."

"This is foolish," Pele said. "I'm going to kill you and devour your pitiful Gift."

Indigo veins lit up all over Daniel's body now as if his blood were on fire. He'd almost completely emptied his Gift and heart into the Tangaloa Bone now and he was fighting to hold on by a thread. He had one thing more to say before the light went out. "Leila, I know you're in there. I want you to know I'm sorry. I failed you. I covenanted to always walk beside you, to keep you safe and never leave you. I didn't do that."

"Stop it," said Pele. "Your talk of love is sickening. I've lived over a thousand years and I know without a doubt, there's no such thing."

"Believe what you like," Daniel said. "But here I am. Please take what I offer. Let my friends go. Let this land live."

He held the Bone above him in supplication and an arched web of brilliant blue light blazed above him, his *ie toga* of entreating apology. Pele saw the parallel. She saw the offering and knew the symbolism of it all. She'd seen it before. With him. On a razor-edged hot afternoon in a dusty village. The humility, the public abasement, the supplication. But most of all, she saw the strength, the courage.

The love.

And she rejected it. It enraged her. "I won't allow it. They must pay for what they have done to me. All of you. And you Ocean Boy, you must pay the greatest price of all."

She unlocked the darkest, most desolate part of her. The one that had been refined over a seeming eternity of volcanic suffering in the very bowels of the earth. Pele unleashed that most lethal part of her on the boy who knelt before her. The flames of hate met the shield of love in a fiery conflagration. Those who believed, prayed.

I am the only god who can hear you

The sky lit up with a blinding flash of energy and crackled so loud that it hurt. Everyone was knocked to their feet and the day went dark as if someone had blasted the very stars from the sky.

A star falls from the heavens and lodges in my brain. Burning, searing, piercing. More stars, so many of them, a haze of light, so bright it blinds me. So hot, hotter than any fire. Screaming. I am screaming. I am pinned to the earth with a lance of pain. I will never fly, I will never speak to the stars. Not when they are lodged in my brain.

I scream and the scream fills the world and swallows it up.

After the darkness comes the light. After the silence, comes the sound. After the death, comes the rebirth.

Talei recovered first. She had been the furthest from the blast center.

"Aaargh." She carefully picked herself up. Every piece of her ached and her ears were ringing still. "Where's everyone?"

She looked. A girl with un-mistakable bottle blonde hair lay in a broken heap beside some rocks. It was Lesina. She had no pulse and her neck was bent at an awkward angle. Talei tried without hope to revive her but soon gave up.

Don't think. Don't feel. Just keep moving. Find the others. See if there's any survivors.

She found Teuila and Keahi. He had sheltered her body with his and now he lay sprawled over her. They were both still breathing, but unconscious. She moved Keahi's weight off Teuila and then left them to go in search of Daniel.

Where are you Ocean Boy?

She stumbled over Pele first. She was a soot covered creature, covered in broken branches. Talei threw the debris aside and checked for a pulse, hoping she wouldn't have one. But thinking of Daniel and feeling guilty for such a hope. Pele was alive. Talei resisted the urge to kick her while she was down and moved on. Still searching. Still hoping.

"Daniel?" There was no answer. No movement. No signs of life in this apocalyptic wasteland. Where was he? "Damn you Daniel. Where are you?"

Then she saw him. Bent and broken in a seam in the lava field. Face down, it was only his arm that alerted her to his presence. She tugged him from his prison place. She was puffing, out of breath with the exertion of trying to lift his rugby player weight. "Come on. Move dammit. A little help here please ..." she said to his unhearing self as much as to herself.

Finally she had him pulled free and lying on the ground. She winced to look at him. His once beautiful features were now marred by a jagged cut that ran from his right cheek up his face and into the hairline and the flesh had peeled back to show the white flash of bone. She bent to listen. *Yes,* he had a heartbeat. *Yes,* he was breathing. A barely perceptible rise and fall of his chest but he was definitely breathing. She smoothed his hair from his face and sat back on her knees. Sweet relief made her weak. She wanted to cry now. Maybe it would be alright to have just a little cry while no-one was awake? While no-one was looking?

"Is he alright?" Pele's voice startled her.

Talei leapt to her feet. Defensive. "Stay away from him. Haven't you done enough already?"

Pele was a ragged mess. She didn't look like a fire goddess. She just looked like a bruised, battered and somewhat scared girl. "Please, I have to know. Is he alive?" she said.

"Why? Do you want to have another go at killing him?" Talei snarled. "Don't come any closer. I will hurt you."

Pele ignored her. Tears streamed down her cheek as she stumbled towards them. "Daniel? Please, let me go to him." She looked up at Talei with agonized eyes, "Don't you understand? I love him."

Shocked, all Talei could do was stand there as Pele fell to her knees beside the boy she had tried to destroy.

Redemption

"I knew you would come for me. I knew you would find me." The words hurt to say. The sound of my own voice is a harsh surprise. But it doesn't compare to the pain that cripples my every breath. My every movement. I welcome it though, relish its pounding ache, the way it intensifies as I try to move. Because pain means I am me. I am alive.

I am Leila.

And he – he is Daniel.

I reach with trembling fingers, to trace the outline of his face. Brow. Cheek. The rough cut of his unshaven jawline. Lips. The mouth that I thought I would never kiss again. There is a deep cut in his face, so deep I know he will always bear the scar. I can see red, pulsing tissue and white bone. There is blood, fast-drying and crusted on his forehead, more matted blood in his hair.

He is the most beautiful thing I have ever seen.

He opens his eyes and stares at me unsmiling. Unsure. Wary. "Leila? Is that you?" He grabs at my hand roughly holding it away from his face. His beautiful face. I can't help the tears "You're hurt. Oh Daniel, who did this?" Again I touch him. I don't want to ever stop touching him. Ever. This time he lets me. Unmoving, his face unreadable. Again I ask, "What happened? Who did this to you?

"You." One word. But it hits me like a brick to my chest.

"What? Me? I would never hurt you. What are you talking about?" Confusion.

Daniel tries to stand, tries to scramble away from me. Why? I see how he is unsteady on his feet, weaving slightly. Weary. In pain. I move after him. Take him in my arms. He winces. "Leila, is it really you? Because I don't think I've got anything left to keep fighting you if it isn't."

His legs buckle and I catch him, help to lower him to the ground. He lies in my lap. I hold him with gentle hands and my tears fall on his face. Blood, sweat and tears. He breathes and then he is still. And in that moment, I remember.

Everything.

I remember the first time I saw you. Red, gold and jade green. A crooked smile. A lazy grin.

I remember blindfolds and mountain springs. Laughter scattering on the breeze like the froth of a waterfall.

I remember salt tears on a liquid silver night by a forest pool. A boy who listened. A boy who carried me. Held me. Comforted me. A boy who made me laugh.

I remember a kiss that set the world on fire. Pain and pleasure splintering the night with red heat. A boy who didn't run. A boy who braved a maelstrom of fury and then helped me calm it.

I remember sending you away. Ripping a still-beating heart out of my chest, stifling the agony with fire. Always with fire. Longing for you. Wanting you. Nights spent crying for you. Daniel.

I remember dancing to earth's song underneath a majestic night sky, before an audience of strangers but with eyes only for you. Skin glistening with coconut oil, the noble warrior of every myth and legend. Guided by your voice as it sings to me. Sings of love, loss and betrayal.

I remember standing against the Sisterhood. With you by my side. I remember watching as they tortured you. I remember dying as they killed you. As they gave your body to the ocean.

I remember silver dolphins dancing on a lace covered blackness, bringing you back to me.

I remember heat. Fire. Longing. I remember you, hard and needing everywhere that I am soft and wanting. '*No, Leila. It means not now.*'

I remember working alongside you in a haze of acrid steel smoke, sparks of blue fire scattering over wet grass, fireworks on our skin. Coils of barbed wire and blistered hands on chain link fencing. Rivulets of sweat glistening on bare skin, overalls looped about your hips. The line of desire that speaks to me, tracing from torso, curve to hip and beyond. You, angry. And yet so fiercely beautiful in your anger.

I remember the bite of the steel tooth against my skin as my tattoo marks me with your story. Strength, resolution, resolve, commitment, laughter, love. Samoa College field alight with a hundred candles, hoping, wishing. *The answer is yes. It's always been yes.*

I remember an ocean on fire, alight with promise, hope and longing as *Vasa Loloa* claimed you as her own. Fire flies of *fanua afi* encircling us with warmth. You. Me. Us.

I remember a volcano. A nuclear battery. I remember what death feels like. White diamonds of pain. The ecstasy of melding with my Mother Earth's molten fire. *Daniel, forgive me.*

And I remember her. Pele. She who enslaved me, melded her spirit with mine.

I remember all that you are to me. I remember all that I am to you. I remember all that we are together.

I am Daniel Tahi. I have your name tattooed in my heart. And you don't even remember who I am …

And I cry.

"You found me. You didn't give up. You came for me," I whisper.

I lean close so I can catch his words. "Always. I promised you, I'd never give up. Even if the ocean burns with earth fire. Always."

His eyes, they are closed but that golden smile, the one that always finds me, catches me in my darkest places, tugs at my heartstrings and lights that slow-burn of heat deep in my secret places. He smiles that smile at me and I know – I am home.

I was Pele, the daughter of Noalani the Covenant Keeper. I was Broken. And now I am whole.

I am Leila, the daughter of Nafanua the Covenant Keeper. I was Lost. And now I am found.

I am Pele. I am Leila.

I am Beloved.

White Ginger

We had destroyed over a hundred acres of forest. The lava scorched field would bear testament to the battle for centuries to come. The smoldering expanse was on all the international news. Media teams from many nations descended upon Samoa to report on a volcanic eruption that was not predicted by any science. A geological mystery. The tsunami generated by Pele's lava landslide had completely wiped out the islands of Manono, Apolima and Nu'usafe'e. Six uninhabited islands of Northern Tonga were consumed by the waves as well. But it could have been so much worse. Those who study such things were baffled as to how and why a mega-tsunami could simply stop in its tracks.

We tallied the dead. Noa was gone. Apollonia and nine of the Ariki were dead. So were two of the telesā from American Samoa. They were dust in the wind somewhere over the ocean. Two telesā each from Vanuatu, Niue and Nauru were gone, one from Tonga, swallowed up by the raging earth. Three of the Sereana of Fiji were critically wounded but they would recover. There was only one telesā left from the atolls of Tokelau and one from Tonga.

In the epic battle amongst themselves and against Pele, the Pacific suffered a great loss of her elemental guardians. It would take time to rebuild the various Covenants and there were wounds of mistrust between the islands which may never heal. The Keawe would not quickly forgive the murder of their Sensate Iolana or the death of her protector. There was even talk the Olohe would seek retribution against all who had conspired against their leader. Betrayal has far-reaching effects.

But those were worries for another day. We had other things far more pressing to worry about. Teuila and Keahi both needed a hospital stay for their injuries. Daniel had surgery to repair his face and the livid rip down his torso. We teased him about the wound that ran from cheekbone, through his eye socket and to his forehead. "*Ka'i tuff*, it's our very own Harry Potter," said Simone.

Daniel laughed from his hospital bed and it was good to hear that rich, golden sound. "No, not the boy wizard," he mock groaned. "Why can't I be someone truly badass, like Scarface?"

Keahi made a derisive sound, "You'd actually have to *be* a badass for that to happen."

More laughter because every moment needed the happiness squeezed out of it. That's what staring death in the face does to you. It wipes out the things that divide you, reveals them as inconsequential. Keahi and Daniel would never be best friends, but they had stood together in battle and that would forge a bond stronger than male ego and testosterone.

When everyone else had gone and it was just Daniel and I in the hospital room, I moved to sit beside him on the bed. He clasped my fingers in his and took them to his lips. With no-one else around, his mask of easy assurance slipped and he looked weary. His smile was tinged with sadness. I knew he thought of his grandmother, her funeral we'd attended the day before, and my heart bled for him. I danced my lips against his bandaged wound, to his cheek and then he turned and captured my mouth with his, bringing his hand up to hold me close. It was a bittersweet kiss but I was hungry for it. We'd nearly lost each other and I would never stop wanting him close, worrying over all the possibilities that could take him away from me.

I gently pulled away from him, a quick glance at my *malu*. He caught my gaze. "Still nothing?"

"No." I rushed to reassure him, "It's a good thing. Fire is what almost took you away from me. I hope it never comes back." Ever since that horror-filled day when he'd offered Pele his *ifoga*, neither of us could speak with Water or Fire. It was as if our Gifts had never existed. There were theories as to why but nothing concrete, like our Gifts had cancelled each other out ... Or Pele took the *vasa loloa* Gift Daniel had offered her and then she died and everything elemental in us died with her ... Or the Tangaloa Bone had negated us both. I didn't care. Thinking about it gave me a headache, a throbbing behind my right eye – so I didn't want to dwell on it. I forced the worrying thoughts away and smiled at Daniel. "What about you, anything?"

"It's gone. Dead and buried." *Like the one's we've lost.'*

Neither of us said anything for a moment as we thought about all our loved ones who had died over our tangled telesā journey. My Dad. Nafanua, Jason, Lesina, Salamasina. Tavake. In the face of so much loss, the fact both of us were no longer Gifted – was a very small thing indeed. I took a deep breath and wished a very little bit for a shred of fanua afi to give me courage for what I planned to do next.

"Umm ... Daniel?" my voice came out all shaky and he gave me a worried frown.

"What is it? What's wrong?"

"Nothing. There's something I want to tell you. Ask you. Since you freed me from Pele's mind prison thing, I've been slowly getting my brain in order, sorting through memories, making sense of stuff, figuring out what's real, which memory belongs to me and which bits are from Pele's possession of me and ..." I was babbling now, nonsensical rubbish. "Dammit!" I moved away from the bed and started pacing, trying to calm my galloping heart rate. Another deep breath. (At this rate, there'd be no more air left in this room to breathe.)

"Leila, it's okay. It's me. Don't worry. I get it."

"You do?" *He does? Well, that's unexpected. I'm not sure I even get it myself ...*

"Yeah. Sure it hurt to see you with Keahi, but that wasn't you, not really. It was Pele and her attraction to him was mostly because they were both *fanua afi*. I know you weren't in control of your body or your feelings. If you're trying to tell me you and Keahi ..." Daniel hesitated with a pained look in his eyes, "got ... together ... got close ... then you have to know, it doesn't change anything. I love you. I always will. No matter what."

It took a few minutes for me to register just what Daniel was trying to say and then it hit me. "What? No, I didn't get with Keahi. At least I don't think I did." An image flashed into my mind. Me and Keahi, kissing, bodies aflame on a lava field ... and then it blacked out. No matter how hard I tried, I couldn't remember any more. *No! We didn't. Please tell me that's all we did.* Fear, panic and rage threatened to choke me. "I have to go. I'll be back."

"Leila, where are you going?" Daniel called after me but I was off down the hall. I had to know the truth.

Keahi was sitting up on the hospital bed watching television, his ankle in a cast. The crash of the door as I threw it open startled him. A smile when he saw me – which quickly disappeared when I yelled at him. "What did you do to me?"

"I've got no clue what you're talking about."

"When I was … absent from my body, when Pele was in charge, what did you do to me? Or with me? Did it even matter to you that she'd stolen my body?" I demanded hotly.

Awareness dawned on his face. Bitterness. "So quick to judge and condemn me Leila. I'm always gonna be the bad guy with you, aren't I?"

"This isn't about you." I was trembling. "This is about me. You don't know what it's like to have someone violate you from in here," I pointed to my forehead. "I was a prisoner in my own mind, she took everything away from me. I fought, I cried for help and no-one came. I was all alone with a madwoman and I could see myself fading away. It was terrifying in the darkness, without a voice, wondering if even my soul was still my own. You don't know what it was like, no-one does." And finally then, I snapped. I'd been holding everything in check, worrying over Daniel, helping to make funeral arrangements, and not wanting to burden him with everything that poisoned me inside.

I couldn't hold it in any longer. My body shook as I cried. I thought about the hours, the days, the weeks trapped in a prison of silence while another lived, breathed, laughed, fought and loved as me. Pretended to be me.

Keahi limped around the bed and carefully took me in his arms. He was tender and gentle as he whispered words of reassurance and comfort, as he held me and let me cry. Then he sat beside me and listened as I told him about the darkness, the visits from a one-eyed woman who was haunted by the spirits of those she had consumed. I told him how my *malu* and the memories of my mother had strengthened me, given me the will to carry on. "At times I was so disoriented I thought I heard her voice," I confessed. "There was even the fragrance of gardenias, her favorite flower. A welcome addition to the slimy cave I was in."

Finally, I told Keahi of my guilt. "So many people died because of me. So many got hurt, even you. Daniel's grandmother would still be alive if not for me. He says he loves me, but how can he ever forgive me for this? I don't deserve to be with him or to be happy or to even still be alive. These hands killed innocent people and caused so many bad things to happen. I just feel so bad inside, evil even." Embarrassed by own drama, I made a lame attempt at a joke. "I'm like Lady Macbeth, floating around the halls in her nightgown, scrubbing at imaginary blood stains on my hands, *Out out damn spot …*"

Keahi interrupted me then with an incredulous look. "Wait up, Leila you've got it all wrong. That was Pele who did those things, not you. Your agency was taken away from you. Your body and firepower were stolen from you. Pele made those choices, not you. She was one messed up woman." He put both hands on my shoulders and shook me. Nicely. "You're not evil, or dirty or bad or whatever. You're an incredibly strong and brave person who's suffered through some crazy shit. You're not Pele. Trust me, I met her, I should know." He hesitated then and moved away from me. "Leila, I'll be honest with you. Pele was dangerous and out of control, but she had a whole lot of hurt inside. I got to see some of it and for a while there, we had something."

"What kind of something," I asked, dreading the answer.

He rushed to allay the fear in my eyes. "Not that kind of something. She was beautiful and umm … kinda hot. Like you. We made out a little. She wanted more. I said no."

It was so unusual to see Keahi embarrassed that I almost wanted to laugh. I was also hugely relieved to hear he and I hadn't done any more than what I'd seen in the brief memory flash. "I'm sorry I accused you of taking advantage of me. Y'know, while my body was possessed by a thousand year old fire goddess demon."

A grin and the old swagger was back. "I only get it on with girls who want it from me. And trust me, there's a lot of them."

"Whatever you say." A roll of my eyes. "I'm just grateful you remembered I'm not one of them, even if Pele was throwing her skank self all over you." I stood up to leave and then dropped the teasing tone. "Thank you."

"For what?"

"For respecting me and my body – even when I wasn't in control of it. And for listening just now."

He called to me just as I got to the door. There was no taunting or leering swagger, only quiet intent in his dark eyes. "For the record, I said no to Pele. But what I wanted to do was say yes. To you."

I left Keahi's room reeling. He'd given me lots to think about – and some things I didn't want to think about. But I walked down the corridor with much lighter steps. It would be a long time before I ever stopped feeing responsible for everything that had happened over the last few weeks but I wasn't drowning in angry guilt anymore. The future looked a little clearer and I was even more certain of what I wanted to do. What I needed to do.

But before I could act, I needed to get a few things first …

The sun was setting when I headed back to the hospital. Daniel greeted me with a hint of relief when I walked in the room. "There you are," he said. "I was getting worried."

"Sorry. I had to get some stuff done." I gave him a quick hug, breathing in the deliciousness that was Daniel. "I need you to do something for me."

"What is it?"

I produced a blindfold with a huge grin. He fake groaned. "No … not that again! You do realize I'm incapacitated and you can't go all Fifty Shades on me, right?"

"You wish," I teased. "We're going on a little trip. Doctor says you can't go hiking all over the mountains yet and even if you could, I don't know where our secret pool is since you haven't ever told me."

He interrupted with a grin, "I never will either. You'll have to be extra nice to me and maybe I'll take you there again." He raised an eyebrow at me with teasing suggestiveness. Seeing him like that did sparkly things to me.

"Stop distracting me, I want to talk to you about something important but I have to take you away first. Put the blindfold on."

He obeyed and I left him sitting on the edge of the bed while I slipped out to grab the supplies I'd left outside the door. A few quick adjustments to the room and everything was ready. I hit the Play button and went to kneel behind him on the bed, with my hands on his shoulders. The sounds of a nature CD filled the room – a dancing mountain spring with the muted call of birds, the rustle of wind through grass and the light hum of insects. I whispered in his ear, "What can you hear, Daniel?"

He went very still and I knew that he knew what was happening. "Water. I hear water," he answered quietly.

"Can you notice anything else?"

"Ginger flowers. I can smell white ginger." He uncovered his eyes and looked around.

A few tea light candles scattered around the room, gave a warm glow to the darkness. A little stereo on the bedside table. And a huge bouquet of gorgeous white ginger. It wasn't much, but it was enough. He sat on the very edge of the bed and brought me around to stand in front of him. One arm curved around my waist and pulled me close so I was pressed against his solid warmth. He gazed into my eyes and slowly traced the outline of my lips with his thumb. "Perfect," he said. "Everything's perfect. Now, what did you need to talk about?"

The nearness of him, the scent of him and that thing he was doing to my lips with his fingers – it was all very distracting. In that moment, I could think of lots of things I needed – and none of them involved talking. *Focus!*

"Umm … I wanted to see if you could help refresh my memory. I think I recall you saying some things to me, but I'm not sure. I need you to verify if these words sound familiar?"

He gave me a quizzical grin. "Go ahead. I'm listening."

"Did you tell me, that when you find the person who makes you want to believe in forever, then you should hold on to them and never let them go?" I asked.

He went very still and the look in his eyes was unreadable. "Possibly."

I continued, "You and I are going to face a lot of storms because of what we are. Heck, we've already faced some pretty awful storms and we know we can handle them, if we face them together."

The world stopped spinning. Time stood still. Everything was this moment, right here in this hospital room with his hands at my waist anchoring me to earth while I drowned in the green depths of his eyes. I whispered, "A long time ago, right here in this hospital, you said we should make every day our forever because we don't know how many days we're going to get."

His voice was low and deep and filled with a taut wonder. "You remember ... Leila Folger, are you proposing to a boy who's all cut up and burnt in hospital?"

"Yes, Daniel I love you. You make me want forever. I'm asking you please, if you'll marry me?"

He held my face in his hands, cradled me as if he feared this moment would shatter into a thousand pieces. "The answer is yes. It's always been yes." A resolute smile. "You're mine Leila. And I am yours."

And then he was kissing me and it was a perfect moment that would never end.

A Song

We were married on a lonely beach at the end of a rough track through the forest bush. The strip of sand gleamed white in the fast-fading sunset, an explosion of cerulean, scarlet and auburn. A river met the sea there and the mangrove trees were home to an abundance of birds and other wildlife.

Simone had made my dress from unmarked siapo cloth, creamy ivory on my skin. A sheathe that skimmed what little curves I had with slits on each side to make striding through sand an easy task. He had grumbled about the strict instructions to keep it simple. Keep it plain. "No veil, no train, no meringue puff skirts – you hear me?!"

A pout. "Fine. But don't expect me to hold back with my outfit. I have to unleash my creative fire somewhere, somehow."

I had wanted Simone to walk with me up the aisle but Daniel beat me to it, asking him to be his best man. "You don't mind do you?" he'd asked.

"Of course not. As long as he's a key part of our wedding ceremony, it doesn't matter whose best friend he walks alongside." I smiled, "Besides, I know he's crazy delighted that you asked him."

It meant Simone got executive decision rights over the men's outfits which worried me a teensy little bit as I contemplated the possibility of my future husband wearing a sequined loincloth and not much else. But I needn't have worried. When I saw him waiting for me by the oceanside in a black *ie faitaga* and white *elei* patterned dress shirt, my breath caught in my throat. He was gloriously beautiful. Even more so with the jagged scar that ran from forehead to cheekbone. And the look in his eyes when he saw me told me that he thought the same of me.

Teuila, Sinalei and Talei were my bridesmaids. Three women who had helped teach me the meaning of sisterhood. They were dressed in gray elei dresses spangled with silver. I didn't want any colors of the fire I had lost, any reminders of the volcano that had held me captive. The pastor from Aunty Matile's church performed the ceremony and the choir's melded voices added reverence to the worshipful natural beauty that surrounded us.

My Samoan relatives weren't happy about my getting married at the frightful age of nineteen. On this my American family was in wholehearted agreement. Daniel and I were young, and fresh out of school. Headed for university in New Zealand and according to their unspoken dire predictions … headed for heartbreak and misery as a couple who were marrying way too early.

"Why don't you two just live together when you go to college?" Aunt Annette had asked, as we went for my dress fitting. Nicely but directly. "You don't need to get married to be together."

I only smiled at her. Some things I couldn't explain. Not to someone who hadn't been through what we had. Not to someone who hadn't lived and died several deaths in the last year. Not to someone who wasn't telesā. The wedding was a formality only. Daniel and I were already covenanted. Bound by more than love, trust and belonging. We were bound by Fanua. Getting married was only because Daniel wanted to 'do things properly.'

And I? I just wanted to be with the one I loved more than life itself. Share the same breath. Walk the same path. Always.

There weren't many guests. The wedding was small by Samoan standards. (Anything under a hundred was considered pitifully cheap and small …) But everyone who meant something to us was there. Simone had set the scene, working on all the arrangements with his merciless energy, to the point where his volunteers wanted to do him bodily harm. Maleko and Keahi had been threatening to have him abducted and delivered to Tafaigata Prison if he didn't cut them some slack.

The final results were breathtaking.

Shell candles marked out an aisle between the rows of seated guests. Their flickering light on the sand was accompanied by the golden stars far above. The river and the ocean shallows were dotted with floating coconut shell candles, lulled by the soft breeze and the slow pull of the tide. The black waters further out were dancing with silver dolphins. Daniel may not have been able to speak to the ocean any longer but clearly her creatures had not forgotten his voice. They filled the air with their high pitched clicks and chirps, reminding him, reminding us – that Daniel had been a Son of *Vasa Loloa*. I bit at my lip so hard it bled, catching at my tears with bitter intensity. I turned away from the boldly beautiful ocean as sadness wracked me. It was too soon for me to miss my fire gift but for Daniel I mourned. It was my fault he had lost his ocean power. It was my fault he would never burn with that same joy of oneness with the liquid earth.

Talei felt my sorrow, guessed at it. She took my arm and gave me a gentle shake. Whispered. "Stop it. This is a happy day. For you and for him. Don't spoil it with thoughts of the past. Thoughts of what could have been. See? He waits for you. He doesn't gaze at the ocean and miss its call. No, he only has eyes for you."

I looked, blinked away my tears before they could ruin the makeup Simone had so carefully applied. Talei was right. There was no sadness on Daniel's face. He stood there, eyes shining in the moonlight. He had that look on his face. The one that spoke of a quiet peace and joy.

'*I loved you before you were a fire goddess. You're the one I want to be with. The one that has me hoping and believing in forever.*'

It calmed me, soothed me. The love we shared had its beginnings long before either of us had walked this earth. I felt that this ceremony, this moment – was a reflection, a memory of another long-ago moment in our mythology. Long ago, when this land was new, when Tangaloa joined man to the earth, through the creation of woman. *Fatu ma le ele ele.* Heart and Earth.

Uncle Tuala and Aunty Matile stood beside me in the aisle of moonlit sand as Daniel sang on his beat up old guitar. He sat on a piece of driftwood in the midst of a scattering of frangipani petals and played his version of 'Falling in Love'. Each note pierced me with sweet sadness because when a moment is so perfect it hurts because you know you can't ever catch it and freeze it. Because part of what it makes it so perfect is its fragile fleetingness.

I didn't know I was crying. I didn't notice lots of other people had tears in their eyes. All I could see was Daniel. As he sang his love to me. My bare feet sank lightly in the powder soft sand as we walked forward. Uncle Tuala had a somber expression on his face as he held my arm and Aunty Matile was valiantly pretending she wasn't crying. We walked through more flower petals that reminded me of a long-ago verandah covered in flame flowers. I flushed at the memory. It wasn't right to be thinking of another boy and his flowers when I was walking to the one who would be mine forever. I raised my head and caught Keahi's eyes. Regret? A flash of pain. That was quickly replaced by a cheeky grin when he realized I was looking at him. *You look hot fire girl,* he mouthed at me. *But not as hot as me.*

Shut up. I mouthed back. He did look very handsome though, if a little uncomfortable in his first time wearing an *ie faitaga*. Daniel had surprised him by asking him to be one of the groomsmen with Maleko and the two of them were an impeccable pair in their elei shirts that complemented my bridesmaids. Simone was also in a formal dress lavalava but his shirt was threaded with gold and he'd gold-gelled his hair to match.

When we reached the front, Aunty Matile gave me a tearful hug before going to sit down. Uncle Tuala bent to give me a quick kiss on the cheek and whispered, "You look beautiful Leila. Remember, you will always have a home with us, if you need one. We love you – even if you are telesā."

Tuala knew?! He knew what I was? Or what I had been, I quickly amended. Before I could react to his words, he moved away to sit beside Matile in the front row where she was dabbing at her eyes with a lace handkerchief. I gave him a watery smile and he nodded his head at me with understanding in his eyes.

And then it was time to take Daniel's hand. A small sigh escaped me at his touch. It felt good. It felt right to stand beside him. To be joining my path with his. Whatever sadness, whatever doubts or nervousness I had felt – it all fled at his touch. I was his and he was mine. Even if we were no longer *vasa loloa* and *fanua afi*.

I looked up in his eyes and they spoke a thousand words. Of love, faith, trust, patience, and all the limitless possibilities of our lives together. I couldn't breathe in that moment as I realized the enormity of what we were to each other. Everything we had endured – it had all come to this moment.

The pastor broke the spell. "Family and friends of Leila and Daniel, welcome. We have gathered here on this beautiful night to witness these two young people make a sacred commitment to one another …"

I barely registered the rest of the ceremonial words. My heart was pounding in my chest and there was a building avalanche of emotion within. *It's really happening. I can't believe it.* I thought of sorrow, suffering, desolate loneliness in a dark cave and so much more – and I was thankful.

It was time to exchange the rings. We had sketched out the designs ourselves with the help of a master craftsman who had fashioned them for us from finest materials of black pearl and whalebone. The pastor pronounced us married. Husband and wife. Would I ever get used to those words? I had expected to feel different. Strange. But I felt the same. His hand in mine still felt like perfection. It was foolish I realized – to think that a few words could possibly improve on what was already perfect. We were what we always had been. Daniel and Leila.

Then we kissed under a flawless sky. His lips were feather soft and gentle. Sweet pineapple and a salty edge of coconut. He was the exhilaration of the rushing falls on a steaming tropical night, the burn of volcanic rock baked hot in the noon-day sun, the caress of a jasmine fragranced breeze as I danced barefoot in a moonlit night. He was all this and more. But unlike that first kiss, there was no explosion of earth's fire, no pain, no burn, no wild rage. It was just Daniel.

And it was enough.

After the completion of the ceremony, everyone came forward to congratulate us. There were hugs, kisses and good-natured teasing. Simone was crying and trying to hide it with exuberance. Uncle Thomas' voice was gruff as he shook Daniel's hand, "Be good to her. Or else ..."

Annette rolled her eyes. "Oh please Thomas! Pay him no mind Daniel. Welcome to the family." Through it all, Daniel was his polite and nobly diplomatic self.

The wedding feast was far less stressful. Aunty Matile had outdone herself making all my favorite Samoan dishes while Annette had gotten everything else catered by a team of chefs flown in from New York. There was food, music and lots of Diet Coke with crushed ice. I'd been too nervous all day to eat, so I was starving but before I could let myself go with the food, Simone dragged me away to get ready for my *siva*.

It was tradition for the bride to dance for her husband. And for him to dance for her. Simone placed a boar's tusk necklace around my neck and tucked my dress up high on each side so that my malu was clearly showing. I danced the *taualuga* meaning every motion and movement as it reverberated a chant of joy through me. My family joined me in the *siva* with enthusiastic cheers.

Then it was Daniel's turn. Cheered on by the music and the encouragement of his friends, he stripped off his shirt and my pulse raced at the sight of his chiseled body. The silver moon painted his *pe'a* white in the velvet night as he retied his lavalava so that it skimmed his calves. He fake posed as everyone hooted and jeered at him, jostling him to the center of the dance area. He searched for me before he started and then he threw me that crooked grin which always yanked at my heartstrings and left me feeling like I'd been slammed by an ocean wave. The music began to play and he bowed with an expansive opening of his broad arms to all, but his gaze marked his dance as being only for me.

Daniel danced under a star-lit sky with the sound of the ocean as our backdrop. Maleko and Keahi were forced into joining him on the dance floor. Maleko was a great dancer while Keahi had a sour look on his face. I laughed at his discomfort knowing full well he just didn't like being forced to share the limelight with his old rival. All of them looked magnificent in the moonlight but I couldn't tear my eyes away from Daniel as he led the dance.

After the dancing and feasting, there were toasts made and we cut our cake – a stunning creation of white and gold-dusted frangipani flowers that cascaded down the sides of the tiered white chocolate cake. Then finally, it was time for Daniel and I to leave. The boys had decorated the green bomb with ribbons, confetti and obscene amounts of whipped cream. We were showered with flower petals as we ran to the truck and everyone waved goodbye as we drove away.

Our wedding night destination was Daniel's secret. I'd tried without success to get him to tell me where we were going but he hadn't budged. "Are you going to tell me now?" I asked.

"No. Nothing you do can get it out of me," he said with a grin.

I sidled across the seat and slipped my hand into his free one. "I would test that but I don't want you to crash this truck," I teased. A quick kiss on his cheek.

We drove for about half an hour before Daniel turned off the road, down a secluded track through the rainforest which led to a quiet strip of sand. A moonlit lagoon and in the distance – an island. Its dark mass rose up out of the sea and on it, a single light beckoned. Daniel pointed. "There, that's where we're going. *Nu'u o le Ia Sa*. Island of the Sacred Fish, the dolphin."

There was a canoe pulled up on the shore waiting for us. Daniel grabbed our bags and then helped me into the boat, making sure I was safely seated before pushing off from the sand and jumping in. He stripped off his elei dress shirt so he could better paddle the canoe. "Do you need any help?" I asked.

He shook his head, "No, just sit back and enjoy the view."

I'm sure he meant the seascape around us but I couldn't stop looking at him. The way the ridged terrain of his torso rippled as he flexed and powered the canoe through the black water with strong, sure movements. He was breathtaking.

Daniel paddled until the boat grazed against sand and coral. Then he jumped into the water and guided the boat the remainder of the way, steadying it until it was partially beached on the shore. I stood up, stretching my cramped legs but before I could climb out, he swept me into his arms, catching my exclamation of surprise with his mouth on mine. He let me go, and my body slid down against his as he kissed me with a slow burning fire filled with promise of things to come. It left me weak and wilting into him. We stood there in waist deep water and kissed with an aching tenderness that made it impossible for me to know where I ended and where the ocean began.

I don't have to hold back. I don't have to stay in control. I have no fire that can ruin this. No fire that can hurt him.

The thought as it came was intoxicating. We were alone under the stars with ocean and earth embracing us – and there were no limits. No more restraints. No more waiting. No nothing. Just Daniel and I.

It means not now Leila.

I could feel him pressed against me and every piece of me that could feel him screamed with crazed delight. And every piece that *couldn't* feel him screamed even louder with wanting. He trailed kisses of fire down my throat, then to my shoulders as he had once before. Only this time I knew he wouldn't stop. He wouldn't hold back. And that lifted me to dizzying heights of sensation. Dimly I felt him hesitate. An indrawn breath. He was looking around us at the water.

"What is it?" I looked where he looked. And time stood still. All around us the ocean was aglow with silver blue luminescence. It was achingly beautiful. "I thought you had no more *Vasa Loloa* powers?"

His voice was hushed with awe. "I don't. It's not me. It's them."

I looked again and then I saw them. Hundreds, maybe thousands of incandescent glowing sea creatures. Jelly fish of all sizes and shapes, lilting in invisible currents, dancing on wires of joyousness. I should have been afraid but I wasn't. I felt wonder at the majestic mystery of it. I breathed, "They're beautiful. Why are they here?"

Daniel turned from them back to look down at me. He held my face in his hands, ran his thumb to caress my bottom lip. He had a half-smile as he tipped his head to one side, like he was listening. "For you. For us. They're here for us." He bent to taste my lips again, his tongue playing with mine in delicious familiarity. His hands held me with the gentle strength of the ocean. "*Vasa Loloa* rejoices with us, congratulates us on our union."

And then all thoughts of the glowing ocean were forgotten.

We never made it up the hill to the glowing light of our honeymoon *fale*. Instead, Daniel spread out his lavalava there on the sand. He helped me unzip the ivory cream dress and it slipped from my skin in soft folds about my feet. He gathered a handful of my hair and lifted it aside so he could breathe a kiss on my shoulder. I was naked in the moonlight and inexplicably shy with this boy who had seen me burn all my clothes off countless times. This boy who had carried my burnt defiled body into a healing ocean and back out again in all its gleaming newness. This boy who's ocean fire had burned in harmony with mine. And yet, I was still shy. He was so perfect. So beautiful. What if he didn't like what he saw? What if he was disappointed with what I had to give?

Foolish me. I needn't have worried. He turned me to him, and his gaze, his hands, his body, his every worshipful move spoke to me of his love.

He laid me down and loosened the clips from my hair so that it framed my face. He whispered my name as I reached for him. I wanted to feel, to taste, all that which I had been wanting for so long. The ocean tugged at our feet with foam caresses as we explored each other. His hands sculpted me, molded me anew. His lips, his tongue – found stories in me that I had never shared with another. His smile, his laugh – teased from me, delights I had never known.

It seemed as if *Fanua* herself sanctioned our discoveries. At one point, we paused for panting breath, hot and slippery with sweat and the sky answered. Lightning seared the sky, thunder crashed and rain pelted us. Exhilarating. Refreshing. We rejoiced in it. We made love in a rain storm of fierceness and we were unafraid. Ocean and sky gave us champagne sparklers of light.

Earth gave us warmth. *Matagi* shared her raw strength and together all the elements helped to make us one.

Again and again.

In a song as ancient as the molten earth and the starlight that bathed us, we brought each other to completeness.

Ten Years Later

"Daniel, can you get the door? I'm still trying to get Moon dressed." Leila sighed in frustration as the most stubborn person she'd ever had the misfortune to meet put on her angry face.

"No Mama. I want to wear my overalls! Be like Dada." The little girl pulled away out of Leila's grasp and tried to make a run for it.

Leila had fifty guests about to descend on her house and no time for stubborn five year olds who refused to wear their birthday dresses. She used her daughter's full name which was always a bad sign. "Dammit! Salamoanasina Nafanua Folger Tahi you get over here right this minute." Leila was chief partner in her own law firm and CEO for a multi-million dollar pharmaceutical corporation, a successful businesswoman who could strike fear in the hearts of her employees if they slacked off on the job. *Surely I can handle one little girl with an attitude?!*

The aforementioned little girl, put her hands on her hips, eyes wide in shock, "Mama, you said a bad word!"

Leila groaned. Exasperation giving way to laughter as her daughter continued to glare at her accusingly. "You're right, that was a bad word and Mama is very sorry. I'll never ever say bad words again. Now come here and please put your dress on." Leila resorted to that tried and true method that mothers the world over knew would have a one hundred percent success rate. Bribery. "I'll let you have ice cream."

Her daughter had a crafty gleam in her eyes. "Now? Before I eat dinner?"

Leila shook her head with a stern glare which turned into a frazzled grimace as the doorbell rang again. More guests were arriving. Now was not the time to negotiate. "Fine, Moon. Yes, now. As soon as you put your dress on, I'll get you some ice cream. Quick, get dressed."

But Moon wasn't ready to give in. "And I don't haf to eat carrots. Or tomatoes. Nuffink yucky."

"Yes, yes no carrots or tomatoes. That's it. No more playing around. Get dressed NOW."

At last, content with winning the battle, the little girl allowed her harassed mother to dress her in the ruffled red elei mu'umu'u style dress. She made horrible scrunched up faces the whole time that Leila whipped a brush through her tangles and pulled her long thick brown hair into two braids. A red hibiscus tucked in her hair was the finishing touch before she tugged her daughter to stand beside her in the mirror. "See? You look beautiful." A sigh at Moon's frown. "Well, you would look beautiful if you didn't have that sour face. It's your birthday party with all your favorite foods and all your favorite people coming to celebrate. Can't you have a smile?"

Moon wrinkled up her nose in distaste at her reflection. "Don't like it. Wanna wear my overalls and hard hat like Dada."

Leila groaned. "I wish you hadn't opened your present this morning!" She knelt beside her daughter. "Baby listen, your Dad promised to take you to work with him tomorrow and you can wear your new overalls then, okay? If you wear it to your party, you might get ice cream on it. Can't have ice cream and cake on your engineer overalls, now can you?"

Moon didn't look convinced. But just then, a loud sing-song voice carried through to the bedroom, "Where's my gorgeous god-daughter? Where's the birthday girl?"

Her face lit up. "Simone!" She wriggled free of her mother and dashed out to the living room. Leila followed with a resigned sigh.

Simone exclaimed dramatically at the sight of her. "There she is! But this cannot be. You are far too grown up and far too beautiful to be MY Little Moon. Are you sure you're her?"

The little girl giggled. "Don't be silly! Of course it's me." A quick flash of a scowl. "Maybe you don't know it's me cos Mama made me wear this ugly dress."

Leila was about to reprimand her but Simone beat her to it. He clapped his bejeweled hands, "Your dress is stunning. I'm breathless looking at you in it. See? Feel my chest. I'm not breathing. You've driven all the air out from my lungs with your beeyootiful dress. Wait, there's something missing. Hmmm … what is it?" He paused with narrowed eyes to consider her outfit thoughtfully. A gleeful smile. "Aha! Of course." He looked around, "Brian? Where's that special something for our special five year old Princess?"

Enter Brian.

Not for the first time, Leila had to marvel at the perfect complement that was Simone and Brian. Brian was everything that Simone wasn't. White, built like a body-builder, quiet, assured, reserved and more comfortable in denim and cotton then anything color, everything about him screamed 'Masculinity.'

While Simone just screamed – 'Simone.'

They had been together for five years now and Brian was Simone's quiet rock while he lived life on hyper speed taking his fashion couture line from Samoa to New Zealand to Australia and then to the world. The pair had just returned from France where Simone had pulled off his first Parisian show with all his pieces modeled by Pacific *fa'afafine*. It had been memorable and headline-grabbing to say the least. Leila was incredibly proud of him.

And slightly envious of the sway he had over her iron-willed daughter. Brian produced the beribboned package to squeals of delight from Moon. Simone wasn't taking a very restrained approach to the gift either, jumping up and down. "Hurry, hurry open it. Oh, I can't wait for you to see it!"

Moon's sea-green eyes were almost as wide as her "OHHHH WOW" mouth of awe as she carefully lifted out the sequined red tool belt, matching hard hat and mini-toolbox. "I love it! Thank you Simone. Thank you Uncle Brian! Look Mama, it's same like my pretty dress. I'm a Princess Builder now. I'm gonna go try it outside right now."

And with that, all disgust disappeared and she flounced away.

"Thanks a lot Simone," Leila laughed in faked disgust. "You've done it again. Shown me up for the loser boring mother that I am."

Simone waved a careless hand at her, "That's what mothers are for. To make life miserable. Now fairy godmothers on the other hand? Our job is to scatter sequin sunshine and joy everywhere. Come here and let me hug you daaahling." Simone gave her an air-kiss and then stepped back to evaluate her appearance. He was unimpressed. "You're planning on changing before all the guests arrive, aren't you?"

She poked her tongue at him. "Most of the guests are here and no, I'm not changing. I'm a mother with twins and a job and two different companies to run and a house to manage and this is as good looking as I'm going to get today."

Brian shook his head at the both of them. "Simone, leave her alone. Leila, ignore him. I do." He pointed to his own clothes, the jeans and T-shirt that was as familiar as a uniform.

"Oh, I gave up on you a long time ago. Thank goodness I just married you for your raw hunk body because otherwise ..." Simone said as he handed Leila a carry bag. "Here you go Leila, a present for the woman who gave life to my beautiful god-babies. Now make sure you wear it. Right now."

Leila smiled as she reached in the bag and tugged out a handful of fuchsia chiffon. "Is this one of your pieces? It's gorgeous. Far too pretty for me to ruin."

"Oh, go on and change. Please. You'll be doing me a favor." He shushed her protests and turned to go. "Now I need to find my godson."

Leila ran into the master bedroom and changed quickly. Time was of the essence. There was a hundred and one things left to do. She ran through the mental to-do list as she smoothed the delicate folds of wispy fabric against her skin. A sigh of pleasure escaped her at the sight of her reflection. A busy mother didn't often get a chance to dress up. And if and when she did, she would never have chosen such a delicate piece for herself. The dress was a masterpiece of symmetry that clung to her in all the right places, ruffles and flounces that left her shoulders and most of her back bare. It was so low it revealed the line of her cotton briefs. Which meant she would have to take them off. "Yikes, that's a bit too revealing for a kid's birthday party!" she muttered under her breath. "Oh well …" She pulled her hair out of its ponytail and let it hang down her back. A quick brush, some lip gloss and she was out the bedroom door on the way to the kitchen when she bumped into something. Hard. Chiseled. Warm. Solid. Someone. Who pulled her close to him with a low growl and a soft laugh, "Hey, I've been looking for you."

His touch, his voice, his heat had her melting. No matter how often he kissed her. No matter how long they were together. No matter the sleepless nights with crying babies or the late nights chasing deadlines and balancing parenthood with work. All of that meant nothing when Daniel pulled her close, nuzzled at that secret tender spot on her neck, and breathed wicked promises of what he wanted to do to her as soon as they were alone. (And the babies were asleep. And all the housework was done.) Ten years ago, Leila had thought she knew what love was. She thought she knew what it meant to entrust another with your dreams, your heart, your everything.

She had been wrong.

Because not until you've walked with someone through the mundane, the ordinary, the sleepless and the painful – not until then, does one truly understand what love is. Ten years ago, they had given their lives for each other. Risked everything to be together. And now ten years and two children later, they knew that while dying for your love was romantic and breathtaking – living *for* your love and *with* your love – was the covenant that defied time.

She looked up into his eyes, delighted in the crooked grin that still had the same effect on her heartstrings – and other parts of her – and slid her arms up around his neck. "Well, you've found me. Now what are you going to do with me?" she teased.

He murmured against her ear, "Everything." Hands caressed her bare skin then paused. He held her back away from him, spun her around. Surprise. A raised eyebrow and an admiring glint in the green depths. "You seem to be missing a piece of your dress, Ms. Leila Folger-Tahi." Hot kisses travelled along the bare curve of her back as fingers explored the line of her spine. "A very essential piece." Exploring hands discovered what she knew they would. Surprise was now shock. Faintly scandalized. "You're not wearing anything underneath this!"

Leila laughed and turned back to face him. "Stop that. We've got guests arriving. We can't be playing around in here."

Daniel faked a stern face. "I'm not playing. I'm merely being a good husband and informing you that in all the rush of preparing a birthday celebration for our children, you have forgotten to put on some underwear."

She pushed away from him, flushed and flustered. "I can't wear any. This dress doesn't allow for it."

He leaned against the doorjamb, still fake-serious but with the edges of his mouth twitching. "And who do we have to blame for such a scandalous dress?" He held up his hand. "No, don't tell me. A fluffy flirty dress that means my wife has to go thong-less? Can only be the work of one person." He backed away, yelling over his shoulder, "Simone!"

Leila poked her tongue out. "Go, check on our guests while I finish getting myself ready."

Daniel came back to take her in his arms one more time, entangling her in a luxurious, long kiss. One that left her weak and swaying for balance. A rough whisper, "I'll be thinking of you all day and what's underneath that dress." He backed away with that tantalizing smile. "Now, to hunt down the person responsible for such an illegal piece of clothing."

A delicious shiver as she mused over his parting words. A mental shake. 'Stop that. Get a move on. You've got a birthday party to run.' One last look in the mirror. It was a mistake.

Because *she* stared back at her. She was Leila, but she wasn't. There was a glint in her eyes and an arch to her hips that was missing from Leila. The woman that wasn't Leila stared back at her, with a gleeful smile. *You can try but you can't ignore me forever.*

Leila hissed, "You're not real. Get out of my head."

Nice try. Is that the lie you tell your husband? Don't you think he deserves the truth? Today's an important day. The children are five years old. Don't shut me out of the celebrating! I'm a part of you. I always will be. We are one.

Leila shut her eyes and grit her teeth. "Stop it. I'm stronger than you are. You will never take over me again."

She stumbled away from the mirror, sat on the edge of the bed and focused on the breathing exercises her therapist had taught her. 'You're over-tired from your late night. That's the only reason why you slipped. You can do this. You are in control. You are in control here.'

Leila breathed and from far away she heard Pele's quiet laugh dying away. *One day you will need me. One day you will need the fire. One day you will need my help.*

When she was sure she was over her panic attack, Leila moved into birthday-battle operations mode. The expansive airy kitchen was overflowing with food. She had ordered most of it from the catering company but the cakes she had insisted on making herself. And then regretted that stubbornness a hundred times over the night before because the stupid things hadn't behaved the way they were supposed to. She'd had to bake new cakes twice because her icing skills left much to be desired. And Daniel hadn't been much use either because he thought a failed culinary experiment was hilarious. Sooo not helpful!

She paused at the table to consider the final results with a worried eye. Two cakes, as per their impassioned requests, a happy dolphin and a fierce fire-breathing dragon. Two very different cakes for two very different children. Twins yet as opposite as the proverbial night and day. Salamoanasina and Ryan. Leila heaved a sigh. Five years old already and about to start school. Where did the time go?

It had hardly seemed possible that they could have made a life together. Could have made a *regular* life together. Daniel himself had said it well. '*You and I are going to have to face a lot of storms because of what we are. We should face them together. And make every day our forever. Because we don't know how many days we're going to get.*'

Yes, they hadn't thought they would get very long. Even after facing off against the Tangaloa Covenant, breaking Leila free from Pele's possession, losing loved ones and both of them losing their powers. Even then, Daniel and Leila had doubted they could have ordinary. Regular. Normal.

After the wedding, they'd gone away to school together in New Zealand. Daniel had surprised nobody by getting selected for the NZ All-Blacks rugby team in his first year of university. He had caused a massive media uproar though when he turned down the contract, instead opting to play for the Manu Samoa rugby team. "I'm honored to be offered the position with the All-Blacks but my loyalty is first and foremost with the country that helped to raise me and make me who I am, Samoa." He'd put his superb organizational skills to good use by playing for the

Manu all the way to their historical win at the Rugby World Cup – and still managed to graduate top of his class in the Civil Engineering program the year afterward.

Leila had surprised herself by doing a law degree. With a minor in Commerce. Her Folger family had been ecstatic. Less so when she moved back to Samoa when she was done, but still proud of her.

Back in Samoa, Daniel and Leila had kept a low profile. Old fears die hard. Daniel's engineering consultancy firm did quiet work and slowly built a reputation for its environmentally friendly focus. His current project was a massive oceanic hydro-electric generator that would produce power for the entire island of Upolu at a fraction of the current cost.

Leila had gone to work at the Attorney General's office and then set up her own law firm, all while continuing her work with the Women's Center, providing free legal services and training. But it was the organic plantations and medicinal research labs which were her driving passion. She spent long hours in the extensive gardens, working with geneticists and biomechanics. She wanted her children to live in a world that had eradicated HIV and found the cure for cancer and she believed the answers could be found in traditional medicine. That was where she poured the inheritance her mother had left her.

But their children were Daniel and Leila's true focus. Unplanned but not unwanted, Leila had been admitted to the Bar "waddling like an overstuffed penguin" she'd wailed. She had been eight months pregnant and feeling like an elephant even though Daniel assured her that he'd never seen her more beautiful. "You're such a liar," had been her rude response. "I'm hideous. I can't stand the sight of myself so how can you?"

The babies had been born after a very long and very painful labor. One where Daniel was thankful his wife was no longer a fire telesā because otherwise the entire hospital would have been consumed in an incendiary ball of fury. Leila had screamed, raged and sworn at everyone, including him. But when the madness was over and she nursed one baby at her breast while he cradled another, Daniel had gazed down at his smiling wife and said, "I was wrong. You here right now with our children? I've never seen you more beautiful."

Their babies were beautiful. (But of course no parent thinks their children are ugly!) A dark-eyed boy they named Ryan after Leila's father. And a green-eyed girl they called Salamoanasina after the two women who had given Daniel life. Simone and Brian were the god-parents, much to Simone's delight. Matile and Tuala were the closest thing to doting grandparents.

Both parents took a year off work to weather the craziness that is the first year with twins. Not for the first time, Leila had given silent thanks for the separate trust funds from both her parents that made such luxuries possible. She and Daniel had been there together to see the twins take their first steps, utter their first words. Together they had endured sleepless nights and endless scuffles with bottles and breast milk. Together they parented babies that wouldn't sleep, Babies that wouldn't stop crying. Babies that smiled and utterly enslaved them. And then drove them nuts the next day. Twins were a fascinating complexity. Especially to Leila because she had been one.

Ryan and Salamoanasina made their differences known from a very early age. Ryan was the quiet one. Easily soothed. The baby who luxuriated in hugs and snuggles. Often content to just sit and stare at his surroundings with wide, serious eyes. His sister was never still, never quiet, never at ease. She hated being held. The only time she was content in your arms was when she was asleep. And that wasn't often enough. Leila often threatened darkly under her breath, that she was going to "dope you up on paracetomol you horrible child."

Ryan had liquid dark eyes and thick curly hair that Leila hated to cut. Salamoanasina had fair coloring, sandy brown hair and her father's eyes that were often storm-filled as she raged against anyone who wouldn't let her have her way. "Salamoanasina is a silly name. Don't like it!" Emphasized with a stamp of her foot and a toss of her tangled hair.

Daniel appeased her with a laugh and an exuberant tickle. "Fine then. Masina means 'moon' in Samoan. You're my beautiful moon princess so we'll call you Moon." Everybody called her Moon after that. So much that even Leila forgot her daughter had another name. There was never any doubt as to which twin was in charge, which twin was the boss. Ryan was content to follow after his sister.

Which is why he didn't tell anyone that he could do funny things with flames. Because Moon made him promise not to say anything …

Accepting that there was nothing she could do to make the birthday cakes look any better, Leila went to join the guests on the deck. Daniel was deep in conversation with Brian, probably about his latest work project because Brian had recently given up a successful modeling career to study engineering. Leila made a face at her husband. There he went talking 'shop' when they were supposed to be having fun. He caught sight of her and teased her flirty dress with a fake smoldering stare and a suggestive arch of his eyebrows.

'Stop it!' she mouthed at him before moving around the room, stopping to greet people. Keahi and Teuila were there. Talei had flown over specially for the birthday from New Zealand where she was based, still playing professional netball. Still single but perhaps not for long? She had brought a 'friend' with her. 'Hmmm, and a very nice looking friend too!' thought Leila as she was introduced to the tall man in a suit that clung to his lean build in all the right places.

Aunty Matile and Tuala were there. Looking very much the same as when Leila had first met them so many years ago. Except today Matile was laughing, a huge smile on her face as Simone regaled them with tales of his Paris show. They were the only grandparents Moon and Ryan knew and they did what exemplary grandparents were supposed to. Spoil their grandchildren rotten. (And then leave their parents to despair of their naughtiness later …) Sinalei had brought her three children to the party and her husband was rocking their newest baby to sleep out on the deck. Sinalei was a pediatrician now and a close friend of the family as the primary doctor for the twins.

Leila greeted Maleko next and was introduced to his new wife. A perky, eager young woman who looked a lot like his last two ex-wives. Leila welcomed them both warmly and then went to check on the food.

She paused for a moment and surveyed the scene. The sun was beginning to set in the distant horizon, the perfect backdrop to the riot of color that was her orchid and bougainvillea garden. The deck resonated with laughter and warm conversation. She and Daniel had worked hard to build a life worth treasuring here. Their children were turning five years old today. They were gathered with all their loved ones to celebrate. Leila felt the warm glow of gratitude.

I am so blessed.

Tears pricked at her eyes. As he always did, sensing her moods even when she didn't want him to, Daniel materialized by her side, slid an arm around her waist, whispered against her hair. "What's the matter? You okay?"

She nodded, words catching in her throat. "Yes. Everything's fine. More than fine. We're so blessed. We have each other, our children, our family and friends. I just never thought we would get that happy ever after, you know? Sometimes I'm so happy that I'm afraid. I can't believe it will last, you know?"

Daniel's hold tightened around her waist as he pulled her close. She fit him perfectly. Daniel never forgot how close he had come to losing her forever. He never took Leila's closeness for granted. "Believe it, my love. This is what happily ever after feels like."

For a moment they were one, their thoughts in unison. And then Leila shifted, curious, "Where are the twins anyway?"

The children were at the far end of the property beside the little stream that edged the forest. Ryan – the solemn little boy with dark eyes and a shy smile was wearing an elei shirt that matched his sister's frilly mu'umu'u. Or at least the one she HAD been wearing before she stripped it off.

"Ryan, come help me." Moon was imperious. Ryan was obliging. As always. His sister had stripped off her pretty dress and was now wearing her overalls, tool-belt and helmet. The offensive dress was in a bunch on the ground piled high with a heap of twigs and leaves. Now she stood and considered it thoughtfully, "Hmm, I don't fink it's enuff sticks. I want a big fire so Mama won't ever find the yucky dress again." She snapped at him, "Get more!"

Ryan heaved a sigh but did as he was told. Moon was the boss. He gathered more small branches until finally she was satisfied.

She squatted beside the pile and brought out a packet of matches. Ryan was dismayed. "Dada said never play wif matches. You being very bad."

She ignored him and tried unsuccessfully to strike a match. Nothing. Again. Nothing. Ryan watched while she went through almost the entire packet. Then she chucked the box on the pile and stood up, stomping her feet. "Oh dammit."

Ryan's mouth was agape. Moon was breaking a cardinal rule of the house. No matches. And now she was saying bad words? This was very distressing. Moon's lower lip trembled and big tears welled up in her ocean-green eyes. A wail. "Mama's gonna be mad at me for making my dress dirty. She's gonna have a angry face at me."

Ryan tried to get the rejected dress out of the miniature bonfire. "Just wear it again. Mama not be mad." He held it up. Both children looked at it with disgust. It was a crumpled ball of dirty ruffles now. And there was a slug happily slugging away on it.

"Eewww yucky. No, I not wearing it anymore. You have to burn it so Mama never find it. Please Ryan?" Moon gave him a wet, hopeful look. A big sniffle. "Please?"

The little boy nodded with a resigned sigh. He knelt beside the filthy dress and rubbed his pudgy hands together. *One, two, three.* Moon watched in eager anticipation. Sparks leapt from his fingers as she knew they would. Fire hungrily moved from its maker and began to consume the dress, the wood, the leaves, everything.

Ryan moved away clumsily from the flames as Moon clapped her hands with glee. "Pretty! So pretty!" She gave her twin a hug.

The dress was no more. Just then, they heard voices calling for them. It was their parents. "Ryan? Moon? Where are you? It's time for your birthday cakes."

The children looked at each other with panicked faces. Their parents would not be happy if they found them playing with fire. Quickly, Moon ran to the stream and dipped her hands in, raising her palms full of water. She threw it up into the air. It didn't scatter and fall. It coiled and twisted into a ribbon of silver that called to more water from the stream below. Moon reached, pulled at the ribbon and yanked it in the direction of the little bonfire. Water danced, waved and twisted until it was over the fire. Then it sank, subduing the flames in a single deluge. Both children's faces lit up. It had worked.

Ryan took his sister's hand in his and together they ran through the bushes towards their parents voices. Giggling. Just before they reached them, Moon came to a skidding halt, pulling Ryan to stop with her. She gave him her sternest face. "Don't tell Mama and Dada. Okay? Pretty fire and water is our secret."

Ryan nodded. Of course. Because Moon was the boss. And he was in total agreement. This trick they could do with sparks and water? It was their secret.

Daniel saw them first. "There you are – birthday demons! Where have you two been hiding?" Two long strides and he swept Moon into his arms and threw her up in the air. She squealed with delight. Back safe in his arms, she hugged him fiercely. "Dada, you my B.F.F. Best friend forever."

Leila knelt with a frown to brush leaves and dirt from Ryan's pants. "I told you two not to get your party clothes dirty." A kiss and a tickle for her son reassured him she wasn't really mad. She took his pudgy hand in hers. "Come on, all your guests are waiting for you."

It was then she registered what Moon was wearing. "What happened to your new dress young lady?"

Moon grimaced, hid her face in her father's chest. Muffled, "Don't like it. It's yucky. Dada, please can I wear my overalls like you?"

Daniel chuckled and ruffled her tangle of hair. "Of course you can. You're the birthday girl."

Leila objected. In vain. "Daniel, don't encourage her. Her dress was very expensive and she and I had a deal."

She couldn't keep her angry face on for very long though. Not when Daniel pulled her close for a quick kiss before sweeping his son into his arms so that he held both children firmly, one in each broad arm. Both of the children shrieked with laughter as he did his monster Dad routine, pretending to roar and spin them around. "I'm going to eat you up with birthday ice cream!"

"Nooooo Dada. You can't eat us. We're your B.F.Fs."

"But monster Dad is hungry. What can I eat then?"

"We got nice birfday cakes inside," offered Ryan.

Moon nodded vigorously. "Yeah, they very yummy. We can share them wif you."

"Okay, birthday cake time. Let's go!" Daniel spun them round once more before making off for the house.

Leila had to laugh at their antics. She paused to watch them. Daniel, red and gold in the sunlight, striding with confident surety, their beloved children in his arms. Laughter, happiness, delight.

Yes, this is what happily ever after looks like.

The End

A Message from the Author

Thank you for purchasing this book. The Telesā Trilogy Series has been a two-year writing journey of discovery, challenges and many fabulous experiences. I've been delighted (and blown away) by the positive response from readers all over the world to this Samoan story inspired by Pacific mythology.

In between writing books about strong, vibrant Pacific women, fabulous gifted fa'afafine (and with some tattooed, chiseled men added in for good measure), I'm also a blogger, mother of the Fabulous Five, a Demented Domestic Goddess, Wife of Hot Man, Long-Time-Ago-English Teacher, Dancer Only When Nobody's Looking, and Baker of Too Many Desserts. To read more of my writing and to find out what books I'm working on next, please join me at my blog, Sleepless in Samoa.

Storytelling is my passion. Thank you for joining me on this adventure.

Faafetai tele lava,

Lani

About the Author

Lani Wendt was born and raised in Samoa, daughter of Tuaopepe Felix and Marita Wendt. She attended university in the USA and New Zealand, studying English Literature, Women's Studies and Education. She then returned home and worked as a high school English teacher while also writing articles for the local newspapers and building her collection of short fiction. Her award-winning short stories have been published in Samoa, New Zealand, Australia and the United Kingdom. Her collection, **'Afakasi Woman'** won the 2011 USP Press Fiction Award. In 2009 she was commissioned by Hans Joe Keil to research and write the narrative non-fiction book **'Pacific Tsunami Galu Afi'**. The book was funded by the Australian Government Aid programme and all profits go to tsunami survivors who were interviewed for the record. Her first novel in the Young Adult Contemporary adventure romance Telesā Series, **'TELESA The Covenant Keeper'** was released worldwide in both digital and print format in 2011 and then followed by **'When Water Burns'**, **'I am Daniel Tahi'**, and **'The Bone Bearer'**.

Lani is married to Darren Young and they have five children.

Made in the USA
Las Vegas, NV
10 September 2021